# THE BOY
## WITH THE
# BEST LAUGH

# THE BOY
## WITH THE
# BEST LAUGH

### A NOVEL

## NAOMI E. KENNEDY

*The Boy with the Best Laugh* is a work of fiction. Names, characters, places, and incidents are the products of the author's imagination or are used fictitiously. Apart from well-known historical figures, any resemblance to real persons, living or dead, or to actual events or locales, are entirely coincidental and not intended.

First edition

Visit the author's website at: https://www.naomiekennedyauthor.com

Library of Congress Control Number: 2022900048
ISBN 9798409228576

Cover Design: Creative Publishing Book Design
Cover Image: Shutterstock

Many thanks to: BK, my editor and friend, Sophia, and sources who survived their escape to Canada and remained there.

*To my son*
**Eric**
*who gives me endless love and support*
*and my grandson*
**Alex**
*who is the better part of all of us*

PART I

# CHAPTER ONE

# LIZ

## (JUNE 1978)

I watched the woman pick up the melon and smell its fragrance. She added it to her groceries as her two young children ran around in circles screeching. *It wasn't so long ago that Will was that age. He seems so grown-up now. Hmmm…Cherry tomatoes, portabella mushrooms, arugula, baby carrots, purple onion, and anise. Quite elegant taste for an eight year old.* Zeytina's, the new gourmet shop, was my last errand. After putting the food packages in the trunk, I went home still thinking about the events of the day.

*How could I have been so stupid! I knew Adam was calling today. Did I purposely avoid his call? I've got to stop this. I could have come home earlier. Dammit, I'll probably never tell him the truth about Will.*

His letter came two days ago confirming he would arrive at the airport on Friday at 1:37 a.m. He would take a taxi and call me later that morning. It was now 4:00 in the afternoon.

I turned on the stove and contemplated making a steak, but settled on hamburgers with scalloped potatoes. The phone rang just as I started to toss the salad. Thinking it was Adam, I quickly answered. "Hello?"

3

"Hi Mom. Sal's father is driving me home. I'll be there soon, okay? What's for dinner?"

That night there was a torrential downpour. After putting the last of the pots and pans into the dishwasher, I heard Will let out a scream.

"Mom! There's a tornado warning flashing on the TV!"

The sky darkened. The lights began to flicker. I felt a sense of uneasiness creep through me as I grabbed Thumby, and Will and I raced downstairs.

"Meowww!" she screeched, struggling to get out of my grip. At two years old she was a beautifully marked and spirited tabby. I put her down to let her settle into our unfinished basement where she had never been.

"Will, stay close to the stairs! Let her run around. I'll look for a radio." As I searched, a thunderous sky filled with anger created a constant rumbling throughout the house. *I know I left one down here! Where is it?* Only a few minutes had gone by and I was becoming increasingly worried.

"Mom!"

# (1967)

Adam and I were just seventeen when we started gambling on horses. He always bet to "Win", and I – the more practical one – predictably bet on third place to "Show". Then there were those wild and crazy evenings when we both placed "Exacta/Perfecta" bets together, choosing one horse to come in first and another to come in second. If your horses came in exactly in that order your bet was a winner. But, we chose our horses nonsensically causing us to lose over and over again.

One evening on our way to Roosevelt Raceway a storm hit. Lightning illuminated the sky creating an eerie vision of night into day. Because of its flatlands Long Island had the most magnificent aerial views. Thunder roared as we drove further east. We gasped in amazement as pellets the size of golf balls hit Adam's new recently acquired purple 1967 Volkswagen Beetle, which already had little dents decorating its fender from end to end giving it *his* interpretation of a lived-in look. Intermittent sheets of rain prevented us from seeing where we were going. The air was unusually humid, ubiquitously smothering us. We began to sweat wishing we could roll down the windows, but the winds were howling and producing a squealing sound that unnerved us. The roads were becoming worse. Adam adjusted the speed of the wipers as I turned the switch to *defrost*. All of a sudden, out of nowhere, a truck in the left lane sideswiped all three lanes.

"Holy shit! What was that about?" Adam was shaken.

"Look over there!" I pointed towards the darkening sky.

Gasping in unison we realized what was happening. An ominous funnel-shaped swirl was forming. I instantly thought of Munch's "The Scream" as the angry winds veered north, giving us enough time to turn around and seek shelter. It was then that we spotted a dilapidated pathetic-looking shack.

"What is that place? Do you think someone lives there?"

"Wait! I can't pull off yet," Adam shouted.

Adam's brakes screeched as he careened off the road. Hurrying, he grabbed a flashlight out of the glove compartment and we sloshed through the grass and mud praying someone would be home.

"Thank God!" I let out a sigh of relief noticing the door was ajar. It almost fell off the hinges as Adam felt around unsuccessfully looking for a light switch.

A foul odor permeated the air and made us wince. Five candlesticks in a row leaned against a windowpane in their pewter holders. Adam searched for matches in his pocket. One by one he straightened the candles and lit them. Garbage was strewn all over the cracked floor boards. The place must have been deserted for a long time because cobwebs and miscellaneous indescribable rusted objects covered every inch of our new found cottage. But somehow it was perfect. Instead of the constant worry of our parents coming home, we finally had privacy.

It was early spring and we made love for the first time. The worst of the tornado had passed, but it was still pouring outside and there was a chill in the air. Adam spread out the frayed blanket he brought from the trunk of the car trying not to look nervous. We sat down and he kissed me tenderly, opening my mouth with his tongue. He put his hand under my blouse and I felt it go gently up towards my breasts. I shivered. As he nibbled on my ear, we groped for each other's clothing and quickly undressed. We were used to fooling around, but had never gone all the way. All of a sudden I noticed something out of the corner of my eye. I shrieked, "Adam! Look! A mouse!"

I think I was always in love with Adam. We met in our junior year of high school during study hall. He was staring at me as I searched through my pocketbook for the umpteenth time. I was looking for my newest lipstick, the one that tasted of strawberries.

"Hi," said a blond haired boy.

"Hi," I replied awkwardly.

"What's your name? I've never seen you before. Are you new to the school?"

"No, I've been around. My name is Liz. What's yours?"

"Adam," he answered. "What class do you have after study hall?"

"Earth Science; which class do you have?"

"French." He grimaced. "My favorite." They both laughed easily.

"Could I walk you to class?"

"Sure," I smiled timidly, pulling my long brown hair into a ponytail with the gold barrette I was holding.

"Listen," he said as we walked to class, "would you want to go to the pool hall with me after school? Some of my friends are going to the one on Hillside. Do you know where it is?"

Hesitant, I tried to figure out a way to go, but couldn't. "I've never been there, but I know." I sighed. I knew all the kids went there after school on Fridays. "Sorry, I can't. I have to catch the bus on time or my mother will kill me."

"What bus do you take?"

"The Douglaston Parkway one," I answered, hoping he wouldn't leave just yet.

"You're kidding! I take that one too." His brow furrowed. "I guess we go home at different times? Is it all right if I ride home with you?"

"I thought you were going to the pool hall with your friends?"

"I changed my mind," Adam mumbled. Bright red blotches appeared on his pallid complexion.

We rode home together that day and every day after that. It turned out that Adam lived a few minutes from my house. We became best friends as time went on, but when Adam asked me to go steady, I declined.

The tornado hit southeast of where we stayed that evening, which was unusual for New York especially that time of year. Luckily no one had gotten hurt, but trees and lines were down, along with debris that blocked local roads for miles. In the early morning, we followed the designated detours, worrying all the while what our parents would say about our disappearance the previous evening.

"Adam? Did we do okay?" I asked sheepishly.

"What do you mean?" Adam asked, stifling a yawn. "Do you mean us being together?"

"Yes, of course! What did you think I meant?" I snapped without realizing it.

I'm not sure if it was because this was my first time, but going all the way didn't turn out to be what everyone said it would be. Fooling around with Adam was awesome. I was crazy about him. But I wondered if he liked *doing it* more than me. I wasn't about to ask. All I knew was that we were in love.

"Well, yes. I think we did fine for a first time! Don't you?" he replied, putting his arm around me.

## (JUNE 1978)

"Mom, do you think it's over?" asked Will.

"What? Oh, yes it's passed," I murmured, jolted back to the present.

Looking out the basement window, I spotted leaves and branches everywhere; a twisted, tangled wood collage with mottled green-gold loosely interwoven. The garden I labored over and truly adored appeared to be in ruins. To the left of my property lay a battered tree which crossed the adjacent street. Wires hung from above.

"Wow! What a storm! We were lucky!" I let out a sigh. "Go find *Thumby*, okay?"

# CHAPTER TWO

# LIZ

## (JUNE 1978)

*Oh Will! Can't you for once keep your room clean? This is disgusting!*
Will was tall for an eight year old. At 4'1" he overshadowed most kids playing basketball. It was Saturday evening and he'd return from his final game of the year by 9:30 p.m. His friend's father was carpooling today and would drop him off last.

Will's room was pale blue with posters of Reggie Jackson and André the Giant covering most of the walls. The Yankees and wrestling matches were all he lived for these days. As I tidied up, I glanced at the photographs on his dresser. There was one of him at five years old with a shock of red hair in dire need of a haircut. Another photo to the left pictured me in a bright yellow sequined Indian tunic and my hippie jeans with embroidered flowers, which I always wore on our vacations at the shore. My hair, normally straight as sticks, was curled from the humidity and made me look different, perhaps Italian, especially because of my dark brown eyes, olive skin, and prominent nose. This time we didn't go to Long Island but instead took an extended trip for one month and went camping upstate (of all things!). That evening I donned my favorite holiday dress and acquiesced to a "real" dinner in a diner after burning the hotdogs on my makeshift grill. By the end of the summer Will and I were natives to the wild. We learned how to use disgusting wiggly worms as bait, eventually mastering the art of killing the poor things. Then, we'd throw the fish back and succumb to good old burgers and franks.

"I'm home," shouted Will.

"How'd you do?"

Disheartened, Will said, "We lost again!"

"You'll win next time, you'll see. Go finish your homework and get to bed honey."

On Sunday morning, certain that Adam would try to reach me again, I waited for his call before leaving for rehearsal. I had been playing the violin since my junior year in college and was now performing in local churches for the community. The concert was in a week and I needed to discuss some last minute details with Andrew, whom we called "Maestro". "I really don't need this stress", I muttered under my breath.

Will was in his room playing with his baseball cards, so I took advantage of the free time and practiced. There were several measures of the 3rd movement, a Menuetto Allegro, that were still bothersome to me after weeks of working on it. We were performing Haydn's "Symphony No. 102 in B flat major." Some members of the orchestra felt this piece was his most aggressive and loudest; an exciting piece for everyone.

The first time I ever played in a concert I stayed up the entire night panicking at the thought of stage fright. But the violin was my passion and nothing would get in my way. I stopped playing after a little while and lay down on the couch hoping to fall asleep. The soft velvety fabric was luxurious to my touch, and the living room was my absolute favorite. Every inch was decorated in earth tones -- rich sable browns and creamy beiges. I stared into space for what seemed an eternity. Looking around I noticed the walls seemed a bit dull and made a mental note to hire a contractor to paint both the living room and dining room.

It was noon and I was getting hungry. I yelled from the kitchen, "Will, do you want a sandwich?" When he didn't answer I went upstairs and saw him sleeping peacefully. The TV was on low and he was holding his cards in his hands. I tiptoed downstairs.

He looked so much like Adam, from his oval shaped face and his crooked smile, to his unusually squared shoulders. *How could Adam not notice the resemblance? Did he really believe that Tom was his father?* Will didn't look at all like Tom, even though they both had red hair and brown eyes. Tom had drooping shoulders and was stocky. If you looked deeply into Will's eyes, you could see Adam's penetrating blue ones piercing back at you.

Taking the bread out of its plastic wrapper, I prepared a turkey sandwich with lettuce and mayo and sat down. Afterwards, I carefully placed my violin and the music back into its leather case up against the door.

"Will, are you up yet? Do you want to eat lunch?" Not giving him a chance to reply, I shouted, "Hey, have you seen my black sweater? You know… the one with those funky gold buttons. It should be here where I left it in the hall closet." The phone rang just as I spotted its sleeve jutting out, sandwiched between two other garments.

"Hello?"

"Liz, I'm so sorry. I tried you yesterday morning and when you didn't answer…well, I had to leave. And then the meetings lasted much longer than I anticipated…got back so late…," he trailed off. Adam was an executive in a top-notch accounting firm, *Whitely and Hersh*. He had been traveling more and more to California where their other offices were located, but New York was his home base.

"That's okay Adam, don't worry about it," I said feeling guilty. "How are you, besides tired?"

"Just anxious to see you and Will. How is he?"

"He's okay. Listen, I'm running to rehearsal. I'm late. I was hoping you'd call before I left. I wasn't sure which hotel you were staying in or I would have called. I didn't bother leaving a message at your house. I figured you wouldn't retrieve it in time." Adam lived in a beach house in South Hampton and Long Island was too much of a trip for him when he traveled. "I must run, but are you sure you don't want to stay here? It would make Will so happy…and me!"

"I'd love to Liz, but I have to finish up some business, see some clients in the city, and then I'll be by. Can we meet for dinner? How about 7 p.m. in that bistro you enjoy so much on 5th and 53rd?"

It was a trip from Westchester, but Adam was right. The *Candlewick Bistro* was one of my favorites. I loved their food, especially their shrimp and hot sausage.

"Yes, I'll see you then." My voice softened, "I miss you."

"Great!"

"Oh, before I forget, I have tickets for you and one for Will for the concert. I'll give them to you when I see you."

Midtown traffic was light for this time of evening. But that didn't stop the horns from honking and I lost it. I screamed out the car window along with the rest of the morons, "Hey, you idiots! Cut it out!"

Will and I lived in a little house in Northern Westchester. It was a rare occasion to hear horns blasting in the countryside. During the summer we would go rowboating or take out a canoe or kayak. Life was peaceful on Mohegan Lake.

I found a parking space right away and started to walk up 5th Avenue when all of a sudden I felt a hand on my shoulder. I turned around and felt warmed at the sight of him. He was as handsome as ever with his tousled blondish-red hair and striking blue eyes, impeccably dressed in a *Paul Stuart* pinstriped blue suit.

"You look wonderful!" Adam beamed. "Is that a new dress?"

I was wearing a silky slim-fitting black dress that V-necked in the back. My hair was shorter than he was accustomed and suited me well. I nodded and to my surprise felt myself blush.

"How was your rehearsal?" He gave me a tender kiss on the lips. It had been three weeks since we had been together and I longed for his touch. I let all ambivalent thoughts leave me as I leaned forward, reached to kiss him more deeply, and felt his body respond to mine.

"It went well. I was having trouble with a few measures, but... oh, look! Look who's here!" Fred, one of our oldest friends, stepped out of a jewelry store.

For 29 years old, Fred looked much older than he should. He was a plain man with tired looking eyes and funny ears that protruded, and with his bald head it gave him a comic appearance.

"Fred, what are you doing here? What a coincidence! It's good to see you!" We hugged and the three of us exchanged pleasantries. "Is Anne here?"

Fred and Anne dated while attending Queens College where the three of us met. It seemed obvious to everyone that Adam and I would be the first ones to marry, but when Anne got pregnant immediately after graduation, she and Fred eloped without a family member or friend present.

"Anne took the kids to Connecticut for the week… you know, to visit her parents."

The last time I saw Anne, she looked stunning. She had dyed her hair blond, with even blonder streaks, a serious deviation from her mousy brown. Men had always admired her long legs and small waist and now with her new hairdo she was a knockout. This was the happiest she looked in a long time. We met for lunch in a small café on the lakeside near my house and talked and talked about old times. The day was magnificent with sunshine sparkling and dancing on the water.

"Wow! You look fantastic! If I didn't know better, I'd say you're in love. I haven't seen you look this way since…well, since you first met Fred. What's going on?" Inquisitively, I looked at my dearest friend, but she quickly changed the subject.

"I don't understand why you haven't told Adam that Will is his son. You can't go on this way forever."

"It's more complicated than you know." Chagrinned, I looked down. "Adam is still drinking. I don't know if I want him to be part of the parenting. Nor do I know if I want to marry him while he's drinking this heavily. It seems to be a big part of his life, but at the same time he seems sober. Do you know what I mean?"

"I guess so. I assume you mean he drinks all the time and never gets smashed, right?"

"Yes."

"I don't remember…has Adam ever asked you to marry him?"

"No, not since we were kids. We used to talk about it all the time though. Since he's been traveling, and even before then when he first came back, things haven't been the same. He seems different. The truth is, we haven't spent enough time together to consider it."

The reality was that Liz saw the changes in Adam as vagaries. She did not recognize the more serious and obvious issues which affected him. And, she was also oblivious to the changes in her closest friend. After lunch what Anne told Liz shocked her.

That was three months ago.

"Why don't you join us, Fred? We're headed for the bistro on 53rd. Please, have dinner with us," Adam insisted.

"N-NNo, thank you. I'm m-mmeeting someone in a little while." Fred shook Adam's hand goodbye and then left.

"Am I crazy or did I see Fred blush?" Adam looked at Liz, puzzled.

"Nope, you're not crazy, and he even stuttered!"

We sat at a cozy table draped with a red satin tablecloth. A single candle was lit between us creating a warm romantic atmosphere. Subdued music played in the background.

Adam looked at me quizzically. "What was that all about?"

"I'm not sure, but what I do know is that I'm hungry!" At that very moment a tall, lanky waiter with bulging eyes approached our table. I whispered, "He must have heard me!" We both chuckled.

The evening was perfect as it always was when we were together. There were never any pretenses between us. The only thing that got in our way was our sexual tension. It was never the right time and there was never a place to be alone. We made plans to meet again for dinner the next day, but this time in the restaurant at his hotel. He was expecting me to stay afterwards, but I'd have to get home to Will. We talked for a while about a new client I had and then switched to how Will was doing in school.

"He loves math like you always did."

"Oh, yeah? Well, tell him we'll go over any problems he might have when I see him, okay?"

I was quiet, wishing I could tell him the truth.

Interrupting my thoughts, Adam asked, "Do you ever speak to Tom anymore? Does he see Will?"

When Adam first heard Tom's name uttered by Will, he immediately assumed he was his father. He was surprised that he was his stepfather. Apparently, he and Liz had married in '75, five years after Will's birth. Something seemed off, but he didn't quite know why. Adam didn't believe that she became pregnant in college. She didn't seem the type to sleep around, but she kept sidestepping the subject of Will's real father. And Adam kept blocking out the possibility that he, himself, might be the father. He wouldn't allow himself to believe that Liz would hold this truth from him.

After we said goodnight, I headed for Taylor Road where Will was eating dinner with his new friend Billy and his parents. Bumper-to-bumper traffic only gave me more time to reflect on Adam being Will's dad. *Why is this becoming an issue after all this time? I raised Will by myself for eight years. Certainly I could continue to do so. Money isn't an issue. Elizabeth Riley Advertising is doing well and with four clients I'm always swamped with work.*

Shortly after graduating college, I started working in a large advertising firm with the hope of putting my art degree to use. Will was two years old at the time and a handful, but my mom took care of him from birth so I could continue school. I was lucky she didn't work. She was always a stay-at-home-mom even after I was grown, and now she was happy to watch her grandson.

The plan was that I would graduate and put Will in daycare as soon as I found work. It took awhile before I told my mom everything; about how Adam and I fell in love, and my pregnancy. She seemed to understand, after all, she was fond of Adam, too. But she did not seem to hear me when I expressed concern about his drinking. It didn't make sense. All she seemed to care about was that he was Jewish. But, he really wasn't Jewish and she didn't hear that either.

Will's birth went smoothly. I took Lamaze classes and Anne was my coach. We set up a nursery in my parent's home and I saved money like crazy with the dream of one day buying a home for Will and me.

It took only two years before I ventured out on my own doing freelance work and then eventually opening my own firm. That's when I met Tom Riley.

# CHAPTER THREE

# LIZ

## (1975)

Tom was my first client at *Elizabeth Bloom Advertising*. His company, *TR Book Developer, Inc.,* designed book jackets. He was 15 years my senior. I was 25 years old and still learning the ropes. His business with me could be condensed to once a week, but everyday at 12 noon he showed up at my office unnecessarily with a picnic basket filled with assorted goodies: pâtés, cheeses, jams, French bread, salad, pastries, and always a bottle of white wine. I fell for him instantly. Tom Riley was charming and irresistible. He swept me off my feet before I realized what was happening; a whirlwind romance. We only knew each other for three months before we married.

Being with Tom was different. He was brought up in a strictly Irish Catholic home. In the short time we knew each other we were at crossroads. Holidays were especially difficult. Christmas was foreign to me. Chanukah was even stranger to Tom. Will loved Christmas. I was not happy about it. He was five years old and even though we weren't religious, it bothered me.

The three of us went to my parents' home for an engagement celebration dinner. They never met Tom before. He brought flowers for my mother and a box of cigars for my dad.

"I'm glad to meet you Tom." My mother gave him a kiss on his cheek. "Thank you for the beautiful flowers!" She took a whiff and remarked, "Oh my, they smell divine!"

"You're welcome. The feeling is mutual."

He then looked towards my dad who turned away. Tom walked closer. "Sir, Liz has told me a great deal about you." My father turned around, shook his outstretched hand, and then walked off again.

The rest of the evening didn't go much better. My father asked Tom how old he was, and even though he knew, he continued to make as big a stink as he did when I previously informed him.

"Don't you think you might be too old for my daughter?" he asked with obvious attitude.

"I hope it won't be an issue for you sir; your daughter and I are in love."

"Are you now?" My dad left the room.

My mother made up for dad's rudeness with her own take on bad manners by asking every question under the sun, starting with would he be willing to convert? And then continued asking: his place of birth; did the birth go well? His dietary habits; his parents, aunts and uncles, and even his cousins' education, and of course, his education, (luckily, Tom didn't have any siblings); and lastly his income, and was he expecting a raise any time soon?

Initially I didn't meet Tom's family, but when I finally did I was uncomfortable.. They were cold and unfeeling. They practically ignored Will. It was a surprise that Tom and he got along so well considering his upbringing. My family was intrusive, but at least my mother was warm. My dad, on the other hand, never acted that way before. He was always gregarious with Adam and my other friends. I suppose this was different though. His little girl was getting married.

Maybe if Tom was Italian there might have been a better comfort zone. There's a greater similarity in these two heritages. But for the time being the sexual attraction was strong and seemed to be enough. And, at least Tom seemed to be a good stepfather, so far.

We said our goodbyes. Taking Will's hand I walked out the door. I looked up at Tom who was quiet, and said facetiously, "Well, that went smoothly, didn't it."

"Your parents," he swallowed, "they're very nice."

Tom shouted from across the hallway, "Liz, where can I put all these cartons? Is this room okay?" He motioned his head to the left as she approached.

"Sure, that's the guestroom. Why don't you use it as your den? Will that work?"

"It's perfect. I'll start unpacking right away. Maybe Will can give me a hand. What do you think? Will he be up to the task?"

They decided Tom would move into Liz's house in Mohegan Lake so Will wouldn't have to change schools. He recently started kindergarten and was adapting well, considering. But the newness of having a stepdad was another matter. Will was confused about the stranger living in his house. The minute Tom moved in, Liz regretted her impulsive decision to marry.

They got married by a justice of the peace with no one present, except Will. Neither set of parents came, nor Anne. Liz had always dreamt of a large wedding with all the frills; a white lacy gown with a long trail and a veil delicately covering her face. She would enter her temple with lots of family and friends smiling, as they watched her walk down the aisle with her dad. They would engage in the most beloved tradition – the breaking of the glass; and afterwards, a band would play her favorite music as Adam and she danced their first dance together as man and wife. Many photos would be taken for their grandchildren to cherish memories as she and Adam grew old together.

*What was I thinking? How could I not take Will into consideration? Couldn't I have brought Tom into his life slowly and let him acclimate to him?* But to Liz's surprise and relief, they bonded as time went on. She would find them sitting in front of the TV with a bowl of chips between them watching baseball or playing Nintendo. Sometimes when she got home late from work, Will would be sleeping in his lap. Tom was a good stepdad.

Will and Tom were shocked when she ended the marriage. The underlying reason was clear – Adam. She missed him. She couldn't stop thinking about him. She noticed early on that her feelings for Tom were disingenuous. Their relationship didn't have a chance to develop.

But the marriage really dissolved soon after an explosive fight which lasted until dawn. It was during sex. They had come home after an office party to promote a new book for one of his clients. Tom had too much to drink and became uncharacteristically aggressive with her. Since they were married sex had been exciting, but never did she feel nervous when she was with him.

Liz thought back to several weeks ago, a snowy Monday in December, when Tom and she played hooky from work. He rescheduled his clients the night before, and she recklessly put her work load aside in anticipation of the impending storm. Since school was cancelled, Will packed up his knapsack with snow apparel and assorted *GI Joe* guys and went to his grandparents' house Sunday night. His grandpa promised that they would build an awesome snowman with all the features, including a carrot for the nose and licorice for the smiling mouth.

Deciding to take a walk on the lakeside, Liz and Tom dressed with layers of warm clothing. The snowfall was steady forming lacy patterns on the branches of the willow trees, and the sunlight was magnificent leaving orange streaks through the forest. Liz was tempted to go back to the house and get some art supplies, but it was too cold to paint outside. They walked for a while holding each other's gloved hands, shivering in spite of the layers they each wore. In the distance they noticed five deer stealthily crossing the woodland with a yearling following in their path. To the right of them, there were two swans and baby geese with their parents gliding through the water. The geese were dunking their heads looking for food.

"I wish Will was with us. It's so nice here," Liz said softly. Secretly she thought, *I wish Adam was here; how he would have enjoyed this day.* Adam still didn't know she was married. She pondered, *what would he think?* She had so many regrets, starting with not telling him about Will and on top of that losing touch with him.

Tom and Liz walked for over an hour and when it became too slippery for them to continue, they headed home. Before they went inside, he spoke in a voice unfamiliar to her. "Liz, take off your blouse." She felt herself flush, turned to face him, and as they entered the house, she did what he asked. "Now take off your bra". Again she obliged. In spite of herself, she became excited. She thought, *why shouldn't I feel excited? After all, I'm married to him, aren't I?*

# LIZ
## (ONE MONTH LATER
### AFTER THE OFFICE PARTY)

"Stop it Tom," she shouted, "Stop it!"

She struggled to get him off, but he kept forcing himself back on top of her. Liz felt frightened and slammed her knee into his groin. He shrieked in pain and fell over to his side.

"You're drunk! I've never seen you this way. How much did you have at the party anyway?" Panicked, she ran downstairs to the living room trying to catch her breath.

Tom ran after her and with slurred speech said, "Liz, I'm *sarry.* You're so *butiful.* I couldn't stop myself."

"Get some sleep Tom! Leave me alone," she snapped in disgust. "We'll talk about this tomorrow."

Several hours later after a fitful sleep, she hurried out the door and left before he got up. She needed to clear her head. Her parents were expecting her at ten, but she turned around instead and headed north. The roads were plowed well enough for her to drive at a good pace. Spotting a phone booth, Liz pulled over and called her parents and told them she'd be a little late. Things were not sitting right with her and she was becoming increasingly nervous. *What the hell am I going to do? It was a mistake marrying him; there's no doubt about it. I'll tell him I want a divorce, that's all. And Will, well, he'll just have to accept it. After all, he hardly knows Tom. But what on earth will I tell him? Guess what Will? Last week you had a step-dad; this week you don't.*

"Mom, why are you always singing that song? It sounds silly," Will commented, watching his mother dance around.

Liz's happy expression changed. She stopped dancing. "That's *Wooly Bully,* a song Adam and I always used to sing. When we were teenagers we would go to the neighborhood fountain shop with a group of our friends and play that song over and over again in the juke box".

"What's a jukebox?" he asked with his big brown eyes searching hers.

"It's a big machine that plays music. You put money in the big machine and voilá, a song plays."

"What's vowa?"

"No sweetheart, *voilá*! It's a word that people say in a country called France when they want to say, *here it is*!" Will looked confused and changed the subject.

"Mom, when will I meet Adam? You're always talking about him, but I never meet him."

"I'm not sure honey. I don't know where he is right now. But as soon as I hear from him, you will definitely meet him. And I bet he'll be happy to meet you. He might even bring you a basketball."

The week before, Liz tried calling Adam's roommate from college, but he claimed he had no idea where Adam was. It had been six years since she had spoken to Paul, but she was worried and didn't know what else to do. The last time she heard from Adam, there was a bad connection and she couldn't make out what he was saying; something about Canada and coming home. She had no idea what he was talking about. There were several other attempts to reach each other in the last few years, but they never made contact. No one else knew his whereabouts. It had been years since anyone heard from him.

"C'mon Will, let's get some pizza. You want some?"

Will jumped up and down to show his approval. "Yea!"

After several more heated arguments, Tom packed his belongings and left. He wasn't a bit remorseful; he was infuriated.

"Liz, I said I was sorry. What's your problem? I had a little too much to drink. Everyone gets drunk once in a while. You're going to dissolve our marriage because of one incident? I don't get it! What are you doing? Do you think you can turn it on and then turn it off whenever you want, like a water faucet?" Tom bellowed.

"You weren't this way this when we first met. I admit I hardly knew you. We married too soon before I got the chance to know the *real* you. And I don't like what I see. And, I don't want Will growing up with an abusive stepfather!"

"Ah, come on Liz! I'm not abusive. I had too much to drink; that one night!"

"Yeah, sure. You tried to rape me Tom!" she shouted. I won't discuss this anymore. Get out of here. You'll be hearing from my lawyer!"

"Rape you? What are you talking about? I didn't try to rape you! What kind of garbage is that?"

"I am not addressing this subject anymore! Get out of here!"

"Liz, Will and I are real tight. He and I have formed a bond! We're pals. What are you doing?" he pleaded.

This time she screamed. "I said get out of here!"

As she watched him leave the room she found herself trembling. Deep inside she knew it wasn't only about that one night. It was about Adam. She needed to find him. She was falling apart and needed to tell him the truth. Too much time had gone by. Will was 5 years old and she had big regrets.

Liz thought, *Maybe Adam isn't drinking anymore. I wonder if he's married.*

"Mom, how come all the kids at school have dads except me?"

Liz tried to remember the kids in his kindergarten class. "That's not true honey. Your friends Peter and Sally don't have dads."

25

"Yeah, but they have stepdads. Sally even has a stepmom and stepbrother. Now I have nobody. Tom left me just like my dad left me," he whimpered.

It had only been a few days and Will was already feeling the effects of Tom not being around. They were pals and he was missing the father-son things they did together.

"Will, we've talked about this before," Liz snapped, frustrated mostly with herself. In a softer voice she said, "You have me. And I love you so much!" She went over to him and hugged him closely. "Your dad didn't leave you. It's just that sometimes people have trouble doing the right thing. They don't always do what they should. Ok, honey?"

"Will I ever meet him?" he asked in a more subdued tone.

"I don't know Will. I hope so." And she meant it.

"Mom, why did Tom leave us? Did I do something wrong?"

"Of course not! Where did you ever get such an idea?"

Liz's recklessness was affecting Will. He was at an impressionable age and wanted to know his real father. She repeatedly told him that his dad was a good man, but couldn't be with him right now. And even though he missed his step-dad, he wouldn't be able to see *him* anymore, because he wasn't a good person. As soon as the words were out of her mouth, she regretted her candor.

# CHAPTER FOUR

# LIZ

## (JUNE 1978)

When I turned onto Taylor Road, Will was waiting on the porch steps with his head pointed down.

"What are you doing out here? Are you okay?"

"Just waiting for you. I got bored."

"How was dinner at Billy's?"

"It was okay. We watched a couple of movies and watched his brother kissing his girlfriend." Will made a disgusting face and stuck out his tongue. "Gross!"

Suppressing a laugh, Liz asked, "How old is his brother?"

"I don't know Mom. When is Adam coming?"

"In a couple of days, honey. He's going with us to the concert and the two of you will sit together, okay?"

"Will he take me to the baseball game next week like he promised?"

"We'll talk about it in the morning Will," my voice muffled as I let out a big yawn.

Exhausted I walked into the house with the hope of going right to bed. In the corner of my eye I noticed a red blinking light. I had purchased my first telephone answering machine and was excited about using it, but decided I would retrieve my messages in the morning. I was still learning how to operate it.

I woke up refreshed, splashed water on my face, and walked downstairs. *How the hell do I get this thing to work? Oh I see, hit play!* "Beepppp"…"Hello, Mrs. Riley, this is Frank from Fixer-up Plumbing. We have your parts ready and…"Beepppp"… "Hi Liz. How are you? I was wondering if you want to get together Tuesday afternoon and talk over the Benson account. Please let me know."

"So much for feeling refreshed," I mumbled. "Will, time to get up, okay?"

Adam paid the florist and headed for the concert, hoping a dozen roses would ease his guilt. His secret was troubling him for weeks. He quickened his step and searched for a taxi not wanting to be late.

Liz and Will were waiting with the tickets at the entranceway when he arrived. Since the day Adam met her, she was always forgetting something. The other night they joked about her absent-mindedness when she forgot to give him the tickets. "Some things never change!" he teased.

"Adam, over here!" Will ran exuberantly towards him and they gave each other a bear hug. Adam kissed Liz on the cheek and wished her luck as he tried unsuccessfully to hide the flowers behind his back.

"Break a leg!"

"Yeah mom, break a leg," Will giggled and then look concerned. "But don't really do that, okay?"

Adam and Will found their seats. They were seated front row reserved for families.

"Did you get those for mom?" Will asked.

"Yes, do you think she'll like them? Hey, wait a minute! I have an idea. After the concert why don't you give them to your mom? What do you think?"

Will beamed. "You mean she'll think they're from me? Thanks Adam!"

The concert was two hours long with one short break. Will was a bit restless, but impressed by his mom. When it was over, the orchestra received a standing ovation, and Adam and Will clapped the loudest.

"Let's go find your mom." They held hands and walked into the reception area in perfect time to see her. She was one of the first to exit. Adam thought, *doesn't she look beautiful?*

"How'd we do?" Liz asked.

At once they both said, "Great!"

The three of them walked over to a corner while the crowd dispersed. Cocktails and hors d'oeuvres were being served.

"These are for you Mom," Will said proudly.

"Oh, they're lovely!" She breathed in the sweet smelling scent. "Thank you Will!"

She and Adam exchanged a knowing glance.

CHAPTER FIVE

# ADAM
## (SEPTEMBER 1978)

"Hanna, if you're there please pick up the phone. I've been calling since yesterday and I'm beginning to worry. Please! Is Lillie okay?" *Dammit! Where is she? Maybe she took Lillie to the doctor?*

As he finished straightening his tie, the phone rang. *Thank God!* "Hello? Is that you?"

"Yes. Hi Adam. It's me, Liz. What's the matter? You sound funny; are you all right?"

Adam sighed. *Dammit!*

"Should I call you later?"

"Would you mind? I'm late for an appointment."

He hailed a taxi and headed for Richard Pinkley, a pain-in-the-ass client who didn't appreciate waiting. Stuck in traffic, he had time to mull over Hanna's whereabouts.

It was the summer of 1977 when Hanna and I met at a fundraiser for a mutual client, Toole & Toole. Henry Toole's wife died of cancer six years earlier and a yearly benefit was his way of dealing with his loss. Each year the fundraiser was a success and brought in tens of thousands of dollars.

Hanna worked as an HR manager of a legal firm out in Orange County and was representing them. I was on an audit in Los Angeles for over a month, and missing Liz. My presence at this event was expected, but I didn't mind much anyway. After a couple of hours the speeches were over and everyone went inside the banquet room to eat. I went to get a drink at the bar and saw a pretty brunette watching me. She was wearing a sexy low-cut red dress that framed her small figure. Her spiked heels gave me the impression that she was tall, but on second glance I realized how short she was. As I approached her, she smiled and introduced herself.

"Hi, I'm Hanna."

"Hello, I'm Adam; Adam Greenstein. Nice to meet you! Can I get you a drink?"

"Why yes, thank you," she smiled again. "Some white wine would be nice."

Hanna and I went to dinner several nights in a row after our first meeting. One thing led to another and before we knew it we were back in my hotel room. Sex was different with Hanna. Neither one of us felt emotional ties towards one another and I felt freer then I had in a long time. Everything with Liz was so intense. This was good for a change.

One month later Hanna became pregnant.

Hanna wasn't a very organized person. Apparently, she had forgotten to take her birth control pill the following morning. After much deliberation, they decided to go forward with the pregnancy, and Adam spent additional time out west to see if anything would develop between them. The baby seemed to be his only connection to Hanna other than sex, and that was becoming less frequent now that she was four months pregnant. Over the next few months Liz and Adam became more distant and he became more confused.

Adam and Hanna only met recently, but she knew, or thought she knew, he was the one. The one to raise her child. Secretly, she was happy about the pregnancy. In fact, she was on cloud 9. She didn't really forget to take her birth control pills.

Marriage was another story. She wasn't interested in marrying him, or for that matter, anyone. She was always a loner and wanted to keep it that way with no one to answer to. But she was thirty-five and was concerned about never becoming a mother. This was a dream of hers, to have a little boy or little girl.

Hanna liked the way Adam thought. At times he was refreshingly funny and appeared intelligent, but he didn't seem to have any interests. This puzzled her. She was yet to find out what made him tick. And that's what made it exciting. Although she wasn't sure if these were enough attributes for a father to pass on to a child, she went forward with her plans.

When Adam told Hanna about Liz, his involvement with another woman went over her head. She didn't seem to hear him, or possibly she didn't care. Her mind was made up without much consideration for the future.

On the other hand Adam felt trapped. He wanted a life with Liz, but he felt he had to do the honorable thing. He was stuck.

One day Hanna became sick. She hadn't been eating much and was experiencing severe abdominal pain. We just came back from a movie and I was leaving for New York in a couple of hours. I gasped when I found her doubled over in her bedroom clutching her stomach.

"Hanna, what happened? What's wrong?"

"Adam, the baby!"

"It'll be okay; I promise, the baby will be okay," I cried without conviction. My voice was weak with fear.

I dodged several red lights before hearing the sirens behind me. "Jesus Christ!" Exasperated, I slammed on the brakes and pulled off the road.

"Officer, please my girlfriend sh… she needs to get to the hospital right away. She's pregnant and, and…and she's sick," I stammered.

We arrived just in time for Lillie to be born. Hanna was in premature labor at 6 1/2 months. It was a difficult birth and Lillie stayed in the hospital for several months before she was strong enough to go home.

Hanna was distraught and blamed herself which only made me feel guiltier than I already felt. I was torn about not marrying her. And, I was confused over what to tell Liz.

Liz called me a week after Lillie was born. I never told her I was involved with anyone and she would be shocked to hear that I was now a dad.

# CHAPTER SIX

# ADAM
## (SEPTEMBER 1978)

"Adam, hi. How are you? I haven't heard from you lately and I was wondering…"

Liz was accustomed to not hearing from Adam, but she was also guilty of not calling him. Neither one of them could get the other out of their heads.

"Liz, it's good to hear your voice! I'm so sorry I haven't called you back. I got your messages, but…" Adam's voice trailed off.

"Please Adam, tell me what's wrong. I don't understand why we haven't' been seeing each other. I thought we were back together. Didn't you? We lost so much time over the years."

"Liz," his voice subdued, "can we get together next week? I should be back in New York for a few days."

"Yes of course," she said with trepidation.

Dread rose in his throat at the thought of what was ahead. He didn't want to lose Liz. Things had changed for them in the last few months. He was afraid their relationship would end if he continued hiding the truth.

He arrived the following Wednesday and checked in at the Hilton on West 53rd. His clients were near 6th and 44th, so this was perfect.

They met in *Etrusca,* which had the best Italian cuisine around. For an appetizer they shared steamed mussels and clams with fresh herbs in a lobster tomato broth. Liz had sea bass and Adam had veal scaloppini. Neither one of them drank wine. They were quiet. And then the whole damned story came flooding out of him.

"The truth is Liz, I don't know why I slept with Hanna. But I did. It's over and done with. And now there's Lillie to consider."

At first Liz seemed distant and angry. Her eyes became the color of slate. It appeared she was trying to take it all in.

"I don't understand!" Liz spat. "We didn't even have an argument. Why would you sleep with someone else let alone have an affair? I thought we had a future together. I thought we loved each other!"

"I do love you Liz," he said with clarity.

"That's ridiculous! I don't call that love," she said steaming.

"I'm sorry Liz. I really am. I was gone for so long and I guess I was lonely. Don't you remember? I asked if you could come for a weekend, but…"

"Stop it Adam! I don't want to hear anymore. After all the time we've been separated from each other and slowly figuring things out and now you do this to me! I can't believe it! We just needed time together to figure things out," she repeated. "Goddamned you!"

Liz quieted and spoke in a business-like manner. "So, tell me about Lillie. How old is she?"

He spoke about her with a mixture of pride and sadness in his voice and was certain Liz wasn't listening. She was ignoring him and changed the subject.

"Ah Adam, look at that sweet puppy," she motioned towards the street. "I wonder what breed it is. I never asked you before, or did I? Did you ever have a dog when you were little?"

*I finally lost her. I didn't even have a chance to tell her about Lillie's premature birth.*

As they were finishing dinner, Liz said there was something important she had to tell him, but when the waiter presented the bill, Adam turned around and saw Liz walking away. Panicking, he signaled the waiter once more and hurriedly paid the check, but she was already gone.

# CHAPTER SEVEN

# LIZ
## (SEPTEMBER 1978)

After leaving the restaurant Liz went straight home. She was fuming and saddened all at once. *How could he! How could he cheat on me? Why?* She started to sob uncontrollably. *And a baby! A baby girl! We were going to have a …wait, what am I talking about? We did. Oh Adam!*

She thought back to a few months ago when Anne shared some shocking news. It was difficult for Liz to digest what she heard after being close friends for the last ten years, let alone this new revelation from Adam.

*"Liz, sit down. I have something to tell you. I'm not sure how you'll take it."*

*"Anne, you can tell me anything. I won't look at you any differently."*

*"You say you won't, but you might. I don't want to hurt our friendship."*

*"Stop it Anne. Nothing will ever change between us. I love you, unconditionally, and I won't judge you. You know that, don't you?" She*

*looked at her dear friend and thought how pretty she looked. Actually she looked happy. Her eyes were sparkling!*

*"Okay, here goes. I'm cheating on Fred." She paused. "And that's only half of it."*

*Liz took a deep breath and swallowed hard. "How the hell did that happen? I always thought the two of you were fine...well, until he cheated on you that is. I'm sorry, that was stupid! Wait! What's the other half of it?" She braced herself.*

*"This is the part I'm really worried about."*

*"Tell me already," Liz said apprehensively.*

*"Okay." Anne averted her eyes. "I'm in love with someone. A woman!"*

This is crazy! All our lives are topsy-turvy! Adam had a baby with someone else! I had his baby and he doesn't know it. And even Anne. How the hell did she become a lesbian? What is going on with all of us?

I went into my studio and found pastels scattered on the drafting table. I started sketching furiously as I did when I was upset as a child. Once in third grade when a few kids made fun of my Buster Brown shoes, I feigned a stomach ache and was sent to the nurse's office. After my mother picked me up and grilled me with questions about how many cookies I ate at lunchtime and how much candy I devoured, she tucked me into bed. When she left my bedroom, I reached for my crayons and drew pictures of my schoolmates punching each other. Today similarly, ragged angry lines appeared on my pad – reds, oranges, and purples, creating fire-like images with fury. With charcoal I proceeded to draw faces of Adam, and then of how I imagined Lillie.

I couldn't tell him that Will was his son after hearing about Lillie. Lillie, a little girl. I can't believe Adam is the father of a little girl! Will has a half-sister!

One week later, after ignoring Adam's calls, Liz finally arranged to meet him at his hotel.

"Why didn't you tell me about Hanna; about Lillie?" *Why didn't I tell him about Will!* "Why did you wait? Why now? How can you let all this time pass?" *How the hell did I let all this time pass? I'm as bad as he is!* "You never thought to tell me before?"

"Liz, it's done. Can we move on?" Adam pleaded.

"How can we move on? How the hell can things ever be the same?" Liz paused and felt her heart pounding. "Look, there's something *I* have to tell *you*."

"Sure, what is it," Adam snapped, glad to depart from this most difficult subject.

Her thoughts were abruptly interrupted by the phone ringing. It was Will's babysitter letting her know she didn't feel well. Rebecca was 15 years old and a sophomore in high school. Liz grabbed her pocketbook and sweater. Vaguely relieved she said, "I guess we'll talk later Adam, I'm sorry."

Later never came. It was a long time before the subject came up again.

Two days later Will was sent home from school. He had a high fever and sore throat. The pediatrician said he had strep and gave him a prescription for an antibiotic. Apparently he got sick from Rebecca, because when Liz called her the following day to see how she was, she also had strep.

Will's blanket was on top of a heap of his clothing on the floor. In the hall closet she found a lighter one and covered him. His fever still hadn't broken, even though three days had gone by. Evidently the medicine hadn't kicked in and alternating lukewarm baths and Tylenol weren't helping either. Liz was worried. She called the doctor's office and for the second time questioned if she should bring him in again.

"How high did you say?" the receptionist inquired. She came back after speaking with the nurse and told Liz that 105 degrees is considered high after several days and if the fever didn't drop by morning, she should bring him to the emergency room.

Just as she hung up the phone, it rang and she hurried to pick it up so Will wouldn't awaken. It was Adam.

"Please Liz, talk to me."

"I can't talk now, Adam. Will is sick." Anger rose in her again, mixed with confusion and sorrow.

Liz tossed and turned for hours. She finally fell asleep at 4:00 am and woke up with a start two hours later to the sound of the alarm.

"Jesus! This is the most irritating clock I've ever had," she said aloud. She fumbled for the off switch and then walked into Will's still darkened room.

She whispered, "Will, how do you feel?"

"I'm okay Mom," he mumbled, "just thirsty. Could you get me some water?"

Liz came back with a small cup and the thermometer. His fever was still high and he looked ghastly. She hurriedly packed a few things and headed for the hospital, while he slept in the car. Upon being admitted, Liz glanced at Will who seemed even more listless than before. After he was given a room, she started making phone calls. She first reached her parents and then Adam.

Frantically, she croaked, "Will is in the hospital. I took him to the doctor a few days ago for strep and his fever hasn't gone down. It's still 105 degrees. Adam, can you please come quickly?"

Liz watched Will as he slept fitfully in the hospital bed. He looked so helpless and she blamed herself unnecessarily for being a lousy mother. The doctor indicated he would be fine and could probably go home in a couple of days, but they first needed to see if stronger antibiotics would be more effective.

*First I marry Tom and Will's heart was broken, and now Adam turns out to be a jerk. Between his drinking and having a child by another woman….well, how the hell can I explain any of this to Will as he gets older?*

"Liz, how's Will? Is he okay?" Adam rushed into the room and found her crying.

"Yes, he's getting better."

"Come here, let me hold you," Adam said soothingly.

She got up and let him put his arms around her wishing she had had the guts earlier to tell him he was Will's father. She needed to share her worries with him, but what good would it do? Now that he had Hanna and Lillie in his life, she wasn't sure about anything anymore.

Moments later her parents walked in at the same time as the doctor. "Mom, Dad, I'm so glad you're here. I've been so scared." They hugged their daughter and reassured her. Acknowledging Adam, they then walked over to Will who was sleeping soundly.

The white haired middle-aged doctor with a faint English accent looked at the charts and said, "Miss Bloom, I'm going to run some tests, but I'm sure there's nothing to worry about. Your boy is in good hands. We've put him on a stronger antibiotic and that should do the trick. Hopefully, Will's going to be on his feet in a couple of days."

"Thank you doctor, but could it be something other than strep? His fever was so high!" Liz was ashen and looked as if she might faint.

"I'm pretty certain that's all it is, but we should know more tomorrow after the tests results come in." Dr. Nichols cleared his throat. "Please, try not to worry."

Liz's mom signaled to speak with her privately and whispered, "Liz, I've asked you so many times; why don't you tell Adam he's the father? He has a right to know! And, now that Will is sick, don't you think after all these years you should tell him?"

"Mom, please leave it alone, will you? Now's not the time."

"Now is the perfect time." Liz's mom was patently upset. "How much longer can this go on?"

"I don't know Mom, I just don't know. But as long as Adam still drinks, I can't consider it."

Will was released two days later. The antibiotics kicked in by days end and his fever had dropped. The scare was over.

CHAPTER EIGHT

# ADAM

## (SEPTEMBER 1978)

*God dammit! Why hasn't she returned my call?* Shortly after Lillie was discharged from the hospital, Hanna and I brought her for her first checkup with the pediatrician. The doctor told us things didn't seem "quite normal"; her progress was a bit delayed, but that was probably okay for a preemie. He wanted to see us back in his office in another month. But when we returned, it was exactly as he suspected; Lillie wasn't advancing the way she should at three months. When Hanna went to comfort her, she would resist her touch. She didn't make eye contact when being fed; she didn't follow her mobile, which hung colorfully above her crib; and she didn't respond to her name when Hanna and I spoke to her.

One day Hanna confessed her frustrations to me. "I want to give Lillie back," she cried. Like she had a choice! I had my own trepidations. I was falling apart and didn't know what to feel. Liz was my life, my future, and I wasn't about to marry Hanna because of Lillie. Was I?

Adam didn't know his real parents. He had no idea who they were. He wasn't sure if they were even married to each other. And for all he knew, he might have a brother or sister maybe even living in the same town.

He was adopted by a woman who in the early years seemed to care about him, but the very second she kicked her husband out and ended the marriage, she ended her role as a mother. Adam didn't understand why his adopted father didn't leave *her* instead. She was a cold bitch. Any woman who goes through the trouble of adoption and then treats her child like the evening trash, well, she could go to hell. Adam was pissed. He felt lost for a long time and actually hated her.

Adam and his adopted dad got along well; they often played golf together. After the divorce his dad moved to California. Adam was lonely and missed those special days when they teed off. That's when Adam started drinking beer every day, but it wasn't new to him. As a teenager he drank a lot, but not *every* day. And that's when he met Liz.

# CHAPTER NINE
# LIZ
## (1966-1968)

School was out and I was looking forward to the summer. Jones Beach and my bikini; my pedal pushers and my ruffled short blouses with the pink polka dots, and the yellow daisy ones; they were *so* sexy!

One hot summer day I came home from the beach with Sue, my best friend in the world. We were as close as anyone could be. Ever since we were thirteen we were inseparable! Our only goal in life was to meet the boy of our dreams and someday marry him. So when school ended, we made sure to search him out wherever we went. But, I was pretty sure I already met someone.

That day there was so much excitement in my house. Mom and Dad were talking about something going on with the Vietnam War.

"Are you kidding?" My mom gaped. "Americans are being investigated by the *Un-American Activities Committee*?"

"Not kidding! I heard it on CBS; Walter Cronkite was on. The government is concerned that certain Americans have been aiding the Viet Cong. Fifty of those people were arrested for demonstrating against the war! Do you believe it? They're thinking of making these types of activities illegal because the leaders of these groups may be hard-core communists!"

Mom looked from dad to me. "Holy mackerel!"

Frankly, I didn't care what my parents were talking about. I had no interest. What did I know about the war at 16 years old? All I knew was that my friends were in love and so was I. My sweet sixteen party the weekend before turned out to be a success. Adam was there, and so was John, another boy in my class who had the hots for me. He was pretty cute and I had everything covered. Jealousy set in motion! But I was ambivalent about my feelings for Adam. Every time we got together he was drunk. Ironically, my mother was crazy about him. And I must admit, there was something about Adam; I was falling for him.

Two years went by and we were officially eighteen. Every weekend Adam and I would take his purple Volkswagen Beetle and drive to the *Port of Missing Men* in Flushing where his father's 45*rpm* records were stashed in the juke box.

His dad, a disc jockey, had supplied this bar and other local dives with extras which had accumulated in his radio station over the years.

What a hideous color purple was! And the back of the car, well, it was disgusting. It was overflowing with empty beer cans and junk. When I groused, he grinned and exclaimed, "What's wrong with the back of my car? I think it looks really cool."

"Oh nothing Adam. Maybe a little depressing, that's all. I think you *might* have a problem?"

It was June and we finally graduated from Martin Van Buren High School. The auditorium was filled with families as we marched down the aisle in our caps and gowns. I waved to my parents and saw them grinning ear to ear, and knew they were filled with pride.

Adam and I celebrated at the golf course down the road from where we lived. This time we both got polluted. I never had so much fun in my life running up and down the verdant hills with my long legs flying as we sang the words "hallelujah, we did It" over and over again in soprano and baritone drunken voices. It was then that I found out that Adam was adopted.

"You were what? You were adopted? You're kidding me! Does this mean you're not Jewish…or are you?" I asked in disbelief.

"Nope, I'm not Jewish. I'm Irish!" he roared and then started to laugh the best laugh I had ever heard.

"You're telling me that you were Bar Mitzvahed for no reason?" laughing so hard that my stomach hurt.

The slow gruff noises that emanated from him sounded mimicked a donkey's bray. I laughed harder and harder with tears running down my cheeks. Before we knew it the sun was coming up. As we lay in the grass dozing without a care in the world, it suddenly dawned on me how late it was.

I screamed, "Oh my God! My mother is going to kill me! Look at the time!"

Running all the way home Adam and I promised each other to write every day. He was leaving in two days to start the summer semester at Orange Coast College, a small school in California, close to where his dad lived. He would study accounting. I was attending Queens College where I would study art. Later on I learned that Paul Simon was a student here and Marvin Hamlisch graduated from this school. I could have taken the same classes as they had, but I was a few years younger and about to start my freshman year. They had already made their mark and I was walking on their ground! Can you imagine? The other half of Garfunkel, and not only that, Marvin Hamlisch, one of the greatest composers of our time, and I had just missed them!

Before we said goodbye, Adam made it clear he wouldn't marry anyone else. He was in love with me and would come back for us to be together.

"I will miss you Liz. Will you wait for me?"

"Of course I will wait for you silly. But Adam, do you think you might get drafted or something? I feel scared for you. I've heard a lot about the war and so many boys have already left."

"Nah, I'll be in college. Nothing will happen to *me*. We'll be back together, you'll see."

They hadn't talked much about the war. They were young and in love and the subject seemed very distant to them. Besides, there were too many other monumental changes occurring.

# CHAPTER TEN

# ADAM

## (1968)

"C'mon! Play cards already! Get your minds out of the gutter! Is sex all you think about?" Adam questioned irritably.

The six of them were drinking beer and playing cards for hours. Their first exams were coming up and no one seemed to care. And when Adam went to sleep that night, not even Liz was on his mind. The beer had f...ked up his mind enough for him to sleep until noon.

The phone rang interrupting his fitful sleep. *Jesus! How much beer did I drink anyway? My head's going to fall off!* Grabbing the receiver he snapped, "What!"

"Adam, is that you?" his Uncle Harry inquired. "Your father! He's in the hospital! Come quick, okay?"

Uncle Harry was an okay guy. When I was little he always gave me the change that he found in his pockets and he'd say, "Save it for a rainy day, okay kid?" Uncle Harry moved to California years ago after my aunt died. I suppose that's why my dad went there in the first place; to be close to his brother.

It was a fifteen minute drive to Irvine where my father lived. The hospital was two minutes from his house. I hadn't seen him much lately. School was keeping me busy when I wasn't goofing off. Now I was regretting it. *What was wrong anyway? Did Uncle Harry say what happened? Is he dying?* I pulled into the parking lot and frantically looked for the entrance to the hospital as I imagined the worst. Trying to catch my breath I started to tremble. "My father, Adam Greenstein, please, could you tell me what room he's in?" I begged the front desk nurse. All of a sudden she turned around, and ran to the rear entrance door. There was some kind of commotion going on and I screamed for her attention to come back. "Hey, where are you going? I need help here!" It was then that I realized there were two Negro men dragging in a bloodied older man. Everything was happening so fast. The attendants stormed out of the emergency room with a stretcher and rushed back with another man on a gurney. "Will someone please…." There was nobody else there. I waited.

It was too late. His father had died of cardiac arrest. Adam was alone. With rubbery legs he walked out of the hospital and into the street where he stood numbly. And then the sobs came.

"Liz, it's me."

"Adam, what's the matter…Adam?" Her hand was shaking as she held the phone. She knew something was terribly wrong by the tone in his voice.

"My father; he died. My Uncle Harry called me yesterday and told me to come to the hospital. I didn't make it there on time. He died of a heart attack, Liz. I was only a few minutes away. How can it happen so fast?"

"Oh my God! I'm so sorry, Adam. Are you ok?" Liz didn't know what to say or do. "I guess that's a stupid question."

"Liz, I can't move. I'm sitting on my couch staring into space since yesterday. What's the matter with me?"

"Nothing Adam, nothing's wrong with you. People grieve in different ways, that's all."

They talked for a while about the funeral, and his mother. He had no idea where to find her and she probably wouldn't go anyway. He hadn't seen her in ages and didn't care to. His uncle handled all the arrangements. It was set for two days from now. All Adam wanted was for it to be over and done with. There would just be three of them; Adam, Uncle Harry, and Adam's obnoxious cousin Steve. Liz was unable to attend. Since it was also her first semester, she needed to buckle down and study for her exams. But, she called Adam often until one day he no longer answered.

After his father was buried, Adam dropped out of school and drank himself into oblivion. He had been in school for only a short time. Many months had gone by before he contacted Liz again.

# CHAPTER ELEVEN

# LIZ

## (1968-1969)

Liz was doing well in school. She loved all her art courses, and was meeting lots of new friends and starting to date. She didn't know yet what to do with her art, but teaching or advertising were on the top of her list. She had time though; classes just started. At a very young age Liz started sketching with anything she could get her hands on: pencils, charcoal, and Cray-pas were her favorites.

Friday night she was going out with a new guy she met in her art history course. Ron wasn't an art major. He was taking random courses until he figured out what to do with his life. During class Liz questioned her professor as to how cavemen drew pictures during the Paleolithic Era. Ron raised his hand and offered an answer. "Didn't they use the shoulder bones of animals, and even grindstones to produce drawing tools?" The teacher was pleased as hands flew up with more questions about paints and pigments and brushes.

Time passed quickly and at the end of the class Ron approached Liz. "Would you join me for some coffee? I know a place down the street."

"Sure."

They talked for a long time about all sorts of things: family, school, their future. But Liz couldn't get into him. He wasn't her type. Nobody was her type. She only wanted Adam. It had been months since she'd heard from him. After he lost his father, he shut down to everyone, even Liz. She missed him and didn't know what to do.

One rainy day after classes, while fumbling for her keys at the door, she heard the phone ringing. Her mom wasn't home yet from work. She ran inside and nearly tripped over the ottoman trying to make it to the phone in time.

"Adam? Finally! I called you a hundred times. I've been worried sick about you! Are you all right?"

"I'm really sorry, Liz. I've been so lost. I haven't been going to school; took a leave of absence."

"Why? Because of your dad?"

"Yeah, I guess so. I've been drinking a lot," he muttered.

"Oh." Liz's heart sank. "Are you going back?"

"To school? Yes, I have already, since yesterday. But not full-time."

"That's okay, Adam. It will work out, you'll see. I miss you, you know. I wish we could see each other." Liz's soft tone changed without her realizing it. "But, I wish you would stop drinking."

"I will Liz. I'm working on it." He brushed her off and they were quiet for a time.

"How's school?"

"Good! I like my courses, especially music history. It's interesting. The professor makes you think. I've also made some friends," she added excitedly with a tinge of guilt.

"Hey, did you hear about Woodstock?"

"Do you mean the concert, upstate?"

53

"Yeah. I wish I could come home in time so we could go together. It's in August. I heard it's going to be one hell of a time. Every band will be there: Grateful Dead, Santana, Richie Havens, Jimi Hendrix; you name it. Fifty-thousand kids are expected! Do you believe it?"

"Wow! Holy mackerel!"

"Liz, I'm coming home during winter break though. Can we spend some time together?"

# (1969)

For two months I could hardly concentrate on my schoolwork. Adam was finally coming home and I was elated. We had spoken a few times on the phone and made plans for when we would be together. After coming up with lame suggestions of where to "do it", we settled on springing for a motel.

We met at our old hang-out, the golf course back in Douglaston. The place hadn't changed. But why would it? Only six months had gone by. It seemed like years.

"Liz, I'm here!"

She turned around and saw him standing there looking as handsome as ever. She threw her arms around him and held him close. Adam stepped back and looked at her, and then kissed her, first gently and then passionately. They kissed for a long time until they could no longer bare it.

"I made reservations in a motel on Northern Boulevard," she said.

"What about your parents?"

"They think I'm at Sue's," Liz grinned.

"Ah, nothing changes," he laughed too. "Come on, let's go." He put his arm around her, still smiling.

"Liz, I've missed you so much. It will be hard to go back to school," he said huskily.

"I can't believe it! You're already saying goodbye? You just arrived." She tenderly kissed his cheek and said demurely, "I love you Adam. You know, we haven't been together since that first time in the shack. It's been so long."

They drove in silence for a time, each with anticipation.

"I remember every moment of that night." *Shit, I hope she doesn't remember! I only lasted a minute.*

Holding hands they walked into the motel room with two small pieces of luggage in Adam's free hand. After putting everything down, they both fell onto the bed. Liz threw off her heels and Adam untied his sneakers. Simultaneously they got up again, giggled, and stripped down the bed linen. Snuggling up against his medium frame, she started to stroke the hair on his chest as Adam kissed her neck and nibbled tenderly on her ear. Slowly he unbuttoned her cream-colored lacy blouse.

"Adam, could you turn off the lights?" He got up, but clumsily fell backwards before his feet hit the floor. "Oh no, are you all right?" she asked with a soft laugh.

"Yeah, nothing a little beer wouldn't cure right now," he joked, but secretly wished it was so. He dimmed the lamp near his side of the bed, lifted his sweatshirt over his head, and lay down next to her. Reaching for her belly, he unzipped her sequined bell bottoms as she slipped out of them. Slowly, his hand continued downward until he found her softness beneath his touch. He gently spread her legs open while stroking her. She watched him and then slid her blouse off and unfastened her bra. His hand traveled up to her small but ample breasts as he took each one into his mouth, gently at first and then more roughly. He ran his knuckles up and down her nipples teasingly and then took one by one between his forefinger and thumb and squeezed. Liz gasped. Adam watched each one grow as she became more and more excited. She trembled and reached for him where he was pulsing. He hurriedly removed his pants and she shyly began to caress his hardness.

They clung to each other and savored each moment until Liz abruptly stopped. Her breathing uneven, she asked, "Did you bring a condom?"

"Shit! I wasn't thinking! Do you have anything?" Trying to clear his head, he mumbled, "That was stupid. You wouldn't have asked me, would you?"

"No, but I think we'll be okay because it's close to my time of the month," she said wondering if *that* made any sense. Her head was also clouded and she couldn't think.

They kissed until their lips were swollen with love.

"Adam," she moaned softly, "Now. Please."

"Not yet," he said gruffly.

Slowly, his hands traveled up and down her hips, and then drawing her up to him, he finally thrust into her. Minutes later they climaxed together both sinking into the bed fully sated.

They slept soundly until the alarm shrieked in their ears and awakened them. The morning was still part of the night. Adam rolled over and held her against him feeling her softness.

"I love you Liz."

"I love you too. That was wonderful, wasn't it?"

"Want more?" he chuckled.

"Nope! I'm starving; maybe later? I built up a huge appetite. Let's go to the *Scobie Diner*, okay? I want eggs, pancakes, bacon…" Liz's eyes glistened. She was content for the first time in a while. "Aren't you hungry?"

"Yep! I'm starving too! I could literally eat a horse!"

They laughed, remembering his father's silly expression.

Adam had one week to spend with Liz before going back to school and they planned to be together every moment of every day. After they left the diner she went home and checked in with her parents. It was the weekend and they were both home. She promised she would touch base throughout the week.

"Mom… Dad, I'm home."

Liz's mom yelled from the kitchen, "Hi honey. How was it last night? Did you have a nice time at Sue's?"

"Yes Mom, I'm just picking up some stuff," she sighed with irritation, and at the same time blushed knowing where she really was the night before. Her mom meant well, but somehow Liz always felt frustrated with her endless questions.

"Don't forget to get some studying done," her dad added as he walked into the darkened living room.

Classical music was playing loudly on the record player. He turned on the lights and looked at his daughter quizzically. "You *are* going to get some studying done, aren't you?"

"Of course Dad! Stop worrying! I'll be fine. Sue and I are just hanging out together, but I promise I won't screw up. Dad, what is that playing? Is it Mozart?"

"Very good Liz! It is; it's Piano Concerto #21. Do you like it?"

"I do Dad. I think I'm going to take up violin in my junior year. What do you think?"

Right then Liz's mom walked in. "Honey, that's wonderful! As an elective?"

"Yes, I'm sticking with art, but I'll take some music courses too. Listen, I've got to go, okay? Sue's waiting for me. We're going to the movies." She kissed them goodbye and hurried out the door.

Her mother shouted, "Wait Liz! Have you heard from Adam yet?"

Liz pretended not to hear.

Adam set the mood with romantic music and incenses. The aroma of Indian sandalwood filled the air. He was glancing at an economics text impatiently waiting for her when he heard the key in the door. Since he had dropped out of school during the first semester, he decided to start off slowly with only one course. But at least he was going back. In order to graduate on time, he'd have to take summer courses.

"Hi, I thought you'd never come back!" He got up and hugged her.

Liz immediately looked around and noticed the atmosphere. "Aren't we going out?"

"Nope! We're staying right here. Come sit with me," he motioned to the bed.

Grinning, she obeyed. "Hmmm, what do *you* want?"

Liz rolled over on her side totally naked facing Adam. Their clothes were scattered all over the floor. He ran his hand up and down her legs and then started to kiss the inside of her thighs. His stubble burned her, but she didn't care. She turned onto her back and let him please her. Minutes later he lifted himself onto her and penetrated deeply until he could no longer bear it. This time he remembered to bring a condom. Hours passed. They slept and woke again, only to find themselves loving each other again and again.

"Hey, aren't we ever getting out of here?" she feigned disappointment.

"C'mon, let's get dressed and go for a bite. Where do you want to eat?" Adam asked.

It went on like that for three days. They'd make love, run out for a quick bite, and return to make love again. For the remainder of the week they filled up their time with a visit to the Museum of Modern Art, and a foreign film festival.

On the last day they met Liz's new friend in a coffeehouse. Adam never met Anne before. There was a folk guitarist playing when they entered. Anne was sitting in the back nursing a cup of coffee.

"Liz, hi, I'm over here!" she yelled over the music and din around her.

They sat down and exchanged pleasantries.

"So, what's your major?" Adam asked.

She grinned, starting to blush. "Well, right now I'm majoring in boys!"

Gullibly, Adam stared at her.

"No, really, I'm just taking some general courses: English Comp, History of Western Civilization, you know, stuff like that."

"I heard you're dating a guy named Fred?"

Liz started to squirm in her seat wondering if that was okay to have told Adam.

"Yes, I like him a lot! But it's new, so we'll see."

"Well, maybe if you're still seeing him when I come back we can double-date," Adam suggested.

"That's a great idea!" Liz said enthusiastically.

"Actually," Anne said, "I'm meeting him later. We're going to the movies to see *The Boston Strangler*. Did you hear about it? It just came out. It's supposed to be scary, and a true story. Tony Curtis is playing the strangler."

"Isn't Henry Fonda playing the detective?" Liz asked.

"He is. It gives me the creeps and I didn't even see it yet," Anne exclaimed. She became quiet. "I'd do anything to get my mind off my brother. He's leaving in two weeks. He's going to boot camp. He'll be stationed in South Carolina. Eddie just turned 18 last week. I'm frightened for him." Her face paled.

Liz was taken aback. "You never told me. I didn't know you had a brother, Anne. I'm so sorry."

The Vietnam War was hitting home everywhere. Thousands of boys were leaving their families not knowing if they would ever return.

Adam felt a sense of guilt and was quiet at first. "I've been deferred. But as soon as I finish college, I'll be there right alongside your brother," he added awkwardly. "I've heard some pretty horrific stories. I hope he makes it home safely. I'll say a prayer."

"Damned this war! I wish it would end. First Johnson and now Nixon! What are they doing anyway to stop this atrocity?" Liz got up and hugged her friend.

There was an uncomfortable silence between them, but instinctively they knew a bond was formed.

Anne looked at her watch and grimaced. "Yikes, I've got to run! It's really late. Nice to meet you, Adam."

"Yes, same here."

She whispered into Liz's ear "He's so cute. I like him! You're lucky!"

A few minutes after Anne left, Liz and Adam walked out into the crisp, cold January air holding each other's hands tightly. It was a perfect week, but it was time to say goodbye again.

Summer seemed a long way off.

# CHAPTER TWELVE
# LIZ
## (1969)

She couldn't stop vomiting. Exhausted, she crawled into bed but her head didn't make it to the pillow before the next wave struck. "How the hell am I going to study?" she asked aloud. There was a tapping on the door.

"Liz, it's Anne. Your mother let me in. She said you weren't feeling well."

Ashen and disheveled, Liz opened her bedroom door.

"Wow, you look horrible! Hines has been asking if anyone knows where you are; you've been gone for over a week." Their English professor, a short stocky man with an odd moustache that rhythmically twirled up and down, had no patience for absenteeism. "I've been worried about you too. What's going on?"

"You're not going to believe this," Liz whispered, "I think I'm pregnant."

"You're what?"

"Shhh! My mother will hear you."

"Sorry! You're kidding me, right? Why do you think that? Geesh, that's a stupid question. I'm sorry. Are you late?"

"I am, and I've been vomiting since yesterday."

"How late are you? Could it be a virus?"

"That's what my mother thinks. But Anne, I'm at least one month late. I have to be pregnant. The first time Adam and I were together we didn't use protection. I feel so foolish." Liz started to cry. "Now what am I going to do?"

"You love him, right?"

"I've loved Adam since we were 16," Liz exclaimed, "but we're too young to have a baby. And, I want to finish school."

"Don't you think you should talk to him or at least your parents?"

"No, you and Sue are the only ones who know."

"Why? Adam doesn't seem the type to take off. Is that what you're concerned about?"

"No, I don't think so. But I don't want him to feel obligated… or trapped."

Liz knew that wasn't what was really bothering her. She was concerned about something else. Adam's drinking was becoming an issue for her and she wasn't ready to face it or talk about it with her friend.

When Anne left, Liz called Sue one more time and rehashed what they spoke about earlier. She had no choice but to tell her parents. But, first she needed to confirm her suspicions.

The following day Liz reluctantly went to the doctor she had known since childhood and took a pregnancy test, begging him not to tell her parents. It seemed as if months had gone by before she heard the news. She was positively undeniably pregnant!

# CHAPTER THIRTEEN

# ADAM

## (1970-1972)

The mail brought bad news. My birthdate, February 1, 1950, allotted me lottery number eighty-six in the first of the drafts. I was going to Vietnam. Public notices were posted all over the school, but I avoided looking. *Fuck! If only I had gone back to school full-time and didn't drop out when Dad died, this wouldn't be happening. I cannot believe it! I'm to fight in a war I don't believe in? Well, they have another thing coming if they think they're going to take me! God damn it! Why did I bother trying to get my degree? And now I can lose my life? What on earth will I tell Liz? She'll fall apart.*

I haven't seen or heard from Liz in a while, but I assume she's been busy with school. After our time together at the motel I tried to reach her many times, but she was never home. It seemed as if her mother kept making excuses for her. I decided to wait for her to call me. But she didn't and I've been confused and worried.

I took a beer from the fridge and slugged it down. I took another. And another. It didn't help. There had to be another way. A way out. I went to sleep and was awakened by a pounding on the door. My roommate was coming home from the night before.

"Sorry, I forgot my key. I was with Sheila the whole night." His girlfriend had an apartment on the other side of town. "How's it hangin'?"

"You won't believe it! I've been drafted! I'm number eighty-six. Have you received your number yet?"

"No, not yet. I haven't looked either. I don't want to know about it. What are you going to do?" Paul asked.

"I guess I'm going to Vietnam to die. What choice do I have?"

"Why don't you join the Underground?" Paul suggested.

"What do you mean, go to Canada or something?"

The following week, without saying goodbye to anyone, I packed my bags with trepidation. I didn't want to leave, but I was *not* going to fight for a cause I didn't believe in, and privately I felt scared. Tons of students were burning their draft cards as an act of defiance. The antiwar movement was rampant on campuses. Protests at colleges and universities were being held by kids who refused to fight an unjust war, and some of them were getting arrested. I was about to join tens of thousands of draft dodgers in Canada.

The sky was gray with an intermittent drizzle when I got off the Greyhound Bus and stepped onto Canadian soil. Paul had given me several contacts, including a name and address of an anti-draft refuge in Montreal. He told me I could be deported or even prosecuted, but the Canadian authorities would in all likelihood leave me alone. When I arrived, the border guards appeared bureaucratic, but just as Paul said, very few questions were asked of me. Breathing an enormously deep sigh of relief, I headed for 3625 Aylmer Street in the McGill University ghetto district.

The *Yellow Door* was a three story Greystone house serving as a coffeehouse, and several social service organizations, which included

*The Montreal Council to Aid War Resisters.* The atmosphere was new to me. Liz had introduced me to art when we were young, but to be around artists, poets, folk singers, and even philosophers, was a whole other ballgame. Eventually, this is where I spent my evenings and met people from all walks of life.

I began the search for a place to stay. The council provided me with enough information to find an apartment, but not a job. They told me to come back in a couple of weeks, but right now jobs were scarce. The first place I looked at was a dump. It was run-down and devoid of furnishings. After two more undesirable apartments, I settled for one that had a very large room with a small bed; a slightly worn couch; a small TV; and a kitchen table, although rusty and wobbly, would do the trick. There was no phone. The walkup to the third floor was a bit of a pain, but anything was better than going to Vietnam. The selling point was a park that I could walk to within minutes.

For now, I would use the money that was deposited into my savings account for school, but when I reached twenty-one, BINGO! I was to inherit a large sum of money from my father's estate. An inheritance was bequeathed to my dad after his oldest brother Sam, an Indy 500 race car driver, died in a racing accident sometime in the 1930's.

That evening I stocked my fridge with Swanson Hungry-Man TV dinners, my favorite; dip for the chips that were sitting in the cabinet unopened; and a case of beer. Propping up a stack of pillows on the couch, I sat back and opened up the *Montreal Star* and to my surprise it was written in English. The help wanted ads were skimpy. My plan was to work during the day and in the evening I would work towards my degree.

The following day I took a walk in the park. The ground was still wet from the previous day and my sneakers swished through the grass.

I spotted an industrial area on the other side. Walking in that direction, I decided to be bold and inquire within. My father used to say, "Adam, when it comes to seeking employment, nobody is going to find you; you have to find them." Then he jokingly added, "Same for girls!"

Entering the first building to my right, I noticed plaques on each door indicating the nature of their business. There were a few possibilities. I was never big on perseverance, but this time I knew it was *do or die*. Before I left New York, I withdrew all my funds, expecting to be gone indefinitely. I knew I'd have to watch my money during my stay in Canada. I had to grow up fast. After one week of persistent job hunting, I fortuitously landed a junior accountant job at an accounting firm.

The next step was to register for school. Classes began weeks ago and I had a lot to make up. I made friends with several students who were in the same boat as I was. Eventually some of them put down roots in Canada. They were reluctant to go back to the States in fear of being labeled a coward.

I kept reading about the demonstrations back home which made me feel even worse. I heard on the news that 500 colleges, universities, and high schools were shut down after unarmed college students were shot by the Ohio National Guard at Kent State. This was outrageous! Four students died and nine were wounded. Some because they were protesting the Cambodian Campaign military operations, and others were observing the protest, at a distance. Unbelievably, they also were shot! Five days later the newspapers reported that 100,000 people demonstrated in Washington, D.C. I wished I was one of them.

The war raged on and so did the demonstrations. Twelve thousand arrests were made in the month of April. Five-hundred thousand people staged protests. And I'm here in Canada as a draft dodger.

I'm ashamed of myself and feel something I never felt before. Guilt. Every morning I wake up feeling sick to my stomach.

*I wonder what Dad would think of my decision. Back then they felt it was their duty, so why don't I? WWII was global, but this war is different. Why should we suffer? Why are we polarized over this war? Why should we be there; why is it our responsibility to obliterate Communism? I feel so confused.*

Some of the people I've met in Canada believe if one country falls to Communism, then bordering countries will also fall, like dominoes, and this would be enough for them to go to war. This doesn't help me clarify what I'm struggling with. Part of me feels Americans need to take care of themselves by focusing on our country's internal problems. There is another part of me that sympathizes with the South Vietnamese, but I can't visualize Communism spreading like wildfire as they propose. I don't know what I feel anymore. And it isn't helping that I now live in Canada. But hey, if Mohamed Ali dodged the draft, I guess I'm cool with it, kind of.

The Canadian newspapers have been reporting that for the first time in US history the media is providing graphic battlefield footage to the public. Again, my stomach is turning. I feel like throwing up. *How could I watch people I know, or for that matter anyone, shot up by the Vietcong; or our boys killing villages of people, and holy shit, even children! Jesus Christ! What the hell is going on? Do they really think televising is going to help the situation?*

"Hello, Mrs. Bloom? It's Adam. Is Liz there?"

"Hi Adam. I haven't heard from you in a long time. How are you?"

"Sorry, I've been busy with school," I lied, still not wanting to tell the truth to anyone.

"Liz isn't here, but I'll tell her you called. Take care, Adam."

*Shit, why did she hang up? What's going on? Now she seems aloof.*

I regretted not telling Liz about my decision before I left for Canada, but I was ashamed and wondered what she would think. I know how much she cares about me; she would have a hard time if I went to Vietnam. But, I wonder if she would be disappointed in me. It's really time to tell her. *Where the hell is she?*

Before I knew it, another year had passed and graduation was only a year away. It would be a relief to get my accounting degree, but something was missing. I wanted so badly to go home. I missed Liz. I missed my friends. I missed home. I tried calling Liz many times, and each time, either no one answered or I was given the same answer as before.

Gradually, I met new people and started dating casually. I wasn't interested in getting serious with anyone. I was hoping and praying I could go home soon and resume my life, hopefully with Liz. Little did I know that it would be years before I could return to the States. Life had changed me as it did for everyone during these times and I wondered how she might have changed, or if she might have married someone else by now. A lot of time had passed. I finally came to my senses and built up the nerve to write to her.

## CHAPTER FOURTEEN
# LIZ
## (1971)

"Hi Mom".

"How are you Liz?"

"I'm okay. Still at school, studying. Is Will okay?"

"Oh he's fine. I enjoy taking care of him. Listen, you got another call from Adam."

"What did you tell him? Did he suspect I was avoiding him?" Liz asked nervously, her face flushing.

"No Liz, he didn't have a chance to ask anything because I cut him short to avoid his questions. Have you changed your mind? Don't you think you should share this with him after all this time? Liz, what is bothering you? Why don't you want Adam to know that Will is his son?"

"Mom, I don't want to discuss it. And no, we didn't have a fight, nor is he the type to desert me if he found out. Can we please change the subject?"

Liz was afraid to tell her mom about Adam's heavy drinking. If she told her her, she would never hear the end of it. She wanted the option

69

of changing her mind without influence. Her mother cared about Adam and telling her he was an alcoholic would change everything. As far back as she could remember her mother abhorred alcohol.

Liz was well aware of the war. For years it had dominated the news, but it never occurred to her that Adam might have been drafted. Nor did the possibility of him dodging the draft. After all, he would have told her. That she was sure of. She was unaware that he didn't return to school after his father's death. As far as Liz was concerned, he was still a student. It's true though, that she didn't pick up any of his calls, so how would she know? The more she avoided him, the easier it was to forget what was happening. She was angry at herself for being in love with a person who was clearly an alcoholic. Nevertheless, she made up her mind that the next time he called she would stop delaying the inevitable and tell him how much she missed him, and just maybe…just maybe, tell him.

Protests continued at the universities and lives were changing. Many feared their loved ones would be conscripted. For several months Liz had been corresponding with a soldier stationed in Saigon through a pen pal program to support the troops. Benjamin was from Texas. He had enlisted in the Marines right after high school. His family owned a ranch and he was expected to work on it after graduation, but he knew his duty was to go fight the Vietcong.

During the Christmas holiday a package arrived at Liz's house. She hurried to open it to find an exquisite red *áo dài*. She had read about Vietnamese national women's costumes in a periodical she picked up at the library and was pleasantly surprised to see one right in front of her. There was a little notecard in the box. It was from Benjamin.

*Hope you like it, with love, Ben.* It was a bit tight fitting, but she felt incredibly feminine in it. Soon after, she sent a photo of herself donning the costume along with a letter thanking him. As far as she knew he didn't have a girlfriend back home, but either way she didn't want to lead him on. Liz continued to send letters filled with hope for his safety, but nothing intimate. She spoke about Will and even sent a photo of him. Benjamin's letters came frequently. They were mostly sad and frightening. After a while they stopped coming. She prayed for him.

Liz had less than a year of school left before she graduated. She started to search for work. Although she knew she couldn't take a job at this point, she hoped she might land one, or at least she wanted to get an idea of what was available. She started looking at the biggest advertising firms in Manhattan and after a couple of months struck gold. *Wilson POP Advertising* needed a junior designer starting in June. Her art degree had paid off!

Her biggest concern was Will and even though her mom took care of him, it would still be hard for Liz. Her mother promised to inform her of all the exciting new things he would experience. It was serendipity that Liz was around when he first crawled at six months and took his first step at eleven months, but the idea of Will coming home from nursery school and not being there to greet him, disturbed her. And when she thought about Adam never seeing any of this, she felt deeply saddened. She often wondered what type of father he would be.

Next weekend was the college winter concert and Liz's parents would be there, along with Anne and Fred. A babysitter would watch Will. Liz enjoyed the violin and was excited to perform again.

The week went by quickly. Liz's parents arrived at the school in time to find seats, and Anne and Fred followed. They were an item by now and very much in love. Anne was never happier. The program included music from *West Side Story* and was enjoyed by all. Afterwards, they went for Chinese food.

"Liz, what are you looking at?" Fred asked.

"Those kids over there," she motioned with her head.

Anne chimed in, "They're smoking pot."

Liz's parents walked into the restaurant.

"How do you know?" Liz asked.

"Are you kidding? Don't you smell it?" Anne asked cockily. Haven't you tried it yet?"

"No, have you?"

"Once or twice," Anne admitted. "Fred and I did with some of his friends, but didn't like it much."

Liz thought about trying it, but refrained because of Will. Irrationally, she felt if Adam was around she might feel safer smoking pot, but either way she would still worry about being a good mother. She had drifted so far apart from Adam and felt lost without him. What she did know was that times were changing and she was uncomfortable with all that was going on around her; the drugs, the free love, the demonstrations.

Liz finally got her mind off Adam for a few days and felt more relaxed than she had in a long time. She went out for some air in her backyard, where her mother's rose gardens, so beautiful in the springtime, were now covered with snow. When she was little her father had built a treehouse for her out back. He cleverly situated it close to the ground and convinced her that she was the luckiest girl in the world because her treehouse was unique and no one had anything resembling hers. Liz was afraid of heights. The entranceway was still big enough for her to crawl through and she sat for a few minutes knowing she needed to get back to Will soon. Memories of her youth caused her to smile.

Liz wasn't much of a tomboy, but hiding away in her treehouse, her very private place, made her happy pretending to be one. Shivering, she hurried back, but first stopped at the mailbox so she wouldn't forget. Somehow she always failed to remember the smallest things. Adam always laughed at her forgetfulness.

Hesitating, she stared at the envelope in front of her. With her heart pounding, she went inside and sat down at the kitchen table. Her mother wasn't home yet from the market and Will was asleep. She tried to comprehend what she saw. The return address was Canadian. *What on earth is he doing there?* Hands trembling, she opened the letter:

*Dear Liz,*

*I don't know where to begin except to say I feel so lost without you. The last time we saw each other was amazing. I felt so happy when I was with you and when we made love. I never stop thinking about that time, wishing we would betogether again, soon.*

*But for now we can't. I have something to tell you that will shock you. I'm in Canada. I was drafted and decided to run. I know it was a terrible thing to do and also terrible that I didn't let you know beforehand, but it's done with. For what it's worth, I'm sorry. I'm sorry for leaving without telling you. And I'm sorry if it looks as if I'm chicken, but I couldn't fight in a war that I didn't believe in. I've been concerned what you would think of me.*

*I've been living in a tiny apartment in Montreal and working in an accounting firm as a junior accountant. I plan on finishing my degree here. A lot of people have come from the States as draft dodgers. You wouldn't believe how many. I haven't made many friends; only from work.*

*I've tried so many times to get in touch with you. Your mother seems to prevent this. Why is she doing this? Are you getting any of my messages? I miss you Liz, and I love you. Tell me what you have been doing with yourself. Are you still doing well in school? Will you be graduating soon? Do you think about me? Do you still love me? Can you forgive me for not telling you before I left?*

*I want to come home so badly, but I can't just yet. Honestly, I don't know when I can come home. I'm afraid Liz. I'm afraid I'll be arrested. Please pray for me. And Liz, I'll try, really try this time, to quit drinking. I promise. Please Liz, please write back.*

*Love, Adam*

Her eyes filled up as every feeling and emotion she had for him flooded her senses.

"Liz, what's the matter honey? Are you okay?" her mother asked as she entered the kitchen and put the groceries down.

"Oh Mom, I don't know what t.. do". Liz fell apart and finally told her everything. "It's his drinkin… don't know what t..do…" she shrieked. "I didn't tell him about W…. my fault ….could have married….. now…in Canada…. they drafted him." Between her sobs, hiccups, and gulps, her mother only heard garbled noise.

"Liz calm down and explain to me what's going on. Is he drinking? Is that what you said? He drinks?"

"It's not as if I didn't tell you Mom. I told you awhile back that he was drinking, but you weren't listening to me. You only seemed to care that he was Jewish, but he's not Mom. He's not Jewish. And you're not religious, so why does it matter to you?"

"What? What are you talking about! Of course he's Jewish. He was Bar Mitzvahed, wasn't he? And what did you say he's doing in Canada?" Her mother was obviously getting annoyed.

Liz pulled it together and snapped. "Forget it! I shouldn't have said anything. Leave me alone!" She ran up to her room, where Will was sleeping peacefully in his crib. Looking at his sweet face, the image of Adam, she sat down in the rocking chair to read the letter once again.

*He did say he would try to stop drinking. That was good. But would he?* Liz was relieved he wasn't going to Vietnam, but ambivalent about him being a draft dodger. She tried to imagine Will being conscripted and immediately knew she would drag him to the ends of the earth to protect him if she had to. This war didn't sit right with her either.

Her mother waited before coming upstairs to barrage her again with questions.

"Liz, have you calmed down?"

"Shhh…Will is still sleeping!"

Complying, her mother whispered, "Then come back to the kitchen and we'll talk, okay?"

Liz acquiesced and gently closed the door.

They both sipped on mint herb tea as she poured her heart out to her mother. In the end, Liz knew what she had to do.

# CHAPTER FIFTEEN

# LIZ

## (1972)

I found out about the VA Hospital from my dad. Volunteers were needed for the overwhelming number of soldiers returning home. The hospital wasn't far from my parents' house where I was still living. If I planned it right, I would still have plenty of time to be with Will. Every Sunday morning after I dressed him, we ate breakfast together and played for a little while. Afterwards, I left him with grandma and grandpa who were happy to spend more time with their grandson. Will was just as content.

When the staff learned about my credentials, they asked me to work as an assistant to the art therapist. On my first day as a volunteer, I introduced the vets to different forms of art. Oil paints and canvases, along with brushes of all sizes; watercolors, crayons, pencils, colored pencils, and charcoal, and pads of all sizes, were scattered everywhere on tables. Easels were dispersed throughout the room.

Many of the men had come home from Nam with Post-Traumatic Stress Disorder and art therapy was healing on many levels. They were suffering from flashbacks and nightmares. Many had become alcoholics and drug abusers and now were in treatment programs; some were hooked on heroin. To my horror, a few attempted suicide, and succeeded.

Creativity was pouring out of them as they expressed their physical and mental wounds on canvas and paper. After what I saw at orientation, I knew I must help them. There were too many men in wheelchairs without a leg or an arm, and sometimes more than one limb was missing. But apparently that was nothing compared to what they endured mentally. They saw their friends mutilated and killed in action. They witnessed Vietnamese children being murdered by their own troops. They had to live with these atrocities for the rest of their lives. Mental illness was rampant. Their future was grim. Their families' lives were jeopardized.

One Sunday morning, a new patient came into the art room and sat down, his face void of expression. I walked over to him and said hello. He did not reply. He was unapproachable. For the two hours allotted, he stared into space. The following week the same thing reoccurred. The third Sunday, I sat next to him and started sketching with charcoal. He watched me draw for a while and then asked, "How do you do that?"

"Do what exactly?"

"Make the drawings look realistic?"

"Here, would you like to try?" I handed him some charcoal and paper.

"Sorry, do you think I could have some colored pencils instead?"

"Sure!" Excitedly, I handed him the supplies. He was finally showing some interest. Extending my hand, I said, "My name is Liz. What's yours?"

"Alex, thank you." He looked straight into my eyes. "You're very pretty."

I felt myself blush. "Thank you Alex. That's sweet of you."

He had the most gorgeous eyes I had ever seen. They were green with specks of grey and were still staring into mine.

He started to draw. Not the still-life I arranged, a rose patterned vase with a scalloped edge and three pieces of fruit in a basket, but horses instead!

"Where did you learn to draw horses?" I asked mystified.

"I didn't. I've never drawn anything before. But I do live on a farm with many of them," he laughed. "So tell me Liz, do you ride?"

"I've never been on one."

His eyes seemed to twinkle as he sidetracked and asked without awkwardness, "Do you have a boyfriend, Liz? Or, are you married?"

"Well, kind of," I answered. "Have a boyfriend, that is. But I haven't seen him in a long time. I have a son though. His name is Will. He's two years old and a handful!" Looking down, I once again took notice of his sketch. You would never have known this was his first artwork.

Week after week, Liz watched Alex draw more horses, always fantastical with rainbows in the background, and every now and then he deviated and painted cows in a paAdamre. Occasionally, she gave suggestions. "Why don't you add a little more *Indian red paint* right here to accentuate the rainbow?" And, "If you lighten this a little, you'll see how the whole painting will brighten up." Sometimes he stared deeply into her eyes and flirted. However, nothing came of their relationship; although, they did become good friends. She never learned what he went through in Nam. He didn't talk about it, so she decided to leave it alone. When she walked around to assist other veterans, she felt Alex's eyes on her and secretly enjoyed it.

A year had passed and Liz was learning how to work with challenging patients. One man was without both of his hands and attempted painting with his feet, and sometimes alternated with his mouth. Another man was blind. It was truly amazing how he compensated for his loss. He would ask her to seat him directly in front of an easel and hand him specific colors so he could apply oil paint to the canvas. She would come back later and find a spectacular abstract painting before her eyes. Somehow in the face of their adversity, they painted. Their work was extraordinary.

CHAPTER SIXTEEN

# LIZ

## (1972)

"Mommy! Mommy! Wake up!" Wake up! You're crying. Are you okay?"

I opened my eyes, but felt disoriented and closed them again. *Am I dreaming?*

*"Hi Liz! It's good to hear your voice! I've been home for a week and wanted to call you, but I've been busy looking for an apartment. I finally found one on Bowne Street in Flushing. Do you think we can get together? I want to meet your new husband and baby."*

*"My God! You're in the old neighborhood? Sure! Let me arrange it and I'll let you know. By the way, Will's not a baby anymore."*

*I cringed when I saw Adam. "You've lost so much weight. What happened?"*

*"I'm sick. I have diabetes," he said matter-of-factly.*

*Confused, I said, "I don't understand. Why haven't you told me? When did this happen?"*

*"I wanted to tell you, but I didn't want to burden you."*

80

"Burden me? What are you talking about? You look so sick! You'll get better, won't you," I nervously asked just as my son walked in. "Will, this is Adam. Remember I told you my friend was coming to visit us?"

Adam handed a basketball to our son. "Nice to meet you. I bought this for you. Your mom said you like basketball. Maybe we could play a game later?"

He called frequently after that, but kept discouraging our visits. Several weeks later he had some news.

"What is it?" I asked.

"I just came from the doctor and he told me that my diabetes has advanced. He told me I better lay off the sauce because I'm killing myself; literally."

"You mean you're still drinking? I guess I hoped that you would have enough brains to stop once you heard you had diabetes!" I started to weep. "Oh, Adam".

Adam began dialysis treatments shortly afterwards, but that didn't stop the next thing from happening. Months had gone by and he still discouraged me from visiting him. Perhaps he's seeing another woman?

I became so immersed in my own life that time went by without me realizing what was happening to him. One day I decided to go to his house uninvited. I was tired of him putting me off. I stopped dead in my tracks and nearly fell over. Adam was in a wheelchair. But something else was wrong. I heard myself scream. "Where are your legs?"

Uncharacteristic cheery phone calls began. Adam had a mission. At last he was accomplishing something fruitful with his life. From his wheelchair he was helping other people with diabetes cope with their disease. I was so proud of him. Never before had he done anything that productive.

*"What do you do when you're there?" I asked. His duties seemed curious to me while working from a wheelchair.*

*"Oh, I talk to people; try to encourage them to stop drinking beer and take better care of their health," Adam said enthusiastically.*

*"Do most of them drink beer?" I doubted this was the case and wondered why he was mentioning this. I knew diabetes struck people from all walks of life. Alcoholism was not on the top of the list, was it?*

*"Yes most of them do. We have AA meetings up here in heaven," Adam laughed.*

*"What are you talking about?" I shouted as my body began to tremble.*

"Mommy! Mommy!" I heard Will's voice and shook myself awake. Slowly, I tried to focus. "It's okay honey, it's okay. I was dreaming." I held him tightly. It was dark and I felt strangely sick to my stomach. *What time is it?* Something in the back of my mind was gnawing at me. After tucking Will back into bed, I walked into the kitchen and brewed some tea. *What was I thinking! Adam's not helping others; he's killing himself. I feel it in my bones. He's still drinking.* Anger rose in my throat. *Damn you Adam!*

She couldn't put it off any longer. It had been three years since they had been together and almost a year since the letter came. It was eating her alive. His calls eventually stopped. What did she expect? She didn't respond to his letters, nor did she return his calls. After her dream, she knew she had to contact him and see if he was okay.

*I'll write him. That's what I'll do. I'll write him. I should have as soon as I received his letter. What was I thinking! But, what if he's no longer at that address? Will he want to hear from me after all this time?* She sat down at her desk and started to write.

*Dear Adam,*

*It's good to hear from you. I apologize for not contacting you sooner, but I must tell you something that will change things forever. Please believe me, I don't want to hurt you. I've moved on. I met someone else and we have a baby. And, I'm happier than I've ever been…..*

Nervously, she crumpled it up and aimed for the garbage. After several more attempts, she ripped up letter after letter, and when the pail was nearly filled to the brim, she then summoned the courage and began again, with all but one tiny detail.

# CHAPTER SEVENTEEN

# ADAM

## (1973)

Between work and school I had no time for a social life. I'd come home late at night and practically fall into bed. Every weekend was spent studying. I found myself escaping into drink. I didn't know how I could exist without one. It began to consume my life. It seemed as if everyone at work drank too much. They'd come back from lunch with a couple of drinks in them, and after work they'd all go out for burgers and beer. Afterwards, some would stay. At first I joined them thinking this was proper protocol for accountants, but by the time I'd get to school, I was too tired to keep my head up. I'd barely make it home and I'd start drinking again. How I ever graduated was a mystery to me.

I was lonely. Lonely for Liz and lonely for home. The whole time I was here I didn't call any of my old friends. A few had been conscripted and lord only knows where they were stationed. I lost touch with my roommate from college. Last I heard, Paul was exempt from the draft. School had saved him. If only I had used my brains and continued full-time, this wouldn't be happening to me and I would be home where I belong.

One Friday night I went to a local bar. It was a dive. As I entered, I noticed a young couple clinging to each other while they slow danced to the music. They were playing the Bee Gee's big hit, "How Can You Mend a Broken Heart," on the jukebox. To the left there were two old men laughing and drinking, and to the right were a bunch of unruly men arguing. I walked over and sat down on a barstool and ordered a beer, and then several more. After an hour or so passed, a girl around twenty wearing a mini-skirt, with long blonde hair and a figure to kill, approached me. I offered her the stool next to mine and bought her a scotch straight up. We talked for a while and discovered we were both from New York. She was from a small town upstate near Saratoga and never heard of Queens.

"I've heard of Long Island though," she said in a ditzy voice. "My cousin went swimming at Jones Beach, but I've never been there."

"Why did you move here?" I asked. "Or are you visiting?"

"I'm here with my boyfriend. He's gone AWOL," Silvie offered. "But you and I can still get it on. Do you want to?" She smiled seductively. I was drunk. She leaned over and gave me the hottest wet kiss I had ever had. My response was immediate. She was so damned slutty. I reached over to kiss her back, and wouldn't you know it – in walked her boyfriend, a big mother fucker dressed in army garb. That didn't make any sense at all. He deserted our troops. Go figure!

There was literally no time to think. He slugged me right in my gut. I fell over crashing into the window as blood splattered from my head. Luckily the glass didn't break. Unsteadily, I lifted myself up and hit him smack between his eyes, but with very little force. The boyfriend grabbed Silvie roughly. "Come on, let's get the fuck out of here."

I spent the next few hours in the emergency room explaining what had happened, leaving out the details of the fight and fabricating a plausible cover story. The bartender was nice enough to ignore the incident and didn't report it to the police or I would have been back in the States and headed for Nam. Two days later I went to work with stitches on my forehead, and a sore stomach and swollen fist, once again contriving a story.

My drinking was out of control and I was in trouble.

Adam had begun to realize how dodging the draft was affecting him. He felt ambivalent about what he had done. It had taken time for him to digest he was in another country away from everything he knew. He wondered what would happen when he returned home. Would people understand? Would Liz understand that he couldn't fight for a cause he didn't believe in?

Most of the people he hung out with were from work, and not only were they drinking, they were also smoking pot. At lunchtime he overheard them talking about a party they were going to at a senior accountant's house. Supposedly the guy was filthy rich, but didn't flaunt his wealth. He preferred to work his way up in the company.

"Adam, are you going to the party tonight?" one of his co-workers asked.

"Nah, that's not my thing."

"What do you mean? We're just hanging out. Smokin' some weed. Come on, haven't you ever tried any? It's groovy. This is good stuff. It's pure Columbian Gold."

Adam thought for a moment. "Okay, cool. I'll go. Where is it?" He wrote down the address and time, and then went back to work. Throughout the day he wondered who would be there and what it would be like. One thing he was sure of, he'd drink some beer before he went.

At 8:30 p.m. he hailed a taxi. It was Friday and he didn't have to get up early the next morning. The cab pulled up to an old brownstone on a populated street downtown. A buzzer let him into a vestibule where he stagnated for thirty minutes. He was a sloth in the tropical rain forest until the door finally opened and he was ushered in by the maid.

"Are you here for the party?" she asked.

"Yes, thank you," Adam replied. *That's weird! A maid? Isn't this a pot party? Hope no cops come!*

He entered a high ceilinged room with a fancy chandelier. Looking around he noticed paintings adorning the walls; almost museum quality, he thought. A sweet aroma of peppers deliciously roasting filled the air. *Jesus Christ! I could get high just standing here without doing anything!*

"Adam, come on in. Meet some people," Ralph, one of the accountants said. "You want a joint? Or a drink? Or both," he chuckled.

"Sure. So what do you do with this thing?" Adam asked.

"Here, watch, take a toke and breathe it in," he demonstrated.

"Far out." Adam inhaled the thinly rolled joint and got an immediate buzz. He looked around and saw some familiar faces. Some of the girls had flowers in their hair and one was dancing around singing the words *Flower Power, Flower Power* over and over again. Everyone was stoned. To his left he saw joints being passed around and he could have sworn he saw something else going on. *Are they popping pills? Holy shit!*

He didn't talk much to anyone that night and instead listened to the tunes and chilled. *Suite: Judy Blue Eyes* was playing when Ralph walked over.

"Hey man, are you diggin' it?"

"Like, just chillin' man. It's really bad; I'm stoked."

"Peace!"

Adam heard a commotion on the other side of the room and turned around to see what was going on. Apparently a girl was hallucinating. He felt edgy and uncomfortable watching her.

"Look at the colors! Look," she screamed. "There, over there…and there! Go follow them." She started running around in circles. "Catch them," she cried again. And then she edged near a tall window and another girl shrieked, "Stop her!" A boy grabbed the girl in trouble and told her to chill, but she headed the other way and started to flip out. She kept blurting out gibberish, something about the colors meeting the snakes. And then, she laughed and in a singsong voice chanted over and over again, "I am *so* happy. I am *so* happy. *Happy!* Everything is *so* beautiful." She started running around in circles, out of control, and the same guy grabbed her and told her in a harsher tone to chill. She finally listened.

Adam went home that night feeling mellow. Other than the incident with the girl, he enjoyed himself. It was different. And, for the first time he didn't think about Liz.

# CHAPTER EIGHTEEN

# ADAM

## (1973)

It was Sunday and I had the day off. *Pierre and Fontaine, Accountants* had been good to me. I was given two raises in the last year and got along well with my boss. Planning a relaxing day in the park, I stopped at a café to pick up sliced pork on brioche with chips and beer, and a newspaper. The grass was wet from the night before, so I sat on a bench, spread out my lunch, and began to eat a pickle. The sun was soothing. Children were running around; some were on swings, some on monkey bars. I watched for a while and started to read the sports section. More than an hour must have passed, because when I looked up the sun had shifted, still bright. I turned my head from the sunlight and spotted a boy on a bike who appeared to be about eight or nine years old. He seemed to be going a little too fast down a hill, which was surprising because the grass was still damp. I stood up to see where he was headed and noticed the street ahead of him. *Oh my God! He's losing control of his bike!* Without thinking I started to run as fast as I could. *What's happening? Oh my God!*

Suddenly I heard the brakes of a car screech. A blue sedan hit the boy and immediately took off. The impact sent him flying into the air, and just as quickly, he came shooting down with force. The boy was lying still in the street. His bike was scattered in pieces all around him. Deep shock enveloped me as I momentarily stared at the boy lying on the desolate and cold looking ground. Shivering, I instinctively bent to pick him up, but then thought better of it. *What should I do? Get a blanket! Pick him up! No, I don't know what to do.* I frantically looked around and spotted an elderly man across the street.

I heard myself scream, "Help me, please! Help me! Get an ambulance! Please, hurry!"

The man yelled back, "What did you say?"

"A boy's been hurt! Please hurry! Get an ambulance!"

*Where the hell did the car go?*

The boy's eyes fluttered and he let out a moan. There was blood all over his head and seeping from his mouth. His leg seemed detached.

"You're going to be all right! You're going to be all right! " I was shaking all over. The boy was turning blue. The little good it might do to warm the boy, I removed my shirt and covered his chest. *Why is he turning blue? Is he dying?* I screamed again, "Where's the ambulance? I wildly searched the streets in front of me wondering if I should start running somewhere, anywhere, for help. I reached down and held the boy tightly as blood stained my clothing. Finally, I heard sirens in the distance. A police car appeared to be coming from another direction.

The ambulance pulled up several minutes after the police arrived. There was so much commotion everywhere. Everyone was bombarding me with questions. I started to sob uncontrollably. "I'm sorry, I'm sorry!"

"What happened?" the officer inquired. "Do you know this boy? Did you see what happened? Is he your son?"

The paramedics lifted the boy onto the stretcher.

I cried, "No, I never saw him before. Please, let me go with him! Please!"

"The boy is dead sir."

Adam's legs became jelly. He felt faint. The police let him go in the ambulance with the paramedics and met him at the hospital where they again bombarded him with questions.

He described the car as best he could: blue with non-Canadian plates.

"The car sped away. I don't know why." Adam's voice trembled and his body shook. "The boy went right in front of the car, but the driver didn't seem to stop in time. I think he stopped afterwards, but then he took off. I don't know why. I just don't know why. Do you think he was drinking?"

Before leaving, the attending nurse informed Adam that when the boy's head hit the ground he suffered an extreme blow which caused a concussion, which then led to bleeding in his skull. And then, an injured artery led to epidural bleeding, which caused his sudden death. She shook her head and stared at Adam. "I'm so sorry! Was he your son?"

Adam went home in a stupor and cried all night. *He died in my arms. How could this be? Why couldn't he have been spared? How could you let this happen, God?*

The following day he went back to the police station and found out that they located the driver of the car. He was a 20 year old male from New York who *had* been drinking before the accident and didn't hit the brakes in time. Adam was right.

He asked the dead boy's name.

"Edouard," they replied. "Edouard Anniele."

He asked his age.

They said, "The boy was ten."

They told him the parents of the boy wanted to meet him. Adam was numb. He absent-mindedly wondered if the driver was also a draft dodger.

My life changed in an instant. I started a 12-step program to help me quit drinking. The idea was to go to meetings and get support by sharing personal stories. Some were lucky enough to succeed, some were not.

Before I left for Canada the doctor had given me a warning. I was diagnosed with pre-diabetes. He told me to stay off the sauce or I'd be headed for a fall. I went to AA for six months and listened to horror stories. One man told his tale of growing up in a home filled with alcoholics; his mother, his father, and even his four siblings. One day his youngest brother was drinking too much and had been in a brawl with his older brother who accidentally pushed him down the stairs. It was a tragic accident. At 22 years old, he became a paraplegic. This vision was enough to make me want to quit. Another person told her story of how she slept with men to acquire alcohol. She would find herself waking up in strange men's beds. Apparently this was an oft-told tale. Then it was my turn. I talked a little bit about my adoptive mother and how I disliked her, and about my father dying and how I missed him. But, privately I knew these weren't the reasons. I had been drinking as far back as I could remember. Liz was always upset with me. The last time I saw her right before we said goodbye, she made me promise I would stop. She claimed I was different when I drank; that I wasn't *me* anymore.

*I have to stop drinking. I can't keep going this way.*

# CHAPTER NINETEEN
# ADAM
## (1973)

It was 1973 and I was still missing everything about the States, but had adjusted to living in Montreal. My graduation six months before was disappointing without friends or a party which I had looked forward to since high school. Sometimes, I lost focus on the war and when I might be able to return home.

In November I went to see a doctor. I didn't know what the hell was going on, but I was urinating constantly. It was getting ridiculous. When I'd go to the bathroom at work, by the time I went back to my desk, I was ready to return. The running joke was that I was pregnant. I wasn't going to do anything about it anyway, but I guess I wanted to know if it was related to the pre-diabetes.

It had been four years since I had a check-up and the last report was worrying me. The doctor in California even talked about difficulties with me getting it up if I didn't take care of myself. There was no improvement; in fact, I was worse. He informed me about poly something or other, and because my glucose levels were higher now, it was obstructing my kidneys. So when I was diagnosed with diabetes, it wasn't a surprise. Since it could be hereditary, I wondered if either one of my *real* parents, whoever they were, also had this affliction. Another reason to curse them.

Undoubtedly my drinking had exacerbated the situation. AA was long gone. I can't say I gave it a good try, but I did go to meetings. The constant drinking wasn't the only issue though; my lifestyle contributed. I was supposed to watch what I ate. I couldn't be bothered.

After I left the doctor's office, I threw his prescription in the waste basket. *There's no fucking way I'm going to take drugs. What was the point of going to him anyway? I'm drinking, aren't I? It's a done deal.* He told me about new breakthroughs in treating diabetes, but I wanted no part of that either. I wanted to forget the whole goddamned problem.

Although my dad left me well provided with his estate in money market funds, I was living a poor existence. He taught me a great deal about being frugal and since I fled to Canada, I knew this was the precise time for me to grow up. After four years of living in a cramped apartment, I was finally in a position to move. I had been given a lot more responsibility at work, which in turn led to a promotion. A larger apartment was now affordable.

It was hard for me to spend time in the park as I had before Edouard's death, but I eventually dealt with my anguish, and started to enjoy it once again. One cloudy Saturday, I was taking a brisk walk in the park and bumped into my old landlord walking her dog.

"Adam, how nice to see you!" Mrs. Peatreé said in her thick French accent. "How's your new apartment?"

"It's okay; I like it! " I bent down to pet *good old* Sam. "It's a few minutes from here. How are you?"

"I'm well, thank you! I'm so glad to bump into you! I would have sent it to you, if I knew where you were," she rambled.

"Sent me what?" I asked nervously, although not knowing why.

"Oh, yes. I didn't tell you yet," she chuckled. "After you left, you received a letter and fortuitously I didn't discard it." Her smile widened. "What a coincidence we found each other! I discovered it under a pile of papers just a few weeks ago. I'm such a dingbat when it comes to filing," she chuckled again. "Why don't you come over and get it and we can have a nice little chat?"

It was from Liz. Nothing could make me happier. Anxiously, I ripped open the envelope and noticed the post date. It was six months ago. I checked my math. *Did I count correctly? One, two, three, four, five.... Why would she wait over two years before writing me back?* I thought she'd never contact me again. Lucky for me *good old* Mrs. Peatreé and Sam were out for their afternoon stroll. I decided they were both old. Now it was my turn to chuckle.

*Dear Adam,*

*I'm so sorry I haven't written you all this time. Please forgive me. There isn't a day that goes by when I don't think about you. I have so many memories. I was shocked to read you're living in Canada. I assume you're still there and my letter will reach you. Is there any word yet what will happen to draft dodgers when they return home? Can you return home? I will continue to pray for you, as I always have. I believe you made the right decision. I'm happy to hear you're working as a junior accountant. Did you get your degree?*

*As for me, I'm doing well. I graduated college two years ago and immediately started working in an advertising firm in the city. The day came when I was able to go out on my own. I am now the proud founder of Elizabeth Bloom Advertising. I have three huge clients. And, I have more news for you.*

*I met someone in college and somehow…I don't know… things just happened. I'm sorry! We're not together anymore, but Adam, I have a baby! Well, he's actually not a baby anymore. Will is almost four years old! Up until recently my mom took care of him during the day. He's now attending nursery school. I am very blessed. Wait until you meet him! You will absolutely love him!*

*I am living in Mohegan Lake, upstate in Westchester County. I bought a house! Do you believe it? Me; a house! It's what you and I used to dream about….owning a house together. I wanted to live deep in the woods far away from everything and everyone. You wanted to live by the ocean.*

*It's beautiful here. There's a lake where we could go rowing. There are so many awesome places to see. The Bear Mountain Bridge is close by and has incredible views! The river and mountains surround it. I've never been so happy!*

*What are your plans when you come home? You are coming home, aren't you? Have you met anyone? Adam, have you stopped drinking?*

*And yes, I still love you and always will.*

*Love, Liz*

She wrote me, she finally wrote me! There's hope. Sure she has a baby, but no husband. Wait a minute…four years old. Will is almost four? We were together then, weren't we? No… that can't be. She wouldn't lie to me; not about something like this!

I wrote Liz back and waited.

I felt better than I had in a long time. In fact, for the first time in a while, I went to work in a decent mood. Even my co-workers noticed.

"Hey, Adam, what's happening? You seem different; you almost seem human. Did you get lucky last night?"

"Cut it out man! Mind your business," I joked, but really meant it.

When lunchtime came the accountants went out for the usual burgers and beer. I stayed behind. I was making a conscious effort to stop drinking. I only drank at night when I went to the *Yellow Door*. Tonight there was folk music and the band was playing some of Dylan's tunes; feet were tapping to *The Times They Are a-Changing*. I thought, *Dylan didn't know the half of it when he wrote that song!*

In walked the classiest woman I had ever seen. *Man is she hot! Get your head together, now. Now's your chance.* Trying to build up my nerve, I walked in her direction, but instead marched right past her, got some chips and returned to my table. *Go to her now, you fool. Yeah, you're a fool all right; you just got a letter from Liz. Is she wearing a wedding band? Ah, screw it.*

"Hello, may I join you? I'm Adam." I put out my hand and she held it. *She is wearing a wedding band. And, holy shit, look at that rock!* I looked up into her dark huge eyes. *I can't believe it; I'm getting hard. Screw you Dr. Coffe, you're dead wrong!* Her full mouth was in a half-smile, questioning my presence.

I was pissed at myself for changing out of my suit after work. Unthinkingly, I looked down at my jeans, slowly back up to my black dress shirt, and then at her. She looked as if she belonged in a jazz club, not here. She seemed out of place.

"Bettina," she replied.

She patted the chair next to hers indicating I should sit. Her French accent made her all the more desirable, and with the tailored pale cream suit she was wearing, with a black blouse peeking out of her collar, well, there was something about her that moved me. Her dark brown hair was chicly cut in a short bob.

"Are you from around here?" she asked. "You sound like a New Yorker."

"I'm originally from New York, more recently living in California, but my company transferred me here temporarily," I lied. There was something that told me to keep the truth to myself.

"Oh, I see. What do you do?"

I filled her in on my job and we talked for hours until the place closed. She spoke impeccable English and I was impressed. As I suspected, she was married; to a tycoon! She met her husband when she was young and never had children. She told me she was 31 and a great deal younger than he was. Bettina was lonely and she let me know it. Before saying goodnight she gave me her phone number with instructions of when to call and when not to call. Dutifully, I respected her wishes right up until the end.

The following Friday morning I called suggesting we meet in the evening for drinks at the *Yellow Door*. This time she wore jeans. Tight fitting ones. We hit it off again and talked until closing, and then went to my apartment. She took off my clothes before I had a chance to grab a beer. You could say she jumped my bones; literally. We did it three times that night and when morning approached, she was gone.

Two nights later she knocked on my door and surprised me. I closed the door behind her and pushed her gently up against the wall. Hungrily, I kissed her with my tongue exploring every part of her mouth, and this time I ripped off *her* clothing. Her breasts were big and full, and as I sucked on each nipple, my tongue alternately darted in and out causing her to have multiple orgasms. My hands ran up and down her body, slowly. I stopped and lingered where she was incredibly wet and hot. She came again. The animalistic sounds that emanated from her were something I never experienced. One thing I was sure of... I would try to keep her in my bed as long as I could. It was her turn to please me and she did. She rolled over and whispered in a low sensual voice, "Let me pleasure you." I lifted the short silky strands of hair off her face and watched. She moved down my body slowly, and deftly worked her hands and mouth as I moaned and cried out until fully sated. Afterwards I thought, *I could do this forever if it weren't for the guilt. She is so damned good down there. What am I supposed to do? Be celibate until I get home?* When we were finished she gave that half-smile of hers and walked towards the door. I grabbed her arm and pleaded, "Come on, please don't go, not yet. We're having so much fun."

"I must go my love. My husband is waiting for me."

It was mid-summer and the air was thick with humidity, common for this time of year. We met in a park on a Sunday afternoon far from her home and mine. Dogwood and cherry blossom trees were everywhere. It was awesome. Bettina was wearing a black halter top with red short shorts and killer heels. I didn't expect her to dress this way. She looked *so* sexy. Before meeting her, I picked up a couple of sandwiches and a salad, and some beer which I knew she liked. She surprised me the other night when instead of a glass of wine, which seemed to fit her better, she ordered a Labatt 50 beer at the *Yellow Door*.

Bettina opened up a black and white silky throw cover which she brought from home and we settled onto the grass.

"Where's your husband today?" I asked.

"He's where he always is; work," she replied and looked nonchalantly down at the two ants crawling in front of her.

I couldn't tell if she was indifferent or sad, but she became distant for a few minutes, so I digressed and asked where she worked. The last time I asked her this question she avoided the subject. It seemed the more questions I asked, the more she withdrew.

She looked up at me with those dark haunting eyes that made my groin ache. "I've never worked. I've been David's wife since I'm nineteen. All I've ever known is to instruct the servants, and entertain his clients at the parties we host. This is all my mother did too. Does this seem odd to you? You know, with women today educating themselves and going to work?"

Apparently she was brought up in wealth and was accustomed to this way of life. I didn't know what to reply. In truth it did seem odd to me. I was brought up with an average lifestyle. My parents weren't wealthy, nor were they poor. In fact, all my friends including Liz were brought up the same way. Everyone had to go to work. It's the way it was. In order to keep Bettina in my bed, I avoided controversy by showing admiration for her devotion to her duties.

I don't know why but I sensed Bettina's disapproval of draft-dodgers before we even got into a political conversation. It turned out I was right. Her viewpoints on Vietnam were surprising. She believed the United States should fight for the South. And not only that, she also believed that Canada should be involved. She was adamant about ending Communism. Bettina's home life, one of submission, made her feel controlled. Communism frightened her. Most Canadians were opposed to the war and supported American draft dodgers, but she commended those Canadians who enlisted.

She questioned if I had been drafted, so I led her to believe I was older than twenty-four. For as far back as I can remember, people always thought I looked older than I actually was. She seemed to accept this.

We were both starving and started to eat. I remembered the last time I ate in a park. A chill ran through me and she noticed the color drain from my face.

"Are you okay my love?"

"I just remembered something, that's all."

"Do you want to tell me about it?"

I needed to talk. Ever since it happened, whenever I saw children or anything that reminded me of him, I felt anxious and increasingly sad. The accident was troubling me.

"What an awful thing to happen to you! That poor boy!" she exclaimed after hearing the story. She moved closer and wrapped her arms tightly around me.

We sat quietly for a time. Several white clouds decorated the sky and for a moment we were able to get lost in their beauty.

"Did they ever find the driver?"

"No," Adam sneered. He should pay for taking his life, the bastard!"

We were quiet for a time, and then went back to my apartment.

This time I couldn't get it up. I was embarrassed. We both knew it was because of the boy. He was in the way and there was nothing I could do about it. I didn't want to give myself pleasure, or Bettina.

Bettina and I saw each other for months. Things went back to the way they were; ardent sex whenever it was convenient for her. And me...well, I was crazy about her, even though I knew nothing would ever come of it. I even considered marrying her, if she would leave her husband. But, deep down I knew it was mostly about the way she made me feel as a man. I also knew I couldn't give her the lifestyle she was accustomed to. I had the money, plenty of it, but I didn't have the class she breathed. She saw me as a bourgeois, and had her own modus vivendi. Sadly, I reminded myself that I was only a diversion from her humdrum life.

And, then one day it was over. She stopped coming just like that. I searched for her night after night in the place we first met, the *Yellow Door*. She was never there. I asked the other patrons if they saw her; if they remembered a classy, striking woman, describing her from head to toe. Nobody had.

She was gone. No explanations, no goodbyes, and no way to reach her. Her phone was disconnected. It was as if she didn't exist and never had.

# CHAPTER TWENTY
# LIZ
## (1973)

Adam's letter came two and a half weeks later. I was glad to be back in touch with him, but the ambivalence I always felt had deepened.

*Dear Liz,*

> *I thought I would never hear from you again. It's been awhile. I guess I understand now why you waited this long to write. A baby. Wow. I didn't expect you to say that. I can't wait to meet him. By the time I get home, he'll be grown. Well, not grown, but you know what I mean. Okay, I guess I'm a little disappointed. But I'm really happy for you. I have to admit though, I hoped you and I would have a baby. I know it's my fault for leaving without first telling you. But it's done with. I'm sorry if I sound bitter; I miss you and regretting my mistakes. At least you didn't marry the guy. Please tell Will when he's old enough Uncle Adam will bring him a basketball.*

> *Another wow. Your own business and house. Very impressive. I'm proud of you. I've never been to Westchester County. Sounds*

*nice. How did you land up there? Remember when we talked about starting a company together? You knew exactly what we should do and how to get started, but we couldn't think of what type of enterprise. We were young. You always had good business sense. You would think I would be the one who knew what to do…being an accountant and all. Well, anyway, we were good together…at the race tracks.(Haha)*

*So here's my big news…I've stopped drinking. I had to. Things were out of control. Liz, there was an accident. A boy on a bicycle died because of someone else's drinking while driving, and it shook me to my very core. I tried to save him, but he already died. In my arms, Liz; in my arms. After that I went to AA. You know, the program to help drinkers. Everyone sits around telling their story. Really depressing.*

*Of course I'm coming back. There's talk of amnesty, but nobody knows when. I wish you could come here. Could you for a short time and visit? I know you have Will to consider, but could your mom possibly watch him? I don't know if I could wait another couple of years to see you again. Look Liz, I made a mistake not contacting you before I left. I'm not sure why I didn't. But you didn't return my calls either. A lot of time has passed. Can we forget it and move on? I still believe we could be good together. Don't you?*

*Love, Adam*

I shivered. Adam always played basketball and loved it, but hearing him repeat what he said in my dream, a dream I could not shake from a year ago, was unnerving. He sounds different. I can't put my finger on what is wrong. He seems impressed that I opened my own business and bought my own house, but he seems bitter, and maybe a little bit jealous. Probably about Will.

She never explained to Adam why her mother had stonewalled his calls. She never told him about her father helping with a down payment for the house; about her struggles being a single mom. Or about how difficult it was to keep her business afloat. She never told him anything about her life without him; her insecurities. She decided unequivocally that unless she saw for herself that he stopped drinking, she wouldn't commit to her true feelings. As it was, she revealed too much. She told him she still loved him.

*I wonder what he will think of me when he reads my letter. Will he believe I slept with another man? Maybe he'd know I would never do such a thing; that I'm lying. But wouldn't he wonder why I would lie? Would he suspect Will is his son? I wonder if he slept with anybody else. He didn't mention anyone in his letter. That would kill me. He's going to ask questions about Will and his father, and I better have the answers. But for now I can leave it alone.*

She took a deep breath and slowly let it out.

Anne called one evening and we set up a time to meet for the following week. I took an extended lunch hour and met her across town. Other than Will and my parents, I felt alone since Adam was gone. My childhood friend Sue and I had drifted over the years, so I was glad my friendship with Anne had grown. As capricious as she was, catching up with her somehow always centered me.

However, this time her news was unsettling. She talked about her marriage and how unhappy she was, that it was a mistake to marry Fred only because she was pregnant. And now a year later, she was pregnant again.

"Boy, you don't waste any time." I realized my *faux pas*. "I'm sorry, that wasn't nice. What are you going to do?"

"He's still smoking pot," Anne said.

"I didn't know he smoked other than that one time you told me about. How often?"

"I think he's a pothead, Liz."

"How far along are you? Does he know you're pregnant?"

"No, I haven't told him yet. I only found out a few days ago; two months." Anne looked at her untouched food.

I couldn't eat either and picked at my salad. Having gone through it myself, I knew what it was like to bring up a child without a husband and didn't want this to happen to Anne. Although, it was different; she and Fred were already married. But a divorce could be devastating.

"I hate to ask you, but would you consider an abortion?"

"I could never do that. Sammy is going to have a little brother or sister with or without his father. You brought up Will alone. I could do it too, don't you think?"

"Sure, but Sammy is nine months old. Plus a new baby. How would you handle all this? Wouldn't you have to work or something? You know, to help Fred out? Living in two different places would be financially difficult."

"I'm not divorcing Fred. You misunderstand. I want him to stop smoking pot. I was thinking though, maybe we'd separate for the time being."

"Do you think that would help?" I asked, nervously twisting my hands. The whole thing made me uncomfortable.

"I think it might scare him, you know, with the baby coming and everything. Who knows, maybe leaving him temporarily might shake him up. What do you think?"

Liz searched for the right advice to give her friend. "I think you should take your time and think it over." On one hand she felt Anne should leave Fred since he was smoking pot, and on the other hand she was concerned the children would suffer without their father.

"Yes, but I'm already two months…." Anne sensed her uneasiness and changed the subject. "Liz, did Adam write back yet?"

"Yes, he wants to know if I can visit him…without Will."

"What did he say about him? Does he suspect he's his?" Anne was on the edge of her seat and started to eat.

"No, I'm pretty sure he bought it. He seemed shocked and hurt. You know, that I had a kid with someone else."

"Will you go?" Anne asked wide eyed.

"Nah, I can't leave Will with my mom for that long, and I can't get away from work. I'd lose money. But I guess the real reason is, I won't be able to look him in the eyes; not yet anyway. I'm afraid he'd look at me and figure it out in a split second."

They talked for a while mostly about Will and Sammy, and then paid the bill and hugged each other goodbye. Anne had to pick Sammy up at her mother's house and Liz had to get back to work.

"Maybe we could get together again in a few weeks?" Liz asked.

"Groovy." Anne waved goodbye as she got into her 1968 blue Chevy.

Liz didn't envy Anne. She tried to put herself in her place. To bring another baby into the world was pretty heavy. One thing she knew for sure; she wouldn't tolerate Fred smoking pot either, just as she couldn't handle Adam's drinking.

Liz didn't want to reply to Adam immediately. She wanted time to think about his letter. But after hearing about the accident, and his reaction to Will, she knew how much he must be suffering…and drinking. She couldn't envision how the boy's parents might feel. And she didn't want to. It was too unimaginable to lose your child. Will was her whole life.

*Dear Adam,*

*I am so sorry about the little boy. You did your best to save him; I'm sure of that. I can't believe he died in your arms. How horrible! And his poor parents…my God, what they must be going though. This whole thing is dreadful. Do you think you should talk to someone about it to help you cope? Has AA helped?*

*I wanted that too, Adam; a baby with you. Life is funny that way, don't you think? You were my first love and always will be. I miss you. I want to believe we'd still be good together, but it's the drinking that has me concerned. I've never been comfortable with people who drink. You know the way I was brought up. Alcohol was forbidden and now that I have Will, well, I feel even more strongly about it. I know you said you stopped drinking, but did you? I guess I sound insulting. I should trust you, but alcoholism is hard to beat. And you're going through so much.*

*I have more news for you. Anne may be leaving Fred! She's pregnant again, and he's smoking pot. She thinks he's a pothead. Have you ever tried any? I don't see what all the fuss is about, but I guess I don't know what getting stoned is. I have to admit though, I am curious. Do you remember the time I drank beer with you at the golf course? Whew, was I a mess! Do you think I'd act differently with pot? Well it doesn't matter anyway. I now have Will and will never screw up again.*

*It must be strange being away from home for so long. Have you been in touch with any of your friends from school? Do your uncle and cousin know you left?*

*I wish I could visit you, but a couple of my clients are in need of immediate attention. Maybe if things lighten up, ok?*

*Please let me know if you hear anything more on amnesty. I'll keep trying to find out too.*

*I love you Adam.*

# CHAPTER TWENTY-ONE

# ADAM
## (1974-1975)

Since their last correspondence, a year had gone by and once again he hadn't heard from Liz. In some ways he was getting used to her lack of communication and couldn't help but wonder if she really cared about him.

*If she really loves me, wouldn't she come to Canada? Maybe she's playing games. But why would she do that? I don't remember her that way. She's too honest and upfront. After all, I did say I stopped drinking..*

Adam felt out of touch with everyone and everything at home. He was lost and alone.

*I wonder if Anne and Fred are still married; if they had a boy or girl. And Paul, I wonder how the hell he is; if he finished college? The lucky bastard wouldn't have gotten drafted if he stuck it out.*

*Jesus Christ, it's almost 1975! How the hell did that happen? I can't believe I've been here for four years! I'm freakin' Rip Van Winkle and just woke up. What will happen when I get home? Will people hate me? If I were them, I would hate me for deserting my country. Liz says she understands, but does she really?*

*Oh, shit! Will I be able to get a job? Maybe I'll go talk to Uncle Harry about it. Maybe he'll have an idea. Unless he hates me, too.*

*I'm going to feel funny what I get home. That's an understatement!*

Friends at work told Adam not to second guess himself, but little by little his guilt emanated from everything including the desertion of his country to his abandonment of Liz. Conflicted, his mind wandered back to events in the White House. The Watergate Trial had been going on since May. On August 9 the world woke up to Nixon's announcement of his resignation.

*I can't believe the first person I vote for turns out to be a jerk. I hope to God Ford gets me out of this mess. I desperately want to get back to New York.*

He was thinking a lot about it lately. Nixon screwed up in a big way. But at least he admittted he withheld information about the break-in. Watergate was constantly on the news, and just like Adam's life, everything was falling apart in the States.

After watching the late news about the biggest scandal in decades, and then oversleeping, he hurriedly dressed and ran out the door. Everyone at work was talking about the illegal activities which occurred and the attempted cover-up. His Canadian co-workers were stunned over the conspiracy.

I often thought about Bettina and wondered how she was, but knew not to contact her. She was a great lay, but not worth the trouble if her husband ever found out. In truth, though, I cared about her. She was supportive, and unlike Liz, non-judgmental. Liz was always on my back to do this and do that. Anything to perfect myself and be a better person. I questioned how I could spend my entire life with Liz. I needed to be me. But the truth is, she *is* my life.

One hot sticky evening in late August, I went to the *Yellow Door* with a friend from work.

"Did you hear 'bout John Lennon sighting a UFO in Manhattan?"

Andy rolled his eyes. "Give me a break man! Speaking of Lennon, wish they'd play some Beatle music in here. The music is boring, don't you think?"

I turned towards the band and noticed a woman being seated by a man at a table close to the stage. She tossed her dark silky hair to one side and looked in my direction, right at me. It was Bettina! I jumped up and headed towards her.

"Where you going man?"

I ignored Andy and kept walking.

"Bet…," I stopped mid syllable. She looked up and quickly turned her head towards the man she was sitting with, pretending not to recognize me. Embarrassed, I went back to my table.

"Do you believe this? She ignored me; she acted as if she didn't even know me."

"Who?" Andy asked.

"Bettina, the woman I was seeing for months. You know the one who was great in bed."

"Ah, yes, the one who put a smile on your face every morning!" He looked in her direction. "Maybe that's her husband."

"I don't know man. Maybe it's her new boyfriend. From what I knew about her husband, I doubt he would come here." I felt annoyed and hurt. "Oh well, there are plenty of women around here; let's go find one."

I don't know what it was but lately I'd been unable to keep my eyes open at work. When I'd get home I was ready to go to sleep, but instead I'd eat and then eat some more. That's another thing. I was hungrier than I'd ever been. I checked this out with the doctor and he explained both symptoms to be part of diabetes, type 2 diabetes. Fancy name, huh? One, two, what the hell is the difference anyway? I have it and I'm stuck with it. Well, at least I wasn't gaining too much weight. In fact, I lost weight. I heard about people with diabetes getting obese, but that was probably because of using insulin. That wasn't going to happen to me.

Instead of going home after work or to the *Yellow Door*, I decided to take better care of my health and join a gym. I drove to the other side of town to exercise along with some muscular looking dudes. My routine was: work on my abs, pecs, biceps, and triceps, and then jog on the track. Afterwards, I'd swim.

I had been going for about a month when I collapsed on the track. As I returned to consciousness people were gathering around me. Besides being embarrassed, I was worried. Pretty sure it had to do with the diabetes. One of the guys that worked there suggested that I probably was exercising more than my body was accustomed.

"Hey, buddy. I should add that you were bound to faint, since you were drinking and all," the instructor said disparagingly.

The alcohol on my breath was a dead giveaway.

# CHAPTER TWENTY-TWO

# LIZ

## (1975-1976)

It was only Tuesday and Will couldn't stop talking about the roller coaster and Ferris wheel coming to town on the weekend. Mini-rides for young children were scattered throughout the park near our house. The Fourth of July festivities would be awesome.

When Friday came his excitement was over the top.

"Calm down Will," I reproached, but I was also eager.

"But Mom, there's even going to be cotton candy there!"

We left early in the morning and by the time evening came we were both exhausted. Will had been on every ride and eaten every type of junk food available to mankind.

"Gee whiz Will, do you think you might want anything else to eat?" I grinned as I cleaned off his face covered with chocolate.

"Mom, Mom! Look at that one!" Will screeched and pointed to the illuminated sky.

The fireworks were breathtaking and we were all excited. Anne had joined us later in the day. We had planned to meet by the Ferris wheel at 3 p.m. She had her hands filled with two year old Sammy and Clare, a sweet little girl, 16 months old. Although three years apart, Will and Sammy were best friends. They took each other's hands and started to jump up and down and scream together.

"Look, look, mommy, they're red….now they're blue!" The boys were elated and even Clare was jubilant.

# SUMMER OF 1966

Adam took Liz's hand and held it tightly as they headed from the parking lot jam-packed with thousands of cars. Jones Beach was filled with colorful umbrellas from one end to the other, a kaleidoscope to feast on. Everywhere there were girls wearing bikinis. After driving on the Long Island Expressway for what seemed an eternity, with traffic covering the expanse of Long Island, the sun and sand under their feet were soothing to their senses. They left at 8 a.m., but by the time they arrived both of them were starving. Liz opened up their blanket while Adam spread out their sandwiches and drinks. After lunch they waited a bit and then ventured into the water still frigid from the previous winter. The ocean never seemed to warm up, so they were prepared from previous summers.

"Don't you dare!" Liz alternately giggled and screamed.

"Too late!" Adam laughed hysterically. "Too late!

Big heaps of water were splashed back and forth. They rode the waves with precision, as they were both good swimmers. Afterwards, totally exhausted, they walked back to their blanket clinging to each other while they kissed. Liz turned on the radio to Cousin Brucie and they sang along to *Wooly Bully*. They were in love and couldn't imagine a life without each other.

In the evening the crowds gathered around for a fireworks display. It was spectacular.

"Look over there!" The sky lit up with every imaginable color and the crowds oohed and aahed and then applauded.

Laughing, Adam looked up towards the sky. "Far out! You really enjoy this, don't you?"

"Don't you? It's awesome!"

"Apparently not as much as you do," he chuckled.

When it was over they grabbed their blankets and chairs and empty coolers and headed home. Everyone piled into their cars for the long ride. Wherever their destination, even if they lived close by, it would take hours to get out of the parking lot and hours on the insane expressway headed west.

# (1975-1976)

It was getting late. Anne and Liz got the children ready to leave and said their goodbyes.

"Do you have any free time tomorrow to meet for lunch?" Liz asked. "There's something I want to talk to you about."

Relieved that Anne would meet her, Liz organized her thoughts. Almost a year had passed since she kicked Tom out and he was still calling her. The divorce was virtually done, but nevertheless she was considering an order of protection. He made her nervous. At first she had asked him nicely to stop calling, and then more firmly, but to no avail.

She closed up her office and headed out to meet Anne. They were grabbing a quick bite in a café convenient to both of them. It had rained during the night and was still coming down as Liz ran back to get an umbrella. The phone continued to ring off the hook. *Clients will wait. I need this time for myself.*

116

"Hi, thanks for meeting me."

Anne noticed how tired Liz looked. "What's going on? Everything okay?

"Yes, I guess so." Liz grimaced. "No, not really. Why don't we order first?"

They quickly looked at the menus, looked at each other and burst out laughing; and then ordered the same old thing, hamburgers and fries.

Anne searched Liz's face. "So what's up?"

"He won't leave me alone."

"Who?"

"Tom"

"You're kidding! I thought the divorce was a done deal."

"It will be over with soon, but Anne, he's still insisting that we give our marriage a chance. It scares me that he won't let go. Plus, I never told you..." Liz's voice trailed off.

"Told me what?" Anne looked into her friend's eyes and saw something she never saw before. Fear.

Liz took a deep breath. "He tried to rape me."

"What!" Anne gasped. "What are you talking about?"

Liz related the story as best she could without falling apart. "He was drunk and was forcing himself on me. I know we were married, but there were also other times, times when he seemed strange during sex...or, perhaps it was me, wanting Adam instead of him. At the beginning sex was good for us. Really good. Something changed. Maybe it's in my head though."

"No, believe me Liz, it's not in your imagination. A man should never force himself on any woman, even his wife! So what are you going to do?" Anne was worried for her friend.

"I don't know."

Liz needed time to think and hoped she wasn't waiting too long to take action. Lately she was an expert at changing subjects, so she switched to Anne's marriage.

"How are you and Fred doing?"

"We're still hanging in there, I guess, but we're not the same. Sometimes I think he's cheating on me. He seems different."

"I hope not! What makes you think so? Have you seen him with another woman?"

"No, but I sense it. He never wants to make love to me anymore. And he always comes home late from work. He never used to. The kids miss him. I don't though….miss him that is. I'm glad we don't have sex anymore."

"I'm sorry Anne. Is he still smoking pot?"

"A little, but not as much as he used to. And never in front of the kids. I'd never allow that," she said emphatically.

"Do you think you should confront him and ask him if he's seeing anyone else?"

"Nope, don't want to. Maybe I'll see someone else!"

"Good idea!" Each offered a weak smile, but felt a sense of sadness between them.

"I keep meaning to ask you… how's Eddie?"

"He's not doing well." Anne's face paled. "I've been avoiding talking about it."

"If it will upset you, don't."

"It's okay. He came home from Nam a few weeks ago, but it was scary for a while. We hadn't heard from him in a long time and every night my parents checked the casualties posted on Walter Cronkite. They were sick with worry."

"He's with your parents now?"

"No. He's in a VA rehab hospital. He was home though, for the first week. Liz, he lost three fingers on his right hand, with a bunch of other minor injuries. Do you believe it? Minor! As horrendous as this was, he was one of the fortunate ones. Many of his friends were either POW's or lost in action; some even died. A best friend of his, dead! They were in a trench together when a grenade exploded. The dirt and debris and rocks were flying everywhere. Eddie tried to save him but couldn't. He acted swiftly by pulling his friend's legs towards the opposite end of the trench and yanked as hard as he could, but it was too late. He died instantly."

Anne started to sob and struggled to speak. "Eddie returned a broken man, Liz. The tragedies he endured devastated him. He's severely depressed. He told my parents he wakes up screaming from nightmares. He says he dreams he's back in Nam, back in the jungles. He still feels those creepy monstrous insects crawling all over his body, biting into his skin making it unbearable. Some of them were really big! They actually used cigarettes to burn them out!." Repulsed, Liz squirmed in her seat. "And the heat, the murderous heat nauseating him; and trip-wires in the swamps! And, enemies appearing out of nowhere…like terrifying jack-in-the-box figures! Boom! That's the way he described it. The doctors say he has Post-Traumatic Stress Syndrome.

Liz's eyes filled with tears as she held her best friend and let her cry it out.

"I visit him every Sunday, but I don't know what else I can do. I wish I could help him."

Liz thought back to when she volunteered at the VA Hospital. She heard about men suffering from this condition. The veterans seemed to benefit from art therapy. She wished she could personally help Eddie, but time wouldn't allow.

"I have an idea. Why don't you see if there's an art program in the VA hospital he's staying in; or even music program? I heard they're introducing music therapy to the vets in many of the facilities."

Annoyed, Anne snapped, "They may have suggested that to Eddie, but do you really think that could eradicate what he's been through?"

"Well, it can't hurt to try!"

"I'm sorry Liz. I'm scared for him. It's ripping our family apart. He jumps at everything we say. I'm afraid to go near him. That first week when I went home to visit him…I found him yelling at my mother. Apparently she entered his room to change his sheet without realizing he was there. He lunged at her, Liz! Lunged at her! And then spewed out profanities!"

"Oh Anne, I'm so sorry!"

They were quiet for a time.

Trying to lighten things up, Liz joked, "Hey! Let's turn to *Dear Abby* for all our problems. She'll tell us what to do. Is she still around?"

Anne smiled weakly. "I think her show may have ended."

"Well, now what are we going to do?" Liz was starting to giggle uncontrollably from nervousness. "What on earth will we do without her?"

"We can always write to her column. *Dear Abby, My friend, my best friend Liz, she can't get rid of her ex. He's one big pain in the arse.*" Laughter began to take hold of Anne too. But not for long. Their laughter turned to sorrow.

PART II

# CHAPTER TWENTY-THREE

# ADAM

## (AUGUST 1976)

Carter's campaign to grant amnesty to draft dodgers did not take Adam by surprise. It was all people were talking about and all he was praying for. Confident he would be pardoned, since those who violated the draft from

1964-1973 were eligible, he followed the news closely every day. His life would hopefully change by the beginning of the year. But he knew when he got home there would be hell to pay. The controversy over Carter's decision was alarming. Many felt it was a disgrace to desert the country and offenders should go to prison. Others felt relief for their loved ones. Adam only hoped that Liz would welcome him home with open arms. His fear though was that he would be ostracized by people he knew, or for that matter, anyone. They might even call him a coward. For this same reason thousands upon thousands of men were thinking of remaining in Canada and never going home. But Adam knew he had to go home.

Without hesitation he decided to leave much earlier than advised. There was no turning back. He had to take his chances amnesty would go through. He couldn't take it anymore. He had had it.

*I'm going home! I'm finally going home! I can breathe again. I think I'll go celebrate!*

He decided *not* to drink. He needed to get his act together fast. He needed a plan. From this moment on his every focus was figuring out how to land a job and find an apartment as inconspicuously as possible.

Adam had lived frugally in Canada for a long time and was now starting to think big. *Maybe I should forget about an apartment and buy a house instead. I always wanted to live in a beach house. Wow, those awesome times with Liz on the beach; Jones Beach. Boy, does that take me back. That's it! I'll move to the Hamptons. It's pricey, but what the hell. I have plenty of money. I'll do it!*

He started to ask around. As luck would have it, one of his clients had connections in the States with an accounting firm, a top-notch company headquartered in NY and a branch based in California.

Everything went smoothly and quickly. Initially Adam was interviewed on the phone. He made up some bogus explanation of why he was in Canada. They must have bought it or maybe they didn't care, but either way they seemed to be interested in his credentials. Right before Adam left he had been given a promotion. It was long overdue, but not because his abilities were lacking; his immigration was in question.

*Whitely & Hersh* had an opening for a senior accountant starting one month from now. They were interested in him. The second interview was set up for September 15.

*I'm really going home. But, wait a minute! Where will I live until I find a house? Maybe I'll stay in a hotel; it will be easier. What if I don't get this job? Then what?*

He decided to stop worrying and move forward. He desperately wanted to go home and see Liz and meet her kid, and resume his life. That's all that mattered to him.

Adam offered his goodbyes at the office. They were sad to see him go. It had taken him awhile but he eventually made friends at work. Now he was leaving. They surprised him with a going away party at the *Yellow Door* and promised to keep in touch. There was part of Adam that was also sad, but only a small part. He desperately wanted to go home.

The Amtrak Montrealer arrived a few minutes late. I grabbed my three pieces of luggage and overnighter, and settled myself towards a rear window hoping for a view of the countryside. During my stay in Canada I hadn't accumulated many belongings and took home even less.

One of my co-workers who was sympathetic to American draft dodgers knew someone who knew someone who gave me a new name. Sam Withers. And so it was, three hundred American dollars later. We exchanged the money for my passport under a table in a sleazy bar. As simple as that. Sam Withers from Brooklyn, NY.

One and a half hours later the train made a stop at the border. My heart was pounding. Two military policemen boarded the train and searched each car finally taking a person into custody. My car was spared, but the train didn't move after their departure. *What's going on?* My adrenalin was racing. *Am I next?*

All of a sudden the train lurched forward. I thought it was over, but then a foreboding border patrol agent wearing an intimidating U.S. Customs uniform, with rimmed glasses perched on his smallish nose, approached me. He must have been taller than 6 ft. He scanned a list that probably took seconds, but seemed like hours. I drew in my breath. Beads of perspiration formed on my forehead. My face felt as hot as a scorched hand burned by an iron. I was certain it turned scarlet red. My neck was clammy and I felt sweat trickling down my chest. And then he looked directly at me and nodded. Sam Withers was legit. I was not on the list. My fake ID was accepted. The weight of the world was lifted off me, but I was still numb with fear.

"How-do," a dark skinned boy around twenty thickly drawled as he neared the seat next to me. "Anyone sittin' 'ere?" His long black braided hair was neatly tied back in a ponytail with a red bandana wrapped around his forehead. He wore a checkered brown flannel shirt hanging out of his ripped dungarees, with equally worn out sneakers.

"Nope, it's empty," I motioned.

The boy placed a guitar between his legs as he sat down and offered his hand. "I'm Joe."

"Adam, nice to meet you. You play?" I pointed to the case.

"Yes sir-ee, since I'm a young'un. Folk music. You?"

"Nah, never picked it up. But my girlfriend plays the violin."

"Cool!"

"Why don't you play something?"

"*Shore* thing," Joe said as he unzipped the case. "Where you headed?"

"Home. I'm going home to New York." I sighed heavily. "What about you?"

Joe started to play some tune which sounded familiar.

"Kentucky."

"You have some accent," I remarked, but wondered if I slighted him. "What's that you're playing?"

"'Father and Son.' Cat Stevens wrote it. I reckon it's about Cat and his daddy." He was pensive for a minute. "His daddy tells him he's dying and wants Cat to be a man and not be afraid. He tells him to live his life even after he dies. My pappy, he croaked this time last year," said the Kentuckian. "When I was a little bitty young'un he told my ma, *our boy is going to be a real musician.* The next day he bought this here guitar and handed it to me and said, *you see this here? Play it 'till you learn it and don't ya come back 'till you do.* Lordy, I was fit to be tied. I *din't* know how to play." Joe continued to strum, but this time he played a Woody Guthrie tune.

I thought about my own dad and for a brief moment how it would feel if *I* were a dad.

"Did he play guitar too?" I inquired.

"No, that was the strange part. Ain't never touched the darned thing."

"Maybe he had a hidden desire to play, but he did it vicariously through you," I suggested.

Joe went back to playing some songs as I fell asleep tapping my foot to the music. When I awoke I was startled to see the sun going down.

"Lordy, you slept as long as a month of Sundays." Joe's accent was even more pronounced.

"Boy, you sure have some funny expressions!" I chortled, suppressing a yawn. "I did sleep long, didn't I?"

I glanced out the window. Off to my left I noticed a spectacular looking bridge with mountains close enough to touch its head. The expanse of the river reached far into the distance. *This must be close to where Liz lives. I remember she described this exact scenery.* The conductor approached me and asked for my ticket.

"Excuse me, sir, what's the name of this bridge?"

"Bear Mountain."

"It's really something. How far are we from Manhattan?"

"About another hour." He tipped his cap and walked off, collecting the rest of the tickets.

The excitement of arriving on U.S. soil started to catch up to me. I felt overwhelmed and started to sweat again.

Time dragged on for what seemed like an eternity. Joe kept singing his tunes, but I heard none of them. I was in a frozen state of anticipation, a mannequin about to come alive after six years of holding my breath. After shaking the Kentuckian's hand and wishing him well, I gathered my belongings as the train slowed.

"Penn Station!" the conductor bellowed.

Luggage in tow, I went through the sliding doors and stepped off the train onto the platform. I entered the concourse through the tunnel, and looked around at the crowds with a nervousness I never felt before. I was home. I was truly home. I kept walking until sunlight shone and all the familiar landmarks I grew up with revealed themselves. For the second time in my life, I cried.

# CHAPTER TWENTY-FOUR

# LIZ
## (LATE AUGUST 1976)

"Liz, sit down!" Anne pulled out a chair, placing her purse on the dining room table. "Did you see the news last night? Carter announced his campaign to grant amnesty to draft dodgers!"

Liz gaped. "Oh my God; thank you God! If it goes through, when will it be effective?"

"There's a lot of controversy about it, but he's aiming for the end of January."

Anne was ecstatic to give her friend such good news. But, she felt ambivalent about Adam's decision to dodge the draft. She understood why he was fearful of war, and agreed that this particular one was indeed controversial, but her brother's bravery superseded any other viewpoints she might have.

"Carter's pardon is only for men who have violated the draft between '64 and '73, and Adam left in '70, right?"

"Yes, definitely 1970," Liz stated unequivocally.

"Well, it will wipe *his* criminal record clean, but not the thousands of enlisted men who went AWOL," Anne croaked.

129

Ignoring her friend's anger, Liz replied, "I'm sure Adam knows what's happening. He must be relieved."

"Do you think he'll call you?" Anne noticed Liz's excitement dissipate.

"I don't know," she sighed. "You would think he'd call me in the middle of the night with news like this, but in the last few years he's given me mixed messages. We're so different than we used to be. His drinking has always stood in the way of our future, but now that he's been gone so long it somehow made it worse. The distance and not knowing put a wedge between us."

"I thought you said he stopped."

"That's what *he* said, but somehow I doubt it. I know he's still drinking. I feel it in my bones." She shivered.

Liz had reoccurring nightmares ever since she dreamt Adam died. She hoped he was doing well and coming home soon. She contemplated why he hadn't called her.

"Well, now what?" Anne asked.

"I guess I'll just wait to hear from him."

"You're not going to call him?"

"Nope."

"You know, Adam has money. I bet you he gets off real easy," Anne snidely remarked.

"What's that about?" Liz asked annoyed. "I thought with amnesty they won't need any help from lawyers? And why are you being so snotty?"

"Just in case is what I was thinking. Don't you think I have a right to be upset with the jerks that didn't fight in the war?"

"I can't believe you're talking this way," Liz cried out. "You know Adam is a good guy."

"Look, all I know is that Eddie can't find work. He needs money to live. On one job interview a potential employer told him he's a "nutjob" because he was shaking so much. Another employer said... and I quote..."I don't want anyone working here for me that killed women or children! Get the hell out of here!" Liz, he doesn't get any support from the government. It's as if he is being demeaned for the services he gave. He feels abandoned by those around him. He should be considered a hero!"

"That's dreadful. I'm so sorry!" Liz knew Anne was right, but her misguided loyalties went to Adam.

They argued for a time, but after realizing the sensitivity of the issue they agreed to disagree. Secretly they both had hurt feelings.

The order of protection was set in motion. Liz's worry about Tom was temporarily mitigated. There was something about Tom that made her uneasy, but at least he had stopped calling.

She grabbed her sweater off the makeshift desk where piles of papers were stacked. Will was waiting for her at school. It was his first week back. They were going across town to Dr. Willabie for his annual dental check-up. When she arrived he was at the playground with some other children and a teacher's aide. As usual the kids were hyper and running around as if it was the beginning of the day.

"Mom, Mom! You won't believe it!"

"What Will? What happened?" She beamed, happy to see him as she always was at the end of her day.

"He was here!"

"Who Will? Who was here?" she asked with mild curiosity assuming it was nobody special.

"Tom, mom! Look what he gave me." Will took out a red yo-yo, wound the string around his forefinger, and started to demonstrate by lifting his hand up and down in a mechanical fashion. "Isn't it neat?"

"Stay here Will and don't leave! Okay?"

Will continued to play with the yo-yo watching it rise and fall until he mastered it.

Infuriated she stomped over to the aide who was outside the playground talking to another mother, and rudely interrupted them.

"Why would you let a stranger talk to my son?" she asked heatedly with a trembling voice.

"Your son indicated the gentleman was not a stranger. They even hugged each other," the aide responded.

Liz left frustrated at the woman's lame and indifferent attitude. She waited until they were home from the dentist before she drilled him with, "don't talk to strangers" rules.

"But mom, it was just Tom!" Will was crying.

Liz put her arms around him and in a softer tone expounded on what she had explained to him before.

"Will, I know you liked Tom a lot, and he's not really a stranger, but he isn't a good guy either. So please honey, if he tries to talk to you again, stay away from him. Walk away. Okay?"

He seemed to better understand or at least accept the situation. After finishing chocolate milk and cookies his mood elevated.

"Mom, could I go play now?" Will asked eagerly. She left him in his room happily playing with his Batman action figures.

The following morning after a restless night she uncharacteristically drove Will to school and marched into the principal's office. When she was done ranting, she ended by stating unequivocally, "Unless they are part of the staff, I do not want anyone going near my son!"

Immediately afterwards, she went to the courthouse and this time filed papers for an order of protection for Will. It had never occurred to her that this would be necessary. It would be many months before the divorce would come through, but she refused to be intimidated. *She* was taking action. She had had enough.

# CHAPTER TWENTY-FIVE

# ADAM

## (OCTOBER 1976)

I had been home for two months and still no word from the realtor. She informed me that I may have a long wait. Nothing met my criteria: A house in South Hampton on the water, with nice sized windows facing the ocean, a deck with the same view, and a big kitchen. Although I didn't know how to cook, I was determined to become a gourmet chef.

The hotel I was staying in was fine for now; within walking distance to work. It would be a long commute from the island every day, but I would figure it out. It would be worth it. Plus, Manhattan was an exciting place to temporarily stay.

My new position as senior accountant started immediately after the second interview. No questions were asked about my draft status. Everything was going smoothly. My fake ID was a thing of the past. Hopefully.

I got the call mid-October. It was a shock to both the realtor and myself. There was a house that met my requirements with all but one minor detail. An extra bedroom. The price was astronomically high, but I was able to talk the owners down substantially. It was a steal and gorgeous to boot. A middle-aged couple lived there for just under five years and were anxious to sell. They were moving to Europe and had no time to negotiate. The deal was quickly settled. I was finally on an up streak. There was no doubt about it.

I moved in with few belongings. Furniture shopping was next on the list, but for now all I needed was a bed, couch, and TV. For the first time in my life, I felt content. I sighed and took it all in. The inside and outside were equally magnificent. It's exactly what I wanted. A panoramic view of the ocean was right in front of me. I walked from the deck into the enormous living room. *Wow! This is a far cry from my apartment in Montreal.*

It was a small house compared to the others in the area. There wasn't a tennis court or swimming pool, but there were other amenities to suggest opulence. There was a Jacuzzi in the upstairs bathroom, right off the master suite. Mahogany woodwork was in almost every room, along with fire places in each of the three bedrooms and living room. A spiraling staircase elegantly joined both floors. The kitchen was a little smaller than I hoped for, but still big enough to prepare gourmet meals on the luxurious marble countertop. In the front of the house there was a sizeable sculpture with an intricate abstract design resembling a sailboat. *I wonder who created this; maybe a local artist?* The best part was waiting for me on the outskirts of town – an exclusive golf course. *I wish you were here dad, to play a game or two with me.*

Things were moving along at a steady pace. All the necessary details to connect my phone and electricity were taken care of, so I had time to kill. It was an unusually warm autumn day, so I went down to the water. The ocean was cold but refreshing. I've always been a strong swimmer and dove in. Afterwards, I stretched out on my towel and let the sand run through my fingers as I repeatedly grabbed the granules and watched them fall back onto the earth. My whole body relaxed as I breathed in the ocean and listened to the soothing sound of the waves as they crashed. Looking up towards the sapphire sky, I closed my eyes for a moment. *This is the life I've dreamed of for so long.*

I stayed for hours, sleeping off and on, and then intermittently going back into the water for a brisk swim. Hardly any people were on the beach, only those who lived nearby or perhaps an occasional tourist taking a stroll. To my left I noticed quaint looking houses each one separated by jagged dunes. *Liz will love it here! She revels in Plein Air painting.* The sun was setting and I realized I was shivering. It was time to go back home.

"Liz? Hi, it's me."

"Adam?" Chills ran through her.

He took in a deep breath. "I'm home."

# CHAPTER TWENTY-SIX

# LIZ
## (LATE OCTOBER – NOVEMBER 1976)

"Adam? You're home?" She quickly counted in her head. "You're home four months earlier than you should be. Am I right? Are you okay? Will you be arrested?"

"Slow down Liz. Actually, I've been home for two months." He took a deep breath. "Please, don't be angry. I needed to be alone. It's been so long since I've been home. Please understand."

"What!" She was outraged. *It's happening again. I can't believe it! He left for Canada without uttering one Goddamned word, and now he returned without letting me know.* "Did I hear you correctly? You're home since …August? Is that what you're saying?"

"Yes, I came home in August." He acknowledged so softly that she could barely hear him.

"I'm trying to understand. I knew about Carter's campaign, but it's not a done deal yet. Why'd you take a chance and come home early? Oh, never mind! I guess all that's important is that you're okay. Where are you staying?"

"I was staying at the *Hilton* on W. 53rd, but Liz, I just bought a house! You'll never guess where?"

Liz knew immediately where by the uplifted tone of his voice. "On the island, overlooking the water, right?"

"Wait a minute, how'd you know that?" he laughed.

"Come on Adam, you loved it there since we were kids. Where, Montauk or South Hampton?"

"South Hampton. It's incredible, you'll love it!"

Dubiously, she replied, "Oh Adam, I can't wait to see it."

"I can't wait to see you Liz….and meet Will!"

In spite of herself, she excitedly went through her closet for the hundredth time, finally settling on a red sweater with black trouser pants that complimented her slim but curvy figure. After Will was born, she became bustier and her hips were fuller. She was self-conscious about her body and wondered if Adam would notice. She put on some red lipstick, oversized gold loop earrings, and brushed her long brown hair back into a ponytail.

*I can't believe he'll be here in one hour. In one hour!* Emotions flooded my senses. I was angry. I was overwhelmed. I was elated. But, no matter what I felt I was sure about one thing; after all these years, I was still in love with Adam. He was my son's father. My grandmother used to say: "My heart is racing like hummingbird wings."

"Will, are you ready yet? Adam will be here in a few minutes. Come down and let me see what you're wearing. Okay?"

"Mom, why are you so nervous? I thought Adam was your friend. If he's your friend then you don't have to be nervous. Okay, mom?"

I went over to Will standing by the bottom stair and held him close. "I love you, do you know that?"

"I love you too, mom."

CHAPTER TWENTY-SEVEN

# ADAM
## (NOVEMBER 1976)

The LIE was moving at an unusually steady pace and his mind started to drift. *He won! I can't believe it's finally over! Thank God he won the election! Carter will soon be in office and I will be free.*

Adam watched the results the night before and was overcome with relief. He turned on the car radio to see if he could catch the latest news. Reports were still coming in on men classified as POWs and MIAs. The war may have been officially over a year ago, but the crisis would continue for some time to come.

Obviously he was one of the lucky ones, but that's not to say he didn't suffer. His life became disenfranchised during his seven years in Canada. Although solvent, he chose to live a life of a middle-class college kid to eventually a lost soul living in an unfamiliar country. He left behind all that was important to him. But again, he knew he was lucky. Not only did he secure a job in Canada, and after that come home to a better one, he was not a prisoner of war, nor was he missing in action. He was alive.

Once I hit the Sprain Brook Parkway I decided to take the scenic route. It would only add fifteen minutes to the three hour drive and be considerably more peaceful. As I approached the Hudson Valley, the river surrounded by mountains came into view exactly as Liz described. It was spectacular! It would take another thirty minutes before I'd arrive at Mohegan Lake, but it was worth it to see Liz again.

With a basketball in one hand and red roses in the other, I got out of my rented Riviera and did a quick survey of the neighborhood. *So this is where she lives. Different, very different than I expected. Nice, not bad.*

Her house was small and provincial. I walked up the path where a breathtaking garden with flowers of every imaginable color covered the landscape. *Well, now I know what Liz does with her spare time. This is incredible!*

Liz opened the door, stared into his handsome face, and felt weak at the knees. "Adam, oh Adam, it's been seven years," she murmured and then the tears started to come.

He put the presents down on the antique welcoming bench to his right at the foot of the door and held her tightly. He wiped her tears away and kissed her deeply as they clung to each other. He began to kiss every part of her tear-streaked face as they remembered each other's touch. "Oh Adam, oh Adam" was all she could seem to say over and over again.

"Mommy, mommy, is this him, is this Adam?" Eager to be introduced, Will eyed the tall man hugging his mother.

They released their embrace and faced him. "Yes sweetheart, this is Adam. Adam meet Will." Liz immediately saw the reflection of father and son, as she had seen Adam's reflection in Will's face for the last six years.

"Hi Will. It's nice to meet you!" Adam offered his hand for him to shake. "I brought you a basketball. Do you play?"

Liz stared in amazement. *My God, it's just like the dream!*

"Yes! I'm good at it. Wanna see?" he asked excitedly. "Will you play with me? I have a basketball hoop over there." He pointed towards the garage. "Tom put it up for me."

"Sure, in a few minutes, okay?"

Adam handed Liz the fragrant flowers. "These are for you. I hope you like them." He whispered, "Who's Tom?"

Averting his question, she replied, "Come on in!" Then to Will, "Let Adam get settled honey. He must be tired from the drive, and we haven't seen each other for such a long time. How about we show him your room first, ok?"

"But will you play with me later?" Will pleaded.

"You bet I will," answered Adam.

"Come on," Will grabbed his hand and yanked in the direction of his bedroom.

"Will and I ate earlier, but are you hungry? Do you want lunch? Or do you want to wait for dinner? We're having pizza in honor of you coming!"

"No, thanks Liz, maybe later. I have a room to check out first… and some catching up to do," he grinned.

The three of them walked up the stairs together and Will showed him all his current heroes that covered the walls of his room.

Liz left the two of them to get acquainted and went back to the kitchen to put the flowers in a vase.

*Boy, these are gorgeous. Take deep breaths. That's it, slow deep breaths. Breathe, breathe.*

She walked back upstairs to Will's room and found them playing with his GI Joe guys.

"You've got quite a boy there Liz," he winked.

She felt like screaming. *He's yours Adam! Can't you see that!*

Later when Will was taking his nap, Liz and Adam fervently caught up with their lives. Sitting on the sofa holding hands, they faced each other with Liz's legs tucked under her.

"You look great Liz."

"So do you! Guess we're a little older though," she joked, pointing to her one grey hair on top of her head. "Look!"

"How horrible!!" He laughed. "You look the same; as beautiful as ever."

She blushed.

"Liz, I've missed you so much. It was wrong of me to leave without telling you. Can you ever forgive me?"

"I just don't underst…"

Adam raised his hand to stop her. "I was ashamed Liz, and embarrassed. I didn't know what you would feel about me with our whole country fighting a war I refused to accept. I know there were thousands of men who opposed the war, but not everyone was a draft dodger. I wanted you to always be proud of me and not think of me as a coward." He looked forlorn and seemed to shrink in size.

She put her arms around him and held him tightly against her. "You could have come to me. I never would have thought of you that way. We could have figured it out together." She looked deeply into the eyes that were so much like Will's. "Didn't you know that?" *I can't believe I just said that to him! I didn't turn to him about me being pregnant. And it was his son!*

"Do you have any beer?"

"Adam! It's only 3:30 in the afternoon! And it doesn't matter anyway! You shouldn't be drinking at all!" Disgusted, she walked away and then thought better of it. "Look, I knew you didn't quit and that is why I …." She stopped herself in time.

"That is why you, what Liz?"

"Forget it! No, I don't have any beer. How about some lemonade?"

"Sure, sorry. I didn't mean to upset you."

She poured some for both of them and sat down again.

"Will was so excited to meet you that he got up at the crack of dawn."

For the last couple of weeks Liz had been talking to Will non-stop about how they went to school together and were the closest of friends. But she didn't tell her son what Adam really meant to her; that he was his father, the love of her life.

Remembering the earlier comment that Will made, Adam repeated, "Who's Tom?"

Once again the subject was deflected.

"Mommy, can we have pizza yet?" Will practically flew down the stairs, although still sleepy from his nap.

"Sure, honey. I'll order some right now. What do you men want on your pizza? How about some meatballs and onions?" Her eyes gleamed remembering Adam's and her favorite toppings.

All three nodded in agreement. "Liz, why don't you order the pizza? Us guys have some serious shooting to do. Come on Will."

"Me first."

They walked hand in hand towards the garage. "Do you know how to dribble yet?" Adam asked.

"No, not really. Tom started to show me, but then he couldn't anymore."

"Why not? Who's Tom? Is he your friend?"

"He was mommy's husband, but isn't anymore. And he's not my stepfather anymore either."

"Okay Will, hold the ball like this." Adam demonstrated as he pondered over his remarks. *Liz was married? How could she have not told me? Shit! What else hasn't she told me?* "And you can shoot this way," he demonstrated. "A lay-up, real close, or….like this." He dribbled the ball further away, turned around, and shot the ball right into the basket. "See, I took a jump shot."

"Yea!" shouted Will. "Let *me* try!" He grabbed the ball and dribbled.

"Excellent Will! You just did an open shot."

"How many points do I have?" he asked all ruddy cheeked and wide-eyed.

"You don't have any points yet. You're getting there. Patience Will. Whoever gets a score of twenty-one wins."

"Will, Adam, pizza's here!" Liz shouted from the kitchen window.

"Mom! We can't, we just started, okay?" Will pleaded.

"Come on, pizza with meatballs. Are you kidding? I'm going to eat yours then," Adam joked.

Will ran into the kitchen falling flat on his face. The three of them burst into laughter, each grabbing a slice, eating with gusto.

After they were done eating, Will put his arms around Adam's neck as he carried him upstairs. Liz and Adam tucked Will into bed, which made all three of them very happy. Out of nowhere, one of them started tickling the other, and all at once the three of them were bouncing up and down on the bed in hysterics.

"Time out," Liz shouted, holding her stomach from belly laughing.

"Oh no, we're not through with you yet," Adam yelled, "Right, Will?"

But Will closed his eyes and pretended to fall asleep. And just as they started to leave, he jumped up and surprised both of them by tickling his mother all over again. "Why you little faker," Liz tickled him back and kissed his forehead.

After a few minutes, she covered him with his GI Joe blanket and turned off the lights whispering goodnight. Exhausted from the day, this time he had really fallen asleep before brushing his teeth or getting into his pj's. With a little snore, Will curled over.

Adam whispered, "I haven't laughed this much in years."

She mouthed back, "You! What about me? You both ambushed me." They both quietly giggled as they proceeded downstairs.

Once in the living room, Adam brought up the subject of Tom again. "Why didn't you tell me Liz?"

"Tell you what?" She settled herself on the couch caressing a pillow.

"Tom."

"I guess Will told you? Well, now you know."

Adam was obviously hurt.

"Liz, I'm confused. He told me you married a guy named Tom, but he's not his father. Who is?"

"I wrote you about that. Don't you remember I met someone in college?"

Liz wanted so badly to tell him the truth, especially after having seen Adam and Will together. They looked so much like father and son, not only physically, but in their mannerisms. She thought, *maybe soon. Maybe soon I'll tell him.*

# CHAPTER TWENTY-EIGHT

# LIZ

## (NOVEMBER 1976)

Thanksgiving was finally here and I was as flustered as ever. I had so much to do. This would be Adam's and my first holiday together in many years and Will was over the moon with him being in our lives. My parents were coming too, and Anne and her children. I was a bit over the moon myself.

I put on my most festive attire for the season, a slim fitting burgundy velveteen dress that V-necked in the front; the heart shaped necklace engraved with our names, which Adam bought for me when we were seventeen; and my favorite, hopefully sexy, heels. I was sure Adam would be pleased. I usually wore my ripped up jeans on the weekends and my tailored suits during the week for work. Today was special!

"Hurry Will, are you dressed yet?"

"I'm coming Mommy!"

"Wow, Will! You look mighty handsome in your red sweater and new cords!" Liz nodded approvingly.

His face turned a shade of red. "Mom, stop!"

"Okay, okay. Come on honey, let's check how the turkey's doing before our guests…Oops! Too late! They're here!"

The doorbell rang three times in succession.

"We're coming, one minute!

Everyone piled in and exchanged pleasantries as they entered.

"Adam, it's nice to see you after all these years." Liz's mom kissed and embraced him and her father shook his hand with relish.

"How the hell are you, son?"

Both of them knowing what Adam did not.

"Anne? These are your two children? They're adorable!"

"Thank you Adam! I'm glad you're okay. Liz has been so worried!"

As they entered the living room, a cozy and welcoming feeling overcame all of them. The house was filled with love and joy.

Everyone sat around and talked as they nibbled on the hors d'oeuvres spread out before them.

"Boy, these are delicious," Anne commented. "What are these?"

"Just something I threw together; some mushrooms…whoa, *Thumby*!" Our two month old kitten, whom we recently adopted from a shelter, flew over the table. Laughing at her antics, I continued, "Bread crumbs and apple slices, and… a little bit of cat hair to add to the texture!" They burst out laughing. I looked around and noticed Dad talking to Adam in earnest as they hungrily devoured the chips. "Dinner's soon," I hollered across the room. On the rug sat Will and Sammy with coloring books and crayons, and Clare, alongside them, was playing with her favorite stuffed animal, a giraffe.

"Honey, the turkey smells scrumptious. Can I help with anything?"

"No thanks, mom. I'm good!"

"Anne, I wanted to ask, but I've been so busy in the kitchen. Where's Fred?"

"He has a cold, or so he says. I really question if he stayed home or went somewhere else. You know what I think, so what's the point of ruining Thanksgiving, right?"

"I'm sorry Anne, you're right. Let's get our minds off this ugliness. What are you doing for Christmas?"

They all gathered around an elongated oak table, covered with a lacy tablecloth embroidered by Liz's maternal grandmother. Two elegant candles were lit in the center. Everyone sat down, laughing and joyous to be together. The meal was delicious with all the usual trimmings: squash soup was served first; the turkey stuffed with hazelnut was tantalizing; gravy, seasoned with rosemary, thyme and parsley (a recipe from her mom) was mouthwatering; cranberry sauce with orange bits; sweet potatoes, with marshmallows on top for the kids; a green bean casserole and glazed carrots, and hot apple cider, awaited their ravenous appetites. Afterwards, apple crisp and pumpkin pies baked by Liz's mom and Anne were spread out for dessert. It was a glorious Thanksgiving.

One week later when Adam returned, he found Liz helping Will on his bicycle.

"Will, be patient, you'll get it," Liz said resolutely patting him on the back.

"I am patient! I can't do it," he screeched in frustration. "I'm not doing it anymore. Give me back my training wheels." He started to whimper.

"Here Will, let me help." Adam kissed Liz hello and motioned for her to leave.

She whispered, "I tried everything; even my father tried to teach him. He's so uncoordinated….like you were when you were a kid. Didn't you tell me that you learned to ride at the same age?"

"Yep, it was a difficult time. All the kids rode bikes except me. Now get out of here so I can help him," he grinned.

An hour had passed and still no results. But, then all of a sudden…

"You've got it," Adam said excitedly. "You've got it…keep going… keep going." He ran alongside of him. "You did it!"

"Mom! Mom! I did it! I rode my bicycle without falling!" Will beamed.

Liz came running out. "Oh Will, how awesome! You finally did it! I'm so proud of you!" She hugged him tightly.

"How did you get him to stay on without falling?" she asked Adam.

"I didn't do anything. He did it all by himself; he needed confidence, that's all."

But something was terribly wrong with Adam. His face was beat red, and sweat was pouring down his cheeks. And, he was visibly trembling.

"What is it Adam? What's the matter? Are you okay?

"It's nothing Liz. I'm okay."

"It's cold out Adam. Why are you sweating?"

That night when Adam went home, he had nightmares of Will crashing into a car while on his bike. When he awakened he frantically dialed Liz.

"Liz, Liz!" The panic in his voice rose and he shouted, "Is Will okay?"

"Adam! It's 2 a.m., what's the matter? Will's okay. He's right here with me."

"Oh thank God! I thought…I guess… …it must have been a dream I had," he stammered. "I've been struggling with the Montreal incident lately. Having a lot of nightmares. And when Will was on his bike last night, well I…I guess I fell apart."

"Maybe you should go for some help Adam, don't you think?" She tried to shake herself up from her deep sleep. "You know, I didn't have a chance to tell you this, but while you were away, I did some volunteer work in a VA hospital. I worked with an art therapist to help the veterans. It was incredible. Many of the vets had Post-Traumatic Stress Disorder and creating art seemed to help them. Are you familiar with it?

"Wow Liz! I'm proud of you! That's a really nice thing to do. And yes, I've heard about it. I have had flashbacks."

"I'm not a doctor, but I wonder if you are suffering from this?

"Maybe. I'll look into it, I promise."

But, Adam had other things on his mind. He wondered if he should tell her about his diabetes.

Thanksgiving had barely past and Chanukah was imminent. Liz wasn't very observant, probably because her parents weren't. It was more about gift giving when she was little. And even though Adam wasn't really Jewish, in their eyes they felt he was. He was raised that way and would remain that way. So when Chanukah came this year, and they were finally all together, it was a jubilant time.

Adam drove up the driveway and got out of the car with Chanukah gifts in both hands. Will came running out of the house shouting, "Are those all for me, Adam? Are they?"

"Well, there are a few here for your Mom. Is that okay?" He laughed heartily and then the packages started to fall one by one as he gave Will a hug with his emptied arm. Both Will and Adam were in hysterics by the time Liz walked over to them.

"Mom, do we have to say the prayers and light the candles first or can we open the presents? Please, please."

Liz shook her head vehemently."Absolutely not!"

A horn honked twice. Liz turned around to see her parents pulling up to join in the festivities. Will's attention was momentarily diverted by his grandparents' arrival. "Popsy, Grandma! Look at all the presents Adam got me! And Mom."

Soon after sunset, Liz's dad placed one candle on the far right side of the menorah representing the first night. He recited the blessings and lit that candle with the *Shamash* candle, which was then placed in the center. Afterwards, songs were sung and presents were exchanged. When the wine was poured, Liz made sure to pour grape juice for Adam. Although she didn't know about his diabetes yet, she didn't want the evening ruined with his drinking, so he acquiesced. There were terrific presents for Will, including dreidels and chocolate gelt, coins wrapped in gold foil. The traditional foods of potato latkes, a savory brisket (with the family's recipe of orange jam and spices), and challah bread, were enjoyed by everyone. All in all, it was a moderately quiet season, with the best part – Adam was home.

# CHAPTER TWENTY-NINE

# ADAM

## (JANUARY – FEBRUARY 1977)

That autumn day in early November when he first met Will, Adam was changed in ways he didn't understand, at least consciously. He saw a great deal of himself in this special little boy. In fact, he sensed an innate similarity. He assumed it was because Will was Liz's son.

They had returned from a movie and the three of them were immersed in a heated discussion.

"What would you do if *you* were the schoolmate watching *your* friend get beaten up?" Liz inquired of her seven year old son.

"I would beat the bad kid up," Will replied smugly. "And then I would get the principal."

Liz countered, "Well, I think the point is that the schoolmate was a lot bigger than the friend in the movie and he didn't have a chance. Plus he had bad influences in his family. His mother was…."

"I know! I know!" Will interrupted and repeated matter-of-factly, "The mother was doing bad things and not coming home."

"I honestly don't know how they could rate this PG. Next time we get a babysitter, or it must be a child appropriate movie. This was for older kids, don't you think?" Liz looked at Adam, realizing she was consulting him for the first time. It's as if he was part of their little family.

"I don't know, Liz. There's a message in there for children of all ages, even Will's age."

"Oh? Like what? Do onto to others, as they do onto to you? Beat up your friends as your friends do to each other?" she asked exasperated.

"No Liz! Bullying should be stopped; that's the message! All kids go through this. I was bullied."

"Yeah mom! Don't you know that? Adam was bullied and that happens in my class too." Will stopped to think. "How were you bullied, Adam?"

"Well, when I was ten years old the kids in my class didn't like me because I was Jewish. They ganged up on me, pushed me against a wall, and made fun of me."

Will was on the edge of his seat. "What did you do? Did you beat them up?"

"I stuck up for myself and told them to bug off or else, and then told them I was proud to be Jewish."

"Wow!" Will exclaimed.

"Okay honey," Liz said giving Will a hug, "Why don't we talk some more about this tomorrow after we get a goodnight's sleep? It's getting late. Go brush your teeth, okay?"

They both tucked him in after a bedtime story, which they took turns reading. After saying goodnight, they went downstairs.

"Adam, did that really happen?"

"Yep, it did. Bad time for me." He looked down averting Liz's gaze.

"But you weren't really Jewish," she kidded, but knew Adam was serious.

"But I was, Liz. My parents raised me that way."

"I'm sorry you went through that," she said teary-eyed. "Maybe you shouldn't be alone tonight. You know, you could sleep here instead of going back to the hotel, but in the den of course, because of ….," she cocked her head towards Will's room.

"I'd love to, but I have work to do…prepare for a new client. I'm okay Liz, really. But, can we make some time for the two of us, soon? Maybe at my house?" He took her in his arms, kissing her tenderly at first, and then ardently. She readily responded, but sighed deeply afterwards "What's the matter, what's wrong?"

When Liz approached her parents, she was pleasantly surprised at their willingness to watch Will for the weekend as she and Adam celebrated his amnesty. Oblivious to the ramifications Adam might suffer, they also seemed to be nonjudgmental, or perhaps they were unaware of his draft dodger status, but either way there was no mention of it. Liz never understood their apparent ignorance and felt embarrassed.

"Oh nothing, really, except… I have to figure out what to do with Will. My parents don't seem to mind, but they're always helping. Don't worry, it will work." She kissed him goodbye, but this time with more longing.

"Stop, stop!" Giggling she escaped his grasp. "Stop tickling me!" This time her voice was filled with lust. "Kiss me."

He leaned in and took her face into his hands. "I love you Liz. I always have."

"I love you too Adam, and I really love this house!" she teased.

Liz had not been to Adam's house before and was filled with anticipation. She couldn't envision him living in such opulence, since they were both brought up in a middle class neighborhood. Amazed at his furnishings, she asked, "Did you do all this yourself?"

"Yep, all by my lonesome. I'm not done yet. Would you consider helping? Perhaps give a woman's touch?"

Liz looked around one more time and nodded in approval.

"Well, which is it?" Adam's lips pressed together, feigning chagrin.

"Which is what?"

"The house or me? Which do you love more?"

"Oh, gosh…gee… I don't know….hmmm…let me think about it." She paused for a moment and looked around. "The house of course!"

"That did it!" He grabbed her and pulled her into the bedroom. "Come here, sit down." Adam patted his dark satin sheets as she now considered the room where they would share his bed.

In a near whisper, she said, "I do approve of your décor. Very masculine."

One by one he took off her heels, then her stockings.

"Hey, what are you doing?" Her voice rose and cracked.

"I'm kissing your toes. Don't you like it?"

They hadn't been together in seven years and she missed him. She could no longer wait to be with him.

"Hmmm…now what are you…umm, yes, umm, I do like… umm," she purred as his hand moved up her skirt and massaged her between her thighs. He took off her panties and stroked her everywhere, and she reciprocated, as they kissed passionately. Desire overwhelmed them and neither could wait any longer. They moved to their rhythm as waves of pleasure took over. It had been a long time, but they were the same, as one. Exhausted, they fell asleep in each other's arms for several hours and were gently awakened by the peaceful sound of falling raindrops.

He looked at her sleepily. "Hey, are you hungry? Do you want a steak?"

"Yes, I'm starving! Like your dad used to say, "I could eat a horse!"

"You remembered!" Adam smiled widely in his memory.

They both went into the kitchen to prepare dinner. Adam put the steaks on the grill which was protected by the enclosed deck for the cold months, and Liz sautéed vegetables and cut up slices of garlic bread. She would have enjoyed a glass of wine, but said nothing, relieved that she didn't see any around. "I'll be back in a minute. I'm going to call my parents and say hello to Will."

"Say hello for me, and tell him next time he's coming too and we'll play some basketball."

Adam smiled thinking how wonderful life was turning out. He quickly grabbed a beer from the back of the refrigerator and slugged some down, afterwards popping several mints in his mouth.

I decided to buy Liz an engagement ring and surprise her for Valentine's Day. She was far from ostentatious, but I had the money and wanted to do it right. After work I went to the diamond district and shopped around. Several days passed with no prospects, so I gave up and went home. Nothing seemed to suit her personality. Liz was special and she deserved something extraordinary.

On the weekend I searched around my area. Southampton was known for unique wares and there were one or two jewelry stores close to my house. I knew the minute I walked into the first one, this was the place I would purchase the perfect ring. Everywhere I looked there were interesting pieces. Nothing was ordinary here. In fact, the gentleman who approached me was a bit quirky. It almost felt as if I had entered a Parisian storefront. I half expected him to converse in French as he wore a beret on his mop of bushy jet-black hair, with a well-groomed moustache above his dainty mouth. His wide colorful suspenders displayed juxtaposed dancing girls.

"Can I be of service to you sir?"

"Why yes, thank you! I'm in search of an exceptional diamond engagement ring for the woman of my life."

When February came, I applied for amnesty and was one of the hundreds of thousands never formally charged before receiving my pardon. I was overwhelmed with relief. It was finally over.

Since my return home, I've definitely been on a lucky streak. Liz and I have been back together, and after all these years I'm about to propose marriage. And, now with Will in the picture I could become a stepdad. That is, if Liz agrees to be my wife. Will may not be my real son, but it sure feels that way. He has become very important to me. I even put a basketball hoop up at the rear of my house, in case he wants to play. And, I bought him some golf clubs in the hope he'll want to learn once we all live together as a family. As my father taught me, I hope to teach him when he's a little older.

CHAPTER THIRTY

# LIZ

## (FEBRUARY 1977)

"Happy Valentine's Day sweetheart."

"Here mommy, I made this for you in school. Do you like it?"

Liz held the card in her hand and beamed. Perfectly rendered hearts covered the entire front and middle part of the card. In between each heart was Will's illegible handwriting spelling out the words *I love you Mom.*

"Do I like it? Are you kidding me? It's wonderful Will! It's the nicest card anybody's ever given me." She hugged him tightly. "Wait let me grab the phone."

"Hi Liz. I'm running late, but I'll be there very soon, okay? Happy Valentine's Day!"

Liz was a little nervous about what might unfold today; the most romantic day of the year. Finishing up the dishes, she put the receiver on her shoulder and dialed. "Anne, can you talk for a minute?"

Anne looked at her watch. "I'm out the door in a second, but what's the matter? Everything okay? Your voice sounds funny."

"Oh, I don't know. It's just that it's Valentine's Day…and you know…he might propose. Don't you think?"

158

"So that would be awesome, wouldn't it?"

"Yes and no. He's on his way here now. I'd feel badly if he didn't, and if he does …," Liz paused. "I can't say yes. He still drinks. I wish I wasn't still in love with him. And to complicate matters, he's so good with Will. Isn't that ironic? Oops, there he is…got to go. Let you know later!"

I let Adam in and right away noticed he was carrying roses in one gloved hand and a rectangular shaped box in the other.

"Hi. Thank you! They're beautiful!

I smelled the sweet fragrance and went over to my china cabinet to look for a vase.

"Adam!" Will ran right into his arms.

"Hey buddy. How ya doing?"

"Look what I made for mommy!" He ran to find the card and came back in a flash.

"Wow, that's great! You made that all by yourself?"

"Yep."

Pensively I glanced at the red wrapped gift box with a small gold bow atop. *Well, it can't be a ring in that box. Unless he put in in there to surprise me. Nah, he's not that clever.*

I remembered when we were in high school and so much in love; we always talked about getting married and having lots of kids. My eyes got misty.

# 1966

It was almost the end of summer. This was the year I would finally see the Beatles. We had seen them on the *Ed Sullivan Show* a couple of years ago, but this was different. They were coming back to Shea

Stadium and this time I wouldn't miss them. So far 1966 was turning out to be glorious! Adam and I had talked about it for months and now we were going to the concert of the century. Nothing could make me happier.

Mom shouted from the living room, "Honey, are you ready? Adam is here."

"I'm coming! Tell him I'll be right there."

I put the finishing touches of my make-up on, brushed my hair for the umpteenth time, and ran down the stairs.

"Wow, you look very pretty! We're only going to a concert. Why the dress?" Adam asked, uncomfortable with his own attire after looking at her.

"Are you kidding? It's a Beatles concert! What else would I wear?" Bell bottoms?"

We hopped into his car and were off.

"Aren't you excited?" I asked enthusiastically.

"The only thing I get excited about is you." Adam swung his arm around me and I moved over so I could be closer to him.

Boldly, I asked, "Do you think we'll get married after college?"

"Yep, I do. You're the only one for me, Liz. I want lots of kids with you. How 'bout you?" How many do you want?"

"Oh, maybe nine or ten," I said nonchalantly.

"Nine or ten!" Adam laughed in a way that only he could laugh. As we approached, we saw the lights illuminating the stadium. "Oh my God! Look at all the cars! There must be a million people here. We'll be lucky if we find a parking spot."

The concert was unbelievable. Girls and boys were screaming everywhere and some of the girls were even crying. There was no doubt about it; the Beatles were the hottest group ever known to mankind. The crowds sang along as they played all my favorite songs including, *And I Love Her* and *Norwegian Wood*. On the way home we sang every song we could think of until our voices gave out.

I knew I would always remember this night; the night we saw the Beatles, on the same evening that we planned our future.

"Open it up Liz."

I felt my heart sink; there was a gold pendant staring at me.

"It's very nice Adam. Thank you. Oh, look. It's even engraved with our names." *What's with him anyway! After all these years, and nothing; a lousy pendant!*

Even though deep in my heart I knew this would happen, and I *was* angry, at the same time, I was strangely relieved.

"Mom! Yuck! Do you have to kiss? That's disgusting! " Will started to giggle.

"Just you wait, Will. When you are a little bit older you will have a crush on a girl. You'll see." I smiled at Adam.

Sitting in his dresser drawer at home was the most spectacular diamond engagement ring with a sparkling round cut and magnificent platinum setting. Two days prior, Adam had chickened out and decided not to give her the ring after all. He still wasn't ready to take the plunge. He kept making excuses in his head. First it was his parent's marriage. What a disaster! They were always at each other's throats. Marriage didn't seem to work, in Adam's eyes, anyway. His fear of commitment became overwhelming. He was apprehensive about being a stepdad because of the incident in Montreal. He was heartbroken to see a child's life taken so soon. But what did that have to do with Liz? Then he worried about his job. What if he got fired? How would he support them? But, there was no threat of that. Whatever the reason, he wasn't ready.

CHAPTER THIRTY-ONE

# ADAM

## (SUMMER,1977)

I finished packing for my trip to California. They needed me more than in New York and it was happening often now. I liked it there, especially the ocean on my days off, but the traveling was getting to me and the length of time I'd be there had me concerned. Liz and I had finally gotten back together.

As I held the receiver between my ear and shoulder, I hurriedly searched for the number of a taxi in my kitchen drawer; a sea of business cards. "Hi, Liz. I'm leaving for Los Angeles in a little while. I have an audit that will probably keep me there for at least a month. I tried to reach you yesterday, but I must have missed you before you left. I'll call you when I get there. I'm sorry it's so sudden. Oh, and by the way… please tell Will I'll catch up with him later."

I arrived early Saturday evening to a crimson sunset. There was nothing more beautiful than twilight in LA, since it was a rare occurrence given the smog. The first thing I did was arrange for a rental car for the following day. I wasn't expected at work until Monday, so tomorrow I would visit my father's grave. I called Uncle Harry and asked him to join me.

The next morning I awakened to the TV's fuzzy white lights. Trying to focus, I fixed my eyes on the hotel clock. *Yikes!* It was past 9 a.m. I was to meet Uncle Harry in less than an hour. *No time to call Liz. Maybe later.* After showering and dressing, I grabbed coffee in the lobby where they had a serving table filled with assorted breakfast pastries.

Adam pulled into the all Jewish cemetery that had been around since the Civil War. He saw his uncle from a distance. He was a short wiry man with a large balding spot at the top of his head. Adam felt taken aback at how much he had aged since he had last seen him.

"How ya doing kid?" They awkwardly embraced. "It's been a long time."

"It's good to see you Uncle Harry. How's Steve? What's he up to?"

As they talked, they reached down to pick up pebbles off the wet grassy ground to place on top of the grave, an old Jewish custom. Hours before, it had drizzled and everything was still damp.

"Upkeep here seems okay, don't you think?" Uncle Harry seemed distracted as he looked into the distance. "Your cousin has some serious issues. He's addicted to some kind of dope. I tried to get him into rehab, but he runs every time."

"Where does he go?" Adam was stunned.

"Looking for more drugs, what d' ya think?"

"I'm sorry Uncle Harry. Why do you think he does this?"

"Who knows why people do the things they do. All I know is that I'm sick of it." And then he whispered, "I'm scared for him, Adam. I'm really scared for him."

He thought he saw his uncle's eyes get watery, and then they rimmed over with tears. He took out a handkerchief and quickly wiped his eyes and blew his nose.

"You still drinking kid?"

"How'd you know that?" Adam was caught off guard.

"What are y'a kidding? That's all your father talked about and worried about."

Adam looked down at the grave. "Yeah, I know."

They chatted for a while and exchanged goodbyes, each lost in their own thoughts.

"I hope Steve stops his crap."

"Thanks kid, take care of yourself."

Deeply saddened, Adam reached down and touched his father's grave.

The next day Adam stopped at his office to pick up some papers for his client. Before he had a chance to collect himself his boss rushed into his office.

"Adam, hold off on the preliminaries for the audit for a day or two. There's a fundraiser in memory of Henry Toole's wife I'd like you to attend."

"What, no hello?" Adam grimaced. "How the hell are you Gene?"

"Sorry, things are crazy here this morning; any problems, let me know."

He walked out as fast as he walked in.

# CHAPTER THIRTY-TWO

# ADAM

## (SUMMER,1977)

That is when I met Hanna; at the fundraiser. Shortly after, Lillie came into my life. The birth was daunting, being premature at 6 ½ months. At 2 lbs. she was as small as the stuffed bear we bought when we heard the news that Hanna was pregnant. We weren't allowed to hold her which caused us to feel envious of the other parents who instantly held their infants. But, we caressed her precious little face with our fingers over and over again. Lillie had tubes dangling from her which were connected to all sorts of equipment. It was the most disturbing sight we ever saw.

I hated myself. She was my daughter and I felt helpless standing around doing nothing. I'd ask myself repeatedly what I did to cause this atrocity. Though never big on prayer, I now prayed several times a day thankful she was alive. I even stopped drinking for a while.

Hanna slept in the hospital until Lillie was discharged. Every morning I stopped by before work. There was this cranky old nurse who objected to me flouting the rules, and I didn't need any more stress, so in the early evening I rushed there before visiting hours were over. I was exemplary when it came to wearing a mask and not touching the equipment, but the strict visiting hours were ridiculous. I was Lillie's father and should have the right to visit her when I wanted to.

I stopped calling Liz. She had no idea what was going on and was probably pissed off that once again we weren't seeing each other. I was pretty sure I was losing her, but couldn't do anything about it. There was no time or energy to get into it with her.

Although the doctors informed us Lillie was making improvements, we were still profoundly shaken. I found myself crying at work. Hanna, also in despair, cried every day not knowing how to comfort Lillie. When she was finally released from the hospital at three months, her weight was 5 ½ lbs., but she was breathing normally on her own and feeding well on formula.

Hanna had two friends with babies; one, a little girl, about to turn six months old. The other, a four month old boy. Irene's daughter would squeal in delight when she played peek-a-boo with her. And, when Tess would enter her little boy's room, the sight of his mother's face was all it took to elicit an enormous grin.

Lillie was different. She didn't smile.

# (1978)

It was July and Hanna had taken a leave of absence from the law firm since Lillie's birth in April. Adam was spending all his free hours trying to get to know both Lillie and Hanna.

Lillie was not making eye contact or responding to her name, nor was she reacting favorably to being held. In fact, she was stiffening up. It was clear she was not enjoying the attention her parents gave her; the enormous hugs they showered on her. Adam and Hanna were feeling rejected, or more to the point they decided they weren't good parents. They blamed one another and also themselves.

"If only you hadn't been drinking," Hanna sobbed.

"What does that have to do with it?" Adam said defensively. "What about the junk you ate during your pregnancy? Don't you think you could have eaten healthy foods instead? Maybe that's what caused her premature birth! I need a fucking drink!" he spat under his breath. But secretly he thought, *Hold on a little longer. Maybe I can quit this time.*

No matter what the doctors did to reassure them it was not their fault, they were guilt-ridden. They couldn't accept what was happening. As the months passed, there was still much more to learn and yet to discover.

# CHAPTER THIRTY-THREE

# LIZ
## (SUMMER,1977)

*Only a message! That's it? One lousy message! I cannot believe he left for over a month and didn't come over to say goodbye. And what about Will? I've had it with Adam!* I reached for the phone.

"…..I tried calling him back, but he's never there. What do you think is going on? Do you think he's pulling another number on me?"

"He didn't do that before, Liz. Back then he was scared and ran." Although she still resented Adam, Anne tried to reassure her friend.

"Will keeps asking about him. After what happened with Tom, I hate to do this to him again. He's become close with Adam. I was hoping things would work out. You know…hoping I could one day tell them that they were father and son; if he'd give up the booze that is." Her composure was changing rapidly. "Maybe he's on a drinking binge," she shouted.

"Calm down Liz. You don't know that for sure. Give him the benefit of the doubt." She paused. "What am I saying? I should talk, right? I never did that for Fred. But, guess what? You won't feel that way after today."

"Oh no, what happened?" They both chuckled as easily as they always had. "What's going on with you two anyway," Liz inquired of her friend.

"I was about to call you, but you beat me to the punch. I wanted to save this for when we were together….in person….but I'll tell you now." Anne hesitated and then sighed. Her breathing became uneven and labored. "He is."

"He is what?"

"He's cheating on me. I caught him."

"You're kidding! What do you mean?" Liz was shocked, although she knew their split was inevitable after everything she'd heard.

Caustically, Anne explained. "I saw him with the bitch! He was leaving his car and entering hers. It was some kind of weird coincidence, because I'm never in that area. They were near his office."

"How do you know she doesn't work with him?" Liz asked.

"I don't, but she kissed him hello and then he laid one on her. And I mean *laid* one on her, the bastard! He's probably *laying* her right now." Anne was weeping.

"Are you leaving him? Oh no….did he leave you?" *The kids*…she thought.

"No, not yet, anyway. Liz, I can't believe this is happening to me. Things were never normal, but I *never* thought this would happen." She paused. "I think it is me. I think this has happened to me before. I'm just wondering if…."

"What… what are you wondering?" Liz asked.

"Never mind." Anne looked away.

"What do you mean though?"

"I don't know. Maybe I'm not attracted to him. For that matter, maybe he's not attracted to me. He never turned me on, do you know what I mean?"

"I'm not sure. I don't have that much experience; only Tom and Adam, that's it."

Anne looked at her watch. "Sorry, Liz. I have to cut this short. I didn't realize what time it was. Can we talk later?"

Trying to decide which bathing suit I should wear, I reached for the copper colored one with the gold trim. I slipped into it, tugging one side up and then the other, and examined myself in the mirror.

*Shit! I need to make a decision. If he's always going to take off like this, then the hell with him! I'll end it, this time, forever. Oh, who I am kidding; I'll never stop loving him. And, he'll always be Will's father. I have to get my mind off this. I'm not going to let him do this to me.*

"Will, are you almost ready?" I shouted down the hallway. "Grandma and Popsy are waiting for us. Do you have your bathing suit on yet?"

The four of us were headed to the beach and afterwards Will was sleeping over their house. I had Sunday to myself! The night before I packed Will's knapsack with his superheroes, pj's, toothbrush, and a change of clothes.

"Come on Mom! We're gonna be late; hurry up!"

"Wise guy!" Liz squeezed him. "I'll miss you tonight mister. You behave yourself, okay?"

We ran out the door into the summer heat. It was only ten o'clock in the morning and the air was already oppressive; a perfect day for the ocean. Even the steering wheel burned to the touch. Nostalgia set in as we listened to one of Cousin Brucie's last broadcasts, just like Adam and I did so long ago.

Stopping the song midway, Will suddenly asked, "Mommy, do you have my pail and my shovel in the trunk? I want to build *very* tall castles with *many* windows for the prince to climb to the top, and then he'll capture the princess," he went on enthusiastically stressing key words.

"Yes, of course I do," I said grinning. "I would never forget something as important as your beach toys!"

I found myself daydreaming about what it would be like if the three of us, Adam, Will, and I were driving to the beach together, as a family. Excitedly Will asked, *Are we there yet mommy? Are we? Daddy, will you play with me and build castles?* And Adam replied, *Of course Will. How about we each build a castle and see whose is the tallest?* Will jumped up and down on his seat. *Yippee! A contest, daddy! Yea!*

I shook myself out of my reverie as I pulled into my parents' driveway and saw them waiting, ice box and chairs in tow.

"Grandma, Popsy, hurry up! We're gonna be late!" Will screamed out the car window.

"We're coming honey. Hurry up Popsy! You heard Will; we're gonna be late," Grandma echoed.

They climbed into the backseat after putting their beach paraphernalia in the trunk.

"Okay, we're all set! Let the fun begin!" Grandma cried out.

The following day, bushed after spending Sunday in the hot sun, Liz caught her breath as she entered an enormous room which appeared to have hundreds of people wandering about in confusion. And there he was, standing right in front of her, looking as handsome as ever, staring right at her. They hadn't seen each other in a long time. As much as she hated to admit it, she was still attracted to him. She chided herself, but to no avail. She tried to avoid him, but obviously couldn't.

She thought, *what am I crazy? Walk away! He tried to rape me.* The nagging recurring thought that had haunted her for over a year, popped into her mind. *Did I exaggerate this? Did he really, or... did I go overboard? Stop this already,* she commanded herself. *Stop second-guessing yourself.*

"Hi Liz. Is it all right if I say hello?" Tom asked hesitantly, offering a smile. "I promise I won't bite."

They were at a book seller convention in Manhattan. Liz was soliciting clients and Tom was promoting his books. They were bound to bump into each other at some point.

"Sure." She regretted her response instantly and frowned. "But only for a minute. I do have an order of protection on you, you know."

"Liz, I didn't try to rape you," he whispered hoping no one heard him. "You know that. Don't you? I had too much to drink, that's all. I'm sorry I scared you."

"And Will? What was that about?" She felt her blood starting to boil.

"I missed him. That's the only reason I went to the school. I wanted to see him." Tom knew he wasn't making any headway, but also knew he was telling the truth. "And I knew you wouldn't let me see him... so I ...look, I know I was wrong. I should have checked it out with you first. I'm really sorry. Please forgive me Liz, for everything."

"I don't know what I feel, Tom. What I do know is, don't do that to Will ever again!" her voice rapidly rising in anger, and then dropping to a normal tone.

"I won't. I promise. Could I sit down?" he asked persuasively as he moved his chair in. "How is Will?"

"He's so big now! You should see him!" Liz was beaming. But, when she realized what she had said, her face turned colors. As an afterthought, she remarked, "He's doing really well in school, except

173

for penmanship." They both laughed. At five, Will was struggling to print his name legibly, and now at seven years old, he was no better.

"Still incomprehensible, huh?" Tom asked.

"Yep," Liz again chuckled.

Heads turned towards the podium as the woman speaker began her presentation and the chaos abated. Liz could not focus on the speech. All she was capable of doing was surreptitiously glancing his way wishing she wouldn't have feelings for him.

"Liz, why don't we go for a drink afterwards?" Tom asked, apparently also lost in thought.

"No. No, thanks. I think I'll call it a night." Vacillating, she said, "Well, maybe. Maybe for a few minutes, but only coffee, no drinks. Okay? I'll be back in a second; I just want to fix my face."

Disturbed, Liz deliberated, *I must be out of my mind. Why am I doing this? Because I'm angry with Adam?*

The stalls in the bathroom were occupied, so she brushed her hair and fished for her lipstick, carefully applying it. She walked back into the convention center and noticed Tom talking to a woman; someone she didn't recognize. Somewhat relieved she headed back into the mass of people and approached potential clients with her business cards, briefly introducing herself. An hour must have gone by when she felt his hand on her back.

"Sorry, I got caught up with an author I knew years ago. I looked for you all over. Why didn't you come back?"

"Well, I did come here to drum up some clients, didn't I?" She attempted a smile.

Tom put his arm around her. "Let's go for that drink now, okay?"

"Coffee, remember? Coffee!" she retorted.

The door shut behind them.

They settled themselves in a booth towards the back of an all-night diner.

"Coffee, please," Liz murmured to the waitress.

"You sure you don't want anything else?" Tom asked.

"No, thank you. I'm not staying that long," she said still mumbling, baffled as to why she came in the first place. *Have I lost my mind?*

There was no doubt about it. She was disturbed about her behavior; any encouragement she gave him was unacceptable and appalling.

"Liz, isn't it possible you reacted irrationally?" he blurted out.

It was as if he read her mind. She knew what he was referring to, although she never admitted it before.

"No, I don't think so! Okay, well, maybe with the order of protection. But not the other stuff."

"Correction. Order of Protections," Tom reminded her.

"Huh?"

"Plural. Order of Protections."

"Yes. Sorry." She was feeling upset and vaguely nervous. "Could we change the subject please?"

"Okay. I've missed you. How's that for starters?" he asked. When she didn't respond, he then inquired, "How's work? Do you have enough business these days?"

"I do. I have plenty of clients. At times too many. But I'm coping. What about you?" She finally started to relax.

"A few interesting authors as of late. One guy, he wrote a book based on a well-known cult. It was pretty scary."

"Wow! Could you imagine your child getting involved with one of those? If Will ever did…oh God, I don't even want to think about it!" Tensing up again, she reminded herself who she was sitting with.

"Will's too smart for that. And, you have such a good relationship with him. Very often kids join cults because they need direction, they need friends, and they think they'll be better off. Unfortunately they get hooked and even more screwed up than they were."

Disgruntled by the direction this was taking, she asked, "Could we change this subject too?" She offered a little smile and they both laughed.

A couple of hours passed and the flow of conversation eased and was similar to when they first met. It was as if they were back together. Liz excused herself to make a call.

"Mom, could you pick Will up after school? I might be delayed a bit."

Her parents were always there for her, especially when it came to their grandson. "Sure Liz, no problem. What are you doing?"

Ignoring her mother's nosiness, she replied, "Thanks. Oh, and Mom, listen, is it okay if I'm back very late?"

Tom stood and pulled the chair out for her. "Liz, are you sure you won't have dinner? Why don't we go to a more…?" He hesitated. He wanted to say, a restaurant with more ambiance, but he knew she would take it the wrong way. "To a restaurant. How about Italian?"

They were ushered into the rear of a quiet darkened brassiere filled with ambiance. Romantic music was playing softly, the type straight from Firenze. A violinist appeared at their table seductively wooing Liz and Tom as they ordered red wine, to which she had reluctantly acquiesced.

"I'm glad you came, Liz."

"Do you remember that snowball fight we once had? Those gorgeous lacy patterns on the willow trees?" Her attempt to divert his attention failed. She wanted to cool off literally and figuratively. The air conditioning wasn't helping, nor was the temperature which had sky-rocketed in the last few hours.

"The snow was beautiful that evening, just as you are now."

Liz felt herself blush and was aroused at the very core of her femininity, an ache for him that she wanted to forget. She couldn't believe that she was feeling this way after all that happened between them. Since their divorce she had never allowed herself to think about that evening; how strange he seemed at first and how scared she was when he forced himself on her. This came flooding back to her now. Tom had a way of controlling her and pulling her in, even when she wanted to pull back far away from him.

He took her hand and her heart raced. Although foolhardy, her attraction for him was undeniable. His fingers were gently caressing each of hers as he leaned over and kissed her with purpose and lust. "Liz", he whispered, "come home with me." They were suddenly interrupted with their dinner thrust in front of them, as the waiter tripped on Tom's outstretched foot.

"I am so sorry sir!" The waiter straightened the plates thankful the food wasn't in their laps.

Stifling a laugh, Liz asked, "Where are you living now?"

"Close by, will you come? It's so nice spending time with you again." He pleadingly searched her sultry eyes.

"Okay, but only for a little while. I'm serious. This is against my better judgment. And don't think we're sleeping together either. That won't happen."

"Whatever you say; I promise!" Tom winked.

*Hmm,* she grimaced; *he never used to wink at me. That's weird. What an idiot I am!* She admonished herself once more and took a forkful of the tender scaloppini, a dish she was unaccustomed to. "This is great!" Liz gushed.

"So what have you been doing with yourself since we parted? Are you still working at the VA Hospital?" Tom asked with genuine interest.

"No. I think I stopped right before we split, didn't I? I can't keep track of time anymore. Between Will and work keeping me busy, I had to stop. Felt real badly about it too."

"I hope you still make time to sketch?"

"Oh, I'm always doodling something. What about you? What do you do with yourself these days… when you're not working, that is?"

"Not too much. Been playing a little racquetball. That's about it."

"Have you been seeing anyone since we split?" Liz asked.

"Nobody special," he answered and motioned for the waiter.

Something told her not to believe him. They talked for a while longer and after a decadent dessert left for his place.

Liz looked around at the antiques tastefully displayed throughout his apartment, a brownstone on the upper Westside.

"Wow, these are incredible. Where did you get this one? It's stunning!"

Liz was admiring a 19th century French sterling trinket box.

"It looks hand-painted. Is it watercolor?"

"Yes, you like it?"

"I love it!"

"It's yours then! Come here, sit down." Once on the couch, he put his arm around her and moved daringly close. "Hmm…You smell good. Lovely perfume."

She blushed. "Did you move here to be near work?"

"Shh…" He kissed her. She responded.

Tom held to his promise. He didn't push her. He took her lead and waited for her to make a move. And she did, all the while privately cursing herself. They kissed for what seemed like hours until she glanced towards the far end of his living room where a late 1700's European wood hand-carved grandfather clock sat gracefully in the corner.

"Tom, look what time it is! I really must run. My parents have been so nice to watch Will this evening, and I have to get up for work anyway," she said wistfully.

They embraced with a tentative date for the following week. Liz left questioning her sanity and her choice of two men in her life, one a heavy drinker and the other a sex maniac.

"Anne, you are not going to believe this!" Liz sounded hysterical.

"Are you okay Liz? What's the matter?"

Liz related all the steamy details to her oldest college friend from beginning to end. With widened eyes, Anne asked, "What are you going to do?" She was shocked that Liz would even consider going back with Tom.

"I don't know what's come over me. I'm sick about it. Well, I think I am anyway," she said with uncertainty. Slowly the laughter came and they broke into hysterics.

"You told me you were afraid of him. Really Liz! What *has* come over you?"

"Maybe I'm reacting to the news of Hanna and Lillie. And, …I miss Adam so much. I think I do, that is." Their laughter became louder and louder. "I'm so screwed up!"

"You think you're screwed up!" Anne thought, *I'm a lesbian!*

"Why, what's happening with you and Fred since you caught him with that woman?"

"Nothing good. A divorce is inevitable. We haven't broached it as of yet. But, one thing is for sure, he's going his way and I'm going mine. It's the kids I worry about. Enough about me. Tell me more about you and Tom."

"We haven't talked about you and Fred yet. Why are you avoiding it?" Liz was confused.

"Leave it alone, Liz. Okay?"

"I'm sorry to push Anne. I don't want you to be hurt, that's all."

"I'm okay. Believe me; I'll turn to you when I'm ready. Tell me more about what you're going through."

"I don't know what I'm going through. Maybe I went overboard, but I don't know why. I mean, it was scary what he did, but not enough to get an order of protection. Two of them, at that! He's so attractive Anne… and I'm drawn to him, like a magnet. He has that effect on me. I swear, I think he has a hold on me. Do you know what I mean?"

"No, I've never experienced that. Wish I had."

"No you don't. He's toxic! The very second I saw him again I knew I was in trouble. Maybe if Adam was around more I wouldn't feel this way. But he's not, and I do." Liz sighed.

"Well, maybe you should give him a chance. What do you think? Just be careful though."

"I probably will. But, like you are with your kids, I worry about Will; what I'm doing to him. I'm a lousy parent, Anne!"

"You're not doing anything to him. If you're a lousy parent, so am I."

They hung up feeling sad, neither of them knowing what to do about their predicaments.

# CHAPTER THIRTY-FOUR

# ADAM

## (JULY-SEPTEMBER 1978)

Adam finally reached Hanna. Apparently nothing was wrong except… as far as Adam was concerned she was an inconsiderate bitch. Here he was worrying about what might have happened to his little girl; maybe Hanna took her to a doctor, maybe something worse than that. But no, she forgot to return his calls. That's all. Just, plain forgot.

*I still can't believe I have a daughter! But what's wrong with her? Please God, help her. She's so tiny.*

Hanna's spacious duplex apartment, located in Santa Ana, was close to the town where she grew up. Her parents, both Columbian immigrants, came to the United States in 1946 when she was 4 years old. Being so young, she had no recollection of her homeland, but oddly enough remembered the lifeboats on the ship. Adam wondered for a long time if there was significance to this memory. Was Lillie now saving Hanna's life in some manner?

Once back in California, he headed for Santa Ana. An eclectic mix of South American and Mexican pottery, paintings of wildlife from Columbia, and large potted plants filled her apartment. Baby toys were scattered on the floor waiting for Lillie to be old enough to enjoy.

"Why don't we sit on the couch, Adam? Quiet though, she's sleeping. Would you like a glass of… some coffee?"

His shopping bags were filled with every type of stuffed animal: giraffes, tigers, puppy dogs, and bears, and pink and white princess dolls peeking in between.

"No thanks. How is she?"

"She's doing ok, I guess. I take her for another appointment in a few days. Do you want to go with us?"

"I'll see what I can do. What day are you talking about?"

Lillie started to cry.

"Can I go in?"

Before entering Lillie's bedroom, he noticed several photos of Hanna's family displayed in the china cabinet. Her younger brother, also dark haired and short, with a neatly trimmed beard, was standing with their parents on either side of him, and the other two pictures were taken in the Columbian countryside, when she was little and he was a baby. It was difficult to appreciate the richness of the landscape as the photos were in black and white; nevertheless, it was evident that their homeland was one of beauty.

"Nice photo of Julián and your parents. I didn't notice it before." As he pointed to the left one, he dead stopped in his tracks. There was a birthday card addressed to Hanna and open for all to see.

"Thanks, that's my favorite picture of…" she started to reply, but was abruptly shut down.

"How old are you again?" he inquired sharply.

"Why?" she asked cautiously.

"Because I noticed the birthday card on your coffee table. Someone congratulated you on your 38th birthday! I thought you said you were 30, didn't you?"

"Sorry, I lied," Hanna's face reddened.

"Why would you lie about your age?" He felt uneasy and wasn't sure why. "Have you lied about anything else?" All of a sudden things started to make sense. "Why you little conniver! What about the birth control pills, did you lie about them too? Did you *really* have a lapse of memory?"

"Look, if you're trying to blame me again...." Defensively, she snapped at him once more and diverted her eyes to Lillie's room. "She's still crying. I should go in."

Warily, he said, "We'll talk about this later. *I'm* going in to her."

"Come here sweetheart, let daddy hold you." He leaned over and gently picked her up, instinctively holding her head. She resisted, but he didn't let her go. "I love you so much Lillie." Adam looked directly into her almond shaped eyes that were exactly like Hanna's. She did not look into his. "My sweet, sweet Lillie. Daddy promises you everything will be all right." As he kissed her tenderly on her cheek, he felt himself getting teary-eyed. She let out a soft little purr and went back to sleep.

"So tell me Hanna, why the lie? Is it because you were getting too old to have a baby?" He started to panic.

"Lill' ok?" she asked.

"Don't change the subject. I want the truth! About everything!"

"Okay, I'll tell you everything, if you would please calm down and try to understand. Lower your voice. Let her sleep. *Please.*"

She took several measured breaths and began.

"I admit it. I lied. About a few things. But all for good reasons."

She looked up at him from the couch. Towering over her, with his dark accusing eyes, he was angrier than he had ever been.

"I wanted a baby. I was getting too old. And now look. We have Lillie. Beautiful sweet Lillie."

"It sounds as if you planned it. How could *that* be?" he asked sarcastically.

"I kind of…" she faltered, "kind of, on purpose didn't take …."

"Didn't take what? Your birth control pills? Are you kidding me? You tricked me? You bitch!" Adam was seething.

"Calm down, Adam. I'm sorry for being deceptive, but I really liked you. And you seemed to be the perfect candidate."

"Candidate! What the hell does that mean? Hanna, Lillie was 2 1/2 months premature! Don't you see what you've done? It's your fault! Don't you see that? It might have been your age that caused her to be premature!"

"You've got to be kidding me!" she shouted. "You're blaming me for that! I wasn't too old to conceive. How dare you!"

Lillie was crying again; this time wailing.

"Now look what you've done!" Hanna still incensed, lowered her voice. "*Please,* stop yelling at me or *please* leave."

They went into Lillie's room together. First Hanna picked her up and then Adam held her. She was inconsolable. Adam wiped her tears and pushed her chestnut colored hair off her forehead.

"Wait, I have an idea." He remembered something Liz had told him. "Do you have a radio or a record player?"

She brought back a beat-up radio from the attic. To her surprise it still worked. "My record player is broken… needs a needle, and this isn't much better, but give it a try."

Adam fooled with the stations until he found one playing a violin concerto; could have been by Beethoven or Mozart for all he knew. His knowledge of music was limited. He had a mild interest in classical music solely because of Liz's enthusiasm, but had never enjoyed anything other than rock, and playing a musical instrument held no appeal for him.

"My girlfriend plays the violin," he informed Hanna. "She told me about how music, especially stringed instruments, can be soothing to babies if it's played softly."

He watched Lillie's beautiful brown eyes become more alert as the soft music mollified her. Her crying slowed and finally diminished.

"Before my dad died he gave me a violin he found in the war. He was stationed in Italy and discovered it in the rubble of an abandoned church which was totally demolished."

Unimpressed with the history of his dad, instead, she obnoxiously replied, "Wonderful. Just what Lillie and I want to hear about. Your girlfriend and her musical talent!"

Hanna didn't *really* care about whether he had a girlfriend or not. She didn't want to get involved with Adam any more than she had. But hearing this news right in front of Lillie felt wrong; it felt demeaning, as if she was the other woman, in some odd sense.

The day didn't get much better. Quarrelling was the only way they communicated and it was taking a toll on the baby. By the time Adam left, they were all exhausted, especially Lillie.

"Let me know which day you're going to the pediatrician. I'd like to go. In the meantime, don't forget to play soft music for her. I'll bring back a record player and some 33's with violin music."

"I love you, Lillie. Be a good girl for daddy." He kissed her goodbye and walked out without another word to Hanna. She said nothing.

❖

Two days later Adam met Hanna downtown at the doctor's office. They sat patiently waiting trying not to argue. An hour passed when they were finally called in.

After thoroughly examining Lillie while she screamed and fussed, Dr. Fredericks looked at both parents with consternation. "You have a special little girl here, Mr. and Mrs. Greenstein.… very, very cute.… umm." He cleared his throat and tried to find the right words. "But, I must inform you…," he paused again, "She still isn't doing as well as she should. We should watch her weight," he nodded to his nurse.

Ignoring his inference to their marital status, Hanna said, "What do you mean?" She was panicking. "Will she be all right?"

"Babies this age usually make eye contact responsively. You also told me that Lillie was avoiding your show of affection, didn't you? But let's not get alarmed. We must take into consideration she was a preemie. And look, it may be nothing. Why don't we revisit this when she's six months old? You'll be here before then, right? So try not to worry."

Adam muttered under his breath, "That's easy for you to say. You just got finished saying she isn't doing well."

The doctor patted Adam on the back and walked out of the room. Hanna gathered Lillie and the baby bag.

"Well, now what do we do?" Consternation spread over Hanna's face. "We go home and accept this?"

Once again guilt ridden they left without answers, baffled and frustrated.

"I don't know. I guess we try to live our lives," Adam said matter-of-factly. But neither of them felt nonchalant. All Adam could think about was having a drink.

# CHAPTER THIRTY-FIVE

# ADAM

## (1979)

"Oops! Be careful Lill'!"

With her face pallid and dusted with freckles, and a mop of uncertain blondish hair which kept changing back and forth to chestnut, Lillie looked up and stared at her mother unwittingly. "Careful. Careful. Careful," she mimicked.

Hanna and Adam watched Lillie as she held onto the ottoman struggling to prop herself up.

"Very good Lillie," Adam smiled fortifying her every effort.

Hanna clapped her hands in approval. "Yea, Lillie!"

They appeared to be having a wonderful time together, almost as if they were a family. But in truth, Adam and Hanna were making the best of a bad situation for Lillie's sake.

All of a sudden it hit him. Adam jumped up realizing what had happened. "Did you hear that? Lillie spoke! See how intelligent she is?" He knew something was different about his little girl. He wasn't in denial.

Lillie hadn't made the typical progress an almost one year old might make, although, she seemed to be talking early. Last week they took her for a checkup with her pediatrician. The doctor seemed baffled. Lillie was parroting her parents and at the same time not understanding what they were saying. She kept repeating words and phrases in an abnormal tone of voice, almost robotically. Her speech had an odd rhythm to it.

"Of course I heard her! She just spoke to me, not you!" Hanna looked away and became teary eyed. "I'm worried, Adam. The doctor has no clue as to why Lillie is not advancing like other babies her age."

"You worry too much!" Adam was pissed as he always was with Hanna. She grated on his nerves.

"Stop ignoring the obvious! Something's wrong! Don't you see that? I think we should go to another doctor!"

"Because Lillie repeated what you said? That's not a reason to get all riled-up."

"Don't tell me what to get. There are lots of things wrong. She still doesn't make eye contact with us. And," she took a breath, "She still tenses up when I hold her." Hanna's eyes clouded over. "You're in denial, Adam!"

"Well, she loves it when *I* hold her." But Adam knew this wasn't true. "Look, let's take this one day at a time, okay?" Years ago, he had learned this technique at AA, but rarely applied it with his drinking. He knew it was important to do this now more than ever. He was scared.

In his hotel room he reached for another drink. He didn't drink the hard stuff often, but today was a rough one. Beer would be afterwards. *Fuck it! How the hell am I supposed to concentrate on work? Look at this mess of papers!* Drunkenly he threw his work on the floor and then fell asleep in the hard leather chair with his head resting on the mahogany desk. He awakened hours later still intoxicated.

He dialed the phone. "Libz? Is zat bou?"

"Adam? Are you all right?" Suddenly, she realized his words were slurred and immediately rebuffed: "Jesus Christ, it's the middle of the night here! You're drunk!"

"It's Lil."

Liz's heart sank. "Is she okay? What happened?"

His phone fall to the floor. "Adam! Are you okay? Adam!"

"Hi Lbz. I biss you"

"Jesus! Call me when you're sober. I want to hear about Lillie. But, when you're sober." She hung up.

Adam fell back to sleep, but was awakened by the tintinnabulation of his alarm and simultaneous clanging of his phone. Bleary eyed he squinted at the clock on his end table and tried to remember what day it was. *Shit! Is it Friday or Saturday?* "Hello? Wait, my alarm is going off." *Along with my head!*

"Adam! Are you coming to work? It's eleven o'clock! Why aren't you here?" His boss's voice bellowed. "We have a meeting at noon with the people from Hanley's."

"I'm sorry Gene; I overslept. I was sick during the night. I'll be there as soon as I can. I'm out the door right now."

He slugged down some orange juice as he gathered the scattered papers from the floor and tried to make sense of them. Running out the door, he realized he forgot his briefcase. The phone was ringing again.

"I'm on my way Gene."

"No, Adam. It's me."

"Sorry Liz, I'm out the door. I'm late for work."

"Wait Adam. First please tell me; is Lillie ok?"

He hung up before she got an answer.

Adam wasn't feeling well. He was in no condition to do his job and his boss was pissed. Both these things were happening a lot lately. He definitely had a hangover, but it was more than that. The drinking was out of control and eating up his body.

"If you don't get your act together soon, we're going to have a problem. What's going on anyway? You're making too many mistakes," Gene said emphatically. "And, I hate to say this, but you look like hell."

Adam gulped. "I have diabetes Gene. Guess my vision is off or something. I get so tired that it screws me up with the numbers. It won't happen again, I promise. I'll take care of this."

"Wow." Gene was stunned. "I'm sorry to hear it. Are you seeing a doctor?"

"Nah. Did once. Maybe I'll go back."

"I don't want to tell you what to do, Adam, but I'm pretty sure you have to go for treatments or something. This seems serious. You lost a lot of weight, too. Everybody's been noticing."

Adam's diabetes had worsened. His fatigue was affecting all areas of his life and the alcohol exacerbated his condition. All he could manage to do was pretend nothing was wrong. But, that wasn't working.

# CHAPTER THIRTY-SIX

# LIZ

## (1979)

"I don't believe this! He calls me up drunk, tells me something's wrong with Lillie, who I don't even know, and he doesn't even know Will is his son yet, and here I am caring about his daughter, and now he lays this on me!" she raged.

Her mind was reeling. It took a while for her to calm down as she tried to put things in perspective. *He made his choices. This is his daughter; not mine, not ours. And, I made my choices. It's time to tell him. Things have gotten out of control. It's time.*

She fell back to sleep.

Slipping off my shoes I sank into the couch after a long unforgiving day. As I had for months, and actually for years, I mulled over my dilemma, but this time it was a done deal. I would tell Adam, Will is his son.

"Mom," Will screamed from upstairs. "Mom, can you come here?" Ever since he was little he needed help with his homework.

"In a minute Will." I grabbed a cup of coffee and headed upstairs as *Thumby* flew ahead of me and nearly tripped me over.

Sitting together we worked on a compound addition problem. I was never good in math and wished Adam was here.

"Are you grasping it yet, honey?"

"I think so. Is this right?" He pointed to the answer.

Liz was distracted, but thought for a moment. "Yes, very good."

"Thanks!"

"Will, I know you like Adam, but how do you *really* feel about him?"

"Mo-omm," frustrated, he stretched out the syllables. "You've asked me this before. I told you! I wish you and Adam would get married. You know you love each other." He gave a disgusted look, stuck out his tongue, and rolled his eyes.

I reached over and gave him a big hug and kiss. "Finish your homework, okay? I'm going back downstairs to make dinner."

*Where the hell is it?* I reached towards the back of the refrigerator while tossing everything else aside. *Do it already!* Grabbing four little red potatoes out of the meshed bag, I proceeded to wash and cut them up, and once in the boiling water, I reached for the phone behind me.

"Adam? I'm sorry, did I wake you? You sound groggy."

"Nah, I'm just tired. How are you?"

"Listen, will you be at your house this weekend, or in the city? I need to talk to you about something important. I'll call my parents to watch Will through Sunday."

"Of course. I'll be at the house. What's wrong? You sound upset."

"We'll talk then. I've got to get supper going." She hung up.

I adjusted the rear and side view mirrors, drew in a deep labored breath, and took off. After dropping Will at my parents, I headed for the parkway.

*There is something I have to tell you. It's going to be a bit of a shock,* I practiced aloud. I changed the tone of my voice and intonations, and also switched the wording around. *There is something I've wanted to tell you for years. You're going to be shocked! stupid, stupid, stupid! I muttered.*

Over and over again I prepared for one of the hardest days of my life. I pictured him sitting back in his brown leather recliner near the window facing the ocean. He was relaxed and content and I was about to shake up his world. Sure he would be happy about Will, but the lies would destroy us. Again I mused, *I'll ring the doorbell. He'll jump up and greet me. We'll embrace, talk, and then: "Adam, please, sit down. There is something shocking and disturbing... I need to tell you, immediately."*

Anxious and fretful, I tried to get my mind off what was about to happen and turned on the radio, but kept returning to my speech; the speech I had feared for so many years. For a moment I was tempted to head back home and forget the whole thing. I almost got off the next exit. Switching stations, I settled on one and sang along as I inadvertently started to cry. After two hours had passed, I pulled off the road to get some coffee and looked at the handwritten directions tucked away in my purse. I had been to Adam's house only a few times before. "Damn! I missed the exit!"

Back on the road cars whizzed by. It was a beautiful day and the sun was shining brightly. *Almost there*, I sighed heavily. Opening my window, I breathed in the sea air and tried to relax. I glanced at the directions once more. *Make a right and another left, and go one mile.* I was finally there.

"Oh, Adam," she looked dreamy eyed. "I'll never get used to it here. It's awesome!" She hugged him tightly.

"How was the ride? Are you hungry?"

"Maybe I'll have a little something. What do you have?"

She opened up the refrigerator and then shut it. "Maybe later, I feel a little queasy." *How can I tell him this news? I will break his heart.*

For as long as she knew him he wasn't great in the kitchen. But, she wondered as she looked at the expanse of the kitchen island.

"Have you been cooking? I mean something other than burgers or franks," she laughed. "I know! We're having peanut butter and jelly sandwiches for dinner. Right?"

"No-oo! Wait until tonight! You will be treated to *shrimp scampi à la Adam.*" He looked at her with a silly grin. "But, for now there is a picnic lunch waiting for us. Come on, let's go. We're off to the ocean!"

They walked hand in hand, his left arm clutching a basket with an old frayed blanket on top of it. Dragging their feet in the sand and alternately kicking them, they talked about nothing in particular.

"This is good, let's stop here." Liz took the blanket and spread it out. They lay down and simultaneously breathed in the fresh sea air. Seagulls screeched overhead as they moved to the rhythm of a soft breeze.

"Look!" Adam pointed to a fish hanging from a gull's mouth.

"Holy mackerel! Oh no!" They both laughed at her unintended pun.

As the tide came in and the waves swished and crashed, they ate their bologna sandwiches with gherkin pickles and chips.

"I can't believe you remembered my favorite sandwich." She kissed him on the cheek and whispered in his ear, "thank you." For a moment she felt content. Then her speech resurfaced.

"Adam… we need to talk."

"Okay." He sat back down. "It sounds serious. What is it?"

"This is so hard. I don't know where to begin."

"Start anywhere. It's okay Liz; don't cry." He had no idea what was going on and was getting nervous. "It's not Will, is it? Is he okay?" She still didn't say anything. "Liz, is Will okay?"

"I hate to do this to you, Adam. I'm so sorry."

"Sorry for what? What did you do to me?" He waited for her to explain, but she didn't. "You're scaring me. Tell me already!"

"I'm sorry, I'm really sorry. This is going to be a shock," her voice quivered. It will change your life," she paused, "our lives, forever."

Adam swallowed hard. He felt unsteady and his blood seemed to rush up and down his body.

She took a deep breath and started to tremble. "It's about Will."

"I thought you said Will is okay?"

"He is. It's about you and Will."

"What about us?" He was getting impatient.

"Do you remember when we first started college and you came to visit me?"

"Of course. We went to the motel on Northern. It was one of the best times we ever spent together; wasn't it? What does it have to do with anything?" He searched her eyes. "You're all over the place. What are you talking about anyway?" He wanted to get the hell away from there. He was starting to connect the dots. It was as if he always knew. His head was shaking back and forth. "Oh no. This can't be happening! What are you saying?" Adam was panicking. "You're not saying…"

Her voice was subdued; barely a whisper. "I am saying that. You are. You are Will's father."

"That can't be, Liz!" he shouted. He got up again and this time started to pace. "You would have told me that the minute you found out, right?" He watched her sob. Screaming, he questioned again,

"Right?" He looked at her terrified, contorted face and knew this was actually happening.

Chills engulfed him. It felt as if the world had come to a dead halt. He ran back to the house without her, without another word, unable to digest what he heard, and started ranting. "I cannot believe all these years she kept this from me! Why? Why would she do that?" he screamed aloud. *Well isn't that a ridiculous thought. I did the same thing to her with Lillie. No; this is different.* "This is my son with her! With her!"

He didn't give it a chance to sink in; he proceeded to drink and drink, first a beer, then the hard stuff, and then more beer. Hours later, he wobbled over to the window and noticed her car was gone. He never gave her a chance to explain and he didn't care. Until morning came.

# CHAPTER THIRTY-SEVEN

# ADAM

## (1979)

Adam awakened to pellets of rain hitting the window. "Perfect! Fits my mood," he muttered as he opened the heavy dark blue curtains and looked out at the dismal sky. After he showered and dressed, he headed for the kitchen and saw her standing in front of him looking disheveled.

"Hi." Her voice was thick and hoarse with sleeplessness.

"Hi."

"You left the door open last night. I came back in, but I didn't want to disturb you; you were dead asleep. I saw you'd been drinking." She picked up another empty beer bottle and added it to the heap. "I made coffee, want some?"

He took two mugs out of the cupboard and poured. "Smells good, thank you."

"I know this was a terrible shock, the way I sprung it on you. I had been planning on telling you for days…for weeks…oh shit, for years. But there was never the right time…or… I don't know, Adam. It's complicated. And then I was angry and hurt when you told me about Lillie. I guess we surprised each other."

"Remember when we used to talk about having kids? I was so excited at the thought of us having a boy so I could play ball with him, take him to games. You said we'd have ten children; whatever it took to have a boy. Remember?" Adam said forlornly. "I can't wrap my head around this, Liz. How could you keep this from me all these years? Don't you know how much I love you, and Will? I would have been a good father."

There was a pretty strong resemblance in Will's and Adam's looks, but it wasn't obvious to him. Adam never considered that Will was his son. Nor did he consider that Liz could keep something of this magnitude from him. He was in his own world; a screwed up world of alcoholism.

"You can still be a good father; if you stop drinking."

"Is that why you kept it from me? Maybe if you told me I would have stopped. If you believed in me!"

"Would you have? Would you have really stopped?"

"Maybe if you told me, I wouldn't have diabetes!"

"You wouldn't have what?" Her mouth dropped open. *This can't be happening; the dream is coming true!* "Diabetes! My God Adam! When did this happen?"

"Right before I left for Canada."

"Are you under a doctor's care?"

"Could we get back to the issue at hand? My son! Does Will know?"

"Adam! Answer me! How advanced is it?"

"Okay already! No I'm not under a doctor's care and I don't know how advanced it is. It's not good, I can tell you that," he sighed.

"How can I help? How about we go to a doctor together?" She knew Adam wasn't thrilled about going to doctors. She remembered when they were kids he refused to go to the dentist when he was suffering from a horrendous toothache. He waited three days before being seen and by then his tooth had abscessed.

"You can't help Liz; I drink. Nobody can help me."

"What about going back to AA?"

"I can't. I tried. It doesn't work for me."

"It didn't then, but maybe it will now," she pleaded.

"Liz, give it up. Stop pushing. I can't do it."

"Maybe Will can help. Does knowing you are his father make a difference?"

"Of course it makes a difference!" he snapped, anger rising again. "Liz, enough already!" Exaggerating the words, he shouted, "Does.. ss Will..ll know?"

"For years he's been asking me. First when I was married to Tom; then when you came back. I kept dodging the issue. Believe me, he's upset with me for not answering him straight. But Adam, how could I? I wanted to tell him since he was little."

"Then why the hell didn't you?"

"Because you're an alcoholic, Adam!"

Ignoring her remark, he said, "Are you going to tell him *now*? Because if you don't, I will!"

"Wait a minute, Adam! Slow down! You can't do that unless we figure out *how* to do it. He's nine years old. I've lied to him for nine years! This could be devastating to my relationship with him."

"We'll do it together," Adam suggested, starting to feel hopeful.

"And say what? Will, meet your father, our friend Adam.'"

"Well, do you have a better suggestion?"

"Maybe he shouldn't be told."

"What! Are you serious? He's my son, Liz! I've missed nine years of his life! I'm not going to miss another second. Do you understand me?"

"Adam, calm down. I do understand, believe me. I've wanted this for both of you since I was pregnant. I needed you by my side at his birth for God's sake! And afterwards… I needed you. I just plain needed you, so much. When he was an infant I wanted to share his tiny fingers with you, his beautiful smile, just like yours. His eyes, just like yours. There were millions of times I needed you by my side in raising him, but you weren't around." Her voice escalated. "Sports, school, birthdays!"

"Because I was in Canada? What about at the beginning? I wouldn't have left."

"That's ridiculous! Would you have stayed here only to be drafted and land up in Nam, and maybe even dead?"

"If I had known we could have married and I wouldn't have gone to Canada! I could have been deferred and granted a 3A status!

"That ended in '65 Adam!"

"Yeah, I know." He stopped pacing and sat down, and put his head in his hands. "Aren't we getting off the subject?"

"Which is what? If it's to tell Will, I say no! He's *my* son and I don't want him to know!" She was starting to panic. "Please Adam, listen. Can't you just be friends with him? You could still do all the things you do with him now; go to all the places that you go, but please…let's leave it as it is, okay?" After she spoke, she realized the absurdity of what she said. "Look, I know how much this means to you. But, I'm afraid what this will do to him."

"You mean what it will do to you, don't you? Maybe this will be good for him. You know, maybe he needs me as his dad. He's had you for nine years. Now it's my turn. I mean it, Liz. I'm going to tell him if you don't."

She took a harsher tone. "Adam, if you do this, I will tell him you're a drunk and a liar. Please, think about it before doing anything. Think about the ramifications."

She got up and walked out the door. He heard the hum of her car engine and then the tires screeched out of the driveway. He reached for a beer, stopped himself, and put it down.

He let a few days pass. The news still didn't sink in, or not entirely anyway. He called her several times. No one was home, so he left a message. After three attempts with no response, he made his decision.

# CHAPTER THIRTY-EIGHT

# ADAM

## (1979)

"Adam! What are you doing here?" Will hopped off his bike, jumped up, and threw his arms around his neck.

"Does mom know you're here?"

"Not yet. I'm on my way to your house. I wanted to talk to you first."

"Mom will be so happy to see you. She's been sad lately."

They walked over to the playground nearby and sat down on a bench. Will placed his bicycle in front of them so he could keep an eye on it. There were big oak trees surrounding the area with huge roots rising above the ground. Two squirrels were chasing each other up and down a tree, abundant with spirally oversized leaves. Acorns were scattered around them.

"Will, I have something I want to talk to you about."

"Okay." He looked up at Adam with big questioning eyes and waited.

"It's pretty big news, son." Adam took a deep breath. "How would you feel if I was your father?"

"What do you mean?"

"Would it be all right with you if I was your dad? Would you like that?"

"For real?"

"Yes, for real! Would you be okay with this?"

"Would I! But, are you *really* my father?" Will hesitated, "I don't understand."

"I am Will. I am *really* your father."

"Wow! All the kids at school have dads except me. When I was little my friends Sally and Peter didn't have dads, but now they do; they have stepdads." Will was talking so fast he couldn't catch his breath, until he remembered and said glumly, "Tom was my stepdad for a while. But he and mom got divorced." He looked pensive. "Wait a minute. If this is true, how come mom didn't tell me? I don't get it. I asked her so many times who my dad was. Why would she lie to me?"

"I don't know why. I wish she didn't. But Will…could we keep this between us for now? Would that be all right?"

"I guess so. But now you're lying, aren't you? How can you be my dad if my mom doesn't know?"

"Of course she knows, but she doesn't want to tell you right now." Adam looked him squarely in the eyes. "I want you to know, Will. Very badly. I love you. I'm not lying about that."

Switching gears as if a light was just turned on, Will said excitedly, "Wow! Wait until the kids at school find out."

"But remember Will, you promised not to tell anyone yet, okay?"

They held each other closely and then went home, to their separate homes.

Adam decided to speak to Liz at some other time.

Will was happy, but also sad and confused. His feelings were raw, new and strange.

# CHAPTER THIRTY-NINE

# LIZ

## (ONE MONTH LATER)

"Don't ever speak to me that way again! Do you hear me?"

"I'll do what I want!" Will screamed.

"What's going on Will? What's wrong?"

He had been acting out for weeks. First Liz got a call from Mr. Henry, the principal of his school. Will had picked a fight with a boy for no apparent reason and could she come to discuss it. Then she got a call from his math teacher saying he had flunked two tests in a row. It didn't make sense to her since he was an excellent math student.

"Leave me alone!" he screamed again.

"Go to your room young man! No TV tonight! And believe me, we will discuss this later."

Liz was shocked at his behavior. Will had never spoken to her this way. Most of the time he was a good boy. She had never gotten a call from his school before. She didn't have a clue what was going on.

One month had gone by and Will still didn't tell his mother about Adam's and his encounter. He remembered her reaction when Tom showed up at the school playground, so he didn't dare let her know about Adam's unannounced visit. It would remain a secret.

"Will, time for dinner. Are you coming down? Will?"

After calling him several times, she went upstairs to see if he was sleeping. Liz entered his room and froze at what she saw. His closet door was open and his clothes, still on hangers, were thrown haphazardly all over the floor. His schoolbooks were scattered on his bed with no schoolbag in sight. In a panic, she started going through his drawers. They were empty. It looked as if his room had been turned upside down. Although she sensed she wouldn't find him, she ran outside to the back of her property and screamed as loudly as she could, "Will! Are you out here? Will!" She ran back into the house and frantically dialed her mother. "Mom, is Will with you?"

"Why would he be with me? What's wrong Liz?"

Stammering, she said, "I don't know Mom. I'm not making sense. I can't find him. I think he ran away."

"Why do you think something so horrible?"

"Mom, please, I want to hurry. Because he's been having problems at school and now his room…." Liz was choking on her words in-between sobs. "His room looks… it kind of looks ransacked."

"It looks what! How long is he missing? Alarmed, her mother's knees became weak. "Did you call the police yet?"

"No, not yet. I only noticed a few minutes ago that he was gone. Let me call his friends first."

"I'll be there as soon as I can. For God's sake, call the police!" Her mother hung up.

After contacting two of his friends' mothers and leaving a message for a third, Liz called the police. Nobody had seen him or heard anything, nor did the authorities, who were on their way to take a missing persons' report. When they arrived, her parents were already there.

"Mrs. Bloom?"

Both Liz and her mom answered simultaneously. "Yes?" Liz then acknowledged, "I'm Will's mother; this is my mom."

"Is there a father?"

"I'm his grandpa," Liz's father offered his hand.

"No. Yes. I mean, yes, but no, he's unaware….actually he just found out." Liz was trembling.

"Found out what?" the officer inquired.

"Liz, Adam knows?" Her mom looked shocked.

The officer interrupted and started rattling off questions: "Your son's full name? His date of birth? His height and weight, ma'am? Color of his hair? Do you have a recent photo? What was he wearing when you last saw him? Where do you think he might have gone? What about his school friends? Does he have any enemies?"

"Enemies? Of course not!" Liz was startled by the disturbing nature of the question.

He continued. "Do you have his friends' parents' phone numbers? Any fights recently with you or his so-called dad, or his friends?"

It slowly dawned on Liz. *Adam…oh no…it can't be….did he actually tell him?*

After 45 minutes of grueling questions and filling out a missing persons' report, the officer said, "Okay, that about winds it up for now. We'll be on this ASAP. If you hear anything, call us immediately; like a person demanding money in exchange for your son, or anything at all."

"A person demanding money? You mean like ransom?"

"Yes, Miss Bloom; like ransom."

"Are you serious? Do you think that could have happened?"

"Anything could happen. But let's not go there. Don't jump to any conclusions. Not just yet."

Liz's mom let the cop out and thanked him. Her father held her while she cried. They were all distraught.

Collecting herself, Liz said, "I'll be back in a minute. I want to call Adam."

"Liz wait! Does he know that Will is his son? You finally told him after all these years?"

"Yes mom, after all these years I finally told him and he didn't take it well. He was angry and hurt." Liz looked downcast and beaten. "I only pray Will is with him, because I don't know where else to look."

Her hand shook as she dialed. *Please God, let him be with him!* There was no answer. She left a frantic message on his answering machine at work. "Adam! Will is missing! I can't find him anywhere! The cops just left. My parents are here with me. I'm so scared. Is he with you? Please tell me he's with you! Adam, I'm frightened. If he's not with you, then I don't know where he might be. Hurry, please call me and hurry here!" She started to tremble again.

Two hours later, the longest two hours of Liz's life, Adam called back.

"Liz? It's going to be okay. I promise. I may know where he is." Adam's voice lowered. "I told him."

"You what?"

"I told him I'm his father."

Liz's breathing quickened. The air around her swirled. Years of denial swirled and surrounded her.

"I also told him that if he ever needs me to call me. The other day he called and asked for my address. He said he wanted to send me a drawing he made. I didn't think anything of it at the time. I thought it was sweet."

"You didn't think anything of it? Sweet! What are you crazy?" Liz was hysterical. "My God! So what are you saying? He may be at your house on the island? He's nine years old! How would he get there?"

"I'm not sure, but I guess he could have taken a train."

"Adam! He's nine years old! Nine! I have to go. I'll see if the police can check out your house. And the trains!"

"Liz, wait! Let me go there first."

"No way! I'm not going to wait any longer! I'm frightened. I don't know where my son is. I don't know if he's okay or hurt...oh God what if he...."

"Don't go there Liz! I'm sure he's fine! I am just as concerned as you are. He's my son too!"

Ignoring him, she hung up.

# CHAPTER FORTY

# WILL

## (1979)

I always wanted a dad. Now I have one. Just like that! I like Adam and I know he likes me. I can't believe my mother didn't tell me all these years he was my dad. How can she hide that from me? Well, she can't any more. I'm gonna live with my dad from now on! But what if he doesn't want me? I know he said he loves me, but he may not want a kid around all the time. Then what do I do? All my friends live with their dads on the weekends and summers. Well, that's when my mom is gonna see me; only then! If she's lucky!

I wonder why my mom did this to me. Adam seems like a good guy. I don't get it. My friends' parents who live together always fight. Once I walked into Billy's house and his parents were screaming at each other. But he didn't seem to care. I felt bad for him.

Love seems so stupid. When I grow up, I won't fall in love with a girl. Well, there's one I like though. Actually, I like her a lot. I think she likes me too. Her name is Rosie. She's not from around here. I think she comes from Florida. She has long black thick hair and sometimes braids it. She's real pretty. Once in a while Rosie smiles at me. It makes me nervous. I haven't told my friends about her. I think they would make fun of me. They always make fun of me. stupid bullies!

Early in the morning while his mother was in the shower, Will quickly packed his school knapsack with all the essentials: his GI guys; a newly acquired transistor radio; some underwear and socks; a pair of pajamas; the remainder of the Oreos from the pantry; a bag of chips; his PEZ dispensers with plenty of candy to fill them; two packages of Twinkies; and the money he had taken from his mom's purse and money he had earned from yardwork he did for Popsy. He knew she would be upset with him for stealing her money, but he didn't care. After all, she did lie to him for nine years, didn't she?

Will walked from his house in Mohegan Lake to the Peekskill train station, a four and a half mile hike. He had never done anything like this before and he was scared. It took him well over an hour, but he was determined to reach his destination. Since his mom and he took the train to Manhattan many times to see basketball games at Madison Square Garden, he was familiar with the route. He knew his landmarks from a game he and Billy made up when he once joined them.

*Lexington Avenue, the one near my house, (he chuckled), not the one in the city, to Route 6 and make a left; then walk forever until I see the library smack in town. First I'll pass the gas station on my right, then the diner that Tom and I ate in when Mom was late from work, and then the library. After that, it will be just a few minutes before I see the train station.* He took a deep breath and sighed. *Then I'll ask the ticket lady for Grand Central. That's the gigantic room with a million people.* He took another deep breath. *That's the part that I don't know how to do.*

One hour later he reached Metro North, and after building courage and feigning confidence, approached the ticket lady. "Ma'am, can I have a ticket for Grand Central please?"

A woman with the yellowest teeth he had ever seen looked him up and down and inquired, "Where's your parents? You're not here alone, are you?"

"Yes Ma'am! My mom just dropped me off so I can go visit my dad." Will had practiced this part of his speech all morning. He was only nine, but because of his height, could easily pass for 13 years old.

The woman with unsightly teeth checked him out again. "You look mighty young to be traveling alone. You sure you're okay son? You're not running away or anything, are you?"

Will took a silent breath and calmed himself. "No Ma'am! I've done this a million times." Smiling, he lied through his sparkling white teeth and asserted, "Don't you remember me? I was here two weeks ago. Went out to see my dad on the island. You see, my parents, they're not getting along too well. So my daddy, he...."

The now unsmiling, but sympathetic woman said, "I'm sorry son; sure, here's your ticket." She took the money from his outstretched hand and placed the ticket firmly in his other hand. "Now you listen; if you're not telling me the truth, I'm gonna be in a lot of trouble young man. But, you go ahead and be very careful. You hear?" She pointed in the direction of the train which was pulling up. Will took off with his knapsack in tow.

Settling into a seat by the window, he let out a big sigh. *Whew! I can't believe she let me go! I almost got in big trouble!* He looked around and noticed that most of the seats were empty. To his left, an old man was drifting off and beginning to snore. The seat in front was occupied by a businessman reading a newspaper. Looking out the window, Will passed familiar sights. In the distance a barge sluggishly traversed the river. He remembered his mom telling him that barges often transported oil. At the other end of the Hudson River he noticed cars as tiny as ants on the Tappan Zee Bridge. Sailboats were floating motionless. He counted sails, *one, two, three, four; a white one, a blue one, a red...* He drifted off into a semi-slumber and dreamt what it would be like to sail across the ocean to far-away lands.

"Tickets!" the conductor bellowed. "Tickets!"

Shaking himself awake, Will rummaged through his bag, but then remembered he placed his ticket in his wallet. He reached for his back pocket and handed the ticket to the gruff man wearing a hat that reminded him of a baseball cap.

Will looked at the watch Adam had given him. It was a thoughtful gift and considering he never owned one, it was gratefully received. *Only a little while longer and I'll be there.* He took out the map that he found the day before in the kitchen drawer next to the sink and studied it. It displayed a time schedule that his mom used when they took trips to the city. *Ok; when I get there, I will ask somebody how to get to Penn Station.* He breathed uneasily and squirmed in his seat.

A half an hour later, the train came to a screeching halt as Will heard the voice on the loud speaker announce, "Grand Central". As he entered the enormous building, he was dumbstruck at the site. "Holy mackerel!" In the past when he had gone to basketball games he was in a hurry. Now he focused on the *millions* of people walking in circles in no particular direction. Something caught his attention and he looked up. *Double holy mackerel! The ceiling has stars on it! And constellations!* Will reveled in using his telescope on summer evenings when the sky was clear, or winter evenings when the birds had gone to sleep and viewing was optimal. He knew that in both seasons the evenings must be moonless. Using a telescope was similar to looking into a person's brain; understanding the depths of both was curious to him.

He walked over to a food concession, ordered a hot dog and root beer, and sat down at a table. Looking around he noticed a crowd forming to his right. Music began to fill the area. A short stocky guy, with long red hair and a red beard equally as long, was hunched over playing the harmonica. People were dropping coins in his hat which was placed on the ground next to him. Will enjoyed the music and tapped his feet. Minutes later, while he was still enjoying the music and finishing his frankfurter, an unruly guy with hooded eyelids sat right next to him, moving his chair too close for comfort. "How ya doing buddy? Want to see something cool?"

Will jumped up and almost fell over. "No sir!" He grabbed his belongings and started to leave. He knew not to talk to strangers and this guy was creepy.

"Cool it man! I didn't mean no harm!" He walked off and Will sat back down feeling shaken.

*Maybe I should get the heck out of here and get to my dad's house fast!* That's the first time he had addressed Adam as his dad and it felt good. It was slowly becoming a reality. Will looked around to see who he could ask for directions to Penn Station. He was apprehensive about walking in the city, but knew there was no other way to get to his destination. It was a big journey for a kid and he was scared even though it didn't show.

He spotted a woman to his far right. She looked harmless as she was holding the hand of her little girl. "Excuse me Ma'am, do you know where Penn Station is?" Within seconds he realized she didn't speak English. He thanked her anyway and kept looking around for someone to help him. A police officer was walking in his direction. *Uh-oh.* He held his breath. The cop walked right past him. *Whew! What am I going to do? I guess I should start walking, but where? Where do I go?* At that very moment, a clean-cut well-groomed man came over to him and asked if he was lost.

"Kind of. I'm looking for Penn Station," Will said relieved. "Do you know where it is?"

"Sure, why don't you follow me and I'll point you in the right direction?"

Will followed the man. Before they reached the exit, he pushed Will inside a telephone booth. "Look, I'll tell you what; you come with me and then I'll take you anywhere you want. And I'll even give you some of this candy." The man pulled out a plastic bag with a tie twisted at the top, and some kind of white powder shone dully inside it.

Will tried to scream, but whimpered instead. "Let me out of here."

## CHAPTER FORTY-ONE

# ADAM

## (1979)

Ever since I was young I dreamt of having a son. That's all Liz and I ever talked about. And now, I screw it up. My son could be hurt, or even worse, because of my irresponsibility! How could I not realize what was going on when he asked for my address?

I took a cab home. I wanted to get there as fast as I could. It took a little over two hours from the city; the most painful moments of my life. The thought of losing my little boy, as I did with ten year old Edouard, was too much for me to bear. I could not go through that again. And certainly not with my *own* son. I would rather die.

I paid the cabbie and ran into the house looking for Will, or any signs of him being here. Nothing. I ran outside hoping I'd see him playing or maybe sleeping in the chaise. Nothing. I ran around back to the pool, hoping, praying. Nothing. I ran back into the house and this time noticed the red light of my answering machine blinking. I hit the play button and held my breath.

"Adam...I mean, Dad, can you please come here? I'm at Grand Central Station and...," Will said frantically and started to cry. "I ran away from home and this man tried to...," he started to cry again. The phone went dead.

I heard myself scream. *Oh my God! Please God, don't let anything happen to him!*

# CHAPTER FORTY-TWO

# LIZ

"This is all my fault!"

"What did the police say? Liz? What did they say?" Their daughter was inconsolable. "Liz, this is not your fault! Why do you say that?" Frustrated, her father got up and walked into the kitchen.

"I should have told Will and Adam this at the beginning! Why did I think I had the right to keep this from them?"

"You did your best." Her father tried to comfort her but it was useless. "Did you call the police on the island or here?"

"I called both. They said they'll alert the officials at the train station, but they can't guarantee anything. There are too many people floating around. They should call us soon."

"You know what I just remembered?"

"What Mom?" Liz was distant; her eyes a forest stripped of its foliage during bitter winter months.

"When you were five years old you were livid with me. I took your *Tiny Tears* doll away from you because you were fresh. Your dad sent you to your room even though you begged for him to reason with me. When that didn't work, you decided to run away from home."

"You're kidding? I don't remember that!"

"You packed all your things. Do you remember the pink bag that you put all your dolls in?"

"Nope." She thought for a moment, "Oh wait! You mean the one with the big purple handle?"

"Yes, that's the one."

"So then what happened?" Liz's eyes widened like when she was little and her father would tell her a scary bedtime story.

"You sat in your treehouse for hours until you had to go to the bathroom."

Liz started to laugh, but stopped. "I miss the old treehouse. I wish it would be that simple for Will." Her face was awash with fear. "I'm scared, Mom."

"Liz, I truly believe Will is fine. You have to believe that. I bet Adam finds him at his home and calls you soon."

At that very moment they were both startled by the phone's jarring ring.

"Liz, try to stay calm. I had to call 911. When I got home there was a message on my answering machine..." He paused. "It wasn't good, Liz."

She felt herself losing consciousness. "Liz!" Her mother caught her just in time.

"What happened?" her father rushed in and pulled out a chair for her.

"I'm okay," she said shakily. "Adam, are you still there? Adam?"

"Yes. Are you okay?"

"Never mind!" she snapped. "Is Will okay?"

"I don't know. When I got home I looked everywhere for him. There were no signs of him. But then I retrieved a message on my tape. He told me he ran away from home; that he was angry at you, and that he was at Grand Central. But then he... Liz, I have to go. The police are here."

"I'm on my way!"

"Liz, stay there; he might call you!" He hung up.

"Liz, what happened?" her parents asked simultaneously.

""I have to go. Please stay here, just in case he calls."

"Where are you going?" her mom shouted.

As she grabbed her belongings, Liz related what Adam said.

"But are you going to Grand Central or Adam's house? Stop and think before you take off. Adam is already there. If you go to Grand Central, it will be like looking for a needle in a haystack."

"So what do I do? Just wait here and do nothing? Will may be hurt! I'm going! I'll find him!"

"Let the police handle it," her father said. "He may not be there anymore. It's a big place. You'll be running around on a fool's errand. Be smart Liz. Sit down."

"What are you crazy? On a fool's errand! That's my son you're talking about! Your grandson!"

"Your father's right. It won't do any good to take off. Wait until we have more information. How about both of you go and I'll wait here? But after we have more information. Okay?" Weeping, Liz's mom said, "Come, let's sit on the couch. See if you could rest your eyes for a little while. Come on, sit next to me."

Her parents sat on either side of her. After a little while, Liz drifted off with her head on her father's shoulder.

# CHAPTER FORTY-THREE

# ADAM

The police came and left with yet another missing children's report filled out on Will. The Grand Central authorities hadn't seen any unattended children wandering about, nor had they received any calls about a little boy. Adam knew nothing more. He reached for a beer. *Only one, maybe two. I must have my wits about me. Damn it! Now what? What? I just sit here?* He picked up an empty beer bottle and flung it across the room. *What the hell did I do? Fuck!*

"Liz? The police were here. They don't know anything."

She made a strangled sound. "What do we do?"

"I don't know. I guess sit tight and wait to hear from him. But we should hang up just in case he calls one of us."

"Wait! Tell me what else Will said to you."

"Liz, let's get off the phone! He could be calling us."

"Don't you think one of us should go look for him?"

"Where Liz? He could be anywhere by now. Let's just sit and wait."

"Wait?" she shouted.

He hung up.

*Who am I fooling? I can't just sit here!* He got up and paced and paced until he tired himself out and sat on his recliner. *Will. What have I done? I swear God, if you find Will and he's okay, I'll stop drinking. I hope.* His thoughts then turned to Lillie. *I hope you're okay, Lillie. Between the two of you, I'm sick with worry.. What kind of father am I?* He drifted off to sleep. He dreamt of Will and Lillie running from a tornado. *Will, help! Run Lillie! It will be all right. Take my hand. Wait a minute; you don't even know each other. I'll save you! What have I done?* He shook himself awake. *Shit!*

He looked at the clock. Only an hour had passed. He reached over for the Sunday paper and opened it to the front page. Apparently a virtuoso violinist had been in a plane crash and died instantly. Response was worldwide. Prayers were being offered to the deceased's family. *Damn it; that reminds me…Where on earth did I put my father's violin? I can't seem to remember. I wanted to give it to Lillie one day if she still likes classical music.*

Icy chills shot up his spine as the sound of the phone thundered in his ears. He ran to it and grabbed the receiver, as if it was his life line. *God, please let it be him.*

"Hello?"

"Adam, have you heard anything?"

"Liz, you have to leave the phone free! It might take awhile before we hear from him. Try to hang in there. I'm scared too, but we must keep our heads."

With terror in her voice, Liz reluctantly hung up.

Bile rose in his throat from fear of what might happen to him. He tried calming himself. *He's smart; real smart. He'll be okay. I'm a horrible father to both of them. I make stupid impulsive decisions. How could I have told Will I was his father without Liz's approval? My kids need stability and security. Who am I fooling anyway? I'm a drunk.*

# CHAPTER FORTY-FOUR

# WILL

W ill flung his arms and wrestled the assailant, although his size
was significantly larger. His broad shoulders were perceptible
in his tailored suit and his height towered over Will's. People walked
by as if this was an everyday occurrence. Perhaps they thought the
incident was between a parent and child. The adjacent telephone
booths were empty. With one last effort, Will's sneakered foot slammed
into the man's leg and shoved him right out of the booth. With a
hysterical sigh of relief Will watched him flee. He trembled fiercely
releasing the trauma with tears. *What the heck was that stuff anyway?*
He had heard about drugs from his friends, but never had seen any.
*It looked like the baby powder my mother uses during the summer.* Still
shaking he dialed his father's number. Before he had a chance to finish
his message, the phone went dead. Defeated, he started to whimper.

A woman appeared in the booth next to him. "Can I help you
honey? I overheard you telling your dad about a bad man."

He looked up at her and noticed her kind looking countenance. She
had grey short hair that framed her full face. Her thin lips were reddened,
as well her cheeks. She was short and plump; a grandmother figure.

Reluctantly he asked, "Could you tell me how to get to Penn Station?"

"I could do better than that," she gently offered. "I can walk with you to the station and help find your dad. Is he headed there?"

"Yes!

"Okay, but only on one condition. If he isn't there, I have to call the police. Okay?"

"Okay, but don't try anything funny with me! I just want to find my dad."

"I won't honey. Why are you alone anyway? Your parents shouldn't have let you travel alone," the nice lady chastised. Apparently she didn't hear the part about him running away.

On their way to Penn Station, the lady named Gladys talked about her grandchildren, ages three, five, and eight. "They aren't as brave as you are though," she confided. "Their parents wouldn't dare leave them alone in such a big place where you can meet all sorts of people." Will and Gladys passed the Empire State Building and Macy's, where his mom bought her sweaters.

"Sometimes my mom and I go to basketball games at Madison Square Garden. It's right over Penn Station."

"Oh, that's very nice!" Gladys turned to face him, and instantly frowned. Will was nowhere in sight! When they turned the corner of 7th Avenue and 33th Streets, he unexpectedly took off in the other direction. "Well... I'll be," she said to nobody in particular. "Where on earth did he go?"

Will knew she would not find his father at the station. Adam was unaware of his son's ill-advised flight until a few minutes ago. Will also knew the nice lady would call the police. When he finally recognized the streets where his mom and he had frequented, he ran at his first opportunity to hide from Gladys.

*Whew! That was a close call!* He looked around and started walking in the right direction. He then hurried down the flight of stairs passing signs pointing to Madison Square Garden in the opposite direction.

I'm scared. What if I can't find my dad's house? *Holy mackerel! This place is humongous too!* I wish I never did this. But, mom screwed things up and now I have to live with my dad. *I miss my mom so much.* Maybe I should call her. She must be so worried. I wonder if she's looking for me. *She must be.* She probably called the police. *I shouldn't have done this.* I hope she's not too mad at me. *Holy mackerel! Look at that man! He must be homeless. He's bony. His beard looks like snakes. Yikes! He doesn't have any teeth. I bet he hasn't washed his hair, ever! I wonder what's in those two bags he's holding. I feel bad for him.* There's a telephone booth; finally! *Please Dad answer the phone!*

# CHAPTER FORTY-FIVE

# ADAM

"D ad?"

"Will? Where are you? Are you okay?"

"I'm at Penn Station. Can you come get me?"

"Yes, right now!" Panicking, Adam screamed, "Are you okay? Wait! First tell me... just in case we get cut off... where exactly are you in Penn Station?"

"Wait, let me look. I'm near... " Frenetically Will searched for a landmark. He shouted, "Track #12!"

"Will, listen to me carefully. I don't want you to move from there. Do you hear me? It's going to take me awhile to get there...maybe over an hour....so I want you to stay put. Don't talk to any more strangers! Adam repeated, "Find a seat if you can and don't move!"

Adam flew out the door, but remembered Liz and turned back. "Liz! Will called from Penn Station. I'm headed there right now!"

'Wait!" It was too late. Adam hung up.

*I can't believe it; he's okay. Please God, let him be okay when I get there.*

He got in his car and prayed traffic wouldn't be heavy. But, that would be like hoping for snow in July. Adam was in for the long haul, stuck on the LIE, the longest drive of his life, with his heart pounding. *Jesus Christ! Move already, Goddamned traffic!*

When he reached Manhattan, he pulled into the parking lot closest to Penn Station and ran the rest of the way. Upon entering the building, he first looked for Track #12, but Will was nowhere in sight. Adam frantically dashed back and forth between the three levels and through the concourses and train platforms below, like a hamster in a cage.

A policeman had already taken Will into custody.

"Are you Will Bloom?" the officer asked as he reached for his 2-way radio and then scribbled something on his pad.

"Yes sir." Will knew immediately his mom had called the authorities. And secretly he was glad.

"Come with me young man. Your mom is looking for you. She's scared out of her wits. Why did you run away from home anyway?"

# CHAPTER FORTY-SIX
# LIZ

"Mom, Dad! I'm leaving," Liz yelled from her bedroom. Adam heard from Will. He's at Penn Station. I notified the police." She ran down the stairs with no sign of relief. It was not over yet. She wanted to see Will with her own eyes, that he was unharmed. She desperately wanted to hold him and never let him go.

Frantically, her mom rushed over to her. "Is he okay?"

"I don't know yet. I've got to run. I'll call you as soon as I know anything."

Her father got up and hugged her, an act he never exhibited. An undemonstrative man, his daughter was nevertheless most important to him.

"Everything will be fine, you'll see."

The door slammed.

Speeding down the Taconic in the middle lane, she almost passed the sign for the Sprain Parkway. Liz slammed on her brakes and made a sudden perpendicular turn in front of another car at the exit nearly causing an accident behind her and the other cars. Horns blared from all over. Shaken, she chastised herself. *Jesus Christ! If you want to get there alive, you better slow down!*

She looked at her watch as she pulled into the precinct. *Probably record time!*

She grabbed her pocketbook, and with her heart pounding she nearly fell over as she entered the vestibule. Surrounding her were a bunch of unruly characters all waiting to be seen. Liz had never been exposed to criminals or prostitutes. The sight was appalling. She felt dirty just being in the same room with them. One of the women's skirts was unpleasingly tight and barely covered her bottom. Liz was certain she wasn't wearing underwear. She cringed. Another woman was made up with a palette of masterful colors thickly applied; resembling a pasty cratered moon on her face.

One hour later a tall rugged-looking cop motioned to Liz. "This way miss." He escorted her into a dully lit room devoid of any atmosphere.

"I'm here to pick up my son. Is he here? Will Bloom; he's nine years old. Did you find him?" she uncontrollably rambled.

"First answer a few questions for me and we'll bring him in."

"He's here?" Is he okay? Please let me see him."

"Your full name, ma'am?"

"Elizabeth Bloom," she acquiesced.

"When did you first notice your son was missing?"

The questions were endless. She started to sob. "Please sir, can I see my son now?"

"One more question. Your kid sure is precocious for his age. I mean, to make it here all the way from Westchester without an adult. That's impressive. Has he done this before?"

Liz gasped. "Will! Thank God!" Are you all right?"

"Mom!" Will ran into her arms. "I'm so sorry!" They held each other for a long time.

"I'm sorry too! I should have told you. I was wrong to hold this from you. Can you ever forgive me?"

"So Adam is *really* my Dad then? He wasn't joking, right?"

"He really is, honey. Come on, let's go home!"

"One minute ma'am." The officer reached over for a pen. "You need to fill out these papers."

Liz held his hand tightly as they walked to the car. "Are you all right honey? Adam said you got disconnected after calling him. What happened?"

Will related the whole nightmarish story on the ride home to Mohegan Lake.

# CHAPTER FORTY-SEVEN

# ADAM

*W*here the hell is he? Did I hear him correctly? Didn't he say Penn Station? Maybe he's in the bathroom. Please God, let him be in the bathroom! Shit! Nobody! Try Track 12 again. Stay calm. I'll find him. I've got to. Nothing! Now what? Maybe he called Liz? Probably not. Oh, what the hell.

He spotted a telephone booth down the other end of the platform.

"Hello? Is that you Mrs. Bloom?"

"Yes, Adam. Did you find him?"

"No. Is Liz there?"

"No, she headed for the police station about two hours ago."

Without saying another word, Adam ran out the front entrance in search of the nearest station. When he arrived, there was a 25 minute wait before he was able to ask where his son was. He watched a disorderly group of boys not more than 18 years old shuffled into an outer room. He watched two prostitutes, one lifting her skirt to get his attention, and the other religiously licking her lips while she stared at him. Finally he was called into the office, only to find out Will was not there, but he had left with his mother. He went directly to his car and cried and cried. *Thank you God.*

# CHAPTER FORTY-EIGHT

# LIZ

"I'm sorry mom. I'm sorry I scared you. I was angry. But I know what I did was wrong. It was stupid."

"I'm not going to punish you Will. I think you learned your lesson and suffered enough. But so help me God, if you ever do anything like this again!" Liz held him tightly. "Now, say you're sorry to Grandma and Popsy."

"We're glad you're okay honey." He hugged both of them and went into the kitchen.

Just as Will sat down with the meatloaf dinner his Grandma had left for him on the counter, a car pulled into the driveway. He lifted the peach and olive green curtains to see who was there. Will went flying out the door.

"Dad!"

Adam ran to him with outstretched arms. They were still clinging to each other when Liz joined them.

"Hi Adam."

"Hi Liz."

It took them a minute, and then they looked at each other. Liz's eyes softened and body relaxed as Adam wrapped his arms around her.

"He's okay, he's okay," he said.

"Yes, he's okay."

"Hello Adam." Liz's mom took in the warm sight of their embrace. "Glad you're here. Thank God all went well." She squeezed Will for the final time. "Well, we'll be off now."

Liz's dad shook Adam's hand, kissed Liz, and patted Will on the head. "Behave yourself young man and don't you do that to your mom ever again."

"I will Popsy. I mean, I won't."

They all laughed and Grandma and Popsy departed.

"So where do we go from here?" Adam looked first at Liz and then Will. They were snuggled on the smaller couch, meant for two, with Will between them.

"Why don't we just sit here and take it in." For the first time in a while Liz felt content.

# CHAPTER FORTY-NINE

# ADAM

## (APRIL 1979)

I nearly missed the flight. The LIE was its usual nightmare with traffic backed up for miles. Leaving Will for a month at this crucial time seemed cruel, but there was no choice. I missed Lillie terribly. Besides, I had been away from work on the coast too long.

As the sun set with silvery linear threads approaching the sky, I pulled up to Hanna's duplex. Dreading her volatile disposition, I unwittingly gulped before I knocked.

"Hello Hanna."

She stood before me in a slinky dress that showed her every curve. But within seconds, any positive feelings I might have were trashed when she bristled, "Hi Adam. It's been awhile, hasn't it?"

Disgusted, I said, "One month Hanna. Only, one month." I looked in the direction of Lillie's bedroom. Defensively, I again countered, "I called you every week, didn't I?"

In the corner of my eye, I noticed Lillie sitting up in her playpen. "Hi sweetheart! Well, when did you start sitting up by yourself? Good for you!"

"She started the other day. If you were here, you would have seen it firsthand."

"I have work to do in New York, Hanna. You know, that's how people pay their mortgage; earning money."

"How dumb do you think I am? You know as well as I do that you were with *her*!"

I quickly changed the subject. "Well, at least Lillie's finally making some progress, don't you think?"

"Slowly, but yes, she's progressing. She's definitely different than other babies her age, though. The doctor said there are varying degrees of when babies sit up, crawl, or walk, but Lillie is *really* slow."

I picked Lillie up and held her. She didn't resist like she had in the past. "Well, let's be hopeful. Watch, soon she'll be crawling!"

"Yes, but Adam, she's turning a year old and only recently sitting up. That's not normal!"

"It's not that abnormal! She's a little slower."

She walked into the kitchen to turn off the stove and came back with her dinner smelling heavenly of roast pork and garlic, without offering me one bite.

"By the way, my parents and I are giving Lill' a birthday party next Saturday. Will you be around?"

"Of course! Did you think I would miss her birthday? Never!"

After trying to involve Lillie in building blocks, without any success, I watched intently as she swayed to the music playing on the record player. Hanna said Bach was it for her. No other composer. She handed me a list of presents Lillie might like for her birthday; exclusively records, all classical selections. Not Sesame Street para-phernalia, not dolls, not the Muppets. Only Bach recordings; sonatas and partitas for solo violin. Lillie's big brown eyes were alert, almost lively; crystal balls shimmering at a dance hall. It seemed she was reacting to every measure with her body.

"How long has this been going on?"

"What?"

"Look at her Hanna! She's dancing to the violins. I mean, it's incredible because the music is intense. It's not light folk music or even rock, which I could relate to more. This is a sonata, isn't it?"

"How'd you know that?" Hanna looked surprised.

"I don't know. Probably from Liz's concerts. I don't know that much about classical music."

"Oh, her again! Please don't talk about *her* in front of Lillie."

It was then that I saw the resemblance between Hanna and Lillie. Lillie had my oval-shaped face and crooked smile just like Will did, but her full mouth, the mouth which resembled her Columbian heritage, stood out. Her skin was creamy white and atop was a mix of my blondness with Hanna's parents and her jet black hair, a chestnut effect.

I took Lillie's hands with mine and moved to the music. She resisted at first, but then she grabbed my fingers with her little hands and started a waltz-like dance. When the record stopped playing, I switched the music and this time turned up the volume. Unexpectedly, Lillie started to wail. I tried to calm her, but she unrelentingly screamed until I lowered the sound. Mollified, she started swaying once again.

"You know, Adam, if it wasn't for your drinking, maybe Lillie wouldn't have these problems. I read somewhere..."

I cut her off. "Don't start this again, Hanna! I could blame you too and say it's your age."

"What about my age?"

"Come on, you know you were too old to have a baby; admit it! Listen, if every time I come here you're going to do this, then maybe I'll arrange to see Lillie on the outside. What d'ya think?"

I was pissed and sick of Hanna's attitude. The few visits I had with Lillie were precious to me.

"Well, no matter what, we're lucky that Lillie is alive."

"Now what are you talking about?" I was infuriated and ready to go.

"The doctors said so! Because of her difficult birth!"

I looked at my watch. "I've leaving Hanna. I haven't registered yet. I have an early morning meeting."

Lillie had fallen asleep. I whispered, "I'll be back soon sweetheart; for your birthday!" I kissed her head full of curls and quietly tiptoed out of her room.

Adam returned to the hotel, ordered dinner, and called Liz. She was pissed and didn't want to hear about Lillie, but she asked anyway.

"How is she?"

"She's sitting up!" he said proudly.

Unenthusiastically, she replied, "That's nice."

"How's my boy?"

"How do you think he is after you left without a goodbye, without an explanation? If you are going to assume the role of his father, you better get your act together!"

"What do you mean assume? I *am* his father!"

Adam couldn't believe he was catching hell from both ends! First Hanna, now Liz.

"Look, Liz, I know I should have contacted him before I left, but...

Enflamed, Liz cut in, "BUT, but, but! That is exactly why I didn't bother for all these years. I knew you wouldn't be there for him. He's hurting, Adam. First he doesn't have a father, then Tom turns out to be an asshole, and now what do *you* do?"

"Liz, listen! I'm new at this. I have my hands filled with Lillie.... wait! What do you mean Tom was an asshole? You never told me that. You said things didn't work out."

"It's none of your business! Don't change the subject!"

"It is my business if it involves Will!"

"Oh give me a break! When you get your priorities straight, give me a call."

"Both Lillie and Will are my priorities. But Liz, something is wrong with Lillie. She needs me. And," he inhaled, "my work is here too, not only in New York."

"Lille needs you! What about Will? He's been without you all these years!"

"That's been your choice, not mine!" Look, can we call a truce for Will's sake? Tell me what I can do. Should I call him and explain?"

"Explain that you are the father to someone else? That he has a half-sister? No thank you Adam, I'll do that."

"Lill', watch *Abuela* light the candles!" Hanna's mother placed one pink candle smack in the middle of her home made strawberry shortcake and a yellow one off center for good luck. The candles were lit! "Blow like this...whoo, whoo." Hanna pursed her lips and demonstrated, and everyone sang happy birthday. But Lillie seemed unimpressed. Instead she watched the rain drops trickling down the window, like fingers raking through one's tangled hair.

Colorful balloons hanging from two ceiling fans decorated the apartment, and from the tops of four chairs, clusters of red, pink and white ones hung high. Presents were gathered all around Lillie, who sat up and intermittently plopped right back down onto the living room rug as she ripped apart sparkly bows on top of the gifts. All of a sudden she turned towards the right and clumsily maneuvered herself onto her knees flopping over and over again.

"Look Adam," Hanna screamed, "I think she's trying to crawl!"

"I told you so!" Adam beamed. "Remember I told you last week things would look up? See!"

They all looked in amazement and excitement as sweet little Lillie was finally progressing.

I spent time on the coast catching up with work and numerous clients, and visiting Uncle Harry and my father's grave. Whenever possible I arranged to see Lillie, but work was all consuming. And, as if things couldn't get busier, I had gotten news from my boss that I would have to stay in LA indefinitely; I would be back in New York by Christmas, if I was lucky.

"Gene, I can't leave NY for that long. Something big happened. I found out Will is my son! Could you imagine that? I now have two kids."

"I'm sorry pal, but this is a done deal. We got three new clients, all of them big, and we need you here. And, Hempsey Corp. just merged with some big outfit out in Vegas and needs revamping I'll tell you what though; if something changes, I'll let you know. By the way, congratulations on your boy!"

Disgusted, I said, "Thanks Gene, thanks a bunch."

It was Saturday. I decided to stay home. Home, my hotel. I fixed myself a drink as I tried to sort things out. What I desperately wanted was to be a good dad to both my kids. But how could I with one kid in New York and one across the continent, in California? I reached for the phone.

❖

"What are you crazy? He's nine years old. Who would watch him during the day?"

"I've given that some thought; I found a sports day camp close by to my hotel. They introduce the kids to every sport Liz; baseball, basketball, soccer, hockey, and swimming! I think he'd love it!"

"I'll think about it Adam, but I don't want to be away from him that long. And I don't want Will living in a hotel."

His enthusiasm was bubbling over. "I'll rent an apartment! It would give us a chance as father and son to get to know each other. And, it would be good for both of you. Don't you think?"

"But that would be only on weekends, right? I'm sure you'll be with Lillie most of the time, won't you?

"So what's wrong with that? They could get to know each other too, as brother and sister."

"Lillie is a baby. She's how old again?"

"She just had her first birthday! You should have seen her. She tried to crawl for the first time! You know, she has a problem; if you remember?"

"Yes, I remember. Sorry. But Adam, you'll be at work during the week. Will you be home in time for Will, when he gets home from camp?"

"Stop creating roadblocks! I'll take good care of him. I promise. Anyway, haven't you heard? Will's a man of the world! He's been all over Manhattan. With *his* experiences, he can handle anything."

"Not funny! I'll think about it and let you know. Maybe next week."

# CHAPTER FIFTY

# LIZ
## (1979)

"Is Dad coming this weekend?"

"No, honey. Don't you remember I told you he's back on the coast?"

"But that was last week. Why won't he come *this* weekend?"

*I can't believe Adam did this to him!*

Not knowing how to answer him, Liz diverted his attention. "Why don't we have Chinese tonight? Would you like that?"

"Spareribs? With orange sauce?" he asked excitedly.

"Definitely!"

"Where's the coast again?"

"California. Remember I showed you on the map?"

"Yeah, now I remember. We worked on that in social studies class with Mr. Goldman."

"Now, get ready for baseball practice and when we get home we'll order some."

"I don't want to go Mom."

"What? I thought you love baseball; almost as much as basketball. What happened?"

"All the kids have their dads there. I'm the only one without one." He looked forlorn.

"What am I chopped liver?" Liz feigned hurt feelings.

"Oh Mom, you're silly!"

"Come on, let's get out of here before your team replaces the great *Will Bloom*!"

"Hey mom, now that Adam is my father, can I have his last name instead of yours? What is it anyway?"

"Greenstein."

He thought for a minute. "Will Greenstein. Sounds good, doesn't it?"

"We'll see Will. Let's talk about this later."

"It's a good thing Tom's last name isn't mine, right mom?"

For the last year and a half Liz had been seeing Tom again. But it wasn't the same. Things were different for them. For one thing, she didn't let Will know that Tom was back in her life. Instinctively, she knew she would eventually end the relationship. Her heart was with Adam, even if things were screwed up.

"It was frightening Tom. I thought I'd never see him again. I would have died without him."

She filled him in on everything since she had seen him last, including Will running away.

"Adam suggested Will go live with him for the summer."

"Are you letting him go?"

"I'm considering it. He wants him to go to a sports camp."

"That's great!"

"Yes, I know." Liz looked forlorn.

"What's the matter? You don't seem too enthused."

"I don't know. I guess I don't want him to meet Lillie."

"Lillie is Adam's little girl?"

"Yes. I know I'm probably wrong, maybe it would be nice for Will to have more family, but...but it's all so sudden." She hesitated. "He now has a sister, but she's not my child. Adam and I were supposed to have children, together. Will has been without his real father, (not that you weren't there for him), for his entire life, and the minute Adam meets him he takes off and spends time with his daughter. It doesn't seem right."

"But Liz, put yourself in his place. He didn't know Will was his son. You kept that from him. What was the guy supposed to do?"

"I know. Anne told me the same thing this morning. I guess it always comes back to his drinking." She stopped herself. "This is ridiculous. I'm telling all this to you, the other culprit. You're not much better, you know?"

"But I'm cuter, right? And you love me." He half-smiled. "Do you Liz? Do you love me?"

"You know that I care about you Tom, but Adam was my first love and will probably be my last. He's forever. I'm sorry, truly sorry. I don't mean to hurt you."

"When we married, did you love me Liz, back then?"

"I thought I did. I tried to make it work, but when you..." She stopped herself, dead cold. "I won't go there. Never again. It's over. The past has been confusing for me too, not just you. But we're friends now, right?"

"I thought we were more than friends. Friends don't have hot sex, do they?" he laughed.

"Well, of course they do!" She laughed too. But privately she felt baffled at her behavior.

"Come on, let's go! It's a beautiful day. What would you like to do? How about roller skating?"

"Roller skating? You're kidding, right? I'll fall on my ass!"

"Well then, I'll make it all better, won't I?"

"Will, hurry! You're going to miss the flight. Stop monkeying around! Are you finished packing yet?"

"I'm looking for my baseball cap. Does dad have room for my GI Joe guys at his house?"

"Of course, silly! I only told you not to bring a lot of toys because it's too cumbersome for the plane ride. Now don't forget...every day at 5 p.m. you're to call me. And make sure you're in bed at 9 p.m. sharp...and don't forget to brush your teeth every morning and every night. Oh, and change your underwear for God's sake. Okay?"

"Mom! Stop worrying! I'm a big boy."

With trepidation, Liz had acquiesced to Will staying with Adam. More than anything she wanted them to be father and son. But having Lillie as part of Will's life was troubling her. Will may have been ready to have Lillie as his sister, but Liz was not. More importantly though, the possibility of Adam reneging on his promise to abstain from drinking, could be devastating to her and end their relationship for good.

She arranged with the airport for Will to sit up front where the stewardesses could keep an eye on him.

"You're not nervous or anything, you know, to go alone? You can always change your mind."

"I'm not afraid. Dad says I'm a *man in the world*. What's that mean? Mom? Mom? Are you listening? I get the man part, but what does he mean *in the world?*"

"No honey, he must have said *man of the world*. He means you've been having a lot of different experiences."

"Can I take this with me?"

"What?" Liz looked over her shoulder and noticed the time. "Will, we have to leave right now. Popsy and grandma will be outside any minute. They each grabbed a couple of bags, two with clothes and two with odds and ends, mostly junk and toys that Will insisted he bring to California.

"Will," she reached for his hand and moved a little closer. "I love you honey and will miss you a whole bunch! I hope you have a super time with your dad, and at sports camp!"

Will squeezed her tightly. "I'll miss you too mommy, and don't cry!" He hadn't called Liz that since he was very little and even he started to get misty. They hurried out the door as the horn honked loudly.

# CHAPTER FIFTY-ONE

# LIZ

## (1979)

"Anne? What's the matter? Your voice sounds funny."

"How is Will enjoying sports camp? You must be going crazy missing him!"

"He loves it. He also loves his sister," Liz said sarcastically. "But what's up with you; what's going on?"

"Can you meet later for dinner?"

"Of course. I feel so badly; I haven't been there for you in a long time, especially since you told me about...*you know what*. It's just that my life has been in upheaval, first with Will and now," she sighed, "Adam."

But that was only part of the truth. For the first time in their relationship, Liz felt awkward with her closest and dearest friend. She didn't know what to feel or how to act. She felt self-conscious; as if Anne might be interested in *her*. These thoughts were so strange and uncomfortable, she purged them from her mind.

"Well, *you know what* has escalated into a nightmare. Fred is taking me to court for full custody of the kids!"

"What are you saying? You can't be their mom because you're a lesbian?"

"Yes, that's what *he* said. And my lawyer feels he has a good case."

"But he's cheated on you! Doesn't that count for anything?"

"Nope! Supposedly that's more *normal.*"

"That's ridiculous!"

"Let's face it, Liz; Fred doesn't want the kids' orientation to be influenced because of me."

"Do you really think that could happen? Do you think children can become homosexual if their parents are? "Jesus Christ Anne! It's not contagious!" Liz was outraged for her friend. "Nor is it proven that it's hereditary. Some people think you're born that way."

"I know, but most people think you're a freak and choose to be that way."

Saddened, Liz said, "What about the march that will be held in October? I heard there will be thousands of lesbians and gay men in Washington. Won't that help?"

"I hope so. In fact, one of the issues in the platform will be to end discrimination in lesbian-mother and gay-father custody cases. But my lawyer thinks we have a long way to go to make a difference. He doubts that they'll get anywhere."

"But at least they're making an effort, and history!" Liz said optimistically.

"Yes, I agree! My biggest worry though is how the publicity will affect Sammy and Ruth. The kids in school can be cruel." Anne was panicking. "What if God forbid Fred wins custody and they grow up without me. What will happen to them, Liz, without a mother?" She started to weep. "I would die without them."

"Don't go there! Things will work out, you'll see." Liz reached for her hand. "Are you attending the march? Do you want me to go with you?"

"I don't think I should go and leave the kids. It would be a bad move at this point with Fred on the rampage, don't you think?"

"Yes, I agree. Stay put and let others fight for the cause. Maybe there are other ways you can contribute."

"That's a good idea; I'll think about it."

"Oh, yum!" Their onion soup was served, with the cheese dripping over the bowl. "Just the way I like it," Liz started picking off piece by piece. They were in one of their favorite restaurants close to Anne's house.

"This *is* good! Thanks for meeting me here. I wanted to be nearby just in case the babysitter contacts me...you know, if Fred calls."

"Anne! You're allowed to leave your house. What's the matter with you?"

"I'm afraid he'll think I'm an unfit mother; that I left the kids home alone while dining with my...you know...lover. I'm even afraid he'll take photos of us."

"Why Anne, I didn't know you had a crush on me," Liz giggled.

"Cut it out." Anne tried to lighten up, but couldn't. "You know what I mean."

"Don't you think you're carrying this too far?"

"Maybe. But I'm not taking any chances; not when it comes to Sammy and Ruth."

Digressing, Liz said quietly, "Adam has diabetes."

"What? You're kidding!"

"Nope. And his drinking has worsened his condition. It seems to be advancing. I'm afraid for him."

"What a mess!"

"What's eerie is that I've been having a recurring nightmare about this for a long time and now part of it came true."

Her interest piqued, Anne asked, "What happens in the rest of the dream?"

"I won't dare talk about it; I'm superstitious."

"I didn't know you were superstitious. It must be bad...does he... oh, forget it; I don't want to upset you."

As the waitress served their hamburgers, Liz noticed from the corner of her eye somebody she thought she recognized but couldn't place who it was. "He's coming over," she mumbled.

""Who?"

"Liz! Is that you?"

"Alex? I thought I recognized you. What are you doing at this end of town? I'm sorry, let me introduce you to my friend Anne." Smiling, they shook hands.

"Please sit, join us," Liz offered. "It's good to see you!"

"You too, Liz. You know, I owe you thanks; I've been painting."

Anne interrupted, "How do you two know each other?" She looked at Liz first, then Alex.

"Alex is one of the VA outpatients that I worked with in art therapy. You should see the horses he draws!" She turned to Alex, "Are you still painting those beautiful horses?"

"I am, but I've deviated and temporarily switched to still-lives using watercolor."

"Wow! Watercolor is difficult. Good for you!"

"So, do you still have the same boyfriend?"

"I do, but I've temporarily deviated and switched to someone else," Liz smiled, amused at her unintended jocularity.

"So, I guess I *still* don't have a chance, do I?"

Anne felt like a third wheel and excused herself to go freshen up.

"Sorry Alex, I could hardly juggle two men, let alone three." *Those eyes!* "Do you come here often? I've never seen you here before."

"No, this is my first time. Nice place!" He scanned the restaurant. "I was passing through on my way to my parents' house; they live in Cold Spring."

"Cold Spring! That's where I live," Anne said returning to her seat. "Small world!"

"It sure is." Alex stood up and stared intensely into Liz's eyes, "I've got to run; I'm just grabbing some take-out food." He hesitated and their eyes met. "Maybe someday you'll change your mind?" Turning his head slightly, "Bye Anne, nice meeting you."

"Wow! He is *good looking*! Anne cocked her head and asked, "Don't you think?"

"Tell me about it!" Liz reddened.

"Well I'll be! You've got the hots for him, don't you?"

"Shhh!" Liz squirmed in her seat as laughter inched its way for both of them.

"Liz, get back to Adam for a second. What else do you know?"

"He told me he's having all sorts of symptoms....he's peeing all the time; he's had to leave work because he's so exhausted; he's excessively thirsty; it's a mess. And now it's worsened."

"You would think he'd stop drinking. What about AA? Has he tried going back?"

"It doesn't seem to work for him."

They both were quiet for a time.

"Anne, could I ask you a question?"

"Sure, what's up?"

"How do you do that?"

"What?" Anne knew exactly what Liz was asking. "Have sex with a woman?"

"I just don't get it. It seems so weird after all these years of knowing you...for you to touch a woman. How can you do that? Liz shuddered.

"Hey, it's not that bad," Anne laughed. In fact, I enjoy it more than touching Fred. Now, *that's* something to shudder about!"

"I'm sorry Anne, I didn't mean to say...to do that. It's just that…"

Anne raised her hand in protest, "You don't have to explain; I understand. It *is* weird for me to have switched genres out of the blue. But, that's not what really happened. I've probably been attracted to women for as far back as I can remember, but I never did anything about it. I had a hard time admitting it to myself, let alone you. And, when I met Rose I realized I couldn't keep denying it. I wanted her. It's that simple."

"Rose? That's her name?"

"Yes. I'm crazy about her."

"What's she like? Where did you meet her?"

"She has the most beautiful blue eyes I've ever seen. I swear, they dance around. I know, that's silly. Seriously though, she's special... smart, funny, and she loves me for who I am. Rose doesn't judge me. Fred had a habit of harping on all my faults. You know what I mean? He goes on and on searching for them."

Liz became lost in thought realizing how much she focused on Adam's flaws since she'd known him. She never took notice of his good qualities; never gave much thought to the possibility of Adam being a loving father. His drinking always stood in the way.

"Are you there Liz?" Anne waved a hand in front of Liz's face.

"I'm sorry, would you mind if we left soon? I want to catch Will before he goes to sleep."

"Hi sweetheart. How was your day?"

"Mom! You wouldn't believe what we did at camp. I love it here! I have so much to tell you!" Will was speaking so fast, that Liz could hardly follow. "Have to tell you later though. I have to go, sorry. I love you."

"Will, wait! You hardly talked to me. Where are you going?" She heard Will's reluctance and asked to speak to Adam instead, feeling lonely and disconcertedly jealous. This was the third time this happened.

Adam's complacency infuriated Liz. "Lillie and Will have been having a ball together! He reads to her and she claps her hands in approval. They really hit it off!"

"For God's sake, Lillie is only 1 years old. How could they hit it off?"

"They have, Liz. Lillie must instinctively know Will is her brother."

"That's ridiculous!"

"They look like each other too!"

"Give me a break! Listen, what's with Will anyway? He never wants to talk to me anymore."

"He's excited, that's all. Everything's new here; he's acclimating."

"Can't you please encourage him to talk to me? I miss him."

"I will. I'll speak to him tonight. I promise."

"Adam, have you been taking care of yourself, you know...your diabetes?"

Acerbically, Adam asked, "Don't you *really* mean, am I drinking with Will here?"

251

"Well that too. But I really want to know how you're doing; honestly Adam. I'm worried about you."

"I'm fine Liz. Leave it alone. I promise you I'm not drinking with Will around."

"Well, I can see this is pointless. Obviously you don't want to talk about it, but you're going to have to do something to help yourself. AA didn't work. You don't want to die, do you?"

# CHAPTER FIFTY-TWO

# LIZ
## (1979)

"Mom, did you know that dad drinks beer? You told me that drinking is not allowed, but dad says an occasional beer is okay. When will I be old enough to drink beer?"

"Put your dad on, *now*, Will." Liz was livid.

"He's not here."

"What do you mean he's not there? Where is he?"

Will was wondering why his mother was yelling at him, since he didn't do anything wrong. He nervously answered, "I don't know Mom. He said he'd be back in a few minutes."

"Make sure you tell him to call me right away, okay? It's important Will!"

"I will Mom. I promise."

"How could you! How could you lie about something like this?"

Adam knew immediately that she had to be talking about his drinking. Liz only got mad about two things: Lillie and alcohol, and Lillie was covered yesterday.

"Look, it was only one beer; calm down."

"Will is questioning when he will be old enough to drink beer and you want me to calm down!" she bellowed.

"Ok, I get it; it won't happen again. I promise."

"Yeah, you and your promises. I mean it Adam. Don't drink while Will is with you. Or it will be the last time you spend any time with him! I'll see to that."

Infuriated, Liz went into her studio, looked around, and tried to focus. Tearing up, she pondered how he could do this to her. *He's an alcoholic, that's why. Damn him! I shouldn't have let Will go. And now he's becoming close with Lillie; his half-sister! This is killing me. I'm letting jealousy consume me. I've got to stop this. We could have another kid, if he ever stops drinking and we marry. But, do I really want that?*

She picked up a brush, thought better of it, and reached for a thinner one with less bristles to fine-tune the edges. Still drifting, her thoughts went to Hanna. *I wonder what she looks like; who Lillie looks like. Certainly not Will! Well, I guess I'll find out from him when he gets home. I miss him so much.* She calmed herself. *I'll try to call him again later; that's what I'll do. There, that looks better!* She picked up a palette knife and added thick vivid colors of acyclic paint towards the bottom half of the abstract; chartreuse, vermilion, a touch of yellow ocher, and globs of cerulean. *Hmmm, long way to go. Better get ready... Tom will be here soon.*

"Tom? Come on in."

Tom walked in pensively and looked around at the house he once enjoyed with Liz.

"It hasn't changed at all. Except, I see you bought some new prints for the living room."

Liz had purchased three reproductions of an artist she appreciated, similar to Grandma Moses, the 20<sup>th</sup> century American folk artist. The snow scenes reminded her of a trip she took to Vermont with her parents when she was young.

"Very nice!"

"You know, I would never ask you to come here if Will was..."

Tom put his hand up in protest. "I know Liz; you don't have to explain. Would you like to go out to dinner?"

"Would you mind if we stay here? I want to call Will before he goes to sleep. Besides, I've made your favorite dish!"

"I thought I recognized that smell; chicken cacciatore, right?"

They were sitting on the couch drinking a glass of chardonnay, with Liz's back snuggled up against him, as he massaged her neck.

"Umm, that feels so good. Hey, you're not letting me concentrate!"

She turned around, and squarely faced him.

"Why do you have to concentrate?" Tom grinned.

"Because I want to talk to you about something."

"Shoot!"

"How would you like to go with me on a vacation? I haven't been on one in a while and I thought..."

"Say no more! Name the time and place and your wish is my command!"

"Next week. California."

Tom's relaxed expression changed.

"Come on Liz. That's not a vacation. I don't want to tell you what to do, but you ought to give them a chance to get to know one another. Don't you think?"

"I can't Tom. I miss him so much; it's been a month. And besides, it's Will's birthday in a couple of weeks! Ten years old!"

"And?"

"And what?"

"We both know it's not only about that."

"What do you mean?"

"Come on Liz. Stop it. Did you forget who you're talking to, your confidante?"

"Okay, you're right. I'm going to die if I don't see what Hanna looks like. Although, I don't know if I can handle meeting Lillie. But I can't go on like this, wondering. And, we'll have fun. I promise. We'll go swimming in the ocean during the day, and in the evening we'll sit by candlelight eating some exotic fish native to California."

"Native to California. You're getting desperate." He laughed. "On one condition."

"What's that? I'm afraid to ask," she smiled coyly.

"We'll talk about that on the trip when there's no turning back. Just you and me in the clouds," he smiled confidently.

"And the other passengers!"

Two weeks later they arrived at the Holiday Inn; Liz eager to see Will, and Tom, well he was focused on only one thing... hot steamy sex.

The hotel was thirty minutes from Adam's newly rented apartment. It was perfect. She didn't want to be too close or too far.

"What do you want to do tomorrow? The beach?" Or, how about we go into town and explore? Although, I think I want to stick around if it's okay."

Tom had a silly grin on his face. "Okay! Sounds good to me! We'll order food in for the entire day."

"That's not what I had in mind, Tom. I meant stay close to Adam's apartment so we can head there when Will's back from camp."

"Oh," he said deflated.

"We'll have time together, tonight."

"All right! I'll order the champagne and maybe some strawberries and cream? What do you think?" he asked uplifted once more.

"Sure," she answered flatly and started dialing Adam's work number.

"Liz, wait a minute. Does Adam know you were coming?"

"Shhh!" she waved him away.

"Adam Greenstein's office. Can I help you?"

"Why yes, thank you. Is he in?"

"No, I'm sorry. Can I give him a message?"

"I wonder where he is."

"Come on Liz, get your mind off Will. You'll see him later. Let's go get some dinner."

Once back in the hotel Liz called Adam, this time at his apartment. It was 7 p.m. and she was sure they'd both be home by now.

"I don't get it! He knew I'd be anxious to speak to Will. Where is he?"

"So he did know you were coming," Tom surmised.

"Wait! Hello? Adam?"

"Yes, sorry we're home so late. I took off the afternoon and picked Will up at camp to go see Lillie."

"Can I speak to him?"

Adam shouted, "Will, your mom is on the phone."

Liz heard Will yell back, "Tell her I'll call her later. I'm watching TV."

She slammed the receiver down. "Let's go! I've had it!"

# CHAPTER FIFTY-THREE
# ADAM
## (1979)

I knew Liz was right. I needed to do quit the booze. But if having Will here didn't make me stop, and having Lillie in my life didn't either, then I doubted anything would.

Several days after Valentine's Day, I visited Lillie. She was sleeping peacefully, so Hanna and I sat in the living room curled up reminiscing about when we met. It was odd, because since our daughter's birth, she was adamant that I not drink around Lillie. And yet, here we were sipping wine and holding hands. Before we knew it, one thing led to another.

It was unadulterated sex; that's all I told myself anyway. But, we did share a child, didn't we? After that, Hanna and I were back in bed a few times; actually, every time I visited, which became more frequent after that night. What can I say? Sex was damned good with Hanna.

When it came to my relationship with Liz, we were always messed up. She claimed it was my drinking. But, I think it is more about her self-righteousness. It turned me off. She lied to me about Will's paternity for nine years. We could have been father and son. What a waste of time! To make matters worse, she married Tom and gave Will a step-father. Damn her!

I can't believe Liz is seeing Tom again. Is she crazy? She told me about the incident. The guy is a jerk. But, I'm jealous too. Jealous and pissed that she married him in the first place and is probably screwing him again. Of course, who am I to talk?

"Will, turn off the TV and come here."

"In a minute Dad."

"Now Will!"

"What is this over here?"

"What?"

"You know what! You've been smoking cigarettes."

"Only one. All my friends at camp do."

"Well you're not going to!"

"It was just one Dad. Lighten up."

"Don't tell me to lighten up! You're nine years old! Your mother is going to kill me."

"Dad! Please don't tell her. She'll make me go home. Besides, I'm going to be ten next week! Did you forget?"

"Well, maybe you should go home if you're going to act this way. And, no I didn't forget."

"By the way, *Dad*," Will said flippantly, "you drink beer."

"Hold on Will, just a minute." There was a persistent knocking and ringing of the doorbell.

"Jesus! Hold your horses! Who is it?"

"Where is he?" Liz pounded the door again.

"Mom!"

"Liz! What are you doing here?" Adam glanced behind her. "Who are you?"

"Tom!" Will flew into his arms and gave him a bear hug.

"Will, don't you want to give your mom a hug first?" Tom asked awkwardly.

Liz started introductions. "Adam, this is Tom. "Tom, ..."

Will approached his mother, looked up at her and said, "Why are you here?"

She ignored the cold greeting. "You don't think I'd miss your birthday, do you?"

"That's next week. Why are you here now?"

"Hey buddy, is that the way you talk to your mother?" Adam chimed in.

"That's okay, Adam." Liz's heart was sinking. *Why on earth is he speaking that way to me?*

"Well, everybody come in. Let's go into the living room. Can I get you something to drink?" *Why the hell are they here?*

"No, thank you." Tom hesitated and instantly changed his mind. "Maybe some water, if you don't mind? Long flight."

"Oh? You just got in?" Adam asked.

"No, sorry. I meant..." *Get me out of here!*

"I'll have some coffee," Liz interrupted, "if you have any made." She glanced at the sofa where Will took a seat in the corner sulking. *Why is he acting this way?*

After the coffee was on, Adam took a seat next to him. Liz and Tom were sitting on the smaller couch facing them.

"It's nice to meet you, Adam. Liz told me all about you before we married."

Adam was fuming from every orifice. "Well, isn't that nice."

Liz sensed a disaster looming and quickly redirected the conversation. "Will, let's plan your birthday party, okay?"

"What a great idea! What would you like to do for your birthday?" Tom asked.

"I think I'm handling that, Tom," Adam said patronizingly.

"Sure Adam, what did you have in mind?"

Now it was Adam's turn to change the course of things. Acerbically he asked, "Why don't we cut to the chase?"

CHAPTER FIFTY-FOUR

# LIZ

## (1979)

*Uh oh!* "Gentlemen, please! Tone it down a bit, for Will's sake. Right honey?" But, Will was gone. Liz jumped up in a panic. Ever since he ran away she was on edge.

Liz walked out of the living room and surveyed the apartment. She passed two bedrooms on the right; the first, a large room beautifully decorated in a pale shade of apple green. The smaller one held pastel blue wallpaper in a pattern partially covered with sports figures; obviously Will's room.

"Will? Are you around?"

"I'm in here, mom."

She scanned the room and smiled. His belongings were covering the floor just like at home.

"Will, what's going on?" He was sitting on the floor in the far corner moping. "Haven't you missed me at all? You seem so mad at me."

"Because Mom, you lied to me. You told me that I wasn't supposed to speak to Tom anymore and that you weren't either. And here you are holding his hand, showing up at Dad's house. Which is it mom, Tom or Dad? Who do you love?"

His voice was elevated to a shrieking pitch. He was angry and hurt.

"I know Will. Calm down. You're right. Things changed and I should have informed you as to what was going on beforehand. But, Will, I'm referring to when I was back in New York. You wouldn't speak to me."

"I don't know, Mom. I'm busy…you know with camp, and my sister, too!"

"Come on Will, you were watching TV when I called. What's going on?" Liz questioned again, exasperated with his circumvention.

"Hey you two, what *is* going on?" Adam peaked his head through the door.

"Adam, could you give us a few minutes?"

"Not really Liz! You left me alone with your boyfriend."

"Five minutes, Adam; just five, okay?" annoyed that he said this in front of Will.

Adam walked away in a huff.

"Will, I've missed you. Come here." They held each other for a time and Liz continued. "Look, if you're not going to tell me what's wrong then I'll guess."

But before she had a chance, Will jumped in.

"I was afraid mom."

"Of what honey?"

"I was afraid if I talked to you I would miss you so much that I would want to go home."

"Oh honey!" Liz embraced her son, the most precious person to her in the world. "But you're having a good time, right?"

"Am I! It's awesome here. And Lillie is the best sister ever! I can't wait for you to meet her."

Liz evaded this news. "Come on Will; let's go back to the living room."

As they passed the door to the master bedroom, the phone rang. Will ran past her relieved to be done with the mother-son talk. Liz paused to hear Adam whisper, "Hanna, I would love to have dinner, but I'm tied up right now. What? Oh, okay, that'll work. I'll meet you at seven at Chico's."

"So Will, how's camp?" Tom asked when they were sitting all together again.

"It's great! We're going surfing in the ocean tomorrow!"

"Surfing? Adam is that safe? He's only nine." Liz asked anxiously.

"They're learning the basics. Don't worry. This camp has excellent supervision....highly recommended."

"Liz, do you think we should be getting back?" Tom asked wistfully.

Ignoring his plea, Liz stayed awhile longer.

"Will, what should we do for your birthday? Can you think of anything special you'd like to do?"

"Yeah, mom. How about we have a party with everyone? We'll have dad and you, and Tom, and Lillie and Hanna. Okay?"

Liz was caught off guard. She didn't know what to say. She wanted to scream, *No way Will! There is no way that I will spend your birthday with your half-sister, let alone her mother! How dare you ask that of me!*

"Sure, honey. That sounds great. How about we discuss the details tomorrow? Tom and I have to go." She jumped up, gathered her belongings, gave a side glance to Tom, kissed Will on the forehead, and left.

"Of all the nerve! How dare he ask that of me!" Liz vented to Tom.

"Liz, he's only nine years old! Give him a break! He doesn't realize that would offend you."

Once back in the hotel, when Tom was in the shower, Liz called the concierge. "Could you tell me where Chico's is?"

"What is Chico's?" Tom asked dripping onto the carpet.

"Shush. No, not you sir. I was ...oh never mind. Where again?" Liz furiously wrote the address down.

"What was that about?"

"Dinner."

"How about dinner right here in our room?" He winked.

"Come on. Get ready. We're eating at Chico's!"

They were ushered into the main dining room when Liz noticed Adam in the corner. *There she is. Disgusting. She's not that pretty. But shit, look at her legs. Jesus! Her dress is so short; why does she bother wearing anything at all? Look at the way he's looking at her. Jesus Christ! He just slid his hand up her leg!*

"Liz? Liz! Don't you hear me? What's the matter?" Tom looked in the direction her eyes were focused on. "Oh; figures."

Without responding, Liz started walking to Adam's table with purpose. "Well, hello Adam. What a coincidence! Introduce me to your lady friend."

*Coincidence, my ass!* "Liz, this is Hanna. Hanna meet Liz."

"I've heard so much about you," Liz said.

"And, I've heard a lot about you," Hanna said.

*Hello, anyone see me?* "And, I'm Tom," he interjected while waving his hands in the air.

The three of them ignored him.

"Well *isn't* this nice?" Liz asked.

"Why don't you join us?" Hanna offered.

Tom said, "Oh, no, we wouldn't want to impose."

Liz sat down.

"I heard you have quite a little girl; the two of you that is," Liz said. "But what's wrong with her?"

"Liz!" Adam said a little too loudly, shocked at her behavior.

Tom squirmed in his seat and grabbed Adam's beer.

"And, your son, what's his name again? Oh yes, Will. What a spunky young man, if I must say so myself," Hana sneered. Adventurous to run away from home at such a young age, don't you think? Something wrong at home?" Hanna suppressed a laugh.

"Will just loves his little sister; his half-sister, that is," Liz said. "In fact, he wants her to come to his birthday party, and of course you too, if you want. But, I'm sure you have better things to do, don't you?" Liz asked snidely.

"I would love to come. I will be sure to make time." Hanna said derisively.

"Okay ladies, let's order dinner. Or, better yet, how about a round of drinks? Sound good?" Adam motioned for the waiter and reached for his drink, but caught Tom downing it.

"You're drinking?" Liz asked with fury.

"Who me?" Adam and Tom said simultaneously.

Liz looked first at Adam and then at Tom. "Tom, let's get our table. It's getting late."

"Well, I never! Do you believe that?" Liz was fuming.

"Try to forget it. Why don't we order?" Tom asked.

"You order. I'm not hungry."

Exasperated, Tom said, "Why don't we leave then?"

Back in the hotel room Liz diligently worked on Will's birthday party. "So what should we buy him for his birthday? Who should we invite? Wait! I forgot for a second...we don't know anyone here. Oh, well. Food, what should we order? And balloons, lot of balloons. We need a theme!"

"Slow down, Liz. Could we do this tomorrow? It's so late. Aren't you tired?"

She wasn't listening. "Where should we have it?"

"I know you're upset seeing Adam and Hanna together, but what did you expect? They have a daughter. Liz? Are you listening to me?" He finally gave up and went to bed, without her.

CHAPTER FIFTY-FIVE

# ADAM
## (1979)

"She has incredible attitude, doesn't she?" Hanna let go of Adam's hand. "How do you tolerate her?"

"I think she's jealous of you." Adam smiled inwardly feeling relieved at the thought. "Don't you feel jealous of her? Just a little bit?"

"Aren't you being presumptuous? Why would I be jealous of someone like her? She's a simpleton. Nothing more. Not even pretty."

"Whoa! You *are* jealous!" Adam was ecstatic. *Two women fighting over me! Alright!*

"Let's get back to Lillie." Hanna was blushing.

"I think she's doing beautifully! She's improving. Slowly, I grant you, but she's doing it," Adam said.

"I know, but I can't help but wonder what's wrong with her. What's ahead for Lillie? Will she ever be like other kids?"

"What's ahead for any child? No parent knows that."

"But she's different," Hanna insisted.

""All kids are different. I'm sure all parents feel that way."

Their dinner was served. They ate in silence, each engrossed in their own thoughts. All about Lillie.

"Do you want dessert?" Adam asked halfheartedly, hoping she would decline. He wanted to get back. He wanted to make love to her. But, he also knew that her mind was on their daughter and sex might take some doing. He was game though. Anything to get her into bed. He needed her, especially after seeing Liz. Except things seemed to be different for him lately. He wasn't as horny as usual, so he knew to take the opportunity when it arose, literally and figuratively.

"No, let's get back. The babysitter will want to go home. I don't like to be too long anyway. I don't think she can deal with Lillie for extended periods. She gets nervous when she cries. Once she starts, she doesn't stop."

"There you go again. That's what babies do; they cry."

Adam paid the check and took Hanna's hand massaging it as they walked to her car. When they settled into its luxurious seats, he bent over and kissed her hard and long. Surprising her, he slid his hand up her skirt and felt her thighs, warm and inviting. With deft fingers he pulled her panties to the side and rubbed her clitoris with a repetitive motion until she aggressively tried to roll over onto him, which sent them into a frenzy of heat. Each realizing there was no room to continue, they considered the back seat, and burst into laughter.

"Nah, we're too old for that. Let's go," Adam said.

"Yes, hurry!" Hanna smiled seductively and started rubbing his hardness. She bent over in an attempt to unzip his trousers, but the seatbelt jolted her backwards. "Later," she pouted.

"It won't matter much though. I already came." He looked over to see her disappointed look. "Kidding, just kidding."

Hanna placed her hand inside his trousers once again and teased with flirting movements all the way home. But it seemed to be over. There was no reaction.

"You did come!"

"No, just distracted driving."

"Come on, you've never been preoccupied before."

The truth was that Adam was experiencing difficulty keeping an erection. It was part of diabetes. But, he'd be damned if he'd let this happen. If he had to fake it, he would. Pretending to be horny though was different than the physical truth.

"Quick, get the money ready to pay *what's her name*. Let's hope Lillie is fast asleep." They ran inside, practically pushing the babysitter out the door.

"Let me check on her for a moment. I'll be back before you're naked. I promise," Hanna said.

A few minutes later she walked out into the living room holding Lillie.

"Oops! Why did you bring her out here?" He hurriedly grabbed his underwear and pants. "Hi sweetheart."

"She was totally awake! I'm going to feed her."

Adam's mood changed swiftly as he picked up Lillie. "How's my little girl doing?"

Hanna came back with her bottle and looked into Adam's eyes apologetically. "Later?"

"I should head back anyway. Will may be a "man of the world", but I promised Liz I'd get back there soon. He's alone."

"Are you free tomorrow then?"

"Sorry, Liz and I are planning Will's party together after I get home. Do you want to join us?"

"No, I think I'll sit this one out. While you're with her, think of me and...," she whispered the rest in his ear.

"Jealousy will get you everywhere!"

He kissed Lillie on her forehead, tweaked Hanna's protruded nipple, and left, relieved to put sex off. For tonight anyway.

❖

"Will, I'm back. What are you doing?"

"Hi Dad. Nothing much. Just watching TV. Mom called again."

"Oh yeah. What did she want?" As if he didn't know.

"She asked if you were home yet. She wanted to go over my birthday party with you. She's making such a big deal over me turning ten years old."

"She loves you. You're the most important thing in her life. But I agree; she's going a little nuts with your party. Especially because you don't have many friends here."

"Dad? Can I invite some of my new friends from camp?"

"I don't see why not. Let's call your mom and see what she thinks."

He reached for the receiver and thought better of it. *What if they're doing it? Oh screw it!* He grabbed the phone again and dialed.

"Busy signal Will." He hung up the receiver and at that precise moment it rang.

"Hello?"

"Adam?"

"Wow. I was just calling you!"

"Oh? Listen, I've been working on Will's birthday party and I think it would be a lovely idea if the six of us celebrate together. What do you think?"

"Sure, but who are the six of us?" He knew damned well who she meant, but wanted to hear her say it.

"Put him on," she said impatiently.

"Will? Would it be all right with you if we celebrate with just you, Dad, Lillie, Hanna, Tom, and me?"

"I guess so, but mom, can my new camps friends..."

271

She cut him off. "Maybe next time, okay? It will be loads of fun! You'll see."

It was a done deal. Both Will and Adam knew there was no arguing with Liz. The party was set for two days from now. Sunday at 1 p.m. at the local pizza place. Liz had reserved the entire back part of the restaurant where normally 20 people could attend.

# CHAPTER FIFTY-SIX

# LIZ

## (1979)

"It's something that our kid's birthdays are only two months apart, isn't it?" Hanna looked over to Liz waiting for a reply.

Taking a bite of pizza, Liz said, "You were lucky though. Adam was with you for Lillie's birth. It's a shame he wasn't there for Will's birth. He was in Canada at the time."

"Lucky! I don't think so. Lillie was premature! A cop car had to bring us to the hospital where she was born, prematurely. My kid was in the hospital for months before she came home."

"Okay ladies, calm down. Are we here for Will's birthday party or to fight?" Adam asked. "And, by the way Liz, I was around when you were pregnant. You chose not to tell me. But that was a long time ago. Why don't we celebrate what is today. I have two wonderful kids and one of them is ten years old today!" He looked at Will and smiled, but noticed he was squirming in his seat, and then to Lillie who was starting to unravel. Tears were rolling down her cheeks as her wails got louder and louder.

Adam picked her up and rocked her. "It's okay sweetheart; shhh..."

"I didn't know you were rushed to the hospital. I'm sorry," Liz said.

"Yes. Adam found me keeled over on the floor. I was only 6 ½ months pregnant."

Tom was quiet, taking it all in. The fighting was grating on his nerves. He was a fourth wheel wanting to get the hell out of there and go home, to New York.

"Hanna, Adam says that Lillie is having problems…that she's different than other babies. Have you thought about taking her to a specialist?"

"Liz! Please! Leave this to Hanna and me." Adam was getting increasingly uncomfortable.

Ignoring his remark, Hanna replied, "I don't know where to take her. Do you have any ideas? The pediatrician says she'll grow out of it, hopefully."

"No, I guess I don't. Wish I did. I'm not sure what I'd do if she were my daughter. Maybe ask around at the local schools?"

"That's an excellent idea! Thank you Liz."

*I don't believe this! They're becoming friends. Give me a break! Just what I need!*

"So Will, how do you like camp?" Hanna asked.

"It's awesome! Tomorrow my team competes against another baseball team."

Lillie was quieting down. Adam put her back in the high chair.

"Camp's been exceptionally good for Will, don't you think, Liz?"

"I wouldn't know." Liz indignantly glanced in Adam's direction.

In order to diffuse the situation, Tom offered, "Why don't we open presents? What do you say, Will?" But things only got worse. Adam was bombarded with insults from both Liz and Hanna for the remainder of the party. Ironically, without them realizing it, a bond was formed between the two women.

"Tom? See you later."

"Where are you going?" He looked at her quizzically. "I thought we were spending the day together, sightseeing."

"I'm meeting Hanna. We're going shopping, and then afterwards, lunch. Meet you back at the hotel at 3 p.m. We'll have dinner!"

"You're kidding me, right?"

But Liz was out the door and Tom was left to fend for himself.

Tom thought with levity, *Great, maybe I should give Adam a call and we could play some golf!*

"That dress looks great on you!" Hanna eyed Liz approvingly.

"Thank you. Do you think Adam will like it?"

"Don't you mean Tom?"

Liz hesitated. "Didn't I say Tom?"

"No, Adam."

"Oh. Sorry!"

"Technically, Adam is both of ours, so to speak." Hanna's pursed mouth opened a little and formed into a wide smile.

Uncertain, Liz smiled too. "He was mine first, so when you're through with him, give him back."

"Touché!"

They both laughed loudly as the storekeeper entered the dressing room.

"Do you ladies need any help?"

"Yes, thank you. I am buying this dress and...," Liz looked over at her new friend.

"I think I will purchase this sweater in pink, if you have it," Hanna said.

They walked arm in arm across the street to a luncheonette, as they chattered and got to know one another. They could be considered an odd couple, but to them, their bond was inevitable. The two woman who loved Adam, the mothers of his children.

## CHAPTER FIFTY-SEVEN

# LIZ

## (1983)

"Are you serious? Tom is seeing someone else?" Anne was dumbfounded.

"I thought he was so devoted to you and rebuilding your future together."

Liz and Anne were sitting outside at their favorite café and enjoying the unseasonably warm weather. It was April and buds were blossoming on the Lilac trees in front of them. Earlier that morning, the proprietor had set up the outside furniture which was usually ready in May.

"He finally gave up. No matter what he does to try to please me... flowers, presents, wining and dining me, his romance doesn't compete with my feelings for Adam. Not even the sex; which happens to be incredible." Liz sighed. "As I said, I think Tom is sleeping around."

"You're kidding?"

"I think he has been all along." Liz's stomach turned.

Lost in her own past drama, Anne remarked, "Holy shit! I can't believe any of this."

Both women were quiet for a time.

"So you and Adam are back together, totally that is?"

"No, not exactly." Liz squirmed in her seat. "I'm sharing him with Hanna."

"What?" Anne was stunned. She didn't recognize the look on her oldest friend's face. "What are you talking about?"

"He's sleeping with both of us." Blushing, Liz looked down at her empty plate. "I can't help myself. And, the weirdest thing happened. A long time ago, Hanna and I became friends. Good friends."

"Oh, isn't that nice. You're sharing the same man in bed," she said sarcastically. "And, does your friendship extend to a threesome?" Anne looked concerned.

"Cut it out! You know I'd never do that. But I have to admit, I truly like and care about Hanna. And Lillie too. Anne, Adam is having trouble getting an erection! I feel really bad for him. He feels ashamed. But, it's the diabetes."

"Are you sure it's the diabetes? Could it be his guilt, or confusion? I mean really Liz – sleeping with both of you! That could... confusing."

"Sexual dysfunction is typical for this disease, for men anyway. And he has so many other things happening to him."

"Like what?"

"He's having a problem with his foot, the right one. Awhile back he stubbed his toe; hard. It's become deformed. Something like that. He hides it from me, and apparently from Hanna too. He seems to be in a lot of pain all the time."

Anne winced. "How come you never told me about any of this, sharing him with Hanna, that is?"

"I was embarrassed. I figured you'd say I lost my mind...or my self-esteem. But honestly, I'm okay with it."

"Okay." Anne stared at Liz. "So how does that work?" Before waiting for a reply, she exploded. "Where the *hell* is your self-esteem? Sharing Adam with another woman! Really, Liz!"

"That's what I just said. Didn't you hear me? I'm fine. When he's in California, he's with her. And when he's home, he's with me. That's all there is to it. I love him Anne. I know it sounds terrible, but it's not that bad. Especially because I'm friends with her. Can you drop this now?"

Anne was far from dropping it. "So are you saying you could do this with me if I was into men?" Anne was astonished.

"Either way, if you're into men, women, it doesn't matter," Liz smirked, about to burst into laughter.

"What?"

"Cut it out! I'm only kidding. You're so gullible!"

Embarrassed, Anne said, "Oh; sorry."

"Anne, he's the father of both of our children so I'm reacting differently than I normally would act, I guess."

"Be careful Liz; I don't want you to get hurt."

"What about you? How's Rose?" Liz countered.

"Don't change the subject, Liz.""

"Come on Anne. There's nothing more to say."

"Okay, have it your way. Rose is doing well. And, she's wonderful with the kids! They love her! The other day we took Sammy and Clare to a toy store. Rose went crazy, first buying a doll for Clare and a truck for Sammy, and then afterwards taking us all out for hamburgers, fries, and a shake."

Unimpressed, Liz said, "And Fred? What's he up to?"

"I don't know and I don't care." Anne looked away.

"How often does he see the kids?"

"He still takes them on weekends, usually."

"Is he seeing anyone?"

"Liz, I don't want to talk about this, okay?"

"Sorry!"

"I'm worried Liz; if we get a divorce, he can take Sammy and Claire away from me...you know, because I'm a lesbian. But if I stay married, well maybe, just maybe, the courts will think...to tell you the truth, I don't know what they'll think. All I know is that Fred is not pushing me and I'm going through life holding my breath anyway."

Apprehensively, Liz asked, "Shouldn't you see a lawyer?"

"I can't afford one."

"Can I help a little?"

"It's too much money. I looked into it. But, thank you."

They left the restaurant feeling beaten. Life seemed unfair.

# LIZ

## (1983)

"Mom, in Mr. Finkelstein's class today we learned about kids who have learning disabilities."

Liz's attention was immediately diverted from a client's file she brought home from work. She looked up at her son's doleful eyes.

"One of the kids in my homeroom class has one and now he has to go to different classes than we do." Will was pensive. "Is that what Lillie has?"

"No, not really. She has something called 'Asperger's'."

"What's that?" Will asked inquisitively.

"It's a disorder which affects the brain and the person's behavior. There's a lot more to it though."

"You could say that again! She has problems, mom."

"I know honey. Just continue to give her support. You've been a good brother." Liz looked at the time. "Have you done your homework yet?"

"Mom, is dad all right?"

"Will, you don't fool me! You're trying to get out of doing your homework." But Liz knew her son was genuinely concerned about his father. "Come here honey." She took his hand and led him into the living room where they sat next to each other on the couch.

"Your dad has diabetes. Do you know what that is?"

"Yes. Dad told me."

"He told you? When?"

"I don't know mom. He told me, okay?"

"Will, what's the matter? Why are you talking to me that way?"

Will eyes clouded over. "Is Dad going to die?"

"Oh honey, I'm sorry. You're scared."

"Aren't you?"

"A little."

"So, he is going to die?" Will repeated impatiently.

"Well, I don't know about that, but he is getting sicker. He needs to take better care of himself."

"You mean he should stop drinking, right?"

"Yes, I do mean that. And other things too... like going to a doctor and maybe taking insulin if necessary."

"What's insulin?"

"It's a drug that can help your dad's blood sugar from getting too high or too low."

"Oh." Will thought for a moment. "I get it. Maybe Lillie and I should talk to him," he said with conviction. "We're his kids and he'll do this for us. I know he will." But Will was dubious. "Won't he mom?"

Liz tried to think of something to say that would make her only son feel hopeful. "Well, it's worth a shot. But Will, your dad is a pretty stubborn man. Hanna and I have been pleading with him for a long time. But give it a try."

"Lillie and I are his kids," he repeated. "You'll see, we'll get through to him."

# CHAPTER FIFTY-EIGHT

# ADAM

## (1983)

"Lill', come here and let me fix your hair. It's all over the place." Hanna arranged her beautiful chestnut curls into pigtails. Long gone was her blond hair; however, traces of it still showed.

It was Lillie's first day at kindergarten and Hanna was more nervous than she was. A year ago she and Adam decided to mainstream Lillie in the local public school, although they did have their reservations and concerns. They knew Lillie was intelligent, but she had problems communicating her needs and understanding directions. She also had difficulty taking things too literally, such as jokes.

"Hanna, Hanna, Hanna. Dad said he will tell my teacher to buy me a dog if I get good marks!"

"Adam! Lillie, Dad was only kidding!"

"Oh." Lillie was crestfallen. "But, can we get a puppy anyway?"

"We'll see Lillie. Let's talk about it later."

Hanna was annoyed, but let it go. Today was her daughter's first day of school!

"Adam, are you coming? The bus will be here any minute."

283

"Oh, Lillie, you look so pretty! Are you ready?" Adam asked with pride.

"I am ready. I am ready. I am ready." Lillie said in a monotone voice. She was talking more normally in the past year, but always fell back on repeating herself three times when she was nervous and upset, or excited.

"Do you believe this? Kindergarten!" Hanna looked mildly chagrinned.

"Are you sure you explained everything to the principal...about... well, you know, *everything*?" Adam asked.

"Mom. Mom. Mom. The bus has arrived."

"Lillie, remember what I told you." Hanna knew Lillie was too distracted to listen, but added, "And, listen to your teacher."

"Okay sweetheart, have a good time. I'll be here when you come home." Adam was teary eyed.

"Dad. Dad. Dad. I'll see you when I return."

With determination, Lillie climbed the stairs of the school bus and then walked straight to an empty seat, just like her mother told her. Hanna was eying her with great concern. The bus driver winked at Hanna. "She'll be fine."

The first few weeks of kindergarten were difficult for Lillie, especially her interaction with the other children. Her peculiarity disturbed and perplexed them. However, there was one girl who seemed to take to her. Robin was chubby and wore unusually thick glasses. She was practically blind. Because she was also made fun of by her classmates, she had compassion for Lillie.

"Why do you repeat everything you say?" Robin asked.

Lillie retorted, "Why do you wear those things on your face?"

But as sensitive as both girls were to each other's remarks, they remained friends. Their camaraderie helped them tolerate bullying from the other kids.

By the following school year though, things had become worse for Lillie and Hanna wondered if transferring her to another school might be in order.

Exasperated, Adam asked, "How will another school help? The same thing will happen!"

Also frustrated, Hanna replied, "I don't know. But maybe it's worth a try. I don't know what else to do. It hurts so bad to see her picked on that way."

"I know." Adam hated to give her more bad news, but there was no choice. "I'm headed back to New York later today. Is there anything I can do before I leave?"

"No, thanks. But, if you can tell Liz I'll be in touch soon. Oh, and take care of yourself, okay? Please, slow down on the drinking. It's obvious your diabetes has worsened over the last few months. Lillie needs you."

When I was little, my father and I used to pray together. My dad prayed for good health and prosperity. I prayed that my mom would leave us. It didn't work. She kicked my dad out instead. He was unaware that I wanted her to disappear, but if he had known, he'd probably would have expressed the same sentiments.

Now I'm praying for Lillie's and Will's health. I have been since Will ran away and since Lillie was born. My prayers worked for Will, but Lillie is another story. Before I left for New York, Hanna and I took Lillie to yet another doctor. We had seen many in the last few years. We finally found out what was wrong with her. We saw a Dr.

Reynolds who's a specialist in something called Autism. He informed us that Lillie has Asperger's, which is on the low end of the Autism spectrum disorder. At least hers is better than most. Some of the kids with Autism don't function at all. She's able to with less difficulty. Or so it appears, anyway. But I am thankful for that. Hanna on the other hand had the nerve to say to me, *I mean, really Adam, this condition is more common in boys. Why the hell did this happen to her? She's a girl! Our luck!*

Surprisingly, doctors have known about Autism for a very long time. Why none of the doctors we saw were familiar with this or Asperger's beats the hell out of me. You would think somebody would tell us, since they realized their similarities two years ago. I was pissed. A lot of time has passed. Lillie could have been helped; maybe even cured. But the reality is that there doesn't seem to be much we could do about it. Lillie is Lillie and she might not change.

I took a long slug of the beer in front of me. Damn it! When will this end?

Adam looked over to the rear corner of his enormous living room. Light shadowed a unique nesting table, where a large porcelain vase painted with shades of magenta and subdued streaks of a Naples hue stood. He scanned the interior. Everything around him was in disarray. Junk was beginning to accumulate and make the room uninviting, even to Adam. Then he spotted the top of something that was long forgotten. His father's violin. It was propped up against the wall, hidden away by the couch. He was in possession of his father's golf clubs, but the violin was an important reminder of his dad's history. He walked over to it and with his hand wiped a thick coat of dust off the blue satiny case.

*Jesus! I forgot all about this.* He thought about Lillie's reaction to classical music; how much she enjoyed it. *I wonder if she will take to the violin when she gets older. Maybe Liz can teach her. Liz had her eye on it, but she's not family; not really. But Lillie, Lillie is my blood. Anything from Dad or me should go to her and Will. I should start thinking about a will for them. You never can tell. I might croak any minute now.*

The phone blared in his ears and interrupted his deep train of thought.

"Hello?"

"Dad? Can you come over today after work? I want to talk to you about something."

Liz was preparing dinner when the doorbell rang.

"Will, your dad's here."

Will flew down the stairs like he did when he was little and came to a halt just in time before he hit the door.

"Hey buddy, what's up? Come here, give me a hug."

They hadn't seen each other since Adam got home and he was anxious to see his son. They walked into the living room and sat side by side facing each other with a big fat pillow between them.

Walking in from the kitchen, Liz asked, "You men want some hot chocolate before dinner? It will be awhile."

"No thanks Liz, but I could use a kiss," Adam puckered up.

Will was still shy about his parents kissing and turned his head. "No thanks Mom, but could you give us some privacy?" His mouth formed a silly grin as she feigned rejection. "I'm leaving."

Convinced that his mom wasn't eaves dropping, Will began his prepared speech. "Dad, Mom says now that I'm 13 years old, I'm a man, in the Jewish religion that is; even though I wasn't Bar Mitzvahed."

"Yeah, what ever happened to that?"

"I didn't want to."

"And your mother didn't put up a fuss?"

"She's not religious. You know that."

"I know, but I thought..."

Will abruptly interrupted him. "So, Dad, since I'm a man I have the right to say whatever I want, right?"

"Well, that depends. What's on your mind?"

Will mustered up the courage and said, "Cut your drinking out... now!" He slowed his breathing down. "Dad, I'm scared. And so is Lillie."

"You and Lillie have discussed this? Come on, she's only five years old."

"We did! Really. We spoke the other day. She doesn't talk much though. But she did say that to me. She did! She said, 'I'm scared. I'm scared. I'm scared, about Adam."

Skeptical, but hoping to mollify Will, Adam said, "Okay. What are you both scared of?"

Will looked Adam square in the eyes, but then looked down. With barely a whisper, he said, "You dying."

"Me, what?"

"You heard me! We're scared of you dying! Dad, you don't take care of your health. You know you don't. Mom says you may need insulin; and yes Dad, I know what that is! Why don't you take it?"

"I'm fine Will. I'm not going anywhere. Believe me." Dodging the question, he continued, "The only place I'm going is into the dining room to eat your mother's amazing dinner. What is that Liz? It smells great!"

"Dad! Stop! I'm really scared. I've only had you in my life for a few years." Will started to cry. "Come on Dad!"

"Okay, I'm sorry. I'm scared too. I'm doing the best I can."

Livid, Will shouted, "You call drinking beer the best you can?"

"I hear you Will; I understand you're upset, but calm down. I'm trying. I've been drinking a long time and it's hard to stop, just like that," he demonstrated by snapping his fingers in the air.

"Tough! I don't care if it's difficult. You always told me that I couldn't get anywhere in life unless I put in effort."

"I'm impressed. You've been listening." Adam was genuinely pleased.

"Dad! You're not listening to me or your own advice. What about insulin? Will you take it or not?" With fire in his eyes, Will looked directly into his dad's eyes, but at that precise moment Liz walked in and announced, "Dinner's ready!"

"What did you make? Please tell me it's my favorite; lasagna?" Adam asked pleadingly.

"Nope! Liver and onions."

"That did it! You're in trouble now!" Adam chased Liz into the kitchen and caught her, giving her an affectionate hug. Neither of them noticed that Will walked off sullen, hurting more than before. His questions were not being addressed and he resented it. As far as he was concerned, his parents were disregarding the seriousness of Adam's illness, and also ignoring him.

"Will?" Liz peered around the counter. "Where are you going?" *No answer.* "Great."

Since he ran away four years ago, Liz's fears had increased anytime she and Will bickered. He was a teenager now and hormones were raging.

"Let him go. He'll be okay." Adam started to pace. "Come on, let's eat."

She grabbed the casserole and started serving. "You're right. There's nothing we can do."

"Of course there is! I could have handled this better, but I'm too damned selfish." Adam's face reddened.

Liz walked over to him and put her arms snugly around him. "You're scared too. We all are. Hanna, Lillie, Will, and I love you. How can we help?"

"Thanks, but I have to do the work myself or accept the inevitable."

"Cut it out Adam! Stop talking that way."

"Dad?"

Startled, they both turned around to see Will was standing right behind them.

"I'm sorry I yelled at you. It's just that I don't want anything to happen to you."

"I know; me neither. I promise you I'll try my best. Now let's eat, I'm starving!"

They sat at the table quietly eating their dinner, each deep in their own thoughts, afraid to broach the subject again.

After Adam left, Liz found Will in his room sulking.

"Will? What's the matter?"

"Mom, in history class last week we talked about Vietnam. It was a bad war, wasn't it?"

"Yes, Will. It was dreadful."

"Dad said he didn't go to Vietnam like the other men. But he didn't tell me why. Instead he changed the subject. Why didn't he go? Wasn't he drafted? Or was he 4F?"

"Wow, Will, that's pretty good. You're learning a lot of important stuff. I didn't know teachers taught about 4F statuses in junior high school."

"Well? Was he 4F?" Will looked directly at his mom and waited for an answer.

"I think you should discuss this with your Dad."

"Mom, will I have to go to war?"

"No Will! Never!" Liz practically screamed the answer and shivered. Vietnam had left scars for everyone, not only those who served.

Will was pensive for a time and then blurted out, "Was my Dad chicken? Is that why?"

# CHAPTER FIFTY-NINE

# WILL

## (1983)

"Mom, is Dad afraid to take insulin? He won't tell me why he doesn't take it."

"He won't tell me either. But, I think it has something to do with his image of what a man should be. He probably thinks he can do this on his own. You know, macho stuff."

"That's stupid! Isn't it?"

"I tend to agree Will, but unfortunately a lot of men are this way. I hope you'll be different."

"Oh believe me Mom, I'll be different than Dad. For one thing, I'll never drink."

"I hope not Will. Your dad started drinking around your age and never stopped."

"Do you think I got through to him?"

"I think you did a good job trying." She sighed.

Will was quiet and pensive for a time. "Mom, Jenny is having a party at her house Friday night. Can I go?"

"Who's Jenny?"

"A girl in my algebra class."

"Will her parents be home?"

"Yes," he lied, his face reddening.

Liz knew that Will was fibbing. Since he was little, he would turn scarlet red when he didn't tell the truth. Like the time when he was ten years old and Liz took him to buy some baseball cards, but forgot to bring her wallet. She promised to bring him back the following day. That evening Liz was doing a wash and noticed an unopened pack of cards that she never saw before sticking out of the rear pocket of Will's jeans. When she questioned him, he did everything possible to cover up his indiscretion. His face turned all colors of the palette, with red streaks outlining his features. Apparently Will had stolen a pack being careful to not let anyone see him. Liz was livid. Early the next day she marched him right back to the store and made him return the baseball cards, hoping the owner wouldn't take any action. Will was lucky. With a thick mid-Eastern accent, the owner mildly chastised Will and explained that the next time he wouldn't be so understanding. After profusely thanking the man, Liz declared Will's punishment: no cards for a month!

"Will..ll?" she drew out his name." Are you telling me the truth?"

"Yes, Mom, honest."

Liz acquiesced for fear of teenage rebellion. She knew things could get rough if she was overprotective. She had heard all sorts of stories of kids doing drugs and she was determined to keep Will safe from harm.

"Okay Will, but I'll pick you up at 9 p.m. sharp!"

"Mom! The kids are staying until 11 p.m."

Liz thought it over and stated unequivocally that 10 p.m. was her final decision.

"Will, want to try some of this?" Jenny's older sister Paula handed me a glass.

Paula was 16 years old and always in trouble. Her boyfriend, two years older than her, was sitting drinking at the far end of the room with two of her friends and their boyfriends.

"Thanks." I took one sip of the horrible smelling alcohol and gagged. Peer pressure was rampant at my school and I wanted to look cool.

"Are you okay?" Paula's face turned white.

"Yeah, it went down the wrong way," I lied. I took another sip.

"Okay, take it easy. I'll be over there if you need anything." She pointed to where her friends were.

Looking around the room, I noticed all the kids were drinking beer and alcohol, and some were smoking cigarettes. A few years ago when I was with dad in California, I smoked cigarettes, but didn't like it much. I'm a lot older now.

Out of the corner of my eye, I saw Jenny walking over to me.

"Are you having a nice time?" she asked.

"Yes, great party!" I lied again." Thanks for inviting me."

In truth I was pissed that I gave into peer pressure. I hated lying to my mom, and worse than that, I wanted nothing to do with drinking or smoking ever again. After seeing what happened to my dad, I promised myself I wouldn't repeat his mistakes.

I was relieved nobody was smoking pot. I didn't smell any, anyway. I never tried pot before and didn't want to, but I knew the weird sweet smell from the kids who smoked outside the school grounds. Many of the kids at my school were experimenting with drugs. It scared me.

Jenny approached looking bleary-eyed. "Did you see Peter in algebra class yesterday? He took out his cheat sheets right in front of Mr. Frye." She giggled.

"I know!" Inadvertently, I reached for my drink, and without realizing it, drank while we talked, until the glass was half-emptied. Jenny's boyfriend then motioned to her and she was off.

The kids around me were making-out. I wished I was one of them. Thirteen years old and I hadn't kissed a girl yet. But I had my eye on one. Pretty sure she had a boyfriend though.

Absentmindedly, I remarked out loud to nobody in particular, "Boy, this is good stuff." But I was becoming disoriented and nervous, and wanted to go home. I glanced at my watch. "Holy shit!" Without saying goodbye to Jenny, I ran outside.

"Hi Mom, I'm on time, right?"

Mom knew immediately I was smashed. She saw my bloodshot eyes, smelled my breath, and let me have it.

"Get in the car right now young man!" she bellowed.

## CHAPTER SIXTY

# LIZ

## (1983)

"I just don't know what to do anymore. I can't believe he came home drunk! Do you have any suggestions? You're his father, after all!"

"As a matter of fact, I do have a suggestion. How about you and I get married."

"What the hell does that have to do with it?" Liz was exasperated. "As usual, you're not taking any responsibility for your son!"

"Don't start that again! You're the one who didn't tell me about Will until he was nine years old; *nine*!" Adam closed his eyes and quieted himself. "Come on, let's calm down and be reasonable. If you and I get married, he will have stability."

"With you drinking? He'll drink more! Why don't *you* be reasonable, and sane, for once in your life?"

"I love you, Liz. I always have."

"Yeah, sure, that's why you slept with Hannah, and slept with her and slept with her."

"I thought you were okay with that. That's what you both said, anyway."

"What choice did we have? It was a done deal."

"Look, think about it Liz. Think about the stability it will give to Will. He'll have two parents, not one, disciplining him in *one* home."

"I don't exactly call this good timing. For God's sake, Adam. Now you propose? After all these years!"

All of a sudden Adam got on his knees and placed a small velvety case in the palm of Liz's right hand.

"Liz, I love you. Please, marry me."

She looked down at the box and stared at it in wonderment.

"Open it Liz."

In it was the most beautiful sparkling diamond she had ever seen. And huge! Liz would have preferred a moderate size, but the setting made her forget about everything else. It was breathtaking! A brilliant four carat round cut diamond was surrounded by tiny baguette diamonds, which glittered and gave the stone a vintage appearance.

"Oh Adam!"

"Do you like it?"

"Are you kidding me? It's...it's stunning!"

"Does this mean you'll marry me?"

Adam didn't wait for her answer. "Put it on Liz; see if it fits. I remembered your size from years ago. Do you still wear the same size?"

Adam had put the ring in a safe deposit box until now, not knowing what to do with it. He knew he would never marry Hanna. He cared deeply about her; she was the mother of his only daughter. But, she was not Liz; the love of his life.

He was filled with anticipation and couldn't seem to catch his breath. Since Valentine's Day six years ago, he had revisited the "M" word many times in his head, but in the last few weeks it had finally come together. He'd be damned if he'd let this opportunity go again. Something was different. He was feeling a bit panicked about his life;

something was wrong. Still young at 35, life seemed short. Maybe it was a premonition. He didn't know. But, what he did know was he had to act swiftly.

All Liz could say was, "Oh Adam," over and over again. She placed the exquisite jewel on her left ring finger.

"It fits perfectly!"

Liz was beaming! She stood on her tiptoes, put her arms around Adam's neck, and kissed him passionately.

"So, when should we do it?" he asked excitedly.

The moment was quickly gone for Liz as she remembered the previous night. Deflated, she replied, "When should we do what?"

"Come on!" Adam squeezed her tightly. "When do we close the deal?"

"Adam, what is the matter with you? Did you forget about Will? His drinking? Can we get back to him before making plans?"

"I think he'll stop drinking once we get married…if he started at all. It was only once. Only one time, Liz! You're panicking for no reason."

"You're not seeing the bigger picture!" Liz was infuriated, but then looked down at her finger and was saddened to cast a pall on such a momentous occasion. "Look, the bottom line is that you are an alcoholic. Will would be exposed to your drinking 24/7. I've wanted to marry you since we were 16 and I still do. But not until you stop drinking." She breathed a sigh of relief having made herself clear.

"So are you saying yes as long as I stop? Because I will, right now. I promise."

"Okay then. I'll make a deal with you. We will set a date for our wedding in six months, and if you haven't touched a drop, not a drop, only then will I go forward."

They closed the deal with a kiss.

"Get over here right now!" Liz practically screamed into the phone.

"What's the matter? Anne groggily answered.

"I have something to show you!"

"This better be important; I'm exhausted. But I must admit you sound frantic."

Although Liz was dubious about the outcome, she was also ecstatic. He had finally proposed!

One hour later Anne came rushing in to find Liz's hand opened, fingers spread out, smack in the middle of her face.

"What? What are you doing?" Becoming aware, Anne screamed, "Oh my God! Adam? He finally did it? Wow, it's gorgeous!" She hugged her oldest friend tightly and tried to catch her breath. "How the hell did that happen? When? No wonder why you called me in the middle of the night! I had to call my baby sitter and tell her it was an emergency."

"Whoa, slow down!" Liz giggled. "Thanks for coming! I couldn't wait until morning. I would have imploded right before your eyes." They both giggled.

Liz filled her in on all the details, starting with her concerns for Will. "If it were just me the decision would be easy. I guess. But Will drank, Anne! He came home drunk!"

"All kids experiment at some point. You and Adam did. Remember? The golf course?"

Anne had a point, but this was different. It was her kid.

"Not at 13 though. He's too young. We were 16." Liz looked miserable.

"Times are different, Liz. What are you going to do?" Anne sat down and sunk into the couch, wishing she could go back to sleep. "Let's talk wedding plans instead." She gave a weak smile.

"Well," Liz mused, "I gave him an ultimatum. Six months of sobriety and then you can all call me, *Mrs. Greenstein*." She gave a little curtsy.

"Okay then. That's a good plan!" Anne gave a sleepy close-mouthed grin. "Can I go home now?"

The next morning, although she knew it would be a mistake and would regret it, Liz reluctantly told her family. First her mother, who screamed into the phone, "When did it happen? How did he do it?" Not letting Liz respond, she jabbered, "Did he give you a ring? Wait! Don't tell me! I'll be over in a jiff." She hung up.

With trepidation, Liz woke Will. The night before he had fallen asleep on the sofa with the TV on and remote in his hand. When Liz came home she gently prodded him upstairs to bed. This morning she let him sleep late.

"Will? Will? Wake up honey. I have something to tell you."

"What Mom? I'm sleeping. Can it wait?"

"Nope! I think you will want to get up to hear this. Your Dad and I…"

Will jumped up and let out a shriek. "I knew it! I just knew it!"

"What?" Liz's mouth opened in surprise.

"Dad proposed, right?"

She grinned widely at her son's delight. "Yes he did! And I said yes. But with one condition."

"Good for you!"

"Wait a minute! You don't even know what the condition is."

"Do you think I'm dumb, Mom?"

"Okay, okay. He has six months."

"Do you think he'll do it?" Will's facial expression was pitifully desperate.

"If this doesn't do it, then nothing will."

"Come on, let's go downstairs and get something to eat."

"I'll be there in a second."

Will rushed to the bathroom, and ran downstairs. His mind was racing. *I can't believe my parents are getting married! This is too good to be true. We'll be a family! Finally!*

Liz was preparing breakfast as Will set the table and asked for details. But her mind was racing too.

Shortly after, the door opened with a thud startling both of them.

"Liz? Where are you?"

"Right here Mom, in the kitchen."

"Grandma, what are you doing here? Did you hear what happened?"

"I sure did! Your mom called me a little while ago."

Liz bent over to kiss her mother's cheek. "Mom, could I get you some coffee? Just made it. And there are extra eggs and bacon if you want. Here, take some orange juice too. I'll put up some toast."

The three of them sat in the kitchen chatting animatedly while they ate a hearty breakfast.

The difficult call was put off for last.

"Hanna? How are you? How's Lillie?"

"We're doing okay? What about you guys?"

"We're okay. Listen, do you have time to talk? Something important has come up."

"Of course. Anything wrong?"

"To the contrary! Everything's right; for me that is. But maybe not for you.

I wished we lived closer so I could tell you in person."

"You're getting me nervous." Hanna's voice faltered. "Wha..t's going on?"

"Well, I shouldn't be the one to tell you. But, I know Adam will procrastinate on this."

"Tell me! What's wrong?"

"Well, as I started to say, nothing is wrong. But..."

"Liz! Cut it out and tell me now!"

"Okay. But, brace yourself."

Hanna let out an exasperated sigh.

"Adam proposed to me last night."

"He what?"

"He asked me to marry him. But, I think it had to do more with Will and his shenanigans lately. Adam wanted to give him security hoping he would stop drinking."

"Wait a minute. Hoping who would stop drinking? What are you talking about?"

Liz related the entire story leaving out details of the exquisite ring now sitting on her left hand.

"Well then, I guess congratulations are in order." Hanna's voice turned cold. "I'll be sure to *not* share this wonderful news with Lillie," she bitterly responded.

"Hanna, I'm sorry! I wasn't thinking of how this might affect her."

Hanna cut in, "Of course not! Why would you? As long as you and Will are happy. Right?"

"No, that's not it! I swear! I was taken off guard, that's all. It was a shock after all these years of wishing and hoping." Liz became quiet. "And, then nothing. Through my pregnancy; through Will's birth, on and on."

"Come on Liz! You never told him about Will until he was... how old...when was it again? Nine years old?"

"Please, Hanna, try to understand. I've known Adam since I was sixteen. Sixteen, Hanna!."

"Yes, Liz. I know all this. But, you try to understand! Lillie *also* needs stability. As far as I'm concerned I don't want to marry the drunk. Goodbye, Liz. I hope you and Adam have a happy life together!"

The phone went dead.

# CHAPTER SIXTY-ONE

# WILL

## (1983)

There was a part of me that was glad I drank at the party. All the kids did. And anyway, I was angry. If my dad could do it, so could I. *I guess.* Yeah; just like what Mom says: *What's good for the goose, is good for the gander!*

Mom's punishment was pretty bad, though. I wasn't allowed to go out at night for one month. That sucked.

But, Mom just gave me the best news ever! She and dad are getting married! I am *spazzing*! This is what I always wanted. *I think.* I kind of like it with just Mom and me. I wonder what it will be like with Dad around. I hope he's not on my back too. He wouldn't do that though. Not if he's busy drinking!

I hated growing up without a dad. I didn't know I even had one until I was nine. That's *crazy*!

I just want to hang out with my friends, but Mom says we'll finally be a family and do things together; like watch TV and stuff. Yuck! Dad should have married Mom when I was a kid. But, Mom was married to Tom, so that wouldn't have worked. *I giggled.*

I wonder what Lillie will say when she hears that Dad's going to live with me, not her. She's too little to understand anyway. Geez, she's only six years old! She'll probably ask if she can visit him or something.

Shit! I can't believe it! Dad just pulled into the driveway. Double shit! I'm getting out of here. He's walking right in without even knocking. What's with him anyway? Man, he pisses me off. He has no right to just walk in.

"Will? Liz? Where are you guys?"

Adam entered the living room, didn't notice any sign of them, and then went from room to room, when he heard a thump behind him. He walked back into the living room and saw Will's foot sticking out from behind the couch.

"Will? Why are you hiding there?"

"I'm not hiding. I always sit here."

"In the corner behind the couch? That's an odd place to hide."

"I told you; I'm not hiding! Why did you walk in without knocking first? *Huh?*"

"Whoa! Why are you so angry? Did I do something?"

"I'm not angry! But, you have no right to walk in unannounced. Okay?"

"Okay, sure. But why not? Your Mom and I are getting married, and, did you forget? I'm your Dad. And, I love you." Adam searched his son's eyes, so much like his own. "I thought you would be happy about this. You're not?"

"I didn't say that. I'm just..." Will looked forlorn. "Confused, all right?"

Adam sat down on the couch and signaled for Will to sit next to him.

"What are you confused about?"

"I don't know. All I know is that I wanted you to be my dad since I was little. I didn't want Tom to be my dad. It wasn't the same thing. You know what I mean?"

"Sure, I get it."

"And now that you are my dad, well, that's okay. But why couldn't you be in my life a long time ago? Like, before Mom met Tom. Like, ..." Teary eyed, Will continued. "When I was being bullied in school, that's when I needed you. Not now! I'm grown up now. I'm a teenager! I don't want you here! Do you hear me? Get out of here!"

Will ran upstairs and slammed the door.

"What happened?" Liz had come home just in time to see Will in a huff.

"Here, let me help you with those."

Placing the food packages on the kitchen counter, Adam filled Liz in.

"Wait, I'm confused. Last night he seemed okay; he was actually excited. I don't get it." She put the rest of the packages away and sat down. "Come to think of it, he was concerned about your drinking. He asked if I thought you would stop."

Pensively, Adam replied, "Well, I hope you told him about our agreement."

"He guessed it!"

"You're kidding? That's pretty smart of him," Adam considered; "intuitive, don't you think?" He continued, "Well then, it's a done deal. In six months we'll be man and wife."

Strangely ill at ease, he turned his head towards the window with a faraway look in his eyes.

## CHAPTER SIXTY-TWO
# ADAM
## (1983)

"How could you do that to Lillie?" Hanna was outraged. "I'm not doing anything to Lillie. I'm trying to do the right thing for Will."

Hanna screamed into the phone, "Like hell you are! You're doing it for yourself, so you can be with Liz. This is what you always wanted and you finally built up the nerve and found a way to do it; through Will!" Her eyes were ablaze, but Adam could not see them, only sense them.

"If I want to be with Liz, all I have to do is ask."

"Look, don't lie to me. I know you. If I hadn't trapped you with Lillie years ago, you and Liz would have been married by now."

"That not true," he muttered under his breath. "That's just not true."

Fed up, he slammed the phone down. He wasn't feeling well, which was happening a lot lately. He was also sick of Hanna and her jealousy. In reality, he *was* concerned about how this change would affect Lillie, eventually anyway. She was still young and wouldn't understand, but right now he had to focus on his health and what

Will was going through. Somehow, he had to stop drinking for Will's sake. Or at least slow down before it was too late.

Goddam, my feet are killing me! I can't take this anymore. There is a freaking ulcer on my foot. It's bleeding! And, how the hell can I walk if my ankles are swollen? The doctor told me if I don't get a handle on this, eventually my feet will have to be amputated. Amputated! No feet! Or did he say legs? He says I need to take insulin. Screw that!

I drank my fifth beer in a row and was on the way to the hard stuff.

Last time I went to the doctor he told me my liver was damaged, damaged beyond repair. My drinking skyrocketed my blood sugar. Wait a minute. What did the doctor say? Maybe it lowered it. I'm fuckin' confused. *Nothing new here.*

I have to shake this depression. This is getting bad. I'm having trouble working. Jesus Christ, I'm having trouble getting it up. I'll tell Liz I need to put the wedding off; that's all.

Come on you asshole! Get your act together! You have a beautiful daughter, a dynamite son. What the hell is the matter with you? Do you want to lose everything?

Okay, so maybe I'll go back to AA. Nah, I'll do it myself. Liz says I shouldn't bring any beer or alcohol into the house. That's easy. Except that won't help when I'm out. I'll just go to a bar. Why the hell am I afraid of the insulin anyway? Maybe I should go to a shrink. Last time I spoke to Uncle Harry he said that might help. I remember though, when my ditzy aunt went to one, she was put on all sorts of meds and was sent to the nuthouse. She went crazy. And I mean crazy. So, no; no insulin, no docs, and definitely no shrinks! I'll do it on my own.

"Liz, can I come over?"

"Adam? You sound funny. Everything okay?"

"Yeah, I'm just tired. Long week. Glad it's Saturday. Five o'clock okay?"

"Sure. Will won't be here though. He's at a movie with a friend."

"Any chance the friend is a girl? He's been talking a lot lately about the opposite sex!"

"Nope. No girls yet. He's still young. Geez! Give him a chance!" Liz winced in spite of herself.

She thought back to when Adam and she first met. They were sixteen and very much in love. But, too young. Liz wanted more for Will. She wanted him to experience life first; meet different people. Not go through what she and Adam went through. Pregnant at 19 years old! They could have been married all this time – if only she had told him. If only he had stopped the booze. If only.

"Liz?"

Startled out of her reverie, she shouted, "Adam? I'm in the kitchen, just finishing the dishes."

Adam walked over and put his arms around her. "Liz, I'm going to do this on my own."

"What, the dishes?" She smiled and kissed him gently on the lips.

"Quit drinking."

"That's great Adam! I hope so." Her stomach turned, as she knew the outcome.

"I need more time though, before we get married. I want to be sober for both of you, not just Will"

"Oh." She didn't expect this and her stomach now roiled.

"Isn't that what you want? For me to totally stop drinking?"

309

"Of course that's what I want! But..." Liz dead-stopped talking.

"What? What were you going to say?" Adam knew what was coming.

"It's just that you always say that. You're procrastinating like you always do; with drinking that is."

"I know it looks that way, but honestly, I will do it this time. I promise. And then we'll plan our big day. But for now I've got to quit the sauce.

"What do you mean he's not paying his bills? Look Gene, just tell him...."

Adam was cut-off with a slew of profanities and orders to be in the LA office in two days or else.

*Oh well. All these plans I had with Will. Down the drain. For now, anyway*, Adam thought to himself. *But, I'll be with Lillie! I miss her. I wonder what she's up to.* And then another thought occurred to Adam which shifted his mood even more. His heart started pounding. *Shit! I don't want to see Hanna. She'll be on my back about Liz and me marrying; even though I put it off. I can't take this anymore.*

After winding up business in his NY office, Adam went home to the island and finished packing. Reservations were set and all that was left was telling Liz and Will that he would be leaving again. For how long he did not know. But what he did know was that he was tired. Tired of traveling back and forth.

What Adam was not prepared for was a surprise waiting for him in LA.

310

## CHAPTER SIXTY-THREE
# LIZ
## (1983)

"Hi."

"Hi," Liz said weakly.

Anne walked in and placed her pocketbook down. She knew her best friend well and sensed a deep sadness.

"What's wrong?"

"He's off to California again."

"Work-related or Hanna?" Anne asked.

"Probably both."

"Sorry," Anne offered. "Did you at least talk some wedding plans before he left?"

"No, but that's okay. I should take it under my stride by now, like Will. He goes with the flow, kind of like a kite." Liz feebly smiled.

"Like this?" Lightening their moods, Anne put her hands in the air and demonstrated fly-like movements.

""Oh no!" Liz made a goofy face and flew with her, as they danced through the air.

They both plopped down on the couch laughing.

"What's going on with you?" Liz asked.

"Nothing much, except Fred wants the kids more often."

"How much more often?" Liz's eyes widened.

"Like, every day! He's playing dirty; actually dirtier. Get a load of this!" she said angrily. "He thought Rose was a passing thing. That my *tendency* towards lesbianism would die. And now that it hasn't he's through pussyfooting around. He has a court date one month from now."

"Oh my God! I'm so sorry! What are you going to do? Do you have a lawyer yet?"

"No, the court will address one to me. I hope."

"Okay. Do you want me to come? You know, to give you support."

"Rose will come." Anne's face contorted. "But I wonder if that's a mistake. Do you think it is? Will it make matters worse?"

"I'm not sure." Liz was concerned for her friend and tried to think of something useful that would help, but couldn't. She said, without conviction, "You're a good mother, Anne. Focus on that."

"No, mom. I am not looking for a wedding gown. There's no point because he's put it off again. And, not only that, he's gone."

Belligerent, Liz's mom cried, "What? Why?"

"Please, just leave it alone. I'll let you know when the wedding is, or if it is!" Liz hung up in tears.

"Mom?" Will shouted from his room. "What's the matter?" He swiftly ran down to the living room. "What happened?"

"I'm sorry to scare you. Your dad left again."

"I know Mom. He told me. Is that why you're crying? He always goes to California. Did something else happen?" His stomach churned and he recalled a similar twinge when he was cornered by the crazy man at Grand Central Station. "Dad's not worse, is he?" Starting to panic, Will cried, "He'll be back, right?"

# HANNA

"Come on Lillie, start putting your toys in the carton. Wait a minute! Maybe put them in this one. It's bigger."

Lillie was just six years old and anxious to help her mother.

"Hanna, Hanna, Hanna. Like this?"

"Yes! Very good!"

Hanna was ambivalent about the move, but it was time. It would be advantageous for Lillie to be near her brother, and more importantly, Adam. She needed her father. Sure, he came to California frequently, but spent much more in New York. She grimaced. *With Will. And yes, Liz.* Hanna was infuriated. *How could he! He has some nerve!*

"Lillie turn off the music and stop dancing! There will be plenty of time for that when we get to New York."

Lillie had stopped packing her toys and turned her attention to the music on the radio. She was listening to classical music on her own volition. Since she was a baby the violin was her favorite instrument.

"Will you buy me a violin there? I want to learn how to play it. It's squeaky just like my doll. Aunt Liz plays the violin and she squeaks too!"

"Ninety-nine miles from LA" kept going through Liz's head, which made her more melancholy than the night before. *God, I love that song. Johnny Mathis' voice is so beautiful!* Liz's chain of thought was relieved by the phone ringing.

"Hello?"

"It's me Liz." Hanna's voice was unmistakable after all these years. But even at the beginning of their friendship, Liz recognized her tone at the onset of a syllable. She had a distinct Californian accent. "I have news. Big news."

"I hope it's good! What's going on?" Liz knew that Hanna's and her relationship was shaky right now, which made her uncomfortable. She wondered what Hanna would share with her.

"Lillie and I are moving to New York. Our flight is tomorrow."

Liz was dumbstruck and struggled to find the right words. "Well, that is big news. What brought that on?" *As if she didn't know.*

"It's time. That's all. It will be wonderful for Lillie and Will, don't you think?" Hanna looked in the direction of Lillie and saw her swaying to the music again, undoubtedly a violin concerto. "Liz, you won't believe this, but Lillie has taken to the violin. Your instrument! She's been swaying back and forth, and dancing to classical music, of all things; especially the violin, since she was a baby. And, all morning long!"

Liz was impressed. "Yes, I remember Adam telling me. That's awesome. Maybe I could give her some lessons after you settle down. Do you know where you'll be living? Will it be close by to me, or Adam?" She silently prayed this wasn't so.

"Not sure yet, but we're renting an apartment in Manhattan in the meantime. I lined up a position there a few weeks ago."

"Boy, that was fast! Well, I wish you luck." Liz paused and changed course. "Look Hanna, I'm truly sorry about everything. I hate that we are at odds with each other. I only want the best for you. I hope you believe me."

"Thank you, Liz. Thanks for saying that. I want the best for you too. But I have to think about Lillie and what's best for her. And, moving is what is best. She needs her dad. If Adam won't relocate to LA, then we will live near him."

"Are you saying that Adam and you talked about him moving to LA?" Liz started to panic. "Is that what you're saying?"

"No Liz, we never discussed that. I guess I wanted to believe that one day..."

Liz cut her off. "Hanna, I have news for you too."

# CHAPTER SIXTY-FOUR

# ADAM

## (1983)

"Adam? What are you doing here? I was just speaking with Liz… hung up when I heard you at the door. Did she know you were coming here? She didn't mention it."

Not replying, he looked all around the apartment in disbelief. "What is all of this? Why the cartons? You're not moving, are you?" Adam's face was rapidly reddening. "You wouldn't leave without telling me, would you?"

"Calm down Adam. We are moving, but to you. To New York!"

"You're what? When were you going to tell me this?"

"Adam, Adam, Adam!" Lillie ran to Adam.

He ached to pick her up in his arms and hold her tightly, but knew better.

"Lillie, sweetheart!" How are you?"

"We're going on the airplane, we're going on the airplane ride, up in the clouds, near the moon! And, Adam, Adam, Adam…"

"That's super! But slow down Lillie, take a breath," Adam said lovingly.

"And, we're going to live with you!"

"You are?" Adam asked, stupefied.

"Well, that's even more super!" he said, feigning enthusiasm.

He walked over to Hanna and whispered, "You can't move in with me. Where did you come up with that stupid idea?" he said incredulously.

"I know Adam. Lillie means we're moving to New York."

Relief flooded his senses. "Why the big move? I will be here, actually for a while," he said wearily.

"I think it's about time that Lillie be near her father. That's all."

"Bullshit!"

"Watch your language in front of her, please," Hanna reproached.

"Look, I know you're upset about Liz and me, but that's no reason to go to such extremes." Adam was too tired to argue anymore.

"It's a done deal. We leave tomorrow. I have an apartment set up in Manhattan and I also lined up a position. It will be good for all of us, including Will. After all, it's his sister."

"Which company?" Adam knew it was unlikely their firms would have reason to interact, but the thought unnerved him. He wanted peace, and as much as he wanted to be near Lillie, Hanna's new revelation had shaken him.

"I will be the HR manager of 'Bennett and Brewster'. It's a large legal firm, close by to you actually."

"Yeah, I know the place," he said dismayed.

"And where's the apartment?"

"I feel as if you're giving me the third degree. Sorry you're unhappy that Lillie will live close to you!"

"Shhh...Don't let her hear that! That's not true! I want peace, that's all. I want to start a life with Liz. It's a long time coming. I'm tired Hanna. Tired of leading two lives. I care about you. You know that. Don't you?" Not giving her a chance to answer, he continued. "But it's time to make a choice, and it's always been Liz. From the beginning I've tried to be clear on that."

"I understand. We had a good thing you and I. The sex was great. But you know what Adam? Lillie needs more than your occasional visits."

"But Hanna, that doesn't make sense. I'm not in New York all the time. So why make our lives more complicated by moving to New York? The kids will feel the friction."

"Do you really think that Lillie and Will never felt friction between the three of us before? Come on! It's a done deal Adam, so accept it."

"Jesus Christ Hanna! Must you always get your way? This time you're involving other people's lives, not just yours. And, one of those people is your own kid! I can't believe you're doing this!" Without a word to Lillie, he slammed the door and left.

"Hanna, Hanna, Hanna. Where did Adam go?" Lillie ran to the door. "Daddy?"

Hanna ignored her daughter and grabbed the phone to dial Liz.

"I'm sorry Liz. Adam walked in just as you were about to tell me something. He just left. Please, go ahead."

"He called off the wedding," Liz blurted out. "Or at least postponed it," she mumbled, embarrassed.

"He what? Then why....." Confused and baffled at the irony, Hanna abruptly ceased talking and placed the receiver back on the hook, leaving Liz in a quandary.

# PART III

# CHAPTER SIXTY-FIVE
# ADAM
## (1986)

I had to leave. I couldn't let them see me this way. They would pity me. Liz deserves more. I'll be damned if I hurt her again. Leaving was best for everyone.

Montreal seems different now. Several buildings were recently erected, but many old ones remain. The atmosphere is post-war, devoid of "hippies", American and Canadian; however, I detect a more freewheeling environment wherever I go. No one is afraid anymore.

I checked out some of my old friends at *Pierre and Fontaine.* Some had moved on, including Gene, but it was good to see the rest of the gang even though they were startled to see my radically changed appearance. Twelve years is a long time, but I hadn't only aged; I was unrecognizable.

I am thinner now; like a skeleton. I avoided shaking hands, as mine are yellowed and sickly looking. My overall skin color is another matter; it is deathly white. My hair has thinned, and what is left of it, has an unnatural dullness. My cheekbones are bony, and cheeks hollowed. I have trouble walking, even with a cane. My feet, which purposely wear a size too large, have numerous sores and ulcers which make it difficult for me to balance myself. My right eye wears a patch, as it has lost its vision; my left eye is blurry at best. I am not a pretty sight. And yes, I still drink. The doctors are amazed I have lived this long without insulin. The inevitable is near and I am scared.

Several times I visited my old hang-out, *The Yellow Door*, secretly hoping to bump into Bettina. She never appeared. I will always care about her and wonder what happened. It was a good thing anyway, because I wouldn't want her to see me this way.

I have so many regrets, starting with not being man enough to stop drinking. How could I have done this to the people I care about? I had so many dreams; dreams of watching my children grow up to be adults. What will Will become? Maybe a teacher? He expressed interest in that a while ago. I forget what he wants to teach though. What did he say? Math? Wouldn't that be a kick if he also became an accountant? I'll never know though, will I? Damn it! Why did this happen?

And, Lillie. What will become of her? Will she find her way? She needs me, although, she has her mother. Hanna will help her; I'm sure of that. But what *will* happen to Lillie? What kind of future does she have with that damned disability? Music makes her happy. Maybe... just maybe...something will fall into place for her.

Liz, the love of my life. I wish I could tell her how many regrets I have. I've loved her since I was...how the hell old were we? Sixteen? Holy shit! It was always Liz; nobody else compared to her...except, *perhaps in bed*. She may have been my first, but damn, Bettina... Hanna...whoa! I hope Liz meets someone soon. She's spent too many years waiting for me. Shit! I feel so bad. She's been patient with me. I'm a prick! Maybe I should call her? Nah. Let her forget about me. Anyway, it's been four years. She probably moved on.

Hanna. The mother of my sweet Lillie. It wasn't meant to be. But, we sure were good together, weren't we? In bed, that is.

Two years ago, when I called Uncle Harry and swore him to secrecy about where I was, he sounded as if he was crying. He lost Steve to drugs and now he's losing me. I loved the old man with his jingling loose change. He's been a good uncle. But, he's so damned old what does it matter? He's going to croak any day now. Can't believe he's not in a nursing home. Good genes, I guess. Damn, I bet I croak before him. How old is he? Ninety, what? I felt the sting of tears in my eyes.

Edouard. I wish I could have saved you. You were a kid, so young, with a future ahead of you. I wonder what would have become of you. A doctor? A lawyer? A teacher, like Will might become? I'm so, so, sorry. I would have done anything for you not to have died. That damned asshole driver! Let him rot in hell!

Well, now what? I've got to figure out a way to get around in this Goddamned wheelchair without people pitying me. Maybe I'll stay home; never go out. After all, I only have one eye. Can't see very much. What's the point? I should probably wind up my estate and will. and make sure my life insurance is in order. Ha! Can't get very far too quickly. It will take a year or two with these fucking wheels. I've got to do something to stop this from happening. But what? What can I do? Too late to stop drinking. Too late for insulin. Too fucking late.

A strange guffaw emanated from Adam as he fell asleep. He dreamt of wheels flying free of his chair, reaching for his hands and grasping them, as he was lifted into the stratosphere and into the heavens, almost a "Chagall-like" vision, where he finally found peace. It is there that he ministered those in need. One by one, alcoholics everywhere came to him for help. Slowly, each wretched soul began to celebrate their sobriety. Surrounded by emptied bottles of scotch, bourbon, and gin, and thousands of beer cans, they rejoiced with song and danced on top of crushed broken bottles. In the background, Cat Steven's "Moon Shadow" played, telling us all to be hopeful in the face of adversity; to not fear losing one's eyes, one's limbs.

*"Halleluiah! Thank you King Stuart our savior!"*

Adam bowed from the waist, and then walked off into God's parlor where Liz, Will, and Lillie awaited his presence. God was sitting in a throne, drinking a beer. Simultaneously, Liz, Will, and Lillie smiled at Adam and said, *"Good job, Dad."*

*"Liz! I'm not your dad! I'm your savior, aren't I? Don't you know that? Don't you love me anymore? Liz? Liz?"*

*"Not until you stop drinking!"* she cried.

*"Will, don't leave me! Don't listen to her! I'm your dad, aren't I?"*

Adam grabbed the arms of the wheelchair. *"Lillie, where are you? Lillie?"*

When Adam awakened, he was still in his living room where he dozed, anxious and disoriented.

# CHAPTER SIXTY-SIX

# LILLIE

## (1988)

"Hanna, when will Daisy arrive?"

Lillie had evolved. She no longer repeated names or words unless she was under stress, good or bad. But on occasion, she still called her parents by their first name. It was apparent she had outgrown some of her foibles, but much of her disability still needed special attention. It was obvious to those around her that Lillie was different. The kids at school shunned her. She was an outcast. At ten years old, she was unnaturally formal. One day at school, Lillie's schoolmates ganged up on her against the schoolyard fence and taunted her. They expected her to cry, but instead Lillie spoke in her robotic monotone voice and said, "This is inappropriate; please stop this right now." One by one, each girl walked away and although they were still mocking her, they left nonplussed.

Lillie's academics suffered. She struggled with all subjects, except one. Unlike most Autistic children, she thrived in math. Although intelligent, she couldn't focus on anything other than math and music and how they related to each other. It soothed her. Hanna would find

Lillie in her room with scores of music on her lap, while working on complex mathematical equations and equating the two. She was obsessed with harmonies and melodies and how they interplayed with each other. While children were riding bikes, or taking ballet and tap lessons, she was immersed in a world of music and her violin.

Soon after they moved to New York, Hanna hired a violin teacher who was known to work with the disabled. Lillie, however, was far from disabled when it came to the violin. Daisy taught students who eventually became highly proficient with their instrument. At the young age of eight, Lillie started playing as if she were a pro and was considered a prodigy by the time she was ten.

"In twenty minutes Lillie. Did you practice your scales?"

"Yes mom, all six of them. And the Beethoven sonata, No.1 in D, Op. 12," she said matter-of-factly, "My favorite! Listen!"

Lillie picked up the bow, applied rosin to it, and played the first four scales for her mother; the A# minor scale and its relative, Gm; and B major and its relative, G# minor, and then performed the sonata.

"Very good Lill'! Oh, wait, here she is! I'll get the door."

"Well, hello Lillie! Good morning Hanna! I hope this bright cheery morning finds both of you well! So sorry I'm running late. Dreadful traffic, just dreadful!"

Daisy walked in and settled herself in her accustomed chair. She was a woman of great stature, elegantly dressed in a navy blue suit, with a silvery coiffured pixie haircut; and although she lived in the United States most of her adult life, Daisy's English accent was still perceptible.

"Good morning Daisy! I will leave the two of you alone for your practice session. Enjoy your lesson Lillie. Play well, as you always do!" Hanna walked out of the music room.

Hanna looked out her living room bay window, partially closed off with a rose colored scalloped curtain, as she listened to her daughter play the Beethoven sonata. *Splendid! She is brilliant! If only Adam was here to hear her play,* she thought.

Hanna was lost without Adam. She knew he wasn't *totally* hers, but she counted on him. And needed him. She would lie to herself and others that Adam's presence was necessary for Lillie's sake, but the truth was that she cared deeply about him. He had been omnipresent in her life for many years and she needed him to be part of her life once again.

Hanna and Liz regained their friendship out of solidarity, but things were never the same. She almost lost Adam to Liz in the most humiliating way, through marriage. But, there was no marriage for either of them. They both lost. Hanna and Liz waited by the phone every day with no explanation forthcoming.

*Oh look!* A blanket of pigeons covered the cobblestone of Chambers Street. Exactly one year to the day, after living in a rat infested apartment, a common scenario, but one classier than most in Manhattan dwellings, she and Lillie finally moved to Tribeca into a three story condominium. It was complete with two bedrooms, two bathrooms, a parlor which she used as Lillie's music room, and a living room, all with polished hardwood floors and elegant high ceilings, extraordinary to most.

It was the weekend and Hanna was due back to work tomorrow. She was going to lunch with a coworker she hadn't met yet. She overheard a woman talking to her boss about her twelve year old nephew who had Autism, and by sheer coincidence was a violinist. She hadn't met any parents of Autistic children and was excited to share stories and hopefully gain helpful information. But, this was too good to be true; a violinist, same as Lillie. Hanna was desperate for support, especially since Adam was gone.

Hanna looked at her watch for the second time. Ten minutes had gone by.

She glanced again; another ten minutes. The anticipation was killing her. Abruptly she rose and left her work in disarray.

They were meeting at a Mexican restaurant at 12 noon, three blocks from work. She sat down at a table for two and ordered a whiskey sour.

*Whew! Strong!* She looked up and saw a woman staring at her.

"Are you Hanna?"

"Yes; Adrienne? How did you recognize me?" Embarrassed, Hanna said, "I'm sorry, please, sit down."

"You mentioned you would be wearing a brown tailored suit; remember?"

Hanna looked down at her clothes. "Ah, yes! I did at that. I was excited to meet you, so I left early." Feeling intimidated, she looked at her watch again. "I see you did too."

The first thing Hanna noticed was Adrienne's broad smile with egregiously buck teeth; however, perfectly aligned. Her jet black hair was wild and concealed the rest of her smallish face. She wore a dated paisley dress falling just below her knees, equally outrageous.

"I ordered a drink...hope you don't mind."

Adrienne sat down. She looked at the whiskey and then up at Hanna. "Early in the day for one of those, don't you think?" She motioned for the waitress. "I'll have the same."

Hanna inquired, "How long have you worked for the company?"

"A long time, maybe 20 years. After my sister died, though, I decreased my hours in order to take care of my nephew."

"Oh, I didn't know you were his primary caregiver." Hanna paused. "Well, that makes it even better." Mortified, she mumbled, "Sorry, I meant..."

"Don't worry about it." Adrienne sneered at Hanna. "Tell me about your Lillie. How old is she?"

"Lillie is ten years old. And your nephew?"

"Matt is..."

"Twelve, right? Oh, sorry, didn't mean to interrupt." Hanna's face flushed. The woman was staring coolly at her, in fact she was glaring. "I'm sorry, did I do something to off...ffend you?" Hanna began to stutter, possibly for the first time in her life, and cringed. "I mean prior to my last comment."

"No." Adrienne continued to glare.

"Okay." *Shit. What's her problem?* Hanna was getting pissed.

"So, let's get down to business. What information would you like from me? I will tell you that Matt is a violinist, same as your Lillie. As a matter of fact, in a few weeks he is attending a program in Canada to better his skills. And from there we hope to present him as a concert pianist."

"So fast? Wow!"

"Yes." Still glaring.

"Well, that is precisely what I'd like to know. How do I get hooked up with this program?"

"Well, you don't get hooked up with them," sneering more fiercely. "You have her auditioned. I will give you the number and then I must go."

"But, you haven't eaten yet."

"Yes." Adrienne fished through her purse with a highfalutin air, pulled out a pad, and scribbled down the number. "Here you go." And she was off.

*Pompous ass!* Hanna drew out a breath.

When Hanna got home after work, she immediately dialed the number of the music program. *Closed! Damn!* She looked down at her watch. *Missed them by two minutes. Oh well; they open early.*

"Lillie? Are you doing your homework? Dinner's soon."

The following morning promptly at 8 a.m. she called them back. "Hello? Bonjour. Could I speak with someone about the music program designated for disabled children? My daughter is Autistic."

# CHAPTER SIXTY-SEVEN

# LIZ

## (1988)

"Mom, do you think Dad will ever come back?"

Will was having trouble concentrating lately. The more time passed, the more restless he became. He even thought about dropping out of college. But it reminded him of his dad's beginnings, after *his* father had died, the grandpa he had never met. Will didn't want to repeat his dad's mistakes. He would tough it out in school, and trust that his father would return one day to see him graduate.

Liz had given up hope, though. Adam had been missing for nearly four years. She and Hanna had used every resource they had to find him, but to no avail. The police; Gene; his old boss; his work buddies and contacts; and even Uncle Harry, who was now old and ailing, had no clue to Adam's whereabouts. He was on the missing person's list.

"Will, which course did you switch from? Was it economics?"

"Yes, I decided to take the accounting one instead next semester. Mom, please answer me. Why are you ignoring me?"

"Your father would be so proud of you...you know, following in his footsteps." Liz sighed. She had given up all hope, but secretly prayed he was at least, alive. *Please Adam, be okay! Come home!*

331

Annoyed, Will shouted, "Mom!" Why are you doing this?"

Liz flinched. "I'm sorry Will. It's still hard for me. Four years have passed and I still miss him so much. And, I can't stop wondering if he's hurt, or even...."She stopped herself.

"Say it Mom! Say it! Dead! Right?"

"Yes, dead." Liz paled and sat down. "I'm so sorry Will."

"What are you sorry for Mom? It's not your fault. It's nobody's fault, I guess." Will rose from the beaten up wicker chair and started pacing. "You know what Mom? I'm pissed! Pissed as all hell! It seems to me that Dad is a coward." Will's voice was intensifying. "When all the other men went to war, what did my dad do? He was a draft dodger, for God's sake! A damn draft dodger! The other men didn't want to fight in Vietnam either, but they went. What the hell was wrong with him? I'll tell you why he didn't go! Because he's a sissy! He was even too scared to take insulin and save his own life for his kids' sake," Will said sarcastically. "And now? Now he doesn't even have the balls to at least say goodbye to us! Why didn't he have the balls? Huh? Go ahead! Answer me!" he screamed. "Answer me!"

"Will, please, watch your mouth." She got up and walked over to him and put her arms around her sobbing son. "I know. I know. I'm so sorry honey. I'm so sorry."

I looked down at my engagement ring still sitting on my ring finger and wept. It was the most beautiful diamond I had ever seen. Flawless. At least he did something right. How could he leave us like that? How the hell could he leave Will and Lillie? No explanation! Damn him! Please God, let him be all right! Where is he? Please tell me!

For the first few months after Adam was gone, I was angry and confused. I was desolate. My feelings were jumbled every moment of the day. Memories engulfed me and ruled me. Each day I got up for work and walked through the motions, numb. My parents suggested I seek therapy. I didn't go. I didn't care. I was lifeless. I lost sight of what was happening to Will. He became a man overnight, without my awareness, without my guidance. And now he's in trouble and I don't know how to help him because I can't even help myself. I've tried to solve the mystery: *where is Adam, where did he go?* But nothing makes sense. Years have passed and I'm still in mourning. I need closure.

Adam is my heart. But Will is right. He may be dead and I must live my life without him. Four years is a long time to be missing. But, it happened once before and he came back. Maybe, just maybe, he'll come home again.

"Anne, are you seeing the kids this weekend?" Liz asked reluctantly. "Want to go to a movie Saturday, bring them along? There's a *James Bond* one at 3 p.m. I could really use the company."

Four years ago, Anne had lost custody but was granted full visitation rights. Ruth and Sam were now teenagers, 15 and 16 years old respectively. With much criticism from those around them, she and Rose were living together making a life for themselves.

Anne had changed. She had become cynical of everyone and everything, especially the law. How children could be forcibly taken from their mother was beyond her. She was a good mother. But according to the courts, not good enough. She had a shortcoming. She preferred women and one in particular. Rose. Anne fought hard in the courts; so damn hard, she was almost arrested. The proceedings ended unfavorably.

# FOUR YEARS PRIOR

Anne rose from her seat, lunged towards the judge, arms flailing in the air, and screamed, "You will not take my children from me! You will not! Do you hear me?" She fell to her knees sobbing and begging.

An officer of the court grabbed her arms and held her, while the judge slammed his gavel. "Order in the court. Order! Do you hear *me*?" In the end her protests were unheard and unrecognized. She was damned lucky not to have been thrown behind bars. And, equally as lucky to have full visitation rights. But, that decision nearly destroyed her. She fell apart.

"I hate you, you son of a bitch! These are *my* kids, not yours! You cheated on me, you bastard! And now you're taking my kids away from me! Over my dead body! Do you hear me?"

"Calm down! You got full visitation rights," Fred said. "Stop getting hysterical or they'll declare you unfit to have any rights. You wouldn't want that to happen, would you?"

Rose took Anne's hand and led her out the chamber doors to their car. "Come, let's go home sweetheart." She practically had to carry her out. Anne was devastated and in terrible shock. "It'll be okay. We'll take it to the Supreme Court." But Anne didn't hear one word Rose uttered. She wanted to die.

One week had passed and Anne still wouldn't get out of bed, nor was she eating. "Please, try some of this soup I made for you. It's your favorite; chicken! You need nourishment," Rose pleaded.

"She's despondent," Rose remarked to Liz one day when she came by. "I don't know what to do. Do you think I should hospitalize her?"

"No. let's talk to Fred first. Maybe we can reason with him. Have the kids visit her. That will cheer her up," Liz said unconvincingly.

"Liz, I hate to say this. It's so horrible. But she's talking about suicide. I'm scared for her."

"Ruth will probably want to go, but not Sam. I'm not sure he's even coming. I think he has a girlfriend!"

"Wow!" Liz immediately turned her thoughts to Will and his new steady.

"They're growing up so fast!"

"Too fast! Let me ask Ruth, but either way, I'll go."

"By the way...how's Rose doing?" Liz asked with genuine concern.

"She's been in remission for a while now; thanks for asking. It was a long haul for her. I think she became sick not long after I started recouping from my disaster."

"Well, maybe in some providential way it got you back on your feet. You know, maybe it was God's way of saying 'Get your act together.' I was so scared for you. I never heard you talk that way before. I mean really Anne! Suicide? I don't know what I would do without you and your friendship." As an afterthought, Liz said, "Tell Rose I'm so glad she's out of the woods. Cancer is nothing to sneeze at."

"So, I'll meet you at the movies at 3 p.m., okay?" Anne hung up before Liz responded. *What the hell is wrong with her anyway?*

Ashamed, Liz reproached herself, *Dammit! I am so stupid! How could I have been thoughtless about something as serious as suicide? I'm an insensitive jerk!*

# CHAPTER SIXTY-EIGHT

# LILLIE

## (1988-1989)

"Lill', hurry up! We're late!"

"I am hurrying! Do you have my violin?"

"Yes, hurry!"

"Is it in its case? Is the bow there? Hanna, Han... the resin!" Lillie was having a meltdown since early morning and started to run in circles. She had only done that two times in her young life. Once, after Adam and Hanna argued, he had slammed the door in anger without saying goodbye; the second time was in reaction to Hanna's news of his disappearance.

Exasperated, Hanna shouted, "Lillie! Please calm down. Take a deep breath." She was trying to get her ready for what seemed like hours. "Now, let's go before we miss the train! Everything is waiting for you by the door." Hanna looked around one last time as she turned off the lights. "There he is! The cabdriver is honking the horn."

"Hanna, Hanna, Hanna," Lillie raised her tired looking face and with pleading eyes looked directly into her mother's. "I'm apprehensive."

Impressed by her daughter's choice of words, Hanna couldn't help but smile. She was also anxious, but reassured her. "That's understandable, Lillie. You will be fine!"

Six months prior to their departure, Hanna filled out the necessary paperwork to present her daughter to the illustrious panel in Montreal. She then brought Lillie to the school where she was tested and accepted into their prestigious program designed for disabled children. These children, of both genres and similar ages, and with comparable talent, also played stringed instruments. Along with their newest enrollee, Lillie Greenstein, many would go on to become world prodigies.

I'm excited to attend my new school. My mother told me I will play my instrument every day. My instrument is the violin. The music I play on my violin makes me happy. Especially the squeaky noises, as long as they're not too loud. Loud noises bother my ears. I get headaches and feel confused. *Squeak!*

I will also attend my academic classes. Math, English, social studies, and science. I like math the best. My brother Will likes math best too. My father also likes math. But, my mother says my father is dead. I don't think he's dead. I think he's alive. Will thinks my father is alive too. But, he's angry at my father for leaving us. I'm perplexed. The other day I looked this word up in the dictionary after reading a book about math and science and how perplexing they are if you don't pay attention to the way they interplay with each other. Then I looked up the word "interplay" and felt perplexed.

I knew I was different than my friends in school at home. They made fun of me. My father told me that they weren't *really* my friends. I call them my friends so I won't feel different. I had one *real* friend though. But she moved, and now I moved.

337

My mother told me the kids in my new school are different, just like me. The best part is that they play musical instruments. They play the violin, viola, cello, bass and piano. The violin is the best one. It calms me down when I'm nervous, as long as those squeaky sounds don't get too loud!

My father once told me he had a special violin saved for me when I get older. But, he didn't know I liked the violin. So why did he want to give it to me? Another perplexing matter! I haven't seen my dad in four years. My Aunt Liz said he's dead too. I don't understand the word *dead*. But I know I don't like it because my father is never here to see me play my violin and I've been playing since I'm six years old. That's a lot of years! My mother told me that. But my father didn't know that. Maybe that's why he didn't give me his violin before he left. I wonder if he ever played it.

My Aunt Liz plays the violin. She's not really my aunt though. Perplexing! She plays in an orchestra in front of an audience with *a lot* of people. I don't think I'd like that. It might be too noisy. My mom says I'll be a vir-tu-o-so and play solo. *SOLO! So Low. Soo-loow.* I like the way that word sounds. I hope a vir-tu-o-so doesn't play in front of an audience. Unless the audience is different like I am. Then they won't make fun of me.

My mom says I will meet famous violinists; maybe Joshua Bell, and I should prepare my questions. I don't have to prepare them. I know them by heart. I know who Joshua Bell is because Daisy told me all about him. He started playing violin when he was four years old, even younger than me. I want to be just like him, except he plays other types of music, not only classical. I only want to play classical pieces. I have lots of questions for him. One of my questions is: do I have to play in front of an orchestra? My new violin teacher says I can play in a quartet with three other instruments: a cellist, a bassist, and a violist, and me makes four. My mother said she is proud of me for pronouncing these musical terms.

Miss Grahm is my new teacher. She has a funny hairdo. It's big. *BIG!* She plays the violin *really* well, without too many squeaky noises. *Squeak!* She's okay, but I miss Daisy. Sometimes Daisy played too loud. She said she'll come to my concert one day. That makes me happy. But, that means I'll have an audience! Maybe Will and Aunt Liz will come too.

Will is going to visit me during the summer. He'll be finished with his schoolwork from college. But, then he goes back in August. When he visits me we will take a bus ride and go to an amusement park. It's on the World's Fair grounds. I've never seen one, but I know it's not there anymore. But the rides are! Roller coaster rides and carousel rides and a haunted house and a pirate house. *SCARY!* If it's too noisy, Will says we can go back home to my school.

I'm sad because my mother is leaving me here alone at school. I've never been alone. I feel nervous. She has to go back to work in New York where our new home is. I don't want to go back there. It's like Los Angeles. The kids don't like me. I like being here with my new friends and my violin!

Lillie's world had changed. She was meeting children whom she could relate to. She was no longer a pariah. She found a home with other gifted disabled children. Lillie did not realize how gifted she was, though. All she knew was that the violin was important to her very being. But more than that was happening. She was on her way to becoming a renowned violinist in later years. She also was unaware of the magnitude of the gift waiting for her. And, the devastating news which would follow.

# CHAPTER SIXTY-NINE

# LIZ

## (1988-1989)

"Mom?" Will walked from room to room, and yelled out again, "Mom? Are you home?"

"Yes Will, coming! Be there in a second."

Liz came flying down the stairs. She was still experiencing empty nest syndrome and sorely missed her son, although he did come home often. The college was only a little over an hour away. Will was sharing an apartment near the school with four of his friends. Two of them had part time jobs, and the other two, including Will, were getting help from their parents. His decision to stay close to home had everything to do with his anger towards his father. He was determined to be the first to confront Adam when he showed his guilt-stricken face. Will had no idea what lay in his future, only that he no longer wanted to follow in his father's footsteps and become an accountant.

"Hi Mom." They hugged and kissed and chatted animatedly, until Will dropped the bombshell.

"How's school honey? The accounting class any better?"

"Nah, I'm dropping out."

"You're doing what? I thought you wanted this so badly Will! What happened?" Liz's heart was pounding.

"Not anymore. Dad ruined that for me." He lowered his head somberly and then raised it to look directly into his mom's eyes. "Look, I don't want to talk about it anymore. I'll find another major. Talk about something else, okay?"

"Like what?" Liz was pissed, but mostly concerned. "Okay, but focus on your future, not your anger."

"Mom, I promise you, when I get back, I'll consider going to an advisor. But for now, no deal. I'm through."

"Get back from where? Where are you going? You can't stop school! Is that what you're doing?" Liz's stomach was turning. She wanted the best for her son. She had planned for his college education since he was a baby and was determined for him to succeed.

"I'm not dropping out of school, only accounting. No way! I wouldn't do what Dad did if my life depended on it!" He searched his mother's worried face. "It's okay Mom, I'm just visiting Lillie when I'm on my summer break. Mom, really, I'll be okay. Besides, I have some other possibilities in mind."

"Oh!" Liz breathed a sigh of relief and muttered, "Thank God!"

It didn't occur to Liz to ask her son what he was alluding to. She was too consumed with his anger towards Adam.

"Anne? Hi, how are the kids?" Are they adjusting to Fred's new idiot wife?"

Fred had remarried shortly after the court decision. Ruth, at fifteen, was a beauty; her brother, a year older, was hanging out with the wrong crowd and becoming a handful. Their new stepmom, a bit of a flake, had no children of her own and was disinterested in her step children's comings and goings.

Anne oozed sarcastically, "They're not; they hate her! It works well for them though. She can't stand them either. Ruth and Sam do what the hell they want. And Fred lets them! Do you believe this? And, not only that, Fred indelicately told them that their mom is a dyke. A *dyke*! Do you believe *any* of this?"

"Oh lord! What was their reaction?"

"Well, I think that's why Sam is doing drugs, and Ruth, well, I think she's sleeping around."

"But she's only fifteen!" Liz was perturbed at her friend's shocking news. "Do you ever think about taking Fred back to court and reversing the decision?"

"Yes, but I know it won't do any good. Lesbians are shunned at. You know that."

"Well, hopefully one day that will change."

"May-*be*, but the kids will probably be adults by then, and I'll be dead and gone." Anne's voice became gravelly. "By the way, how's Will doing in school?"

"That's another disaster area!"

She updated Anne on Will's decision. They both were quiet for a time and then Liz said to her dearest and oldest friend, "We turned out okay, didn't we? Maybe our children will too."

I wanted to believe that Adam was still alive, but questioned his sudden disappearance. How could he leave his two children? He abandoned them! And me. We were to be married and live happily ever after. How could he have done this to us? He *must* be dead. Oh well, that was over four years ago. When on earth will I accept this?

Anne says I'll meet someone one day. But, I know I will never trust again. And Will? He's changed forever because of Adam's desertion. Funny word to use; after all, that's what he did to his country. Chicken to fight for his country, and now chicken to stick it out with us till the end. When Adam came back from Canada, I supported him dodging the draft, but I sure as hell don't support him deserting his children. The bastard!

"Hanna, did you know Will is visiting Lillie soon?" Liz asked.

"Yes, she told me. She's very excited! When does he leave?"

"In three days. They're hoping to see some of the sites, especially where Adam hung out." Liz became serious. "Hanna, do you think there's a chance?"

"A chance?" Hanna knew what she was asking, but didn't want to think about it. The possibility was inconceivable. "No, I don't. He wouldn't have done that to us. That would have been heartless."

They met in Horn & Hardart in midtown Manhattan. Liz had an afternoon appointment with a client nearby and Hanna was on her lunchbreak. They were both quiet for a time each deep in their own thoughts.

"I love it here, don't you?" Liz looked around and without waiting for a response said, "My dad used to take me here when I was little. I'd be so excited to put the coin in the slot; a quarter, or was it a dime? Or, wait a minute! I think it was a token. Well anyway, I'd open the glass door and take out a sandwich, and Hanna, it was heavenly! But, I can't remember what it was!" They both chuckled. "Then there was the Chock Full of Nuts restaurant. I remember that sandwich!" Liz grinned widely. "Cream cheese and walnut on date bread. Yum! Now that was the best sandwich I ever had!"

"I never went to either of those restaurants until I moved here. I don't think we had them in California." She was unimpressed, but mildly amused at Liz's enthusiasm.

"Well, you don't know what you were missing. It was the highlight of my childhood to go there with my dad."

They laughed comfortably as they had when they were closer, before all the dissention started between them.

"How's Lillie doing at the music school? You must miss her."

Hanna paled. She was also experiencing empty nest syndrome. "I do miss her; too much. But, I'm thrilled that she's doing something important with her life. I mean, imagine, she will probably become a virtuoso! She's Autistic Liz! Autistic! And look at her now! I wish Adam could see his daughter blossoming. It's a shame. It's a damn shame."

"What are you doing with your time now that she's gone? I mean, besides work? Are you seeing anyone?"

Liz was really thinking about herself. Will had been gone for a while, but she still wasn't used to being alone. Occasionally she thought about dating, but didn't want to get hurt again. At 39 she felt old and was convinced her love life was over. Adam had been her world since she was 16, and Tom took his place later on. But both men had screwed her up. They had destroyed any possibility for trusting any other man.

Hanna looked at Liz and saw a sadness she hadn't realized before. "I'm sorry Liz. Adam did this to you, to all of us. Me? I have a friend. He's only a friend. We go to dinner sometimes, or a show. Fool around. But, I too will never get serious with anyone again. Anyway, I'm not the marrying type. I prefer being single. I'm free to do what I want, when I want. That's the way I like it."

Sadness overcame these two strong, yet damaged women.

344

# CHAPTER SEVENTY

# WILL

## (1988-1989)

William's mind drifted as he looked out the window. Ten years had passed since his trip to Grand Central when his dad had rescued him. This time he was an adult on his way to see his little sister. The Metro North train moved northward with great speed.

I can't believe this! My little sister, Autistic, and she's going to be famous! She's amazing! I'm 19 years old and I don't even know what I want to do with my life yet. Mom says I have time to figure it out though. I thought I would be an accountant, just like Dad, but ...forget that!

When I get to Montreal, Lillie and I are going to the *Yellow Door* where dad used to hang out. That is, if they let her in; she's underage. It must have changed a lot since Dad's been there. Either way, we could probably hang out where they serve coffee and listen to some *cool* music.

Dad told me the name of the street he used to live on. He even mentioned the apartment number. We can check that out too. Neat!

And *good old Mrs. Peatreé*; that's what he called his landlord back then, but she must be dead and gone by now.

I wonder what Dad would think of Lillie going to school in the same city where he ran away to during the war. She's not even eleven years old and a prodigy on her way to being a violin virtuoso! He'd be real proud of her. I've always been proud of my mom playing the violin, but this is different. This is the bigtime!

The train came to a gripping halt and one by one passengers descended and boarded at Penn Station. Will hurried to transfer to the Amtrak train.

Twenty minutes later his thoughts were interrupted as he found himself staring at the most beautiful girl he had ever seen. She had long thick blonde hair, green eyes, with a gorgeous figure, and looked around his age.

"Hi! Do you mind if I sit here?"

Will gulped. "No, please do! Here, let me help you with those."

He noticed she was taller than he was as he assisted her with her luggage. He lifted her two bags into the compartment above.

"Thanks, I'm Suzy." She offered her hand and daintily shook Will's.

"You're welcome, anytime. You going upstate?"

"Yes, to Albany U. I'm an undergrad there, majoring in special Ed. I want to work in a junior high school someday. I was visiting my parents on Long Island. What about you? Do you go to college?"

"Yes, a small college, SUNY New Paltz. Not sure what I'm majoring in yet, though." He hesitated not knowing how much to divulge. "I just dropped out of the accounting program. It's not for me. I'm thinking maybe I'll switch to a psych major. My little sister has autism. She's become an inspiration to me."

"Wow, that's awesome!"

"She's ten, and you won't believe this," he said with pride, "she's in a school for musically gifted disabled students who will more than likely become virtuosos!"

"Wow, that is awesome! What instrument does she play?"

"The violin."

"I always wanted to play an instrument. When I was in junior high I opted for chorus instead. But, now that I'm older I thought I'd learn the trombone."

"You're kidding me, right?"

"No! I am not! I like the *voom-voom* sound." With one hand outstretched and the other hand pulling the pretend trombone inward, she blew out some jazz sounds with her pursed lips.

"Okay," he laughed. "I'll join you!"

Sitting side by side, they played their pretend instruments to *their* jazz song, all the while laughing hysterically.

Over three hours had gone by without either of them realizing the time. They non-stopped talked about their hopes and dreams for the future. They shared their personal dramas: her family, who consisted of her childhood dog and her parents; and their marriage which was volatile. And, then Will alluded to his father's disappearance four years ago.

"I'm so sorry! That has to be so hard on you...I mean not knowing..."

Thoughts and sentiments were abruptly interrupted as the conductor announced the next stop, Albany.

"Hey, would you want to maybe get together on a weekend when I get back? Maybe catch a movie?" Will quickly calculated. "We're only about an hour and a half from each other. I could come upstate and visit you."

As he held his breath, he felt his face flushing with anticipation.

"I'd like that!" She smiled coyly. Her curiosity peaked. "Back from where?"

"I'm headed to Montreal to visit my sister. I'll be back in a week. How about the following Saturday? Are you free?"

Suzy thought for a minute. "I am! Here's my number." She jotted it down on a scrap piece of paper she found in her pocketbook.

Will awkwardly kissed her on the mouth. Embarrassed, he searched her face for a reaction. She looked nonplussed. Suzy hurriedly gathered her luggage and once again gave Will a demure smile. He watched her walk away and as she exited the train, she stumbled, and now it was her turn to be embarrassed. She threw her hands up in the air self-consciously, and waved goodbye. Afterwards, and for the remainder of the trip to Montreal, he worried if the kiss was a mistake; if it was too soon. He also wondered if the encounter with Suzy was love at first sight.

# CHAPTER SEVENTY-ONE

# WILL AND LILLIE

## (1988-1989)

L illie looked up when she heard the rapping at the door.
She bellowed, "Who is it?"

Will banged at the door once more, but this time with the secret code they developed years before. *Rap, rap rap, rap, rap rap rap, rap-it-tee- rap!*

"Will!" she screamed.

Grinning from ear to ear, Will walked in. To his surprise and shock, she flung out her arms and fiercely hugged him.

"Lillie! That is the first time you ever hugged me!"

In response, Lillie gestured, "Oh, I've gotten over that. Besides, I missed you so much!" She then withdrew, but slowly approached him again. This time he gave her a big bear hug.

"I missed you a whole bunch too squirt! So, how's everything?"

## LILLIE

When Will entered, I was exuberant. He is the only person, other than my parents, who accept me. Until I came here, that is. But, everything is still foreign to me. I miss my mother and sometimes my new house, and many times I think about asking her if I could go home. But, I love playing the violin and learning everything about it. It seems to supersede everyone and everything. Another *big* word!

Yesterday, my English teacher told me that my vocabulary is superior to my peers' level. I feel proud of myself! I'm also at a superior level in mathematics! My father would have been impressed if he were alive. But he's not. He's dead. My brother will be impressed though. I'll make sure to tell him. I wish he would stay here with me, forever.

When my mother left me here, I was apprehensive. I hugged her goodbye because I knew I would miss her a lot! This was the first time I ever hugged anyone. She started to cry. I felt badly that I made her cry, but she said they were happy tears. I'm not sure I understand that…it's an oxymoron. Another big one!

"The music lessons are awesome. The kids and teachers are okay too."

Will studied her sullen face. "I sense something is wrong though. What is it?"

"I miss you, and Hanna."

He thought for a minute. "Well, I'm here right now! So cheer up squirt! How about we go out and get some breakfast? We could go to that place Dad used to go to…that is if they serve breakfast…not sure."

"Yes!" Still in her PJ's, Lillie grabbed her outfit she set out for the day and ran to the bathroom.

Will scanned the room and noticed the other bed seemed untouched for so early in the morning. He shouted across the room, "Where's your roommate?"

"Oh, Sara? She's with her parents. They live in Quebec. They come almost every weekend. Hey Will, do you have to tell Miss Grahm that we're leaving?"

"Already got permission from the office!"

"Sara's my best friend! She plays the cello really well."

"That's awesome Lillie. I'm glad you have a best friend."

They headed out the front door with a beaten up half-opened umbrella Lillie brought from home. It was pouring by the time they arrived at the *Yellow Door,* only to discover the doors were closed.

"Will, the sign says they open at 5 p.m.; could we come here later?" she asked wistfully.

"You betcha! For dinner. How's that?"

Nervous and excited, Lillie said, "Will, Will, Will! This is the place Dad went to, right?"

Will's face sobered, "Yes Lillie, this is the place."

As they walked around the streets of Montreal, Will wondered how close they were to *good old Mrs. Peatreé's* house. He took the folded paper out of his pocket and held it tightly in his hand.

"Lillie, let's cross over here." Will took her hand and led the way. "There's a cop over there. I can ask for directions to where Dad's old street is, where he used to live."

The officer indicated a thirty minute walk and gave detailed instructions how to get there. They could have easily taken a trolley, but the rain had stopped and they were both anxious to see the historical city in which their dad once made a home for himself. Happily, Will and Lillie strolled the streets and ate their pork brioches along the way.

"Dad once told me that they have the best pork brioche sandwiches on earth right here in Montreal. He was right!"

"I think there might be a sandwich just as tasty somewhere else. We'll have to ask a world traveler," she said in all seriousness. "Someone who likes to eat," she added. She bit into hers. "It is good!"

Will looked at her in amazement and once again realized how different Lillie was. Her view of the world was unlike most people. She experienced a literal world of black and white, with no room for deviation or embellishment.

"Will, I'm tired. Can we go back?"

"Come on squirt; *good old Peatreé awaits us! Are* you sure? We're almost there."

Disappointed, he looked at her tired face and felt badly for her. "Okay, we can come back in a couple of days. You *do* look bushed."

They settled in the family lounge where parents and friends gathered when visiting the school.

"Want to grab something to eat? We never went to the *Yellow Door*."

"I'm too tired to eat," Lillie answered and let out a big yawn.

"Me too. I'll go soon."

"No, don't go yet," Lillie pleaded. "I want you to stay."

"So what do you do on weekends, when your friend isn't here?"

"My mother comes every other weekend, and I have other friends too."

"I'll try to come more often, but I probably can't until the next semester break. What do you want to do tomorrow? Go on the rides at the World's Fair?"

"Yes!" Lillie awkwardly danced around the room. "This is called my *Happy Dance.*"

"Oh yeah?" He joined in without inhibition as other families jointly smiled and felt their joy.

"Hey, let's go back to get your room. Will you play something for me?"

Lillie practically fell over running up the stairs to her room. She took out her bow, applied the rosin, and proceeded to play a piece by Mozart.

"Wow! I thought you were talented before, but you've improved Lillie!"

Beaming, she asked, "Do you want to hear more?"

For the next hour, without interruption, she performed several pieces for Will.

"Do you learn all about classical music, too?" Will asked with genuine interest.

"I do! We're even learning how to write music. I've written a concerto."

"Seriously? A concerto? Isn't that hard to do?"

"Not really; I've written some before."

Will shook his head in awe.

"Will? What do you do in college?"

"Same thing as you do in school. study boring subjects." Chuckling, he said, "And look for girls!"

"I don't do that silly!" Lillie giggled.

"Lillie, guess what?"

"What?" She looked up at her older brother with huge eyes.

"I met a girl on the train. Her name is Suzy."

"Do you like her?"

"A lot. I am going to visit her when I get home; maybe go to a movie or something."

Not really paying attention or caring about her brother's new turn of events, Lillie switched topics. "Will, I wish I could go camping with you. I want to sleep in a tent and watch the awesome stars."

"Maybe some other time when you don't have school. You just started here. Hopefully, next summer you'll be allowed to leave for a week," Will offered.

He hugged his little sister once more.

"Good night, squirt. I'll see you bright and early in the morning!"

It was only a one mile hike to the camping grounds. With his tent securely packed in his duffel bag, he flung it and his knapsack over his shoulder. Soon after reaching the site, he set up his gear with all the necessary paraphernalia and climbed into his sleeping bag, falling into a deep sleep dreaming about Suzy. It had been a long happy day.

We were off to the World's Fair grounds. It had been closed down for a while, but the rides and assorted eateries were still open to the public. The only relic left on the grounds looked as if it was made of Legos! I was disappointed though. The other building, the *Biosphère*, had previously burnt down. It held Elvis Presley's guitar, and exhibits on NASA's space program!

The deserted expanse of land left me wondering how awesome it might have been to experience so many cultures all at once. My mom and her childhood friend Sue, went to the one in Flushing Meadow Park back home in New York in '64. She said there were eighty nations represented, and over fifty million people attended! It was the most exciting experience of her life! Except for giving birth to me of course, ha-ha.

"Lillie, don't run off! Hold my hand."

We walked and walked until we found the rides Lillie had been asking about. But once there, she chickened out. There was too much confusion for her. Kids were running all over the place and the noise was practically deafening. I felt badly about it, but didn't blame her. It was a nightmare! We did find one ride, though, that she liked. The merry go round! We each got on a pony, held tight, and waited for the ride to begin. Lillie looked a little scared, but I reassured her it was tame compared to the other rides. She nodded. All of a sudden, four teenagers were screaming and running towards us, as one after another jumped on board and took hold of a pony.

One of the boys looked at Lillie. "Hey, how old are you sweetheart? Want to come for a ride with me?"

Lillie was not even eleven yet, but could pass for thirteen. She was very pretty and tall like me. She looked scared and said nothing.

"Hey! What's your problem? Leave my sister alone, right now, or else!"

I stood and when they saw my height they backed off, but only after getting the last word in.

"Oh, yeah?" the shorter one bullied.

"Oh, *yeah*!" I lunged towards them, but thankfully they ran.

"Want to go?" I asked Lillie. She was trembling.

"No way! I remember what you taught me about bullying and what you said happened to dad."

Little did she know they were doing more than bullying; one of the boys was coming on to her.

# WILL

Shortly after the incident, I took Lillie back to the school. She was exhausted. Our plans to stop at the *Yellow Door* were again postponed. I decided to stop there for dinner by myself.

It was a bit eerie knowing Dad used to come here. I stepped into the foyer of the well-known coffeehouse and anticipation and anxiety

355

overwhelmed me. I guess I hoped my dad would *pop* around the corner and say, "Son, what the hell are you doing here?"

Within minutes I was seated and looked around. It was semi-dark and had a cozy atmosphere, although jam-packed and spacious. Up front, a band played some cool music. I tapped my foot in rhythm, trying to relax.

The food was outrageously good. I took a bite of my hamburger, smothered with onions and a sauce unfamiliar to me, ate a few fancy-looking French fries, and sat back watching people come and go. I hadn't enjoyed myself in this way for a long time. My studies were time consuming. *Wish I was sitting here with Suzy. I hope she likes me as much as I like her.* All around me people were talking and swaying in their seats to the music, and dancing on the dance floor.

Over a couple of hours passed and I was beginning to feel tired. I ordered an expresso, with chocolate soufflé for dessert. I was planning on leaving for the campsite when I noticed a woman staring at me. We locked eyes. *Who is this gorgeous woman? She's kind of old for me. Why is she staring at me? Shit, she's coming towards me!*

"I'm sorry, do we know each other? You look so familiar." She stared again, more closely this time. "Wait, I know! You remind me of someone I once knew, and cared about."

*Whoa, she has a French accent.*

"Oh, yeah," was all I could manage to say. My heart was pounding… thumping…coming out of my chest! *She is sex-y, for an old lady that is. She must be 40, or even older. Should I ask her to sit? What the hell do I say to her?*

"Who was it?" *What a jerk I am! Who was it? You idiot!*

"Oh, just somebody I met here once, a long time ago. His name was Adam. You look exactly like him."

My heart stopped.

"Are you okay? Oh my! You look white as a sheet. Would you like some water?"

"I...I...." Nothing came out of my mouth.

"You look as if you might faint. Should I get some help? I'm so sorry if I upset you."

"No. Thank you." I searched for words. "I believe you are talking about my father. We looked alike. And, he used to come here."

"Did you say, 'looked alike'?"

"He died." Scanning her now pale face, I asked, "Now you look like you might faint. Are you okay?" I rose and offered her the seat next to mine.

Still shaken, Bettina said, "This must be *destinèe* that we met. How did he die?"

"We don't know for sure, but one day he disappeared. It's been over four years."

"Oh my! Was he back in the states when this happened, or here? Is that why you are here?" Bettina was saddened.

"No, back home." Will had a gut feeling that they were lovers, but asked anyway. "How did you know my father?"

"Your father and I were friends. We met right here." Bettina pointed at a table close by. "It was during the war; Vietnam. I guess you knew he took refuge in Canada? Or did I speak out of place?"

"Yes, I knew. I'm not sure what I feel about that...you know, deserting our country. Well, mine anyway. But, wait a minute...my father told me that he never told anyone in Canada he was a draft dodger. He said he was ashamed. And, also afraid he'd get caught. You knew?"

"Yes, I knew. I figured it out. Your dad and I had our political differences, but he was a decent man. And I knew he was scared to go to Vietnam. It's okay *Mon Cherie*, I'm sure he did what he thought was right for him." She paused to think a minute. "What is your name?" She held his hand, softly. "Mine is Bettina."

Will and Bettina talked for a long time; about college, his future, Lillie, and Bettina's sad life, although one of privilege and wealth. Never once did they speak of Liz. And then, they said their goodbyes and parted ways, never to see one another again.

# WILL AND LILLIE

"Com'mon lazy bones! Rise and shine!"

Lillie opened her sleep filled eyes to see Will standing over her, smiling.

"What time is it?" Lillie yawned and grunted. "Go away."

"Oh yeah?" Will bent over and tickled her until she helplessly relented. "Com'mon, we're off to Dad's old apartment!"

Suddenly her head popped up. "Yes!" She ran to the bathroom, quickly dressed, and was ready ten minutes later.

"Are you hungry? We could grab something along the way."

Arm in arm they walked briskly, this time with purpose.

"Will?"

"Yes? Here, put this on." He offered his jacket. "Aren't you cold?" It was starting to drizzle and the wind was kicking up, unseasonable for this time of year.

"A little, thanks. Will?"

He studied her forlorn face. "What's the matter?"

She gulped before answering. "Do you think Dad's alive?"

"Why? Do you?" Shocked at her question, his jaw dropped open.

"You first!" Lillie looked at her brother's startled expression.

"Frankly, I don't know. So many years have gone by. I don't see how it's possible. But, ..."

"But what?" Her face was turning beet red.

"Sometimes I think he might be," he blurted out, "but then I realize it's wishful thinking. What do you think?"

"I always told everyone he's dead, but in my head I always believed he's alive."

"You're kidding? Why? What makes you think so?" Again Will was surprised.

"I just know it, in here." Lillie pointed to her heart.

"Wait, I think it's this way," Will said excitedly. They hooked a right and randomly started looking at apartment numbers.

"Will! Here it is!" Lillie practically screamed, "Let's go!"

"Lillie, give me a moment. Okay?"

"What's the matter?"

"Nervous, that's all." Will took a deep breath, and then another one. "Okay, let's go."

Directly facing them stood a directory on a platform. The names were worn off and illegible to the average eye. But, Lillie was able to decipher some of them and started rattling off names, when all of a sudden a bleached platinum haired, scrawny woman with a thick French accent appeared.

"Excuse me Ma'am, but does ...I mean did, my father, sorry," Will rambled, "Did a Adam Greenstein once live here? Would you know?" Will was beginning to sweat profusely.

Although still unaccustomed to touch, Lillie reached for Will's hand and held it tightly.

"Who's asking?" The woman eyed them suspiciously.

"We're his children," Will answered.

"Nope! Nobody here by that name. Now get out of here. Don't need no intruders or vagrants."

"I assure you Ma'am we are neither," Will said politely.

"I said get out of here, before I call *les keufs.*"

"What the hell did she say?" Will whispered to Lillie.

"The police," the scrawny woman screamed at them. "The police!"

"Come on, Lillie. Let's go."

"But, Will," Lillie protested.

"Lillie, NOW, before there's trouble."

They both ran out the door.

"Will, please listen, please!" Lillie burst into tears.

Exasperated, Will said, "What is it Lillie? "Keep walking though; keep *walking.*"

"I saw something."

"What do you mean you saw something?" This time Will stopped dead in his tracks and stared at his sister.

"I thought I saw Dad's name."

"Are you serious? How can that be? That horrible woman would have told us, wouldn't she?" Puzzled, Will's heart was like a drum beating loud and hard.

"What should we do?" Wide eyed, Lillie looked at her brother.

"We should go back, of course!" Will said resolutely. But he didn't let Lillie know, as determined as he was, that he was also scared. Scared to find what, or who, would be there. Scared the crazy woman would call the police if they were caught. Just plain scared. "But, not now; later. We'll sneak in."

# CHAPTER SEVENTY-TWO

# LIZ

## (1988-1989)

"Liz? How's everything?"

"Okay, mom. I guess I forgot to tell you, though. Will's in Montreal visiting Lillie. He's on summer break."

"Oh, how nice! Well, say hello for me when he calls. Tell him I miss him and that I have some of his favorite cookies waiting for him when he returns. Those applesauce ones he loves."

"I will Mom, thank you. How's Dad feeling?"

"Oh, you know...his arthritis is kicking in, but...oh, wait, someone's knocking at my door."

"It's okay Mom, I have to run anyway. I'll call you later."

Liz walked into her den, lifted her new chestnut colored curtains, and let the sunlight in. It was a beautiful warm July morning. She noticed Will's apple green bicycle, with all the fancy gears he used as a teenager, leaning on the shed door. She made a mental note...*shed door sorely needs a paint job.* Inside lay his tricycle, navy blue with a stark white stripe down each side. She thought about giving it to the *Salvation Army,* but never did. She couldn't part with it. And there was his first bike, with its training wheels removed. Bright blood red; a bit worn, but still eliciting strong memories. *Mom, Mom! Adam helped me stay up longer than yesterday. Three full minutes! He timed me!*

Will was a man now, in college and driving a car. She was immensely proud of her son. And missed him.

Liz hadn't heard from him in over a week. She decided to call the campgrounds where he was staying, and as luck had it they spotted him walking up the laborious steep incline towards his site.

"Mom, hi! I'm sorry I didn't call you. I've been so busy with Lillie. You wouldn't believe how tall she's grown...and her music.... phenomenal...and Mom, I have news for you....maybe..."

"What? Did I hear you right?" Liz was hyperventilating. "I'm coming! I'll be there in two days! I'm coming!"

Liz scribbled the address down in a flurry.

"No, Mom, wait! I don't know for sure!"

But Liz had already hung up.

# CHAPTER SEVENTY-THREE

# WILL AND LILLIE AND ADAM AND LIZ
## 1989

The following morning, at the crack of dawn, Will and Lillie went back to the dilapidated apartment building. Years before, it had a certain charm to it, but since then it had fallen apart as many apartment buildings and houses had in this area.

"Shhh!" Will put his finger to Lillie's mouth. "Walk quietly! Don't make a peep!"

Considering Lillie was a klutz, this was an impossible feat. With heavy hearts, they proceeded up three flights, walking as if there were a bed of feathers atop each stair. They were surrounded by graffiti filled walls and crumbled plaster, which left white marks everywhere on the worn-out stairs. Lillie clung to him avoiding a mishap.

"Will! There it is; 3A!"

They looked at each other in disbelief. The apartment number actually existed! Taking a second deep breath, Will knocked. Not a sound was heard from the adjacent dwellings, nor the one facing them. He knocked again; still no answer. Will placed his trembling hand on the rickety door knob. It was unlocked.

"Will?" Lillie croaked.

"Hello? Is anyone here?" Hyperventilating, Will repeated, "Hello?"

Sickening odors permeated throughout the narrowed vestibule as they entered; Urine? Vomit? Will was overcome with nausea and Lillie made choking sounds as she attempted breathing more evenly. He moved forward past the entranceway, all the while squeezing her hand. As their eyes adapted to the light, they became fixated on the vision in front of them.

Barely a whisper emanated from Will's drawn mouth. "Hello. I'm sorry. We must have the wrong apartment number." He looked at Lillie with enormously concerned eyes and motioned with his head. "Let's get out of here!"

"WAIT!" The skeleton of a man screeched. "WAIT!"

They turned and saw one eye searching theirs.

"Will?" the man cried out. "Son? Is that you?"

*This isn't my dad. He looks nothing like him. Why does he know my name and why is he calling me son?*

"Dad?"

"Yes, come here son. Who is with you?"

Will was dumbfounded. His entire body was shaking.

"It's Lillie, your daughter."

"My daughter! Is that really you Lillie? You've grown... into a young woman. You were a little girl when I left." It was difficult to determine if Adam was happy or sad at this revelation. His face was void of emotion.

Confused, Lillie said in a monotone voice, "My name is Lillie. Are you my dad?"

"Dad, what happened to you?" Will intervened. "You're, well, you're...not you. I mean..." he started to cry. "Your left eye...it isn't... it isn't there."

"I didn't hear you son, what did you say?"

"You don't look like my dad," Lillie said. "My dad had hair and was fatter than you, she said assertively.

Adam lifted himself upward into a semi-sitting position. "Help me, Will, would you, into the wheelchair?"

It wasn't much of an effort on Will's part. Adam couldn't weigh more than 75 lbs. Will gently moved the gruesome looking tubes off to the side of Adam's bony and discolored left arm, and lifted his blanket to expose his upper body. He then adjusted the tube on the side of his chest and lowered the blanket once more to reveal his upper thighs.

The shock was too overwhelming for Will. He was incapable of speaking. Blood rushed throughout his entire being as he steadied himself avoiding a fall. *This can't be! Where are his legs?* Unprepared for this unnatural site, both Lillie and Will gasped for air.

Lillie screamed out, "Will!"

"It's okay Lillie, go sit over there." He pointed to a chair off to the right of the bed, closest to the window. "Go sit, it will be okay."

Will desperately sought air. *How the hell could anything ever be okay again?*

"Dad? How did this happen?" Bile rose in Will's throat as he tried to adapt to the horrific sight before him.

Adam questioned in a slow gruff voice, "Oh, this? Sorry. I'm used to it. Is Lillie okay over there?"

Will looked at his father and then towards Lillie. "Lillie? He walked to her with the deliberate strides of a protective brother. "You okay squirt?"

"No!" she sobbed. "Is that my father?"

"Yes, Lillie. He's our dad. Pretty upsetting site; I know."

"I want to go home. Right now!" she demanded.

"Me too, so do I. But Dad needs our help. Don't you want to help him? I want to." Will reached for his little sister's hand and held it. "Come on squirt, let's go sit over there."

Practically crawling, they both edged up to Adam's bedside. Will then assisted his dad into his wheelchair and covered him up again.

"Why do you look like this?" Lillie's voice quivered.

"I got very sick."

"Is that why you left us?"

Will cut in, "Dad, what's wrong with you? Is it the drinking that did this to you?"

Lillie looked up in confusion. "Drinking?"

"Yes. Mostly. I'm sorry Will. Really sorry. I tried. Believe me, I did." Adam closed his one eye to rest it, or possibly to advert his gaze from his children. "How did you find me?"

"You told me. Don't you remember? You told me where you used to hang out, and where you lived. But Dad, we thought you were dead. Mom thinks you are dead."

"Wait a minute! You came here to find me? But you thought I was dead? I don't get it."

"Not exactly. Lillie's in school here. It's a coincidence. So I came to visit her and we decided to check out your old hang-outs."

"School? In Montreal?" He turned to Lillie. "Why's that sweetheart? Did your Mom and you move here?"

"No. Mom's not here. I'm alone. I go to a school for the gifted."

"Gifted? How wonderful!" With his one sickly looking eye, Adam looked at her inquisitively.

366

"Mom says I'm a prodigy. That's means I'm very gifted, and one day I will become a violin virtuoso!" Lillie beamed.

"A what? A violinist virtuoso?"

"Yes! I will play in concert halls," she took a breath, "and meet famous violinists like Joshua Bell!"

"Well, how the hell did that happen? I'm so proud of you Lillie!" Adam looked at Will for confirmation of this incredulous news.

"Yes, Dad. What Lillie says is true. All of it."

*What is going on? Why did he leave us? Because of this atrocity?* Will looked down towards his father's legs hidden by the blanket. All of a sudden out of nowhere he shouted, "Dad! Why? Why did you leave us? We could have helped you!"

Adam's head dropped. "Because you couldn't help me. Nobody could."

"How do you know? You didn't even try!" Will's hands were tightly fisted by his sides. Infuriated, he said, "You left without a word to Mom or me."

Adam tried to respond, but the exertion overcame him.

"Or me!" Lillie's voice rose in anger.

"Here Dad." Will reached for the glass of water sitting on his night table. "Sip on this." He placed the straw between his dried cracked lips.

As the minutes ticked on, Adam became visibly weaker. Hardly audible, he struggled for words. "Lillie, I ....I...want you...have... somethin..." With effort, he lifted his bony forefinger and pointed to the sequestered closet to his left. "...violin it's..there. Remem...ber, I promised you. You always loved classical music."

A knock at the door interrupted them. "Excuse me, anyone home?" Cautiously, Liz entered the vestibule just as she heard a scream.

"Dad, don't!" Will cried out. "Don't leave us! Please!" Sobbing, he dropped to his knees.

"I'm sorry Edouard. I should have saved you."

"No, Dad it's me, Will!" Will knew who Edouard was and felt embarrassed for his father calling his own son another boy's name.

Adam rambled in and out of consciousness as blood oozed from his nostrils, and dripped from the side of his mouth. "Will, I'm sorry I disappointed you. I should have fought with the other soldiers. I was chicken. I dodged the draft and was a chicken!" He hacked a deep sickening cough.

Startled at the noise behind them, Will and Lillie jerked around. "Aunt Liz! My dad...he's not dead!" In slow motion, Liz scanned the dismal room that was saturated with stench and then gaped at the vision before her. Her knees buckled.

Too much for her to assimilate, Lillie walked off to claim her father's last wish. She lifted the shiny instrument into her small hands, placed it under her chin, and moved the bow along the strings. She then stopped to adjust the strings to the proper pitch and proceeded to play the 2$^{nd}$ movement of Brahms Violin Sonata No. 3. The tranquil music soothed her, so she continued as if no one was there.

"Mom, Mom! Are you okay?" Will ran to Liz's side and cradled her.

"Dad? Thank you for my violin. How did you know I played?" I never told you. Did mom?"

"No, sweetheart. I just knew. I love you Lillie."

"I love you too Dad." Lillie stared blankly.

Words never spoken before comforted Adam. His daughter told him she loved him, and with one word, gave him peace; *Dad.*

Liz came to her feet and hobbled over to Adam's bedside. Convulsive sobs emanated from her once supple body, now stiff and deadened, as she embraced him.

"Don't Liz, don't cry. I'm so sorry. I've loved you since we were kids. I didn't mean to hurt you. You will always be the love of my life." Tears ran down Adam's cheeks. Take care of our son."

"We were to be married!" she cried. "You left without a word! Why didn't you trust me to help you! I hate you, you bastard!" She pounded on the arm of his chair, but instantly stopped when the blanket fell to his side. She gasped. *Oh my God! It's the same as the dream! No legs! Oh my God!* "Adam! I'm so sorry! I'm so sorry!" She fell to her knees. "I love you Adam, please, please..."

"Will, come here," Adam managed to say. "Help your mother. Liz, I love you."

"No! Adam!"

Will faced his father. "Dad?"

"I love you son and always will. Take care of your mom and Lillie. Have a good life, okay?"

"Will? Will!" Lillie screeched as she lifted her chin and dropped the violin.

"It's okay Lillie, it's okay."

Adam took one last look at his family.

# ONE WEEK LATER

Liz leaned over, kissed Adam's hollowed out cheek, and gently placed a 45 *rpm* record between the palms of his hands. *This is for what we once had; 'Wooly Bully' Adam, 'Wooly Bully'. I love you Adam Greenstein, I will always love you. You were the boy with the best laugh.*

Attended by his loved ones, Liz, Will, Hanna and Lillie, the unorthodox funeral was held in Queens, NY near their childhood home where they met so long ago.

# LIZ

*Just like the dream! I can't believe it! How could that happen! It's really ironic. When we were kids he told me he feared going to Vietnam because he didn't want to lose his legs like so many other men, and now Goddamn it, he lost his legs to alcohol, to alcohol! And then died!!*

"Mom, are you okay?"

"Yes, why?"

"Because you're mumbling, and I keep on talking to you and you're not there."

"Sorry, honey. What did you say?"

"How long will we be there? I want to call Suzy."

"Who?"

"Mom! I told you! She's someone I met on the train to Canada."

"Yes, sorry, you did tell me. I don't know. Probably a couple of days. We'll get moving men to dispose of the rest of his belongings. For now we'll take what's important." Liz's eyes were misty and distant. "Do you want to tell me about this girl?"

"Not yet. Let's see what happens."

"You know Will, I think there's a chance that the violin your dad gave Lillie might be worth something. During WWII the Nazi's hid valuable paintings and musical instruments. Some were discovered years later. Your grandpa, you know, your dad's dad, found the violin in Italy in the rubble of an abandoned church. Hanna is getting it appraised just in case my theory is right."

"Wow! That would be awesome for Lillie. I can't believe it; a violin from WWII."

They pulled into the driveway with heavy hearts and walked past the art sculpture and into the house.

"What?" Will was horrified at the site before him. "What the hell happened here?"

The once lavishly decorated Long Island home looked like a tornado hit it. As they entered Adam's living room, a disturbing sight shook them to their very core. Papers were strewn all over the place; on the floors, end tables, coffee table, everywhere. Beer cans were crushed and thrown haphazardly. Food and garbage in untied bags were lying on the floor, and in the kitchen unwashed dishes lay on the counters and island, possibly for months. The stench was unbearable, different than Adam's room in Canada though.

Bewildered, Will asked, "Do you think someone trashed this place?"

"Yes. Your father."

"You're kidding, right?"

"No, unfortunately I'm not."

"Unbelievable! He was really sick Mom, wasn't he?"

"In more ways than you understand." Liz said.

"Okay, where should we begin? What do you think?"

"I guess you take one room, I'll take the other.

Mustering up all the courage she could, she walked into his bedroom. Memories flooded her. "Look Will," Liz called out, "A photo of you and your dad when you visited him in Los Angeles. You were both wearing those silly sunglasses." Then she spotted another photo to her left. It was one of Adam and Liz when they first met, celebrating her sweet sixteen birthday. She was wearing her red velvet dress and he was holding her hand looking directly into her eyes. She remembered that moment distinctly. It was the moment she fell in love with him.

"Mom! Mom!"

"What is it Will? What's the matter?" Liz ran into the living room alarmed.

"It's Dad's will!"

Liz opened the document with trembling hands; Adam's *Last Will and Testament*. She looked around for a place to sit, closed her eyes for an instant, and carefully read, and then re-read. His inheritance was left to Will and Lillie, and one million dollars was left to Viet Nam veterans.

"Where did you find this?"

"In his safe. He gave me the key the day he died."

"What does it say?"

"It says that your Dad did right by you and Lillie; and did the right thing for other people too."

# WILL

My dad was a decent man after all. Maybe he *was* chicken, but in the long run he did the right thing. I don't know…if I was in his place, what would I have done? Run? Or fight? It was a war of the unconscionable.

*I forgive you dad, I truly do. I hope you can forgive me for being judgmental and criticizing your decision. I wasn't in your shoes and have no idea what you felt. I would have been scared though; I'm sure of that, but I'm not sure what I would have done. As far as the little boy goes, you did the best you could. It wasn't your fault. I know you tried to save him. Please Dad, rest in peace. I love you.*

"Mom, sit down. I have something to tell you."

"Oh no! What now?" Liz held her breath and braced herself.

"It's good Mom. You can breathe!" Will laughed heartily. "I hope you approve."

Liz sat back and felt her body relax. "I could use some good news; tell me."

Hardly able to contain himself, he blurted out his news. "I'm going back to school to become an accountant!"

Liz jumped up in excitement. "Oh Will!"

"Wait, there's more! After I graduate, I will honor Dad by representing our POW's and MIA's families, and aid them financially with the money he gave me."

"Oh Will! How wonderful! I am so proud of you! Your Dad would be very pleased too. This is the right thing to do, a noble act!"

Liz embraced her son for both her and Adam as they talked about his plans for the future.

After Liz left, Will made a phone call he had been putting off for too long.

"Hello, Suzy? It's Will, Will Greenstein. We met a few months ago; remember, on the train to Albany? I'm sorry it took so long to call, but...."

# CHAPTER SEVENTY-FOUR

# LILLIE

## (1990)

"Mom, how'd I do?"

"Brilliantly! I am so proud of you! The reviews come out tomorrow…just you wait," Hanna said excitedly. She looked down at her daughter sitting in the red velvet chair trimmed with gold. "What's the matter? You should be happy. In fact, you should be ecstatic! Take a look at this Lillie!" Hanna handed her daughter the entertainment section of the newspaper from the previous day.

*Preview: Autistic 12 year old Ms. Lillie Greenstein will perform at Lincoln Center, Saturday, September 8 at 8 p.m. Word has it that this young lady will be the newest Isaac Pearlman of the century…*

"What about Joshua Bell? Will I be the newest Joshua Bell too?"

"Maybe! Keep working hard!" Hanna smiled, knowing that Lillie didn't realize the magnitude of what she read.

"I wish my dad was here to see me perform though," Lillie said sullenly.

"Oh, your Dad was here Lillie! Didn't you feel him? He was watching over you with that crooked smile of his, and tremendous pride! After all, you were playing a *1.6 million dollar* Stradivarius violin from the 16th century at Lincoln Center for God's sake!"

Lillie stood up and gave her mother a huge crooked grin and hugged her tightly.

# THE END

Printed in Poland
by Amazon Fulfillment
Poland Sp. z o.o., Wrocław
29 April 2022

b0f51967-e80d-4b1f-bfec-e493267b5336R01